Nirim

Book Four of
the Outsider series.

by
Aiden Phoenix

Nirim

ISBN: 9798399834962

Cover created by Aiden Phoenix.

Table of Contents

Welcome to Collisa!

Collisa is a new world brimming with opportunities for adventure and growth. It is also brimming with chances for romance and fun. This is the story of Dare and the life he builds for himself with the women he meets and falls in love with.

As you can guess, it is a harem tale, with all that includes. Be aware that it features varied and explicit erotic scenes between multiple partners. It is intended to be enjoyed by adults. All characters involved in adult scenes are over the age of 18.

Prologue
Forward

Dare reined in outside the wrought iron gate to Montshadow Estate, relieved to see that unlike his last visit here it bustled with activity again.

Looked as if the Baroness of Terana and her staff were back from whatever had called them to Redoubt. Which meant that his trip to town would be productive for more than ordering more building materials and hiring more laborers for the whirlwind of renovations and improvements on Nirim Manor.

The guard at the gate recognized him, and to his gratification let him in without a word; it seemed Lady Marona's invitation to visit when he was able had been sincere.

A stable boy was waiting to take his horse, and the large doors of the mansion opened at his approach. Miss Garena, the Head Maid, appeared in the doorway and curtsied. She wore a black and white ruffled dress that inexplicably looked almost exactly like a French maid uniform from back on Earth.

"Welcome, Master Dare," she said, stepping aside. "Please, come in."

"Thank you." He stepped into the grand entry room, with twin staircases sweeping up to a balcony to either side and a crystal chandelier looming high overhead. "I hope I'm not intruding."

"Not at all, the Baroness will be pleased at your visit. She's been looking forward to speaking with you." The severe older woman gestured curtly. "Miss Marigold, if you'll see our guest to the Baroness's sitting room?"

Dare tried to hide his surprise. If he remembered correctly, the sitting room was usually a comfortable living area right outside the bedroom in a lady's chambers. That was unexpectedly informal of

Lady Marona. Almost intimate.

He wondered if he should be nervous.

At the Head Maid's summons another maid popped into the room, looking a bit flustered. It was the gnome Dare had met on his first visit to the mansion.

Or more accurately who'd met *him*, when she snuck under the breakfast table to give him a blowjob beneath the tablecloth in front of half a dozen people, without getting caught.

Marigold was a bit shorter than Zuri, plump and adorable with a friendly round face and big blue eyes. She had silky pink hair flowing freely down to her ankles, which swished against the floor as she curtsied. "If you'll come with me, Master Dare."

Her pouty rosebud lips were quirked upward in a slight smile as she said that, and her eyes sparkled mischievously as if she'd made a double entendre. Which, considering his last encounter with the adorable little woman, was probably the case.

Dare momentarily forgot his nervousness about being called to Lady Marona's chambers, heart thumping with excitement at the prospect of more fun with the naughty maid.

Marigold set off at a brisk pace, long pink hair swishing from side to side with every step, and he hurried to keep up as she led the way down a few hallways and up some stairs to the third floor. Then he stifled a surprised noise when she abruptly grabbed him and pushed him towards a tapestry, then through it to a secret servant's passage beyond.

"Hi!" she whispered, round cheeks flushed as she beamed up at him. "Glad I was the lucky one on duty when you visited . . . Belinda's going to be so jealous."

Belinda was a dragon girl maid who'd boldly given Dare a bath during his first visit. Along with some incredible sex.

He smiled down at the adorable gnome. "I'm glad you were, too. I've been looking forward to seeing you again."

Marigold giggled. "Good! But we have to hurry before the Mistress wonders what's taking us." She wasted no time untying his laces and pulling his cock free, gasping at the sight of it. "Wow, I forgot how huge it is."

If she was already impressed at Dare's semi-rigid state, she became astounded when he rose to his full nine inches. Her eyes greedily took him in as she opened wide.

Like Zuri, the little gnome could walk face first onto his dick, and her small mouth strained mightily to fit his tip inside. Although unlike the goblin, who as a carnivore with pointy teeth was used to swallowing food in large chunks or even whole (and was easily able to do the same for his cock), Marigold couldn't fit more than his tip inside.

But she made up for it by enthusiastically drooling all over his shaft, then getting to work with both small hands to pleasure him along his length, making him groan appreciatively and run his hands through her soft pink hair. Her tongue worked just as diligently over every inch of him in her warm mouth, and she made muffled sounds of enjoyment the entire time.

Given her haste and her wholehearted effort, it only took a couple minutes before Dare groaned in release, grabbed two handfuls of her hair, and began spurting down her throat. She greedily swallowed every drop, making contented noises, and when he was done pulled back and licked her lips.

"Thanks, I've been wanting that ever since I got to taste you last time," she said with a giggle. "You're delicious."

He grinned down at her as he stuffed himself back in his pants and tied the laces. "I'd love to return the favor sometime. I bet you taste delicious too."

Marigold clapped her hands eagerly. "I do!" With a naughty grin she reached under her ruffled white skirt and wiggled, sliding an adorable little pair of lacy white panties down her pale, plump thighs. She nimbly stepped out of them and held them up, a rich scent of cinnamon and heady musk wafting from a large damp spot on the gusset.

"Here," she said, biting her lip. "Something to remember me

by."

Dare could honestly say he'd never had a girl give him her panties before. Although he supposed Zuri, Pella, or Leilanna would happily do so if he asked. But that would sort of take the fun out of it.

"I'll treasure them," he said solemnly, neatly folding the soft little bit of cloth and putting it in his pocket.

The pink-haired gnome giggled again. "I don't want you to treasure them, silly, I want you to jack off to them." Her big blue eyes twinkled with mischief. "That way you'll be excited to see me again. Next time you stay over I'll be the one to give you a bath, or even sneak into your rooms late at night if I have to." She batted her eyes coyly. "And you'll love it . . . there's no pussy as tight as a gnome's, you know."

Considering that Zuri's crushed him like a vise when they made love, he believed her. "I can't wait." Dare lifted the adorable little gnome in her sexy French maid dress and kissed her plump, glistening lips.

"Mmm," she moaned, kissing him back hungrily and teasing his lips with her small pink tongue. Then she gave a guilty start and squirmed out of his arms. "Shit, we need to go!"

Marigold hurriedly led the way out from behind the tapestry and down the hallway, frantically smoothing her black and white ruffled dress and combing her hair with her fingers as she went. Dare followed, making sure he was also presentable.

At the end of the hallway the little maid rapped on a pair of double doors, got a muffled response from within, and opened both in front of her with a bow. "My Lady, the adventurer and landed gentleman Dare." She gracefully moved aside and motioned him through with a deep curtsy.

Dare stepped through the doors into a cozy, elegantly appointed room dominated by a loveseat and two overstuffed chairs around a coffee table. Lady Marona was reclined on the loveseat with a book turned facedown on the table, as if she'd been interrupted reading.

To his surprise she looked far different from when he'd last seen her.

Still elegant, of course, with slender, aristocratic beauty in defiance of the fact that she was probably in her late 40s. But now her graying hair was raven black, sleek and shimmering in a waterfall around her shoulders and down her chest and back. Her face had been subtly but expertly made up, smoothing away or covering slight wrinkles around her eyes and at the corners of her mouth. Her dark brown eyes looked large and mysterious thanks to delicate touches of mascara, and her lips were painted red and glistened invitingly.

She wore a stunning gown of clinging yellow silk that accented her slender curves, and had what looked like a matching set of emerald-studded truesilver tiara, choker, bracelets, and rings.

The baroness had been beautiful before, and he'd even appreciated the signs of elegance and maturity her age lent her. But now she could've been any of the breathtaking mature actresses walking the red carpet in Hollywood. If he hadn't known better he might've believed she was in her early 30s.

Which begged the question of why she'd gone to so much effort.

"My Lady," Dare said, bowing low. "If I may be so impertinent, you look absolutely stunning today."

A blush struggled valiantly to show through her serene composure. "Thank you." She motioned to the overstuffed chair beside her loveseat. "Please, come sit down." She turned to Marigold. "Thank you, that will be all."

The pink-haired gnome looked startled at being dismissed, no doubt especially when it meant leaving a man unattended in her lady's quarters. But at a stern look from her stately mistress she curtsied hastily and left, shutting the doors behind her.

"All alone this time, Master Dare?" Lady Marona said politely as he sank into the comfortable chair.

"I'm afraid so," Dare replied. "I was just in town to make some purchases and see if you'd returned from your trip. Leilanna is leveling with a friend, Pella is managing the laborers at Nirim Manor, and Zuri is . . ." He trailed off. "Actually, that's one of the things I wanted to talk to you about. I've extended an invitation to a tribe of goblins to rent a portion of my land for a new village."

The Baroness of Terana pursed her lips, clearly displeased. "Did you, now."

"I did. They're indebted to me for aid I've given them in the past, and call me a friend. I have their assurances that they'll keep the peace." He awkwardly scratched at his jaw. "And I've also agreed to cement our friendship by marrying the daughter of their chieftain."

In spite of her irritation the noblewoman looked amused at that. "Another addition to your harem?"

Dare blushed. "If all goes well."

She smiled, then sobered and shook her head with a sigh. "The land is yours to do with as you please, and while goblins are looked down on it's not forbidden to take them on as tenants." Her expression became stern. "But if they cause trouble it'll be on your head."

He nodded. "I understand, and I'm prepared to deal with it should any issues arise. Zuri is acting as a go-between for now, and she seems confident the goblins will make productive use of the land and stay out of trouble. That's where she is now, preparing for their arrival today."

"Very well." That seemed to settle the matter for Lady Marona, and she relaxed back. "How is Zuri, by the way? I understand she's getting very close to her due date."

"She's a couple weeks away, still," he said. "But yes, she's very close. At all of our insistence relegated to pottering around Nirim Manor doing light tasks and resting." He chuckled. "Honestly, she's happy for the chance to go out with the others and welcome the newly arrived goblins as a change of pace."

"I can only imagine how that must feel." The older woman's expression was oddly wistful, and she seemed eager to change the subject. "Nirim Manor, did you call your new home?"

10

Dare nodded. "Leilanna's suggestion. According to her the Nirim flower only grows in rare and special places, or in gardens cultivated by skilled elves. It never loses its petals, and as the ages pass regularly grows a new ring of petals. The oldest ones are apparently enormous and breathtaking."

"An appropriate name for a man so clearly eager to grow his harem." Her lips quirked upward in a subtle smirk. "I take it your current consorts are okay with the idea of sharing you?"

He couldn't help but laugh. "If anything, they eagerly encourage it, and pump me for details of any encounters they weren't there for." He abruptly remembered who he was talking to and hesitated. "Forgive me for my impropriety, my Lady."

The baroness laughed richly. "It's quite all right. I begged the answer with my question, and in any case I'm not such a prude as you might think." Her dark eyes glittered with amusement. "Tell me, do you have any tales for them from this trip?"

Dare felt his cheeks heat as he considered how just minutes ago he'd emptied his balls down her maid's throat just down the hall. Probably not the best thing to admit. "Most likely."

"Well, that dovetails nicely into my purpose for inviting you," she said, straightening briskly to a seated position. "I'm glad to hear work on your manor is going well, and things seem to be well in hand. But it wasn't the main reason I asked you to visit when you had the chance. Although I suppose it's a good thing you came alone."

Well that was mysterious. "To what do I owe the pleasure of this invitation, my Lady? If I can be of service please let me know."

"It's good to hear you say that," Lady Marona said, biting her lip. "I did in fact wish to make a request. Something . . . unorthodox."

Dare leaned forward attentively, waiting.

She took a deep breath, low-cut bodice proudly displaying her small breasts, and then spoke quickly and firmly. "Master Dare, you'll find that as you get older you have less patience for beating around the bush. So I'm going to come right out with it."

"All right." He thought he had an idea of what she wanted, but if he was wrong he didn't want to make an ass of himself.

The baroness smoothed the lap of her elegant dress. "I love my departed husband, but to my lasting regret I was barren and never able to bear him children." She paused. "Although it could be argued that the problem lay with Orin . . . he enjoyed dallying with many of our maids, and though they were not always particularly careful none of them ever became pregnant with his child."

Interesting. And salacious. And Dare was now pretty sure of where this was going, although he wasn't sure whether to be eager or nervous.

"In any case," she continued briskly, "whether I am barren or not, I'm afraid age has taken its toll. Women of my advanced years often have very great difficulty conceiving a child, and often suffer complications in the pregnancy." She leaned forward, dark eyes intent. "Which was why I felt a ray of hope when I learned from Belinda that my handsome guest has a fertility stat of 51."

Well, it looked as if the draconid maid wasn't terribly worried about discretion.

Lady Marona's full red lips curled in amusement at his reaction. "Which doesn't seem like something he would lie about while trying to get between her legs . . . most women merely looking for a good time don't find the possibility of getting pregnant just from touching his dick a good thing, and men are smart enough to realize that."

"Yes, I have 51 fertility," Dare admitted.

"That's good to hear." The beautiful noblewoman nervously brushed a strand of dark hair from her cheek, looking off to one side of him as she hastily continued. "Because with fertility that high even a barren old woman might have some hope. I wanted to ask if you'd consider helping me conceive the child I've always longed for, before it's too late."

Okay then. It was his turn take a breath. "What exactly were you imagining here, my Lady?"

She blushed again. "I suppose I'm willing to consider

alternatives, based on what you wish. We could keep the child's parentage unknown and I will raise it by myself. In that case you would have no responsibility for the child and no role in its life.

"Alternatively, if you wished to acknowledge the child as your natural born offspring you might visit and have a role as its father. Although in terms of inheritance the child would be solely mine, I must insist on that."

"And what of us, Lady Marona?" Dare asked quietly. "Is giving you a child your sole interest in me?"

The baroness shifted on the loveseat and bunched up her fancy dress in her fists, looking far younger and less assured than she had just moments before. Suddenly shy, she met his eyes and quickly looked away.

"It . . . would not displease me to have you as a lover, Master Dare. I would look forward to spending time with you, should you pay me visits." She abruptly smirked. "And my maids would certainly be overjoyed if you had more excuses to come to the manor . . . the ones who don't get to spend time with you sulk for days after you leave."

Dare coughed, reddening. "I hope you don't mind the impropriety, or me taking them from their work."

Lady Marona threw back her head and laughed freely at that. "Not at all. My husband used to be the same way with them, his own little informal harem." She smiled sadly off into the distance. "Besides, it makes them happy . . . this place hasn't been so lively and full of chatter since he died."

She abruptly sobered. "Which is kind of my point. I merely assumed that since you're surrounded by beautiful, fertile young women throwing themselves at you, you'd have little interest in a fading flower almost old enough to be your grandmother."

That wasn't quite accurate, going by his age on Earth. "In the land I came from," he said with a smile, "many women are blessed to retain their beauty as they enter the golden years of life, and often find lovers even in old age, including younger men." He met her eyes boldly. "And most of them pale in comparison to you, my Lady ... I would be honored to be with you."

The baroness smiled back as if she didn't quite believe that, but seemed pleased nonetheless. She relaxed and settled deeper into her loveseat. "It could only be the occasional dalliance, you understand. I'm not interested in replacing my husband, and of course you have your harem." Her lips quirked. "Not to mention my maids need seeing to."

Dare got the impression he was really going to enjoy his visits to the mansion. Not that he wasn't already, of course. "Then I suppose it doesn't need saying, but to be clear it would be my pleasure to help you conceive a child, and if you'll allow it I would like to be part of the child's life."

"Good." The beautiful noblewoman stood gracefully, showing some nervousness as she smoothed her clinging dress. "I daresay you have more experience with romancing strangers than I do, seeing as how I married my husband soon after I came into womanhood and was never unfaithful."

She nibbled her lip. "So how would you like to begin, um, proceedings?"

"I believe this is a good start." He stood as well, stepping close, and met her eyes as he gently reached up and cupped her cheek with one hand. She sucked in a sharp breath, eyes widening and lips slightly parted in eager anticipation.

Dare leaned forward and gently pressed his lips to hers.

Lady Marona kissed him back with surprising passion, wrapping her arms around his back and pressing her slender body against him. Dare wrapped his arms around her as well, supporting some of her weight as she lifted one foot behind her as the kiss deepened.

Wow, he thought women only did that in movies.

She didn't seem to be ready for tongue just yet, and when he trailed a hand down her back to her hip he felt her lips hesitate. So he broke the kiss for a moment. "We don't have to rush if you don't feel ready," he told her, gently rubbing her back. "We can spend more time together, get comfortable in each other."

Lady Marona shook her head with a slight smile. "I appreciate the sensitivity, but remember I'm racing the clock with infertility here." She stepped away and gracefully slid the straps of her dress over her shoulders. With a whispering rustle her lovely yellow gown slithered down her slender frame to pool around her feet.

She was naked underneath.

Dare stood in awe, taking in her beautiful body. She'd obviously taken care of herself over the years, with barely a sag or fold in spite of her age. He'd seen women in their 20s with less stunning figures.

An even more arresting sight was her clearly recently shaved sex between her toned thighs, flushed with arousal and glistening with her nectar.

The baroness snickered. "The fact that your jaw's on the floor seems like a good sign."

He raised his gaze to her soft brown eyes, smiling. "Take this as flattery if you wish, my Lady, but I find myself having difficulty believing your claims about your age."

She smirked back. "Then do I arouse you as much as your beautiful young consorts?"

In answer Dare took her hand. "By your leave." He pressed her palm against the bulge straining against his pants, his cock twitching at her touch. "Does that answer your question?"

"Mmm." Lady Marona's long, elegant fingers traced his length through the cloth. "Belinda and Marigold did say you were huge." Suddenly daring, she unlaced the ties and pulled his cock free, fingers soft and grip firm. Her eyes widened and she gasped quietly. "I see their descriptions don't do justice to reality . . . I hope I'm ready for this monster."

He trailed his hand down her side and cupped her firm ass, kneading the soft flesh. "I can help you with that."

Dropping to his knees, he bent and pressed his lips to her hairless mound.

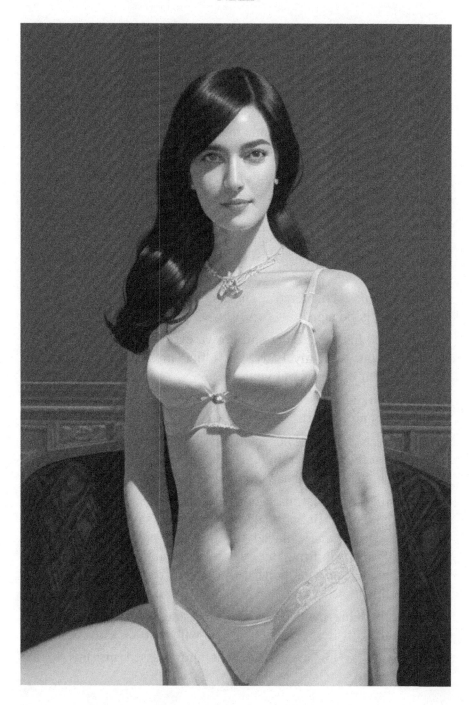

作

"Oh!" the baroness cried breathlessly, clutching his head with both hands and stroking her fingers through his hair. "I'm a bit surprised you're interested in doing that with me."

Dare had a hunch about what might please this elegant lady. He'd be best served by taking inspiration from Victorian romance novels. Although unfortunately his only real experience with those were a few book clubs he'd attended with a prospective love interest that had turned out to be a disappointment.

Although maybe not a complete waste of time.

"If you could see how beautiful you are right now, my Lady," he said as he kissed his way over her mound and down her slim thighs, "the only thing that would surprise you is that I'm able to hold myself back from ravishing you like a beast."

"Oh!" she said again, sounding scandalized yet pleased. "The things you say, Master Dare."

"And do, my Lady?" Grinning, he finally stopped circling the prize and pressed his lips to her glistening sex, tasting her nectar, rich and musky like aged wine.

Lady Marona gasped and spread her legs to give him better access. Or maybe because her knees had suddenly gone weak. Dare gripped her firm ass with both hands to support her as he made love to her elegant pussy with his lips and tongue, making her moan and squirm.

He wasn't sure if she climaxed, but she abruptly pulled away and fell back on the loveseat, small chest heaving with her panting breaths. "Does my flower please you, Master Dare?" she asked, draping one leg over the back of the loveseat to present herself to him.

Dare leaned over and kissed her nearer knee, looking up into her dark eyes, which were slightly glazed from lust. "I could worship it until I collapsed from exhaustion, my Lady, and dream the sweetest dreams."

The baroness bit her lip and dropped a finger to trace her folds. "You have my leave to take your pleasure of me."

Holy shit, that was the most refined way of saying "fuck me" he'd ever heard.

He hastily tossed aside his shirt and pants and positioned himself over her, tip grazing her entrance. In response she wrapped both arms around his neck and looped a leg behind his, looking up at him expectantly.

He leaned down and kissed her softly, rolling a nipple with one finger, and gently pushed into her soft warmth.

"Oh!" She moaned. "Gods rest my husband, he was never this large."

Her walls were tight but yielding, lovingly caressing every inch of him that sank into her until he finally bottomed out with inches still outside. Dare went slow at first to give her time to adjust, stopping frequently to kiss her, play with her small breasts, and rub her sensitive pearl.

Finally he felt her relax and begin to undulate her hips against his thrusts. He sped up, letting himself enjoy her velvety pussy.

While Lady Marona wasn't as wet as most of the other women he'd been with, her juices flowed steadily to lubricate his shaft. She seemed to be enjoying herself as much as he was, sighing and squirming against him.

Finally she began letting out the most delicious whimpers as she held onto him desperately, kissing his shoulder and neck as her velvet walls began rippling over his length in a powerful orgasm. "If you're ready, Master Dare," she panted in his ear. "Would you kindly release your seed in me?"

Hard to refuse a request like that. Dare grabbed her slender hips and gave a last firm thrust, pressing his tip against her core, then began emptying himself inside the mature noblewoman.

Her fingernails delicately scraped his back throughout their shared climax, not quite hard enough to draw blood. Finally he collapsed beside her on the loveseat, still sheathed in her warmth, and gathered her up in his arms, kissing her hair and inhaling the scented oils she'd combed into it.

"Thank you, Master Dare," she said, demurely nibbling his neck in turn. "That was . . . very nice."

"That was incredible, my Lady," he said. "I'm blessed to taste of your sweet flower."

Lady Marona laughed softly. "Our lovemaking is done with, Master Dare. You can stop talking like a lady's private reading."

Dare chuckled as well, trailing his fingers along her arm. "Flowery terms or not, I enjoyed that."

She sighed and settled in against him, soft and flushed with satisfaction. Then with a reluctant noise she pulled away, straightening briskly. "I would like to spend more time with you, and perhaps in the future I'll have time. But I've got a thousand things to catch up on after my trip to the region capitol and I'm afraid I can't spare another moment."

"Maybe just one?" he asked, rising and pulling her back for another brief but fierce kiss.

The noblewoman's deep brown eyes looked up at him warmly as she pulled back. "Until next time, Master Dare. You and your lovers are always welcome." She smiled. "And even if I'm not available, feel free to stay as long as you like, even the night if you wish. I'm sure my maids would be pleased to attend you."

Dare had to wonder if he'd died and gone to heaven, not only blessed with a harem of three beautiful women who genuinely loved him, but also to find a beautiful lady who wanted a lover at her convenience and had zero issues with him fooling around with her staff the rest of the time.

Although technically, he supposed he *had* died, back on Earth. And while Collisa wasn't exactly heaven, he was very lucky in the life he'd found here.

* * * * *

Nirim Manor was almost a full day's ride from Terana, making any trip there an investment in time.

It was afternoon of the next day before Dare came in view of his

19

manor. Although he passed it by and headed on to the land he'd picked out for the goblins he'd invited to live on his estate. It was an area of plains dotted with a few woods and a stream running through it, suitable to support a small village.

He was relieved to see that the goblins had arrived, most likely the day before as promised. They were members of the Avenging Wolf tribe, mostly women and children and laborers uninterested in combat and seeking safety.

Avenging Wolf was a tribe that had combined from several smaller tribes who'd been living in a nearby ravine leading through the Gadris Mountains. When slavers had begun raiding the ravine, kidnapping and killing and plundering, they'd banded together for mutual protection. Even then they'd been steadily driven back towards the north end of the ravine.

Dare and his lovers had killed the group of slavers that had been persecuting the goblins, freeing 41 innocent captives in the process. But although the immediate threat of slavers was gone, when Dare had offered the tribe his protection on his lands, many had chosen to come.

Chieftain Gar and most of his warriors had opted to stay in the mountains, as well as most of their families, but that still left over a hundred goblins willing to move. As well as a few hobgoblins, or the hybrid offspring of humans and goblins. One of Chieftain Gar's mates and her two children, to be exact.

One of whom happened to be Dare's betrothed, Se'weir.

He'd expected Zuri to be there helping, of course, and Pella as well if she could get away from her duties at the manor. But he was pleasantly surprised to see that Ilin and Leilanna had taken a break from leveling to also help out.

Which was good, because both were well suited to helping the goblins with their fledgling settlement.

Leilanna had an almost supernatural affinity for growing things thanks to her elvish heritage. She'd already worked a miraculous transformation on the manor's gardens, and was currently giving dozens of goblin laborers advice on planting fall crops.

As for Ilin, he'd spent the last decade wandering and assisting in charitable efforts everywhere he went. He had the best grasp of all of them of what the relocated goblins needed, not just short term but long term, and how to organize efforts to help them.

All three of Dare's lovers rushed towards him when they saw him riding up, even Leilanna looking happy as she broke away from the goblins toiling in the soil and trotted over.

"How did it go?" Pella called, her fluffy golden-furred tail wagging eagerly as she reached him first.

At two months pregnant she was already starting to show, her tall, muscular body's womanly curves becoming even softer. That was partly because they were almost certain that, of the 50/50 chance to have a human or canid child, the coin flip had landed on canid, and canid pregnancies lasted about six months rather than the almost ten for humans.

The other reason was because dog girls tended to have twins, triplets, or even more children at a time. Apparently their stomachs were capable of stretching more easily than human women to accommodate the larger number of children, and almost always without stretch marks (which Zuri and Leilanna were clearly envious of).

All signs pointed to the fact that Pella was having at least twins, and Dare couldn't help but look forward to seeing the beautiful dog girl with a huge pregnant belly and her already generous breasts swollen even larger.

She was waiting to throw her arms around him the moment he dismounted, and he kissed her warmly and rested a hand on the gentle swell of her belly. "How are you and these little guys doing?" he asked.

His golden-haired lover gave him a warm smile and rested her head against his shoulder, soft floppy ears pressed to his cheek. "They're doing great, and so am I. Although I missed you the last few days."

21

"I missed you too," he said, nuzzling her hair and ears. She smelled fantastic, as usual.

She giggled and gave him an impish look. "But you weren't too lonely, right?" She playfully grabbed his crotch, feeling the outline of his cock, large even when flaccid, through the cloth. "You found someone to keep you company in Terana, right? There's a sweet-smelling gift in your pocket."

Dare felt his cheeks heating at the mention of Marigold's panties. Camping alone last night he may or may not have used them for the purpose she'd given them for. And he was definitely looking forward to seeing her again.

Thankfully he was interrupted from having to answer by Zuri's arrival, with Leilanna close behind. Which was good, since they would've pressed for details too and it saved him from having to repeat himself.

Zuri expectantly held her arms out so he could pick her up. Which was sort of necessary if they wanted to comfortably hug or kiss, since the beautiful goblin woman barely came up to his belly button.

He had to be more gentle these days in picking her up, careful of her belly, which looked even more hugely swollen on her small body. She was only weeks away from having their baby, which with four months of pregnancy meant it would definitely be a goblin.

Dare cradled her gently and kissed her and then her round tummy. "And how are the mother of my firstborn and the little one?" he asked.

She beamed up at him, big yellow eyes loving. "Ready for the birth, but otherwise healthy and happy."

"Hey!" Leilanna complained, holding out her arms. "Do I have to get knocked up before I get any attention from you?" She almost sounded like she didn't mind the idea.

Dare laughed and gently set Zuri down, stepping over to the beautiful dusk elf and wrapping her in a firm embrace. Her return hug was surprisingly fierce, engulfing him in the warmth of her soft, curvy body as she lifted her face expectantly for a kiss.

He obliged, her plump lips soft against his, mouth opening to offer a warm welcome to his invading tongue. She tasted like sweet blackberry wine, and as he pulled back a thread of their mingled saliva connected them for a few inches before snapping.

"You two are so cute together," Pella said, tail wagging as she wrapped them both in a hug.

"We're all cute together," Zuri agreed, wiggling her way into the center of the group embrace.

"So speaking of getting together," Leilanna said, dark pink eyes smoldering playfully, "I thought I heard Pella asking you about your adventures in Terana before we arrived. Did you finally get with that sexy guard and her shackles?"

Dare coughed, embarrassed. "No. But Lady Marona and her maids were back. I was able to clear up the last bit of business with the estate, and get her approval to rent some land to the Avenging Wolf goblins." He brightened. "Speaking of which, how are they settling in?"

"Uh uh uh!" Zuri scolded, grinning. "It's no fun you going off and having a good time if we don't get to hear about it from you. Come on, what happened."

"Weeeellll," he said, grinning. "I got to see Belinda again after my meeting with the Baroness. She pulled me into her room and we had some fun. And that pink-haired gnome, Marigold, tugged me behind a tapestry on our way to my meeting with Lady Marona and gave me another blowjob."

"That's pretty hot," Leilanna said. "You'll have to give us all the details tonight." She grinned impishly. "Maybe we can try some of it."

"Hold on, you're saving the best for last," Pella accused. "You smell way too satisfied." She grinned hugely, tail wagging. "Also you smell like someone else."

Dare laughed; hard to hide anything from a dog girl's keen senses. "All right. I may or may not have become Lady Marona's

23

lover and agreed to father her heir."

"Really?" Zuri asked eagerly. "Is she going to join our harem?"

He gently stroked her soft black hair. "That would be a bit hard to work out with her ruling Terana Province. She's more interested in the occasional tryst, and of course a child." He grinned around at them. "And she's offered us the run of her manor, and basically said outright she doesn't mind me fucking her maids."

"Oooh, we'll have to visit Montshadow Estate soon then," Leilanna said. "Their food is delicious."

"So are their maids!" Pella said. "We need to see if they just want to play with Dare, or they'd be willing to play with us, too."

Their banter was interrupted by Ilin's arrival. The Monk had politely given them space for their reunion, but since they seemed to be talking he'd finally made his way over. "Welcome back," he said, smiling wryly. "You'd almost think you were gone for a year, not a few days."

Dare chuckled as he clasped wrists with the shorter man. "You and Leilanna gained a level while I was gone. Congratulations."

"Up to 24," Ilin agreed, sounding satisfied; as he would, after the issues he'd had leveling on his own. "Just a few more levels to catch up to you." For some reason Leilanna made an irritated noise and dug an elbow into the Monk's side, and the man flushed and hastily nodded to the northwest. "So, ah, how did the trip to town go?"

"It went well," Dare replied, wondering what that exchange had been about. "I checked in on the orphanage like you asked and construction is going at a good pace. I also checked in on those families and made sure they got their provisions."

His friend looked relieved. "Good, thank you. Saved me a trip."

Dare turned to include his lovers. "The supplies and laborers we need will be coming with the next shipment from Terana." He couldn't help but grin. "Including the pipes for plumbing and sewer and the toilets. I can finally start trying to get the septic system working."

"Hurray," Leilanna said, rolling her eyes; much as she loved the idea of indoor plumbing, she wasn't sold that he could actually make it work. "Speaking of ordering things, we need to discuss finances."

"Wait, wait!" Zuri said hastily, tugging at Dare's hand. "First you need to go and say hi to Se'weir and spend some time with her. She's been looking forward to seeing you again ever since you betrothed her two weeks ago."

"No no no!" the fiery dusk elf snapped, stamping her foot. "If you put Dare in the company of a beautiful woman he'll forget everything else, and he's already got enough reasons to put this off." She grabbed his arm, pink eyes flashing. "We're talking about finances *now*. He can meet with Se'weir after."

Dare couldn't help but wince. "Don't worry, I haggled aggressively in Terana. We got great deals."

"It doesn't matter how well you haggle if we're spending more than we're bringing in," she shot back, putting a hand on her lush hip. "You all agreed to put me on finances since Dare's busy with other stuff, and Zuri and Pella are a bit weak when it comes to math. So if you're going to give me the responsibility, the least you can do is listen to me."

"Fine, fine," Dare said soothingly, wrapping an arm around her waist and kissing her gently. "So what do we need to discuss?"

His beautiful lover didn't seem mollified. "We're going overboard with the renovations," she said with a frown, tucking a strand of soft snowy hair behind one of her long tapered ears. "It's my fault as much as anyone's . . . we let the fortune from the dungeon go to our heads, and didn't consider how hard it would be to earn that amount in the future."

That was a good point. And a troubling one, since they'd be relying on that gold to support Zuri and Pella and the babies until they could level enough to start making more.

"So we scale things back?" Zuri asked.

Leilanna nodded. "Especially since so many of the expenses are for Dare's fancy *bathrooms*." Her tone wasn't completely teasing.

"Whoa whoa whoa," Dare protested. "We can hold off building

another guest house or adding another wing to the manor for a while, but I want you guys to have the best comforts available."

"We can get by with drawing water from the well and pooping in an outhouse," Pella said, patting his arm.

As opposed to working toilets, bathtubs and showers with hot water, sinks for the kitchen, and everything else? Dare threw up his hands in exasperation. "I'm telling you, once you experience indoor plumbing for yourselves you'll see that everyone else is living in squalor in comparison. It is the single greatest luxury a house can have, aside from maybe central heating and cooling."

Leilanna smirked at him. "There you go making up nonsense phrases again."

The group chuckled, although she was exaggerating since he'd already explained the concepts in detail.

Zuri hugged him warmly, pregnant belly pressing against his legs. "We all believe you, Dare. You're usually right about this stuff. We're just having fun."

"Although we really do need to consider finances," Leilanna insisted. "My share of the loot me and Ilin bring in with our leveling can barely cover basic expenses, let alone all the extravagant improvements we're making to what's already a more luxurious home than any of us have ever had. And we haven't even considered taxes yet. And when the babies come we'll be needing even more for them."

Dare found it pretty amazing that his dusk elf lover willingly gave up her share of loot for the family, and had ever since he'd met her. She complained, of course, but that was just her way; she was a lot more generous and kindhearted than she let on.

Of course, she didn't pull punches either. As she proved when she continued. "We can't expect Zuri and Pella to farm monsters, of course, but those of us who can produce gold should." She gave him a pointed look. "Especially when it's your *responsibility*."

He winced. Yes, over the last couple weeks since moving into Nirim Manor he'd been busy with other things; while Leilanna and

Ilin had gained four levels he'd only gained one. But he'd made plans and was ready to leap back into leveling and farming gold.

He'd just been waiting for Leilanna and Ilin to catch up to him. And it looked as if they finally had.

"I know," he said. "Now that I'm back I can join you and we can really dive into it."

His lovers exchanged glances with each other and Ilin. "Actually," Zuri said carefully, "we kind of think it's about time for you to leap ahead."

Dare blinked in confusion. "What does that mean?"

Pella rested a hand on her belly. "It means that Zuri and I are going to be mothers. We're out of the adventuring game for the foreseeable future. Our lives now are the family we're building here." She smiled at him gently. "And honestly I'm all right with that . . . I fought monsters to be with my master, but if he'd given me a baby I would've been happy to stay at his estate and raise it instead. Like I can here, with our children."

Ilin nodded. "And while me and Leilanna can catch up to you, we're ultimately going to slow you down by splitting experience with us." He chuckled wryly. "You proved that by getting a level almost without trying as you scouted the nearby spawn points, while we were busting our asses in the same amount of time."

"Besides," Leilanna said, "I enjoy adventuring with you, but the longer I see Pella and Zuri, the more I want to be a mother with them." She rested a hand on his arm. "To have children with you. I don't want to slow you down only to ultimately take a different path."

"And although I've enjoyed spending time with all of you," the Monk added, "and I've come to consider you like family and this place a second home, eventually I'll be moving on."

Dare felt a surge of helplessness. "We're stronger as a group," he protested.

"Maybe, but you're faster on your own," Leilanna said bluntly. "And you need to be high level to protect us, and also to earn the gold we need to support us." She squeezed his arm gently. "We'll keep on leveling as we can, as long as you scout out the spawn points for us. And we can go after weaker party rated world monsters and even dungeons if we get the opportunity."

Their arguments weren't terrible. But even if they were right that it might be more efficient, it wasn't what he wanted.

Zuri seemed to read his mind, hugging his legs tightly again. "I know you want to adventure with us, my mate, and we want to be with you too. But ultimately if we wanted to have a family and bear your children this was bound to happen. So let us make Nirim Manor a haven for you to return to often for rest and sanctuary."

Pella hugged him as well, tears in her eyes. "We'll have other adventures with you, Dare. Raising children is an adventure. But we all know you dream of being high level, and you have the abilities and intelligence to make it happen. So go, for yourself and for us."

Damnit. Part of Dare thought fondly of his first month on Collisa before meeting Zuri. A lot of that was because it was all new and exciting, but he had to admit he'd loved the independence and challenge of each fight, relying on his wits and skills alone.

And, part of him had to admit, not having to worry about the women he loved being in danger.

He hated the thought of not being with his lovers, not having them there by his side every day and around the campfire with him every night. But a part of him also thought of the independence of leveling alone.

He looked around. "Are you sure you're not just saying this to make the decision easier for me?"

"You're not leaving us behind to go adventure, Dare," Leilanna said, finally joining the hug herself. "We're content here, with our growing family, and like the others have said this is what we want for you. And what's best for the family, so you can protect and provide for us."

They were right. He needed to be higher level to take care of his family, and if they were content here then far from it being selfish to leave them behind, it would be selfish to ask them to come with him.

"All right," he said reluctantly. He smiled and hugged his lovers tighter. "As long as you promise we can still travel and do exciting things. Safe, exciting things."

"And you promise you won't get so caught up in adventuring you neglect us," Leilanna said. "Maybe not half of your time at the manor, but a lot of it. And returning every night, if you can."

"I promise." Dare nodded towards the goblins. "I suppose I should go say hi to Se'weir."

It wasn't hard to pick out his hobgoblin bride-to-be among the smaller goblins. She topped Zuri by almost a foot, which still put her under five feet.

Also she was waiting eagerly for him, surrounded by a cluster of young goblin women who might've been her sisters, friends, or even her attendants. Hard to be sure since he'd only exchanged a few words with her and wasn't quite sure what her situation was, other than that she was the daughter of Chieftain Gar and shared her mother's hobgoblin heritage.

Dare's lovers and Ilin returned to the tasks they'd been occupied with, leaving him to go out to meet the woman he'd be marrying in a year.

With every step towards Se'weir she brightened further, until her face practically glowed with a mixture of excitement, nervousness, and shyness. But mostly excitement; she was genuinely happy to see him.

And he had to admit that while he was still coming to terms with the fact that he was marrying her when he barely knew her, she seemed like a nice young woman. And she was without a doubt nice to look at.

The hobgoblin had green skin similar to a goblin's, although slightly lighter in color than even Zuri's. Her features were more soft and rounded, with just enough sharp angles to lend her an exotic beauty. Most goblins had black hair but hers was a light brown, long and flowing to halfway down her back. Her eyes were a yellow so pale they were almost white, large and open and full of feeling.

She was unquestionably plump, with a soft curvy body that you just knew would feel nice to hold, as he'd already found for himself when she hugged him the last time they met. And no doubt she'd be fun and bouncy in bed.

When she smiled he saw more familiar human teeth, even and white, and when he smiled back her blush added a pink flush to her pale green skin rather than darkening it like Zuri's did.

Se'weir broke away from the goblin women and ran to him, large breasts bouncing invitingly and hips swaying, although she didn't seem aware of it. "Dare!" she said, wrapping him in a warm hug. "Thank you for coming to visit me! I've missed you these last few weeks . . . I long for the day we'll be wed and I can bear your children. It seems so far away."

Damnit; whatever Dare's reservations about the marriage, it was impossible not to be charmed by her sweet sincerity.

He hugged the little hobgoblin back warmly, feeling her soft body through the nice dress she wore. Zuri must've made it for her, because it was a major upgrade from what she'd been wearing when he first saw her.

"Would you like to see the gardens at Nirim Manor?" he asked, offering her his arm. "We can take my horse."

"I would love to!" she said, face lighting up eagerly. Although she seemed a bit confused by the arm he held out to her, so he gently took hers and looped it through his, leading the way to his horse.

Se'weir practically bounced as they walked, she was so happy. "Can I see the manor too?" she begged. "I want to see where I'll live."

Assuming they both still wished for this marriage by the end of the year. Although at the moment it seemed likely they would. Dare chuckled and patted her arm. "Of course, although it's a bit of a mess right now with all the work we're doing."

"That's all right." She leaned against him, expression contented. "I can see the future, and it's beautiful."

Phoenix

He was liking his betrothed more and more.

Chapter One
Long Awaited

As a rule Dare didn't make use of exploits.

He wanted the challenge of a game. Of winning it as perfectly as possible by min/maxing the best gear and stats with just the knowledge he'd earned while playing, without relying on any guides or discussion boards.

Sure, when he'd done everything else he could do he'd sometimes use exploits to fool around before abandoning a game for the next challenge. Or if there was an interesting one that he wanted to see for himself. And there were even the odd visual glitches that were purely cosmetic that he'd play with because it was funny.

But no, usually he played the game fair.

On this world, though, he had three lovers at home who needed him to provide for them, two carrying his children, as well as a potential fourth he was tentatively engaged to; he couldn't ignore opportunities when he found them.

Which was why he was currently trotting through a forest with around 30 pissed off firbolgs stampeding after him, occasionally pausing to loose an arrow at the closest ones to fuel their enraged pursuit.

The firbolgs were all two or three levels above him, while their Alpha and its two lieutenants were all Charcoal to his Adventurer's Eye. Ten levels above him, with a helpful warning from the ability to avoid them at all costs.

Normally Dare would've avoided their camp like the plague, especially since within the camp proper it was almost impossible to aggro an enemy without pulling at least one add, which would've made the fight dangerous with most monsters.

And while he'd been given a lot of powerful abilities on Collisa, the new world he'd been reincarnated on after dying on Earth in an industrial accident, the ability to respawn or come back from death wasn't among them.

But conveniently, the big bear-like monsters were designed to be slow but strong melee fighters, with powerful single target and area of affect melee attacks but no movement buffs. For melee classes they would've been a daunting challenge, and probably even for melee and healer parties.

But Dare was a Hunter who wielded a bow, and had a broken ability called Fleetfoot gifted to him by the unseen benefactor who'd brought him to this world, which gave him a 34% speed increase. He could run circles around enemies, even ones with Charge or passive movement buffs.

Firbolgs were almost zero threat to him.

In fact, they were such a small threat that he'd actually taken the risk of pulling them from the camp itself, since he could kite as many adds as he wanted and easily stay ahead of them, slowly but steadily dropping the high health monsters with a constant stream of arrows.

A task which was made easier by Entangler, the Master quality bow he'd recently gained. Not only did it have nearly three times the damage of the bows he could craft with his basic Hunter ability, but it had a 10% snare proc and 5% root proc.

Which made it even easier to stay ahead of the lumbering firbolgs.

Farming monsters from the camp could be dangerous if one of the sentries that he'd already killed respawned early, which became a possibility when he was fighting enemies from the camp itself. Or on the rare occasions when a wandering monster roamed between monster spawn points. But Dare had once spent almost twenty minutes running around in a big circle shooting arrows while four firbolgs chased him.

That wasn't what he was doing now, of course. He didn't have the arrows to kill so many, and the Alpha or its lieutenants alone would've soaked up his entire quiver and barely lost a chunk off their health bar.

No, Dare had a much better idea.

He'd been farming this camp for days since it wasn't too far from Nirim Manor, and at one point had managed to get close enough to the Alpha to use his Adventurer's Eye on it. He'd discovered that the huge creature had an ability called "Rally the Camp", which pulled *every* firbolg in the spawn point as an add.

The obvious intention was that he clear the camp before trying to take on the boss fight. But to Dare it was a convenient way to gather all the monsters up.

So he'd shot the Alpha right in its stupid ursine face, then turned and bolted.

For the last half hour he'd steadily pulled the firbolgs farther and farther from camp. Kiting like that worked as long as he stayed in sight of them and didn't get too far away, as well as occasionally refreshing aggro so they didn't switch to another target they passed.

By this point, though, they were probably far enough away now to buy him some time. Which meant it was time to rob the stupid monsters blind.

Dare whirled around and began circling the firbolgs at a sprint, blasting past them at better than 25 miles an hour, a speed none of them could touch. Just for the fun of it he also raised Entangler and activated its use on cooldown ability, Vine Lash.

A vine shot out of the center of the bow and stretched 20 yards, wrapping around a sturdy branch ahead. Dare gripped the bow at either end and braced himself. "Retract!"

With a whoop he shot through the air, the vine pulling him not quite fast enough to give him whiplash, and somehow keeping him from dragging across the ground in spite of the low angle. Within moments the vine was stopping him safely at the branch, although rather than grabbing it he let himself drop the ten or so feet to the forest floor below.

Then he took off towards the firbolg camp at a sprint,

maintaining a high speed even while navigating through dense woods. Largely thanks to his Hunter abilities giving him a reduced movement speed penalty while traveling through undergrowth in a forest, and Fleetfoot giving him the agility and reflexes to keep from slamming face first into a branch at car speeds.

The trip that took a half hour while leading the ursine creatures took a fraction of that at full speed, and soon enough Dare was tearing through the crude hide tents, searching for loot worth taking.

Camps always had some. Because of the danger of adds, and the fact that there was usually some sort of higher level or more powerful boss, it usually took a group or a much higher level adventurer to clear them. To make the prospect more appealing the camps had enough loot to share between a party of four or five people for a decent reward.

Or one person who had children on the way and wanted to give them the best possible lives, and was willing to cheese away the guards and yoink the treasure without clearing the camp.

It was sort of a dick move for the next adventurer who came this way and cleared the camp hoping for loot; when you cleared the camp and looted the treasure, the treasure despawned for a short time, a week or so. Then a new treasure spawned with different loot rolls.

Since Dare wasn't clearing the camp, though, the treasure wouldn't respawn until someone came and did so. Only thanks to him they wouldn't get the usual loot as a reward for their efforts.

Well, killing monsters was its own reward. He would probably farm this camp until the firbolgs were too low level to provide experience anyway. He might even try his hand at the Alpha and lieutenants then, especially since it seemed like they were just as slow and "strong" as the others.

He found a few gold and trinkets among the tents, along with some bulkier loot that he might have to drop off later; he was strong, and this world was reasonably forgiving when it came to carry weight. But his pack was only so big, and he still had to run away from the firbolgs once he'd grabbed what he could.

Finally he reached the eagerly anticipated big tent at the center of the camp, where he'd pulled the firbolg Alpha and lieutenants. That was almost definitely going to be worth looting.

Possibly even the only tent really worth looting, considering the meager finds in the others.

The interior had the musty stench of poorly cured hides, not only from the heavy walls but also from a crude bed of more hides in the center. Off to one side was a large shape covered by a crude hide tarp that almost looked like a giant birdcage, and to the other was-

"Jackpot," Dare muttered, running over to an open chest of hide and bones. It was filled with what looked like the looted remains of travelers, trinkets and weapons and armor and coin pouches. None of it particularly high quality, but there was a goodly amount of stuff and it would probably fetch a couple hundred gold counting the coins themselves.

Dare produced his legendary chest, which was enchanted to shrink to the size of a peanut and decrease in weight by the same amount, and set it on the ground in front of the hide chest. "Grow."

It snapped to full size within an instant, easily big enough to hold everything he'd looted and more, and he hastily began transferring things over.

Then he froze when he heard a rustle from beneath the cloth on the other side of the tent. "Who's there?" a frightened woman's voice asked.

Dare spun with bow raised and arrow nocked, then hesitated; somehow he doubted whoever was under there was going to be a threat.

The voice spoke again, sounding on the verge of tears. "You're not a firbolg, right? I heard the Alpha call them all off and they haven't come back. Please, can you help me?"

"Of course," he said, hurrying over and yanking the tarp aside. Then his eyes widened when he saw who was inside the cage.

It was a fox girl. A genuine, honest to god fox girl.

She had sleek midnight black hair, including the silky fur on her large fox ears and her incredibly fluffy tail, a peaches and cream complexion, and big golden eyes that were the best feature of a beautiful face with sharp fox-like features, a small nose, and pouty rosebud lips. She was probably five feet nothing, with a curvy hourglass figure beneath the tattered dress of soft white rabbit fur she wore. Her delicate bare feet were also covered in soft midnight fur.

The poor girl had several claw wounds on her arms and legs, and her delicate skin was covered in bruises; either she'd fought desperately when she was captured or the firbolgs hadn't been treating her well.

His Eye identified her as "Vulpid, adult female. Humanoid, intelligent. Class: Stalker level 19." Her listed attacks and abilities suggested she was a sort of hybrid of a class similar to Pella's Tracker, which was adept at hunting prey, and a rogue with classic Stealth abilities and attacks.

The fox girl was looking at him with wary hope. "Um, hi," she said. "Can you please let me out? I don't want to be eaten."

Dare was already sawing at the rough leather binding the cage's bars together with his knife. "Don't worry, you'll be free in no time," he assured her. "I'm Dare. I live nearby, and my mate is a Healer. She can see to your wounds."

"Thanks, that would be great," the fox girl said with a nervous smile. Her big delicate ears twitched, and she fretted her lip and looked anxiously towards the entrance. "Can you, um, hurry?"

He redoubled his efforts, and finally with a wrench pulled a section of the cage away large enough for her to crawl free. "There you go," he said, turning back to the chests on the other side of the tent. "Just let me grab all this and . . ."

Dare trailed off and turned at a soft rustle, just in time to see the fox girl's adorably soft, fluffy black tail disappear through the tent's entry flaps.

Well, he could hardly blame the poor woman for beating a hasty retreat the moment she had the chance. He still had some time before the firbolgs returned but he should probably do the same.

No matter how fast he was, he didn't want to get caught in here with the Alpha or its lieutenants blocking the entrance, or *he'd* end up in the cage. If he was lucky.

After stuffing his chest with the loot, plus a few of the nicer hides from the bed, he shrank it again and stuffed it into the special reinforced pocket he'd made in the waistline of his pants, which had two different flaps that buttoned in three different places to make sure it didn't slip free.

Then he stuffed a few final hides in his pack, shrugged it onto his shoulders, and got out of there.

Dare could hear distant snarls and roars as he bolted the other way, but he was confident he'd easily be able to outdistance the slow firbolgs until they dropped aggro and returned to their camp.

Minus all their treasure and most of their Alpha's bed. Suckers.

Sure, he probably shouldn't be too proud about tricking a bunch of monsters, which usually tended to be slightly more intelligent than your average cow. But it was always satisfying when a plan worked.

Up ahead he spotted the fox girl, who'd paused between two trees to look back. He waved, and with a flick of her tail she bolted away in a flash.

She was quick, probably faster than Pella, but nowhere near the speed of a bunny girl. More than fast enough to get away from the firbolgs, though, and Dare wished her the best.

Judging by her cautious nature and Stealth abilities he had a feeling that was the last he'd see of her, so with a shrug he bolted off in the direction of the next spawn point he'd planned to visit.

He was close to Level 30, and was pushing hard to reach it by the end of the day. Every 10th level was a big one and he was excited to see what sort of new abilities he'd get, since not only should he get one for the level but also he'd unlock one with his ability tree Student of the Wild, which let him pick a new ability from it every five levels.

Phoenix

Dare gained access to the abilities by killing certain animals, which meant he only had a handful to choose from. But recently he'd killed a large porcupine-like creature that shot quills, and the ability it had provided was the accurately if somewhat unimaginatively named "Quill Shot".

It had been 20 levels since he'd got his last ability for the bow at Level 10, and while a lot of the ones he'd gotten instead were useful for survival or utility, he was looking forward to finally getting something that would help his ranged damage.

Quill Shot was humble, a passive boost that increased the damage done by his arrows by 2-4%, and when he took damage had a 1% chance to choose to instantly loose an arrow at his target as long as he was holding a bow and had an arrow in hand or in his quiver.

He didn't intend to get hit just to get off an extra shot, but passive effects were always nice. As he'd found with Entangler's 10% snare and 5% root; they'd saved his bacon more than once, and made leveling a lot easier and safer.

And Vine Lash was just awesome.

By the time Dare reached the next spawn point he was confident the firbolgs had lost aggro and returned to their camp. He shot the nearest preying mantis-like monster, and as it skittered his way steadily brought it down.

He'd discovered that aside from junk loot, the mantises mostly dropped alchemy reagents and diaphanous wings that tailors could use. In fact Zuri had used the most recent ones he'd brought her to create a sexy transparent nightie for Leilanna.

His goblin lover seemed determined to entice him to the beautiful dusk elf however she could, which was hardly necessary since he and Leilanna were still in their honeymoon phase and he could hardly keep his hands off her.

Honestly, he suspected that Zuri was secretly hoping that if he and his dusk elf lover practiced making babies often enough, they'd spontaneously decide to stop using Prevent Conception and go ahead and make it happen already.

She'd probably get her wish before long, too, since more and more of Leilanna's dirty talk during sex revolved around him impregnating her, to the point that mentioning it was a huge turn on for her.

Dare was more than willing to have a baby with the newest member of their family, but as was often the case Leilanna was slow to acknowledge her own feelings, and wasn't quite ready to take that step yet. Although he'd be there for her when she was, as he was determined be for Pella, and for Zuri who'd be having their baby any day now.

Almost as if his thoughts had been a summons, as Dare was preparing to aggro the next closest mantis he heard hoofbeats in the distance, and turned to see Ilin galloping towards him on a lathered mount, leading two more behind him.

"Dare!" he shouted, reining in hard enough his horse whinnied and danced, on the verge of rearing. "Blessing of Balance I found you so quickly, my friend!"

"What's wrong?" Dare asked anxiously. Everyone at the manor knew where he was leveling in case of an emergency, of course, but this was the first time anyone had come out here to him.

The Monk laughed easily. "Nothing wrong, just the opposite! It's time."

Dare's heart began pounding in his chest, and without waiting for further clarification he threw himself up into the saddle of one of the spare mounts. Ilin transferred over to the other, and without a word they galloped back towards Nirim Manor.

Zuri was having the baby.

Part of him had that panic ingrained from Earth, where childbirth was difficult and painful and could even be fatal if something went wrong. But thankfully Collisa, while cruel in many ways, was a lot kinder about the harsh realities than the world he'd left behind.

First off there was magical healing, which helped prevent much of the pain and danger. Secondly, the world system that allowed

41

women of smaller races to have children of larger races dramatically smoothed the process for everyone.

So there was much less danger and pain involved for childbirth on Collisa.

It usually took less time as well, or maybe he just hadn't rushed to get home fast enough, because as Dare burst into the manor and made his way towards the master bedroom he heard the energetic sound of a newborn crying.

Dare's breath caught at the sound, heart soaring. He had a child.

He burst into the room, ignoring a noise of protest from Leilanna, and rushed to where Zuri lay swimming in pillows near one side of the huge bed. She looked tired and pale but glowing with joy, cradling a baby to her breast, while Pella, Leilanna, and Se'weir hovered over her.

The mother of his child looked up with a radiant smile. "My mate," she said, holding out a hand. "Come meet your daughter."

His daughter. Dare moved forward almost reverently. "How is she?" he whispered. "How are you? Did everything go smoothly?"

Zuri smiled wanly. "As smoothly as it ever does. And our baby is as healthy as we could hope for." She gently stroked the soft fuzz of black hair on the girl's head. "Would you like to hold her?"

He nodded eagerly, and Se'weir carefully wrapped the baby in a soft blanket and offered her to him. His goblin daughter was so tiny that for a human baby he would've thought she was premature, and he felt huge and clumsy as he carefully cradled her in his arms.

Her face was dark green as she continued to fuss and wave her little fists, tiny features sharp and delicate. He looked down at her in wonder, instantly feeling a fierce love and protectiveness for this precious miracle.

"She's beautiful," he whispered, gently brushing her soft cheek. Tears blurred his vision, and he hastily blinked them away so he wouldn't miss a moment of the best day of his life. "Our little Gelaa."

"Our little Gelaa," Zuri said tenderly, tears in her own eyes.

At her insistence they'd agreed to name the baby the male or female variant of the goblin word for "courage", wanting their child to be Dare's namesake. He was honored by the name, and thought it was beautiful as well.

Gelaa kept fussing and he carefully passed her back to her mother, who shifted the blanket around to cradle her at her breast. With a few final plaintive noises the baby latched on and began contentedly nursing.

Dare wanted to stay and experience the joyous moment, but before long Leilanna and Pella and even sweet, timid Se'weir began firmly ushering him towards the door.

Apparently on Collisa fathers tended to be fairly hands off when it came to their babies. They might hold them and cuddle them, but changing and feeding and getting up in the night to tend them was firmly the province of mothers and female relatives. Or in this case the other women in their family.

In fact, when he talked about helping with the baby his lovers all looked at him in baffled incredulity, then politely but firmly told him they'd handle it.

Part of him was disappointed that he wouldn't have those opportunities to care for Gelaa, but another part of him was relieved he wouldn't have to worry about poopy diapers and sleepless nights and all the rest. Also, as they'd fairly pointed out, they were all around the house available to do the work anyway, while he needed to be out leveling.

He found Ilin waiting in the parlor downstairs, a bottle of wine from the cellar opened with a glass poured. The bald ascetic drank water as usual, but he'd obviously anticipated the need for celebration.

Dare accepted the glass and raised it in toast. "A girl. Gelaa."

His friend grinned and clapped him on the back. "Congratulations. And many more to come, I hope."

"Not too close together," Dare said with a quiet laugh. He took a deep gulp, smiling in the direction of the bedroom. "She's beautiful.

And so tiny I'm kind of afraid to hold her with my big clumsy hands."

Ilin laughed, although he looked wistful. "Treasure these moments, my friend."

Dare took another sip, looking at the wandering ascetic. He wondered how the man felt about his celibate life, knowing he'd never have children himself. He had to feel some regrets, surely.

The Monk seemed to sense his thoughts. "We all have our different paths to tread," he said, taking a sip of his water. "Happiness is finding joy in our path, not looking with envy or regret upon the paths of others."

Dare finished his wine and leapt to his feet, full of energy. "You know what?" he said. "I'm going to go work on the plumbing. I want my daughter to have a working toilet and hot water and all the rest."

* * * * *

Five days later, Dare dragged everyone into the kitchen and adjoining bathroom, grinning eagerly.

Zuri looked fully recovered from the labor, cradling a sleeping Gelaa in her arms. Pella was as excited as he was, probably mostly in response to his own feelings, while Leilanna looked hopeful beneath her heavy show of skepticism. Se'weir still seemed confused about the idea of plumbing, but was happy to be along and like Pella had enthusiastically joined the excitement.

Ilin just seemed like he was along for the ride.

"Okay fine, we're here," Leilanna said, folding her arms. "You finally going to let us see why you've kept most of the kitchen and your "bathrooms" and the roof outside covered beneath tarps for the last few days?"

Small surprise she was grumpy, since she'd been up half the night caring for the baby so Zuri could sleep. Although she would've been up anyway since she only slept four hours at a time, so she could refill her mana pool while leveling.

Which was why she'd offered to babysit in the first place.

"Actually, the tarps on the roof are for a completely different reason." Dare grinned and grabbed his dusk elf lover's hand, leading her over to the sink and resting it on the handle. "Go ahead, turn it on."

Rolling her eyes, she moved the metal lever. There was a soft gurgle and water began to flow into the sink, disappearing down the drain.

"Holy shit!" she blurted jumping back. "How did you do this? I know for a fact you haven't hired a water mage."

The others crowded around, making awed and excited sounds. "Where's it going?" Pella asked, peering beneath the sink at the pipe running away.

"To the gray water outflow," Dare replied, although he didn't need their blank looks to know they'd have no idea what he was talking about. "That was the cold water tap. Turn that off and turn on the other one."

Leilanna made a disbelieving noise, although she quickly did so. Then at his urging they all tentatively put their hand under the water. "It's warm!" Zuri said in amazement. "How did you do this?"

"How did you do any of this?" Leilanna demanded. "Did you spend more of our money on expensive enchantments? Or even go into debt considering what would be required for this?"

Dare laughed. "Actually, I didn't use magic at all." He paused. "Well, a couple things, but one was super cheap and the other's an item we already had." He eagerly led the way to the bathroom. "Come on, we're just getting started!"

In the downstairs bathroom he only had a toilet and sink, while in the upstairs one he'd gone all out with a shower and bathtub. Although at the moment the bath was only large enough for one or at most two people; he still wanted to get a pool or bath house, but that was an item for the future.

Also the upstairs bathroom wasn't quite completed, and he wanted to finish it before showing it off.

"There's water in the bowl," Ilin observed, looking into the toilet. "Is it for washing hands?"

Dare chuckled. "Not if you want to clean them. You sit on this seat and relieve yourself into the bowl."

"Into the water?" Pella asked, wrinkling her nose.

"It reduces the smell, and helps remove the waste when the toilet is flushed." Dare pressed the handle to flush the toilet, and they all watched the water swirl away with more exclamations of surprise and amazement. Then he had to push a new lever to refill the bowl; no automatic toilet tanks yet.

"Does this also go into the gray water place?" Zuri asked, seeming genuinely intent on understanding how it worked.

"No, this goes into the septic tank, which empties out into the drainfield. It's a sanitary way of removing waste." He straightened proudly. "We can fill in the outhouse now, and there'll be no more open pits of stinking sewage, no need to empty or clean chamber pots, none of it. You do your business and flush it away."

Leilanna fiddled with the sink, testing the cold and warm water levers. "Okay, let's get back to how the hell you're doing this. How do you make the water move through the pipes? And how do you heat it up?"

Dare grinned, thoroughly enjoying this. "Come with me."

They followed him outside, where he pointed up to the roof. "See those tanks up there? We fill those with water, and gravity provides pressure to move water through the pipes to all our indoor fixtures. And you'll notice one is covered by a black tarp, which collects the heat from the sun and warms the water inside." He paused. "Although in winter we'll probably have to think of a different setup. Maybe you can help with that, Leilanna, using your fire magic."

She grinned eagerly. "Yeah, that would be pretty easy, actually. I use spells to heat bathwater all the time." She abruptly remembered she was supposed to be skeptical and frowned again. "But I thought the idea is to save us effort and be more convenient. If we have to drag water up to the roof to fill the tanks, how is that any better than just using the well in the first place?"

He couldn't help but smile triumphantly. "That was actually the biggest hurdle I had to jump. But luckily I was able to think of a legendary solution." They all stared at him blankly, missing the bad pun. "Come on, I'll show you."

He led the way to the side of the house, where an adjacent shed had been created with pipes leading up to the roof. He opened the doors to reveal a large pump, simple in construction but sturdily built and with a few complicated additions. It had a hand lever that would gradually lift the pump over the course of a hundred or so cranks, drawing water from the well and up to the roof.

The device existed on Collisa, used by miners and on ships and for jobs like that, but it was obvious no one besides Dare recognized it. So he quickly explained what it did, and demonstrated working it and how it would draw water from the well up into the roof tanks.

"Okay great," Leilanna said. "So we don't have to haul the water up ourselves, we just break our backs working this pump of yours inside this little shack."

"Well we can hire a servant to do that," Pella said. "Or take turns. And we only need to do it when the tanks need to be filled."

"Actually, we don't need to do it at all." Dare grinned. "I cheesed a couple magical items for a purpose completely different than what they were intended for, and now they'll do the job for us."

"Okay, I genuinely want to see this," his dusk elf lover admitted. "Although I have no idea what cheese has to do with anything."

"Okay, watch." He'd designed the pump so it could be operated vertically, for a very specific purpose. Which he displayed when he produced the legendary chest they'd gotten from the dungeon, in its shrunken form, and scooted it in the small space beneath the fully extended pump.

"Grow," he said with a flourish.

The chest expanded to full size, pushing the pump up with it. The equivalent of dozens of hand cranks in an instant. "Shrink." It shrank just as quickly, allowing the pump to drop back into place.

Ilin burst out laughing. "You diabolical genius, my friend," he said, clapping him on the back. "You turned a size modification enchantment into a pump."

Leilanna's dark pink eyes were sparkling eagerly, obviously loving all this far more than she let on. But she kept up a stern expression as she crossed her arms, lifting and accentuating her glorious breasts. "Okay, but someone's still going to have to stand here and say "grow" and "shrink" for however long it takes to fill the tanks."

"Wow, Lanna, you'll complain about anything," Pella said, glowering. "Dare just gave us water flowing directly to where we need it, cold *and* warm, and the ability to magically make poop disappear with the push of a lever. And you're complaining that someone might have to lounge around saying a few words to do the work of a dozen men?"

"Actually, you won't even have to do that." Dare produced a chunk of quartz from his pocket and set it on a shelf.

They stared at it. "A translation stone?" Zuri asked, fingering the one hanging around her own neck.

"Not quite. But I asked an Enchanter and it turns out this was not only possible, but far easier to make." Dare tapped the stone.

His voice emerged from it, saying, "Grow. Shrink. Grow. Shrink," at a carefully timed pace. In response the legendary chest pushed the pump up and down with all the smoothness of an automated system, and over the racket of the pump they heard the gurgle of water being pulled up the pipes to fill the tanks on the roof.

Leilanna stared, openmouthed. "You crazy bastard. You actually did what you claimed you could." She stepped forward and wrapped her arms around his waist, pressing her voluptuous body against him as she looked up at him with a very solemn expression. "I don't think you've ever looked as sexy as you do right now. Tonight I'm going to do very, very debauched things to you to show my appreciation."

"Make that two of us," Pella said, hugging him from behind.

"Now that you've given us an easy way to clean ourselves, we can get as filthy as we want."

"Um, what about Cleanse Target?" Zuri asked with a mock frown.

Dare laughed and dropped to his knees, gathering her and their daughter gently in his arms. "What do you think?" he asked, gently kissing Gelaa's soft cheek. "I worked extra hard so our daughter could have the comforts I remember from my old home."

"And I'm sure as a newborn occupied with eating and pooping she appreciates it," his goblin lover said wryly. But her eyes were warm as she kissed his cheek. "It's amazing, my mate. Thank you."

"What about the upstairs bath?" Pella asked, wagging her tail. "Is it almost done? I want to take a bath with you!"

"I can show you my progress on it, at least." Dare retrieved the legendary chest, since obviously they didn't want to leave that around to potentially be stolen if they weren't using it, and led the way back towards the manor.

Before reaching the front doors there was a call of greeting, and he saw a small team of laborers approaching. He'd been expecting them back from Terana today, and he was especially eager since one of the new arrivals was Morwal, the earth Mage who'd been making his ceramic pipes and other plumbing materials.

With his help they should have the upstairs bathroom done within the next few days.

Or not.

"Master Dare!" the Mage called, looking surprised. "I didn't expect to see you here."

Dare exchanged confused looks with his lovers and Ilin. "Where else would I be, so soon after my daughter's birth?"

"Leveling up," Leilanna muttered behind him.

Morwal frowned. "Word must not have reached you. A raid rated monster has been spotted to the north, along the Tangle. Adventurers are gathering in Terana to form a raiding party to kill it."

Oh hell yes. One of Dare's favorite things in MMOs had been raiding dungeons with large groups. He'd been part of top ranked raiding guilds, and had even led his fair share of raids.

Of course, that was back on Earth. Here he was the new guy, with little experience in dungeons or against party rated monsters and none at all with raids. Which just made him want to be part of this all the more.

He had a chance to learn a whole new system, min/max damage and ability rotations, and excel. Make a name and a reputation for himself and perhaps even become a leader.

If that was what he wanted, given his experience organizing and leading raids in games. And this would be real life where the stakes where infinitely higher.

Pella laughed. "You should've seen how your eyes just lit up, Dare."

Zuri nodded, gently rocking Gelaa. "I saw it too. You should go, my mate, and Leilanna and Ilin as well. This is an excellent opportunity."

"Not to mention we'll get a fortune from helping kill a raid rated monster," Leilanna said. "And achievements and a chance for trophies and amazing gear and other goodies."

"And the more important consideration of the fate of the people in the nearby area," Ilin said. "A raid rated monster will eventually begin rampaging, destroying villages and towns until it's stopped."

Dare rubbed his jaw. With the plumbing near completed he had one less good excuse to hang around so he could cuddle Zuri and hold Gelaa. And joining a raid did sound exciting. Not to mention good for his reputation and standing, and his chances of being part of more raids in the future at higher levels.

And more importantly, if it was in the Terana province it could potentially prove a threat to Nirim Manor; he wasn't letting any monster get within a day's ride of his family.

"All right," he said with a grin. "All right, this will be awesome.

Let's go slay a raid monster!"

Everyone cheered, even those staying behind. Pella ran off to gather the horses, Leilanna rushed away to pack their things, and Ilin went to fetch his few possessions and the loot he'd accumulated with Leilanna to sell in town for charitable purposes. Se'weir disappeared into the manor without a word, looking excited.

That left Dare with Zuri and Gelaa.

He took the few precious moments available to hold his daughter while his lover hugged his legs, head buried in his hip. "Be safe, my mate," she murmured. "Raid rated monsters kill adventurers in just about every hunt for them, and sometimes entire raiding parties."

"We will be," he assured her, kissing the soft black fuzz on Gelaa's head as she peacefully blew bubbles. "I need to come home to our baby. And her mom and the rest of my lovers."

"Soon to be wives?" she hinted.

"As far as I'm concerned you already are," he said, wrapping an arm around her shoulders. "And as soon as I can figure out the boondoggle of Haraldar's bureaucracy, we will be."

"Maybe we should just have our own ceremony and call it good," she said.

Dare nodded slowly. "If official channels fail, we will. I promise."

Se'weir came rushing through the front doors, bearing a bundle. "Here!" she said, holding it out to him. "Cooked meals for your journey." She blushed. "I know you're a good cook, but I wanted to show you how much progress I've made."

He couldn't help but smile as he gently passed Gelaa back to Zuri and accepted the bundle. The beautiful hobgoblin was a Level 14 Jeweler as her class, which they'd encouraged her to pursue by providing her with uncut gems and semiprecious stones, as well as precious metals to smith in the small forge they'd had made for her.

But out of all the girls she was also the one most eager about cooking, and excited to share Dare's knowledge of recipes and gain more proficiency in the ability with him. He would've welcomed the time with her even if it had just been a ploy to share his company, but she was genuinely enthusiastic about cooking.

Which everyone else appreciated, since he was so often gone leveling or busy for other reasons.

"Have a safe trip, my betrothed," she said, wrapping him in a warm and more than a little passionate hug. Then she hesitated, pale green skin blushing pink. "Can I kiss you?"

Smiling, he leaned down and pressed his lips to hers, tasting a hint of honey and the berries she loved from their breakfast. She melted against him, luscious body soft and yielding, and it was with some regret that he pulled away.

A year was feeling like a longer and longer time, and he wondered what had possessed him to insist on such an extended wait.

The others arrived, and after a flurry of packing saddles and goodbye hugs and kisses he, Leilanna, and Ilin mounted and set off, those staying behind waving and calling out best wishes from the door of the manor.

Chapter Two
Raiding Party

Dare spent the extra effort to get the final kills needed for Level 30 on the way to Terana.

It was less exciting than Level 20 in some ways, since the main boost for the level came from Power Up. Which was an ability all classes got at 30 that gave a +5 stat increase across the board, not just combat stats but noncombat stats as well.

For most it would be an exciting power boost, but the body his benefactor had given him was already ridiculously overstatted, so the gains felt more humble. Not that he was complaining about getting even more boosts.

The most exciting ones came to Speed and Stamina, increasing his max speed up above 30 miles an hour and letting him run for longer. Which needless to say he was super happy about.

Although if he was being honest the *most* exciting bump was the increase in his fertility stat.

When Pella reached Level 30 they'd enjoyed some incredible sex thanks to her increased fertility increasing pleasure for both of them. Not to mention she'd also produced more copious arousal, orgasmed easier and more often, and had been able to go for longer. As well as increasing her chance of pregnancy.

Speaking of which, that bump increased his fertility to 56. Which thankfully was still below the 60 cap for Zuri's improved Prevent Conception, but if he got another boost like this he was going to have to start worrying about knocking up every woman he was with again.

For now, though, it just meant better sex. Which Leilanna was eager to test out, having heard from Pella all about her experience with her fertility boost.

And sure enough it was some pretty mind-blowing sex; the +5 boost might not've been huge, but it was definitely noticeable.

Although Dare had to reluctantly cut it short after making his dusk elf lover come a few times and emptying his balls deep inside her. He was worried about missing out on the opportunity to join the raid, and wanted to hurry to Terana now that he'd gained his level.

Along with Power Up he got Quill Shot with Student of the Wild, of course, like he'd planned. But to his delight, the big ability for Level 30 was the movement speed ability that Duelist highwayman who'd chased them long ago had hinted at: Cheetah's Dash.

It increased movement speed by 25% for up to 2 minutes with no stamina usage increase, with a 5 minute cooldown. Even better, it increased reaction speed and agility specific to running so he wouldn't bite the dust at dangerously high speeds, or if he did would be able to land in a way to reduce the damage.

Which was going to be a huge deal, since Cheetah's Dash plus Fleetfoot and the Power Up speed increase, on top of his benefactor gifting him with the body of an elite athlete, meant he was now able to run almost 40 miles an hour at his best speed.

Even without Cheetah's Dash he'd felt like a superhero as he ran around at car speeds. With it he felt like he had afterburners.

Shit, he might even be able to keep up with a bunny girl with this.

His companions watched him in bemusement as he zoomed circles around them, although they kept up their steady pace to Terana on their horses. "You realize this means I can now carry you faster on foot than we can go on horseback?" Dare called to Leilanna with a wild laugh as he bolted past close enough to make her horse shy.

"Yeah, yeah!" she called at his back, although he heard laughter in her voice. "But we probably wouldn't get far before I had to stop so *you* could ride *me*. You know how I get turned on by bouncing around on magnificent beasts at high speeds."

That was definitely an application of Cheetah's Dash to look forward to.

Camping that night Ilin took his usual place meditating by the campfire, oblivious to anything but an imminent threat to the camp. Which was good, because Leilanna took full advantage of having Dare to herself as she dragged him into their tent to enjoy his increased fertility some more.

"I almost regret sending you off to level on your own," she panted as she hastily pulled off her Exceptional quality caster robes, which she'd inherited from Zuri with a few size adjustments now that she was high enough level. "We could be doing this every night."

He wasn't sure whether she was serious, and couldn't really pursue the issue because she pressed her lips to his firmly as she lay back and pulled him on top of her, thick thighs spread in anticipation. She practically yanked him down into the bliss of her warm, sopping wet pussy, at which point he found something else to occupy his attention.

And again, and again, for the next few glorious hours; she really was intent on making the most of their time together.

* * * * *

The next day they reached Terana in the early afternoon, eager to join the raid.

The signs of the impending monster hunt were everywhere to be seen, but most notably in a large, martial camp sprawling across a field outside the town's walls that held at least a hundred people. The raiders and their camp followers, no doubt.

By mutual agreement, Dare and his companions headed to the camp first.

There were a few Level 20 guards posted to keep out curious onlookers (or opportunist thieves) from Terana, but at the approach of him and his companions a finely dressed man emerged to intercept them. Dare's Eye identified him as a Level 25 Armorer with an Archer subclass.

The guy had weaselly features and an overly arrogant bearing, clearly displayed as he sneered at three main combat class adventurers at least a couple levels higher than him. "Your business?" he asked with the most punchable voice and tone Dare had ever heard.

"We're here to join the raid going out to kill the raid rated world monster," Dare replied.

The man's sneer deepened. "You're too low," he said dismissively. "The monster's Level 35." He paused reluctantly. "Although the minimum level for recruitment is Level 30, so you barely qualify. I wouldn't hold your breath about getting in, though."

Heart sinking, Dare looked at Leilanna and Ilin. "Sign up," his lover urged him. "We can always go back to leveling."

Ilin nodded. "Maybe we'll have better luck with the next one. But in the meantime you should take this opportunity, my friend."

"All right," Dare told the weaselly man. "I'll sign up."

"How wonderful for us," the man said sarcastically, eyeing him up and down. "At least you seem properly equipped for your level. Your class?"

"Hunter."

Somehow the Armorer's sneer took an even uglier twist. "How quaint." The man produced a sheaf of papers bound to a block of wood, a rudimentary clipboard, and scribbled something down. "And your name?"

"Dare."

A slightly uncomfortable silence settled as the man looked at him impatiently, waiting for more. Then he rolled his eyes. "And the surname, title, or feat of strength you're known by?"

Before Dare could wonder if he even had any of those, or if he could make something up, a list populated on his screen of options he could choose from: "of Lone Ox" and "Master of Nirim Manor".

Being known for hailing from a flyspeck village in the middle of nowhere wasn't exactly thrilling, and wouldn't do much for him. He vastly preferred the second option as a reminder of his home and family, although to his ears it sounded a bit pretentious.

Still the obvious choice, though. "Master of Nirim Manor," he said confidently.

The weaselly man scribbled that down. "And finally, where can we find you to send word in the unlikely event you're invited to the raid?"

"Montshadow Estate."

That drew a derisive snort from the arrogant Armorer. "The home of the Baroness of Terana Province," he said in clear disbelief.

"That's right."

Another derisive snort. "Very well, I'll just jot that down." The man made no move to do so. "Finally, your qualifications to join this raid? Party or raiding experience?"

Ouch. Dare was going to have to spin this hard. "I've slain a party rated world monster, and cleared a Level 23-25 dungeon." He was tempted to mention he'd soloed the last half of the dungeon boss, but decided the man would neither believe him nor care.

"About what I expected," the weaselly man said, tone making it clear that wasn't a good thing. He jotted a few final notes. "Very well, Dare, Master of Nirim Manor. You'll be notified if we have need of you. Don't hesitate to make other plans, however."

"Thank you," Dare said politely. Nodding to his companions, he wheeled his mount and rode on towards Terana.

"Ascendants, what an ass," Leilanna growled once they were out of earshot. "I spent the entire conversation fantasizing about shoving a Fireball down his mouth and another up his ass and seeing where they met in the middle."

Ilin chuckled. "Be prepared to deal with nobility more and more as you reach higher levels. And from my experience, limited I'll admit, his is the more pleasant encounter you're likely to have. Unless of course you have some reason for them to ingratiate themselves to you."

Leilanna reined up close enough to Dare to rest a hand on his arm. "I'm sorry, lover. I know you were looking forward to this."

"Well, maybe I'll get lucky," he said with a shrug. He grinned. "Either way, at least we have a night of being hosted by Lady Marona and her lovely maids to look forward to."

Or not.

Montshadow Estate was busier than he'd ever seen it, horses crowding the stables and spilling out into a side field, servants bustling about the mansion and outbuildings, and people coming and going.

The guard at the wrought iron gate nodded politely as they rode up. "Master Dare," he said. "The Baroness extends her congratulations on the birth of your daughter, and her best wishes for the health of mother and child. She also wishes you to know that she has no news yet but remains optimistic, and hopes you'll offer your assistance in the matter again in the near future."

"Thank you," Dare said, although he wondered why Lady Marona hadn't wanted to express such personal things herself. Perhaps a less than hopeful sign about their welcome at the busy mansion.

The guard continued. "She has also informed me that you and your companions are to be welcomed in on most occasions, even if she's otherwise engaged."

In spite of the cordial greeting the man made no move to open the gate. "I take it now's not one of those occasions?" Dare asked dryly.

The guard smiled apologetically. "Now is not an opportune time. The Baroness is hosting Lord Zor, Lady Ennara, and the rest of the nobility of the raiding party and their entourages. But she bid me to urge you to let her make it up to you when things are less busy."

Apparently Lady Marona's paramour didn't rate among such esteemed company. Dare honestly didn't mind too much, though; he would've felt awkward around all those lords and ladies, without knowing proper etiquette and lacking any title of his own.

Maybe he should take his noble lover's advice about petitioning for knighthood, whatever the process involved. It was probably worth doing for more than just the status bump.

Dare didn't want to make a nuisance of himself, but there was one unpleasant admission he had to make. Which that asshole back at the raiding party camp was probably going to feel very smug about.

So he hailed the guard again. "If you'd be so kind, in haste I provided the Baroness's address as the location where I could be found. I've applied to the raiding party, so if anyone comes looking for me could you redirect them to the Mountain's Shadow inn?"

"Of course," the man said, bowing slightly. "Again, my apologies for the circumstances. Please visit again soon."

As Dare and his companions rode away from the mansion, he did feel some regret about the fact that meeting the raid leader, and likely most of the man's party leaders as well, would've improved his chances of being invited on the raid.

That and disappointment about not being able to enjoy the attentions of Lady Marona and her beautiful maids.

"On the plus side," Leilanna said brightly, taking his arm as they walked away down the street, leading the horses behind them, "at least that means I get you all to myself again tonight."

Dare grinned and wrapped an arm around his voluptuous lover. "How would you feel about sharing me with that sexy guardswoman Helima? I keep on giving her rain checks."

She rolled her eyes. "Again, a term I've never heard of." She playfully pinched his bottom. "As long as you're the only one getting shackled with her manacles. It could be fun to have you at our mercy."

Hoo boy.

Ilin cleared his throat. "Since it looks like our time is free after all, I'm going to check on the orphanage and destitute families." He glanced at a passing group of finely dressed people on expensive horses clattering up the street towards Montshadow Estate. "Also

59

events such as this tend to draw itinerants hoping for opportunities, who generally need succor. I should do what I can for them as well."

"Let me help them with a few meals, at least," Dare said, fishing in his pouch for a handful of gold. Leilanna shot him a dirty look at giving away gold when they were so worried about finances, but she didn't protest.

She'd probably resigned herself by this point that he was going to help people if he could. And honestly he'd seen enough generosity from her to know that her grumbling was mostly a chance to poke at him, part of their banter.

"The ideas you've provided us for plumbing for the orphanage is gift enough, my friend," Ilin said. Although he accepted the gold. "Thank you. I'll meet back up with you two at the Mountain's Shadow inn later this evening."

With a formal bow, palms pressed together, he turned and set off at a brisk pace.

"Well since we've got the time, it's been a few levels since you've gotten gear," Leilanna said. "And Master quality or not, Entangler is five levels below yours now." She rubbed his arm, trying to sound especially cheerful to make up for the series of disappointments. "If we get you the best possible gear for this raid, they'll be more likely to consider you."

"Probably a good idea," Dare agreed. Although he felt a bit wistful at the thought of losing his bow. Its snare and stun procs were incredibly powerful, and Vine Lash was flat out a blast; he'd almost be willing to keep it just for that.

Or not. As it turned out a Level 25 Master quality bow was worth a thousand gold to the right buyer. Which happened to be the Terana Counting House, one of the few groups in town who could afford such an expense.

Dare found a Level 30 Journeyman quality recurve bow for a tenth that price that offered enough of a damage increase to make it worth the trade-in. Granted, when he was soloing the utility of the procs and Vine Lash would offer him enough survivability to make up for the loss in damage. And even for a raid Vine Lash might save his life if things went south.

But he couldn't hang on to Entangler forever, however much he loved it. What eventually decided him, though, was that at his clear reluctance to sell the bow Norril, the proprietor of the counting house, upped his offer to 1,350 gold.

It hadn't even been a bargaining tactic.

Dare shook on the deal, went back to the market and bought the recurve bow and upgrades to most of his other gear with the extra 350 gold, with coin to spare, and dumped the remainder into Leilanna's pouch for her to put towards the manor's expenses.

"Still want to complain about the 11 gold I gave to the poor?" he asked with a smirk.

She just rolled her eyes. "I need to finish selling mine and Ilin's loot," she muttered, stomping off.

Dare trailed after her since he was done with his own business. Although he did stop at a few booths to purchase some cooking spices, as well as a teething ring for Gelaa.

It would be a while yet before the newborn needed it, and doubtless she'd tear through the thing with her sharp little goblin teeth. But he wanted to get her gifts whenever possible, a chance to look forward to her smile when he finally got to see her again after a trip.

Thinking of his daughter, he also bought a rattle and a painted doll. It looked like something you'd see from pioneer days, but at least it was cute.

"Your daughter's a lucky girl," the vendor said with a smile as he bought the items without haggling.

"I'm the lucky one," he replied, returning her smile.

A few hours later they met up with Ilin at the inn. That was when Dare finally got his surprise.

* * * * *

"You know," Lielanna murmured in a sexy voice, scooting her

chair closer to his and cuddling against his side. "You could be down here drinking this piss they call ale. Ooorrrrr . . ." She waggled her delicate snowy white eyebrows suggestively. "If you're thirsty, you could take me up to our room where you could-"

"Drink piss?" Dare teased.

She scowled furiously, pale gray cheeks darkening to charcoal in a blush. "What the serious fuck?"

He laughed. "Joking, joking. It was just too easy of a setup to ignore." He paused just long enough. "Unless . . ."

"You were definitely joking," the beautiful dusk elf growled, straightening in her seat and taking a gulp from her own mug. "Gods, I liked it better when I only *thought* everything you said was perverted."

Dare smirked. "Says the girl who kept asking me to lick her asshole while she was sitting on my face."

This time her blush reached all the way to the tips of her long, pointed ears, her expression absolutely adorable. "I didn't actually want you to do it," she protested unconvincingly. "Anyway don't talk about what we do in bed in public!"

"Turning you on?" he teased, wrapping his arm around her again.

She abruptly brightened, looking relieved. "Oh good, Ilin's here." She arched a delicate eyebrow. "And he's got a *girlfriend*."

He snorted as he followed her gaze. "He's a celibate ascetic, he woul-"

He cut off sharply, not at the sight of a woman with his friend but at the sight of *the* woman with him. And if he had any doubt he might've mistaken her for someone else, it was dispelled by the knowing smile she returned to his shocked stare.

No fucking way.

Dare would judge her age as mid-20s, although she could pass as younger. She probably came up to his shoulder at best, five foot nothing, with a slender, delicate frame and small breasts, a narrow waist and a cute little ass. Her curves were accentuated by the form fitting cleric's robes she wore, embroidered with a planet circled by a comet across the chest.

She had big green eyes that sparkled like emeralds, delicate, almost doll-like features with a flawless peaches and cream complexion, and a little rosebud mouth with lips that might've looked pouty on a less innocent and pure looking face. Her perfectly straight, silky auburn hair flowed loose down to her waist like a waterfall of bright copper, striking and lovely.

She was the woman of his dreams, the type he'd fantasized as his ideal girlfriend back on Earth. And last time he'd met her he'd literally fled a city to escape afterwards.

"Ireni?" he said incredulously. "What the hell are you doing here? How did you find me?"

"So vain, assuming I'm here because I sought you out. Although it's completely true." The High Priestess of the Outsider, who he'd met in a brothel of freed slaves in the city of Kov, smiled wryly and met his gaze unapologetically. "And yes, I'll admit we came on too strong last time. I knew we were, but in the excitement of the occasion it was just too hard to hold back."

Dare continued to gape at her as she settled primly into the chair Ilin pulled out for her across the table from them. When he'd first met her he'd thought she was a bit bookish, like a librarian, but if that was still the case she hid it with sheer grace and elegance.

Also, the last time he'd seen the Priestess she'd been several levels lower than him, and he'd been much lower level at the time. But now she was Level 30.

Which was flat out impossible. *Nobody* leveled as fast as him and his companions. To the point that people were constantly blown away when they found out how many levels he'd gained so quickly.

"Isn't this a pleasant surprise, Dare?" Ilin said, smiling slightly uneasily at the way the "reunion" was going. "I met her assisting a group of destitute refugees fleeing Kovana as part of Lord Zor's camp followers. Of course I had to invite her to come drink with us."

"Yes, of course," Ireni said, grinning at Dare. There was warmth there, and fondness, but most of all she seemed far too knowing for his liking. About him, personally. As proved by her next words. "Congratulations on the birth of your daughter. I hear Gelaa's a beautiful, healthy baby."

"Wh-" Dare started to demand angrily, fear shooting through him at just how much this woman knew about his family.

Ireni spoke over him. "Congratulations as well on Pella's puppies. My best wishes for their good health, they're going to be adorable."

She turned to Leilanna. "Leilanna, good to see you settling in with the family. I'll admit I'm envious that you got to have Dare before I did."

"Who the fuck are you, you ginger cow?" the dusk elf demanded angrily. "How do you know all this, and why was Dare freaked the fuck out by you even before you opened your cock holster?"

"Leilanna," Ilin said in disappointed reproof. "You're talking to someone I respect and admire, who I invited as a guest. To say nothing of her status as High Priestess of the Outsider."

She flushed, but kept her suspicious glare fixed on the Priestess.

Ireni sighed, warm smile faltering. "I suppose I need to explain everything." She stood gracefully. "Come, Dare, I've rented a room. Let's go have a serious conversation."

"Like fuck you're taking him to a room on his own, you smug little slut!" Leilanna snapped. "You're probably going to knock him over the head and steal his coin pouch."

"Leilanna!" Ilin said reproachfully. "Ireni's a good friend and a virtuous person. One of the best I know. I'm not quite sure what's going on here and this situation is . . . unorthodox, but please moderate your tone."

Ireni ignored the other two, eyes fixed on Dare. "If it helps," she said quietly, "I'm the surprise."

Dare jumped in shock. His surprise, as in what his benefactor had been teasing him with? He wasn't sure he liked finding out that it was a person.

"Go with her," his benefactor said in his head, making him jump again. "We do need to talk. All of us."

He sighed in defeat and stood, ignoring his dusk elf lover's incredulous stare. "Lead the way."

Ireni smiled in obvious relief, unconsciously smoothing her robes as she walked beside him towards the stairs. "I realize we haven't had a chance to have a normal conversation yet, but I promise it was never my intention to make you uncomfortable. Just the opposite." She hesitated. "I'm . . . not great at this sort of thing."

That moment of vulnerability actually did a surprising amount to put Dare at ease. "How's Trissela?" he asked. "I should probably warn her, if you don't already know, that she's pregnant."

The petite redhead's eyes danced with humor as she unlocked a door and opened it, leading the way into a plain but clean bedroom that was probably one of the nicer ones in the inn. It had a large bed, two chairs and a table set with a bottle of wine and two glasses, and an unlit fireplace with a bearskin rug laid out in front of it.

"Yes, she's very excited to have her son," she admitted. "He'll be a merfolk, by the way. If you haven't figured it out by now all your first children with a woman of another race will be of their mother's race. A gift from your benefactor, you might say."

Realization dawned, and Dare narrowed his eyes. "You knew," he said. "Back in the brothel, you knew I had a fertility rating of 51, and I'd impregnate Trissela right through the Prevent Conception spell." He thought of the odd things the mermaid had said and grit his teeth. "And so did she, didn't she?"

"She knew," Ireni agreed. "And she was overjoyed about it. Knowing you, I'm sure you'll want to visit, or even have Trissela come live with you at your manor. She'd be amenable, as long as you can see to the health and comfort of her and the baby . . . she's been told just how wonderful you are, and is eager to give you her heart if you'll accept her. You could say you and her were set up as a good match, and she's more than happy with it."

"Set up by who?" he demanded furiously. "Who the fuck are you? What do you want from me?"

The petite redhead grinned at him. "You know who I am, Dare. There's no secrets there. I'm a High Priestess of the Outsider who formerly oversaw a brothel in the slums of the city of Kov."

She paused, taking a deep breath. "As for set up by who, and what I want from you . . ." She settled down in one of the chairs and nodded at the one across from her. "You'll probably want to sit down for this."

Dare glared at her suspiciously for a few seconds, then grudgingly moved to the chair and plopped down.

"Thank you." Ireni took another deep breath. "Me and Trissela knew who you and Zuri were, and she was told about you and made excited by the prospect of carrying your child, thanks to our Goddess, the Outsider."

She paused significantly. "Who, as you really should've figured out by now, is your mysterious benefactor."

Chapter Three

Outsider

Dare jerked in his seat as if struck by lightning. "What?" he demanded in a strangled voice.

Ireni continued calmly. "Given your desire to bed women of every race, it was convenient that our order had a brothel staffed by just those sorts of women in Kov. It would've given you a chance to sleep with women of ten different races, as well as me, and all of us a chance to receive your seed." She grimaced. "If only we hadn't come on too strong and spooked you."

"Forget all that," Dare said. He pulled up his system commands screen as well so he could speak to his benefactor. "You're telling me I could've known more about you all along, contacted your followers, but you didn't bother to tell me?"

His benefactor's, or the Outsider's he supposed, voice responded to him, soothing and warm. "I wanted to see how things played out."

"And on top of all the other women I knocked up before I learned about my fertility stat, you would've blithely tricked me into impregnating at least ten more?" he demanded. He waved at Ireni. "Including this weird girl?"

The Priestess looked hurt. No, actually closer to devastated. "That's not a nice thing to say," she said in a small voice.

"It really isn't," the Outsider agreed. "You should be ashamed of yourself."

Dare flushed, feeling guilty in spite of his annoyance. They were right, Ireni didn't deserve that. "I'm sorry, High Priestess."

"It's quite all right, Dare." She gave him a warm smile. "I know we sprang this on you. All things considered you're handling it very well."

"Good, I'm glad that's settled," his benefactor said. "I care deeply about both of you and want you to come to feel the same about each other. Especially since Ireni is going to become one of your harem living at your manor."

Dare jumped again, scowling. "Excuse me?" It wasn't that he hated the idea, since Ireni seemed like a sweet person. Not to mention she was beautiful and had that sexy librarian vibe going and was just what he'd wanted in his past life.

But it was hard not to feel like he was being tricked every which way here.

Ireni sighed. "Here's the thing, Dare. The Outsider has to expend a lot of effort to create an incarnation. So as much as she enjoys sleeping with you, it's just not a realistic solution if she wants to regularly do it. So while she might still make the effort every now and then, and continue to improve her incarnations, she needed another option."

She pointed at herself. "The solution was for me to become a vessel for her, so she could come to you in the flesh and be with you as she truly wishes to be, and carry your children as she truly wishes to do. It was good fortune that not only am I and the Goddess already very close and have been for years, and we wish to be together in this way, but out of all her followers I was also the one most similar to your preferences for human women. So I was the ideal candidate."

"So let me get this straight," Dare said, rubbing his temples. "My benefactor, the Outsider, sent you to join my harem so that whenever she gets horny, she can possess you and jump my bones?"

Ireni blushed. "She also promised that I'd be able to be with you intimately as well. Sometimes she'd dwell within me, sometimes she'd be content with just feeling what I feel." She absently rested a hand on her belly. "And although the Goddess may claim my children as her own, ultimately they'll be mine as well. My flesh and blood. I'll get to have the honor, and the joy, of bearing and raising them when she is not dwelling within me."

Dare had experienced some bizarre things since coming to

Collisa. He'd fucked an entire spawn point of slime girls, while using them as bait to hunt all the male monsters who also came to fuck them. He'd romanced a goblin, a dog girl, and an elf, unwittingly impregnating two of them, and they'd become his lovers and members of his party.

He'd had some of the most intense and draining sex he'd ever experienced with a demon Succubus. He'd fucked a goddess in the form of a shadow woman and alabaster mannequin.

And now that same goddess wanted one of her followers to be his fourth lover, so she could vicariously make love to him and bear his children. And the Priestess she'd sent *also* wanted to make love to him and bear his children.

Essentially two new lovers sharing the same body.

This felt seriously messed up, though. How could two people share a body? How could that be fair to Ireni?

"No," he said, standing. "I'm sorry, Ireni, but no." He looked up at the ceiling. "And you, Outsider. You know me as intimately as anyone could, watching me and reading my thoughts what seems like every second of the day, and you thought I'd be okay with this?"

The Outsider sighed. "Just the opposite. Looking at it without a better understanding of me and Ireni and our relationship, I could see how it would be very easy to judge it as terrible. Like I'm using the poor girl for my own benefit."

"What?" Ireni demanded, eyes huge as she also looked up at the ceiling. "No, my love! You built me up when I was broken, and you shelter me every moment of the day. You held my hand in support until I could finally stand on my own and go back into this cruel world. You're more close than a friend, than family. Having you dwell within me is the greatest comfort I could've asked for."

She turned pleading eyes to Dare. "Please don't think ill of the Outsider on my account. She was there for me long before you even came to this world, and we've been close the entire time. In fact, the reason I love you is because she confessed her love for you to me as a confidant, and through her eyes I saw you and came to share those feelings as well."

69

The petite redhead gave him a shy smile. "I know all about Earth and the life you had there, and your circumstances in coming to Collisa, and all your adventures since. The Goddess has told me everything about you, and I can see why she loves you. We were both excited at the prospect of being with you, and when she expressed frustration with the difficulty of creating incarnations to be with you in dreams, I asked her to use me as a vessel so we could both be with you as we dreamed."

She paused and gave him an intent look. "I mean that Dare. I asked her. She would never have asked such a thing of me, and every time I let her take the fore it's with my full permission and support, otherwise she couldn't do it."

"She's telling the truth, Dare," the goddess said firmly. "That's the depth of the trust between us. I love Ireni with all my heart. To the point that, much as it pains me to say it, if she failed to win your heart and you sent her away, I would leave with her."

"What?" Ireni whispered, tears filling her eyes. "But all your hopes and dreams are with him-"

"Shh, my love," the Outsider soothed. "I hope it won't come to that. Because I know Dare and I trust that he'll give us a chance."

Dare looked between them, or at least between her and the ceiling, then scrubbed his fingers through his hair before covering his face with his hands. This was too much, all at once. Like cramming for a huge test only to discover in the moment that it's an entirely different subject and you have to scramble for answers.

"What did you hope would happen here, Outsider?" he asked as patiently as he could.

Her soothing voice laughed wearily. "Honestly? I'd hoped you'd be overjoyed to finally be with me in person, and we'd make passionate love on that bed over there. Also that you'd be excited to get to know Ireni better, and welcome her with open arms as a companion and future consort."

Ireni was nodding along, eyes shining with hope.

Godsdamnit. This was even harder to navigate than his arranged marriage with Se'weir. Dare was indebted to his benefactor, and he enjoyed her company and had strong feelings for her as a lover. And everything he'd seen of Ireni showed her to be kindhearted and genuine in her feelings.

Under most circumstances he would've been overjoyed to have both of them as lovers and members of the family. But with them sharing a body it was all muddied.

"You're really okay with this?" he asked Ireni.

"Okay with it?" she repeated with a shy smile. "A life with you and the Goddess is everything I dream of. I know she wouldn't lie to me about you, so all I fear is that you won't accept me."

Dare wasn't sure whether he was worthy of that trust and high regard. Although he certainly wanted to do everything he could to become worthy. "What happens to you when the Outsider takes over?" he asked.

"I'll sort of ride along, experiencing everything she does," Ireni replied. "Just like she can experience everything I do, when she wants to." She cocked her head. "Here, maybe it would help if we showed you."

The petite redhead's entire demeanor abruptly changed. She'd been leaning forward earnestly, eyes full of feeling and expression intent and hopeful.

But as if a switch had been flipped, she suddenly became regal, expression warm but slightly remote. She sat up, seeming to suddenly become taller even though her height didn't change, and casually crossed her legs and clasped her hands on her knee.

Dare had seen her before. In the movements, the expressions, even the bearing of his shadowy and alabaster lovers. Both representations of the goddess. And in spite of the circumstances his heart leapt and he couldn't help but smile tentatively. "Benefactor?"

"My beloved," she said, voice richer and more melodious, full of confidence and authority. "It's so good to finally speak to you in person." She reached forward with a small hand.

He took it, feeling her soft, warm skin. To his surprise she leaned down and kissed his fingers.

"So, the Outsider huh?" he asked. "You really were a goddess all along."

"Small surprise, I think." The Outsider grinned at him. "Ireni's right, you really should've guessed before now."

Dare laughed sheepishly. "So does that mean you're from another world like me?"

"No, I'm from Collisa." She grimaced. "It's a bit of a deceptive name. I'm called that because I'm the only god who regularly goes outside and visits other worlds."

He frowned. "You're called Outsider because you go outside? I don't think that's how the word works."

"No, that's definitely not how it works. But that's the reasoning I use, because it's better than the real reason." She shook her head wearily. "You see, I didn't choose the name, it was forced on me. The other gods began calling me that because they thought I was abandoning my duties when I left to explore. They said I'd become an outsider, no longer with any loyalty or attachment to Collisa, and my followers would all abandon me.

"That didn't happen, of course. But what *did* happen was all *their* followers started calling me that, so when my own followers used my real name nobody even recognized it. I was stuck with the choice of either having to be reintroduced to every single person my followers met, or just giving up and answering to my new name."

"That sucks," Dare said.

The Outsider laughed and shook her head. "I love your people's penchant for brief, flippant evaluations. Which are usually either gross understatements or seriously overblown."

"Well if you ask me, Outsider is a pretty badass name."

"Thanks, I've come to consider it that way too."

He gave her a curious look. "What's your real name? Now that you've finally revealed who you are, isn't it about time I know?"

She shook her head soberly. "Maybe I'll tell you one day, when we know each other better." The petite redhead abruptly raised her head to look at him at eye level, voice becoming businesslike. "Now, enough about me. Let's talk about you and our new situation."

Dare bit back a sigh. "I suppose we probably should."

Her green eyes held his, regal and infinite. "First things first, will you give us a chance to make this situation work, in spite of your reservations?"

He hesitated. "Yes. But I hope you realize that I won't be sleeping with either of you until I get to know you better. Especially Ireni. And I'll need to understand her situation so I can know this is really what she wants and she's happy with the arrangement."

"I suppose that's about what we expected." The Outsider idly toyed with a lock of auburn hair. "Ireni will be joining your adventuring, of course. She's an appropriate level, and as a Priestess has many spells to strengthen you and protect you with shields and barriers. She has no attack spells, but you won't need them."

The beautiful woman abruptly smiled fondly, leaning back with a contented sigh. "I just wish we could've arrived to adventure with Zuri. We really want to meet her in person, and can't wait to be able to spend more time with her."

Dare gave her a quizzical smile. "You and your followers really like Zuri. I completely understand why it's so easy to love her, of course, but I'm a bit curious about why *you* do."

The Outsider smirked. "Is it really such a mystery? She was the first woman you really met and had a relationship with on this world, and she continues to be an important part of your life. How could we not fall in love with her at the same time you did?"

Her expression turned wistful. "Especially since I got to see Zuri's perspective as well as yours. I was actually moved to tears by how happy some of the things you've said and done have made her."

He felt a lump in his throat at hearing that. "I'm glad to hear I've made her happy," he whispered.

The goddess leaned forward and rested a hand on his knee. "I love Pella and Leilanna, too, of course. And I'll love all the other women you meet and fall in love with. But Zuri was the first, and the first is always special, isn't it?"

"She is."

She smiled, eyes shining. "You'll come to love Ireni as you love the others, I promise it. Because I know how worthy of love she is, and I'm eager for the day you see it too. Soon, I hope. And all the other women we'll bring into your harem will also be people I know you'll be able to love."

Wow, that was a bit more than Dare had expected.

"One thing," he said gently but firmly. "I'm grateful for you, and I'm beginning to love you for all we've shared. But if you're going to be living with me, traveling with me, leveling with me, you need to understand that you can't just order me around all the time and completely take control of everything. You gave me this second life, I know that, but it's *my* life and I want to live it."

"Oh?" the Outsider said in amusement. "Can't I?" Before he could answer she laughed merrily. "Have you really been worrying about that? I sometimes forget how paranoid humans can be."

He frowned at her, and she rubbed his knee soothingly with her small hand. "Darren Portsmouth. Dare. My entertaining transplant from another world. My darling lover." She gave his leg an affectionate pat. "Sometimes I wonder how much you actually listen to me. To what I want."

Dare felt a moment of chagrin. "Right. I guess if you want to watch what I do, what decisions I make, then controlling me like a puppet every step of the way kind of works against that."

"Exactly!" The Outsider clapped her hands in delight. "If it makes you feel better I only plan to dwell in Ireni to adventure with you at times, to make love when you're willing to take that step, to spend time with you and the rest of the harem and their children, and of course to take part in raising our own children when you're ready to take *that* step."

Her green eyes held his intently. "And just as you refuse to be controlled, I have my own limits. Much as it might pain me should harm come to you or the ones we love, I won't bail you out if you get into a bad situation. I don't want to do something that boring, and I couldn't even if I wanted to."

She grimaced. "In fact, on that note I'm going to need to stop using the world systems to talk to you. I've been using loopholes I created when I helped make the system to do so up til now, but eventually it's going to get me in trouble. So I think it's best that from now on we only speak through Ireni."

Dare noticed with vague surprise that she was able to directly reference the world systems, without that same system turning it into an incomprehensible fuzz to uphold immersion. But that was the least of his considerations. "We can't talk anymore?" he asked, heart sinking.

The Outsider leaned forward and gently stroked his cheek. "Only through Ireni. It may seem I can do what I like, but this world has rules even I can't break or circumvent. So you'd better make damn sure you take very good care of yourself and the rest of us, because you have no one to blame but yourself if you get us all killed."

Her solemnity abruptly vanished into her usual levity. "So basically, all you can expect from me is out of this world sex, pun intended, a few memorable adventures, the occasional engaging conversation, and of course loving attentiveness to our children as often as I'm able."

She giggled. "And of course the occasional bump, like I did with the treasure chest, to make sure you're able to pay for it all. I won't have my children raised with anything but the best opportunities." Her eyes narrowed in mock sternness. "But I expect you to be working hard and solving your own problems, even when it comes to our finances . . . I can only bail you out so often."

The goddess abruptly straightened with a sigh of regret. "Speaking of what I'm able to do, I have pressing duties I need to get back to. I'm turning Ireni's body back over to her." She hesitated. "But before I do, I hope you'll be kinder to her than you have been. I love her, and it hurts when others are rude to her. Especially those I also love."

Dare felt a surge of guilt. "Sorry for calling her weird. And for the cool reception. She didn't deserve that."

Her eyes softened. "She understands. We knew this was going to be a lot for you to take in." Her face became stern. "Although you should apologize to her, too."

"I will."

"Then I'll see you soon, my beloved." The Outsider pulled him into a warm hug and gently kissed his cheek, then leaned back again.

From one moment to the next her demeanor noticeably changed to one less bold, less certain, as Ireni came back to the fore. "You probably have questions for me, too," she said with a somewhat shy laugh.

"More than I can think of," Dare agreed. "But first the Outsider's right, I need to apologize to you." He leaned forward earnestly. "I'm sorry, Ireni. You didn't deserve harsh words or insults just because the situation caught me off guard. Whatever I feel about this situation, I can see you're a good person and I was wrong to be so rude to you."

She looked surprisingly touched. "It's all right, Dare. I know this situation is unusual and from the outside can be a bit hard to accept, and we just dumped it on you without warning." Her voice became playfully chiding as her eyes lifted to the ceiling. "All so someone could have her surprise in a situation where more tact would've served better."

He chuckled. "Well, it surprised me."

The petite redhead grinned. "Okay, now let me answer your questions."

"All right, well first I suppose the most important one." He leaned forward and looked deep into her green eyes. "Ireni, I'm not a fan of arranged marriages. You probably know that thanks to my year long betrothal to Se'weir."

"I do," she said with a slight smile. "You seriously lucked out with her, by the way. She's a sweetheart. And Zuri, and Pella, and all the others. Even Leilanna's a sweetheart once you peel away her rough exterior."

He wholeheartedly agreed with that. "Well you can see how your goddess arranging for you to let her take you over and have sex with me is even more troubling to me than an arranged marriage would be. So I need to hear you tell me what this is like for you. Because while I love the Outsider and trust that she has our best interests in mind, I don't want her to hurt you or use you."

Ireni's eyes softened. "I know, and that's one of the reasons I love you." She took his hand in both of hers. "Because while I may be a stranger to you, Dare, you're not a stranger to me. I know you and love you, and I know and love the rest of the harem. And it fills me with joy that I'll be able to be with you, sharing your adventures and hopefully one day part of our family."

That was good to hear, although Dare still wasn't sure how *he* felt about things. Or for that matter how the others would.

"The others will accept me, I'm confident of it," Ireni said; apparently she was either incredibly perceptive, or she shared the Outsider's ability to read minds. "My Goddess wouldn't plan things any other way."

"And the Outsider using you as a vessel?" he pressed. "Tell me honestly, how do you feel about it?"

The petite woman paused, expression very solemn as she seemed to consider her response. "The Outsider is my closest friend and my beloved Goddess," she said quietly. "She was there for me during the worst parts of my life, giving me the strength to get through them. And she helped me put myself together afterwards, taught me how to strive to improve myself and seek new experiences, as she encourages all of her followers to do."

She took a deep breath, beautiful green eyes meeting his firmly. "Many times in my life I've been made to feel powerless, no more than a puppet to the whims of others. I've lived that hell, and will never live it again. But giving myself to my Goddess so she can be on this world and experience its wonders isn't strings to bind me. It's freedom. Fully willingly, and happily. A shared wonder with the person I love most."

She squeezed his hand. "And we get to share it with you, if you'll let us."

Dare was deeply touched, and could admit talking to the two women, even if in the same body, had helped ease some of his reservations. "Give me time," he said. "I want things to work out well for everyone. The best way possible, so everyone can have a happy life."

"I think we all want that, with all our hearts," Ireni said warmly. "And we'll get there. Shall we rejoin the others?" She stood gracefully and started for the door.

He hurried forward to gently catch her shoulder, and she turned back to him with a raised eyebrow. "As unexpected as your arrival was," he told her, "and as odd as your message and the rest of this evening has been, it's good to see you, Ireni."

She relaxed, giving him a genuine smile. "Thank you. I was sad when I learned you left Kov without visiting me, even though I understand why you did. I'd been looking forward to it."

"I promise I'll make it up to you." Dare offered her his elbow. "Shall we?"

Chapter Four
New Adventure

"Are you serious?" Leilanna asked when they returned to the table arm in arm. "After all the weirdness of how she just walked up and started talking all crazy, you're all chummy with her now? Are you *that* blinded by a pretty face?"

"Ireni is far more than just a pretty face," Dare said, giving the Priestess a reserved smile.

Ireni laughed. "Although it makes me happy to know you think I'm pretty. Even though my Goddess had already assured me you would. Some things you want to hear for yourself."

His dusk elf lover wasn't laughing. "What the hell, Dare? I know you like to stick your dick in every warm, wet hole you see, but how the hell did you get from how things were when you left to flirting with her?" She put her hands on her hips. "Were you born with zero danger sense whatsoever?"

He glanced at Ireni and she nodded, so he leaned towards his two companions and lowered his voice. "It's a bit hard to explain, but my benefactor is actually the Outsider, and Ireni is serving as the vessel for the Outsider so the goddess can be with me in real life."

Leilanna seemed only shocked, but Ilin looked flat out disbelieving. "What?" he blurted. "That's preposterous."

Ireni sat primly with her hands clasped in her lap, looking every inch the proper high priestess. "It's not unheard of for deities to incarnate on Collisa in some way or another."

"To fight the great evils of the world, or do some great wonder!" the Monk protested. "Not to have an affair with a mortal."

Dare laughed. "That's pretty much the exact opposite of the lore of many of the gods from back home."

Ireni snickered, the only one really able to understand the joke, which was a pleasant surprise. Since she knew about Earth it would actually be nice to have someone who would get his references, and maybe even be able to talk with him about his old home.

A silver lining to a relative stranger knowing everything about him.

"This is no laughing matter, my friend," Ilin said firmly. "The gods take little hand in the mundane affairs of the world, but they *do* tend to smite those who use their name falsely."

"Ilin," Ireni said warmly, resting a hand on his. "Who are you talking to? I'm a High Priestess of the Outsider. I'm not saying I *couldn't* lie about this, but not only would I never, but I know better."

Her posture shifted to the Outsider. "And I would hardly allow such a farce to go on beneath my very nose," the goddess said with a smile.

Perhaps there was some heightened sensitivity to spiritual matters innate to Monks, or maybe Ilin simply observed the change in Ireni and discerned its meaning. Either way his face paled in awe. "Patron of Explorers," he whispered, standing to bow formally.

She inclined her head. "It's good to finally meet you, Ilin. I've observed you long, and found much pleasing in you."

The bald ascetic looked awed. "You honor me, Goddess."

The Outsider waved curtly. "Enough formality. I'm here not as the Outsider but as Dare's lover. And your friend."

Ilin didn't seem to know how to process that. "I-I'm not sure what to say."

She grinned. "I have to say I thought you'd take this with more aplomb. I've never seen you this nonplussed before."

"Okay, so I guess we suddenly have a new companion," Leilanna said. "Would've been nice to have a vote, but I suppose I can't really argue with it since I was already cool with you being lovers. Guess we'll see what Zuri and Pella and Se'weir think of it."

The goddess smirked. "Don't pretend you aren't secretly wondering what it would be like to fuck me. Believe me, Leilanna, the feeling's more than mutual."

The beautiful dusk elf flushed. "Sure, make yourself right at home in the group. For you this all may be familiar, but remember I met you less than-"

"Dare!"

Dare jumped at the familiar voice and to see a catgirl in her early teens weaving through the tables towards them, pale orange ears pointed cheerfully forward and tail lashing as she waved. She was wearing the surcoat of the Marshal's Irregulars mercenary company she was contracted to, although none of the rest of the group he'd seen her with in Jarn's Holdout, including her older sister Linia, was anywhere to be seen.

He couldn't help but grin as he waved back. "Hey, Felicia. What are you doing here?"

She grinned back. "What do you think? I get to be part of a raid! The Irregulars hired out the services of five dwarvish Archers and Marksmen to Lord Zor." Her good mood dampened a bit. "Although I have to stay safely to the rear fetching ammo and whatnot."

Hardly a surprise, considering her age and the fact that she was only Level 5. Which was two levels higher than when he'd last seen her, granted, but still weak enough a Level 35 raid rated monster would kill her with a sneeze.

"So how's Linia?" he asked.

Felicia grimaced. "Got knocked up and decided to take a two year vacation in our village up north to have and wean the baby." She gave him a level stare very reminiscent of a displeased cat. "By the timing it might be yours."

Dare winced, exchanging a glance with the Outsider. "Actually, unless she was already pregnant I'm definitely the father. I found out after sleeping with her that my fertility stat was high enough to overpower Zuri's Prevent Conception. And also high enough to pretty much guarantee pregnancy."

The young catgirl's stare intensified. "What do you mean you *found out* your stat was higher? Your fertility is right there on your character screen with all your other stats. Unless you didn't bother to learn the stat caps for Prevent Conception, which makes you an idiot. Or you didn't know what fertility even does, which makes you an even bigger idiot."

He shrugged sheepishly. "Guilty as charged. Can I go talk to her? I want to help with the child and be part of its life, if possible."

Felicia waved that away. "Felids almost always raise their children alone, or trade off custody. We're free spirits who won't be tied down, even by people we have strong attachments to. The only exception is our children, of course."

She stroked a hand curled into a cat's paw over her one of her big soft ears, thoughtful. "Although if you really want to help raise the child, and Linia thinks you'd make a good parent, she might agree to giving you custody when she returns to the Irregulars to complete her contract."

Dare perked up hopefully. "I'd like that. If it helps, me and my harem have a manor and land to the southeast. I already have a baby, and more on the way, and we're in a good position to care for her child."

Felicia laughed. "You have a baby? How the hell? It's only been a couple months since I saw you. Was your goblin consort already pregnant?"

He rubbed the back of his head. "And Pella too. I fucked up with my fertility stat and Prevent Conception, remember?"

She laughed even harder, tail lashing. "Wow, Linia's going to have kittens when I tell her about this. On top of actually going to have a kitten, of course." She sobered a bit, although her pale orange eyes still danced with mirth. "I'll explain the situation and give her your offer, though. She liked Zuri and Pella, and you of course, and I think she'd be okay with you guys raising the child."

The young catgirl smirked. "Assuming she doesn't tear your head off for knocking her up like a dipshit."

"But you'll put in a good word for me, right?" Dare asked. His tone was light but he was serious; he wanted to make it up to Linia for his mistake and be there for her and the child. Having Felicia on his side would help.

"I guesssss," she said slowly. "You're not a douchebag like a lot of the jerks she goes after, and it sounds like you're in a good position to take care of my niece or nephew."

He relaxed, smiling. "Thanks. How long do catgirl pregnancies last, anyway?"

"Seven months." Felicia dropped into the seat next to Leilanna and flagged down a passing serving girl. "Pint of ale over here."

"Absolutely not," Dare, Ilin, and Ireni said at the same time.

The young catgirl scowled. "Come on, you're not my parents or guardians. I'm a contracted mercenary, I can do what I want."

"You're a thirteen year old girl," Ireni said firmly, projecting a commanding air even though she was barely taller than Felicia. "Tea for me and Felicia," she added to the serving girl. "Water for the gentleman here, and refills for the others."

The serving girl curtsied and hurried off, and the high priestess turned her stern gaze back to the catgirl. "Where's Irawn?"

Of course she knew about the older felid who acted as a guardian to the catgirl sisters.

Felicia slumped back in her chair and crossed her arms, pouting. "Back in the camp, of course. I was sent as a runner to deliver messages." She brightened. "One's for you, Dare. The raid's under strength in spite of our recruiting efforts, and Lord Zor wants to set out quickly before the monster begins rampaging. You've got a spot if you want it."

Dare perked up hopefully. "Really?"

"Yeah. Since you'll be in the bowmen party you report to the leader of the Irregulars' dwarvish contingent, Gorfram. I can point you to him." She stretched lazily, tail lashing. "Now I just need to find some Priestess named Ireni to let her know she's in too. Probably have to head up to Montshadow Estate to find her."

Dare stared at the petite redhead, who looked smugly satisfied as she picked up the teacup the serving girl set in front of her and placidly blew on it. "You knew you'd be joining me on the raid even before you approached me," he observed.

"We look forward to adventuring with you," she replied with a grin.

"So you're High Priestess Ireni?" Felicia said, brightening. "Great, that saves me running around. You report to Lady Ennara with the support party."

"Congratulations, looks as if you're in after all!" Ilin said. He glanced at Leilanna. "I guess we head back to the manor and keep leveling, then." He didn't seem too disappointed.

The dusk elf hesitated, looking at Dare. "It's okay," he told her. "We'll be back in four or five days, depending."

"Great, that'll give me time to tell the others all about Ireni and see how they feel about her," she said, a little too brightly. "Have fun!"

He got the feeling he was going to need to spend a few quality hours cuddling with Leilanna to mollify her.

They finished their drinks, then said their goodbyes. Dare hugged his dusk elf lover for a bit longer than strictly necessary, stroking her silky hair. "I'll miss you," he told her.

"Hurry back, then. And bring back a big haul from the raid." She briefly pressed her plump lips to his, offering him a taste of sweet blackberry wine, then gathered her things and headed out the door with Ilin.

Ireni had her own horse, a sleek dapple mare as small and delicate as she was. She let Felicia ride behind her as they mounted up and headed towards the raiding party's camp.

On the way the young catgirl filled them in on details of the raiding party and gossip about its members. From the sounds of it the raid would include almost 40 people: a small party of tanks, a party of melee damage dealers, a party of ranged spellcasters, a party of archers, a party of healers, and a party of support spellcasters.

Each party leader would focus on their role under the leadership of Lord Zor, a decent enough organizational structure. Dare had no complaints, especially if his party leader was an experienced mercenary and Ireni's leader was Zor's personal friend and apparently a well loved healer.

Back at the camp they were intercepted by the same weaselly squire from before. "I brought the recruits, Dorias," Felicia told him in a carefully neutral tone that suggested she strongly disliked him. Which wasn't surprising.

He sneered at her. "Took your time, girl. Take care of the new arrivals' horses, then return to your duties."

She glowered at him but reluctantly obeyed, gathering up the reins of Dare's and Ireni's horses. "Come camp with the Irregulars," she invited Dare and Ireni as she led the mounts towards where over a hundred other mounts were tethered.

The squire, Dorias apparently, turned his sneer on them. "It looks as if you'll be coming along after all, through no merit of your own. I expect you to work twice as hard to pull your weight in spite of your levels."

"Of course," Ireni said regally. "We're grateful for the opportunity."

He sniffed and pulled out his crude clipboard again. "You'll be paid a portion of the profits, with an opportunity for bonuses based on exceptional contribution. Profits are weighted by various factors, such as that Lord Zor and his party leaders, along with the armored defenders, will be getting larger shares. Under the circumstances you can probably be expecting a smaller share than everyone else."

Dare felt his heart sink. "Are shares determined by level?"

The weaselly man smirked. "No, by contribution, according to the raiding party's stats after a fight. Which is why you'll be faring so poorly."

Interesting to hear that raid parties got stats for the contributions of its members. In most games Dare had played you needed to have special mods for that. "I have zero complaints about a merit based system."

Dorias gave him an irritated look. "Careful your confidence doesn't stray into arrogance, *Hunter*. Lord Zor has little patience for braggarts."

"Don't worry, he likely won't even know I exist. I plan to keep my mouth shut and do my job."

"That would be for the best." The squire produced two cheap tin insignias in the form of a roaring lion with a long tail forming a circular boarder around it. "Keep these pinned to your left shoulder at all times to signify your position in the raid party." His sneer made a final reappearance. "You'll likely be mistaken for hangers-on otherwise."

As they pinned on the insignias Dorias curtly directed them to the archer and support party leaders. Ireni gave Dare a hug before leaving to report in. "I'll meet you back in the Irregulars camp," she said, kissing his cheek.

"See you soon," he replied, awkwardly hugging her back; he still didn't know the high priestess well enough to be fully comfortable with intimacy with her.

Which was strange, since with most women he slept with he had no issues being perfectly at ease. Maybe because he knew they were just looking for a good time and he could give them that, then they'd both walk away satisfied.

But Ireni was going to be part of his life, part of his family, and that changed everything. Maybe he was afraid he'd fuck it up, or that she wouldn't fit in well with the others, or he wouldn't end up liking her personality for some reason. But there it was.

Come to think of it, he'd had a lot of the same uncertainties with Leilanna. Maybe he should do himself a favor this time and be more forthright with Ireni.

At least they'd have some time to bond during the raid.

In the Irregulars' section of camp he found the archers doing some sort of shoot and move drill. Or no, wait, move and shoot.

Which could only be for a few reasons in a raid, especially with Felicia and other camp followers tossing things at them or making sudden loud noises.

Along with the five dwarven mercenaries, two of whom were women, there were also a human and what looked like a wood elf, likely recruits like Dare. Both of them had recurve bows, but he was surprised to see that the dwarves all used crossbows.

A quick inspection showed that they were by far the slowest of the ranged weapons he'd seen, although still not as slow as the same weapon would be back on Earth. They made up for it, though, with increased range and damage, and most importantly did massively more against targets with heavy armor or thick hides.

Dare asked one of the camp followers where he could find Gorfram and was pointed to a Level 35 Archer participating in the drills. The dwarf looked ancient and tough, with long, white hair and an equally snowy beard down to his belt, both braided. He seemed to be moving with smooth competency, by far the fastest and most accurate of the group, and not just because he was the highest level there.

The old dwarf broke away from the drills at Dare's approach. "You're the new Hunter?" he asked, giving Dare's gear a once-over and apparently finding nothing to criticize.

"I am." He held out his hand. "Dare."

"Gorfram." The dwarf's grip was unintentionally crushing, tone businesslike. "With your class you won't have the multi-target attacks of Archers, or the extra range, accuracy, and armor penetration of Marksmen. But that shouldn't be an issue against the beastie we face."

Archers got multi-target attacks? Damn, that would be nice. Maybe even nicer than the survival abilities that he made constant use of. Not nice enough to take the experience penalty to change classes, though.

"What monster *are* we facing?" he asked.

Gorfram grimaced. "The sightings were all from low level

adventurers and travelers, so they couldn't be sure. A massive wyrm that bursts out of the ground to devour its victims." He spat off to one side. "We'll get a better idea when we clap eyes on the beast, and Lord Zor's monster lore experts can identify it."

Dare resolved to use his Adventurer's Eye on the monster as soon as he could.

"Anyhow," the dwarf said briskly, getting back to business. "Here."

Dare heard a ringing sound and text popped up informing him he was invited to join Zor Brightshield's raiding party, Physical Ranged sub-party. He hesitated. "Joining a party requires a bit of trust on all sides, doesn't it?"

"Sure, but raiding parties aren't quite so free with your personal information. At least not to anyone but the raid leader, and they usually have too high a reputation to uphold to consider betraying someone's trust." The Archer gave him a curious look. "First raid, I take it?"

"Yeah." Dare reluctantly accepted the invite; he didn't see many other options, and everyone else seemed okay with trusting this Lord Zor.

Gorfram grunted in satisfaction as he joined the party, taking a few moments to apparently read through what he saw of Dare's information. "All right, then. If you don't mind me asking, what compelled you to volunteer for a raid you're under level for?"

Dare couldn't help but grin. "Because I've been looking forward to being part of a raid for as long as I've been on Collisa." He paused, grin widening. "Also I've got three consorts, two of them pregnant, and one child I need to support."

The dwarf looked at him as if he thought he was joking, then shook his head with a laugh. "You're young for that, and fairly low level to support so many. If that's true, I don't know whether to congratulate you or offer you my deepest condolences."

The party leader rubbed his hands together, getting back to business. "Anyhow, haven't run across you before. You new to this area? I've traveled Adventurer's Guilds all through the north."

Actually, Dare hadn't had much interaction with Adventurer's Guilds thus far, although he'd like to. But it wouldn't do much for Gorfram's confidence in him to admit that. "I recently purchased land nearby to live with my consorts and child, yes."

"Well it would be nice to have had experience fighting alongside you, or at least heard something of your reputation. That's going to solidify your status as the newby in the group, as well as the lowby."

"I look forward to building my reputation here," Dare said. "Starting with this raid."

"I hope so." The Archer shook his head sourly. "You've got a few wins under your belt from the looks of things, but I'll want to see for myself how you do." He pointed curtly at where the others were still drilling. "Go join in."

Dare nodded and dropped off his pack, unslinging his bow and using Rapid Shot to bring four arrows to his bow hand. "Looks as if you're practicing getting out of the way of enemy attacks with as little interruption to damage output as possible."

Gorfram nodded. "Aye, lad, that we are. Glad to see you're not a fool, at least." He motioned. "Go on, take my target."

Dare jumped in and got to work, focused on getting as many arrows into the target as possible. As he did Felicia and the others called out impending threats like cones of frost, acid spit, and ice spikes, while also throwing objects at them. He couldn't help but notice that Gorfram joined in too, apparently adding a level of difficulty to test the new guy.

Thanks to both the speed and improved reflexes from Fleetfoot, as well as his general raiding experience, he was able to smoothly navigate the challenge. And when Gorfram abruptly shouted out a change of targets and Felicia and the others threw several painted bags downrange, he was the first to switch and got in the most shots, activating Rapid Shot to burn the "adds" down more quickly.

The young catgirl brought him more arrows when he needed them, and judging by how the old dwarf shouted instructions at her this was as much a test for her as him. She did the job well, though, allowing him to stay on target.

As the sun sank below the horizon the others began dropping out, panting from exhaustion or due to failure of their weapons. Dare was streaming sweat and breathing hard himself, drained from his constant tense vigilance and brief bursts of speed to get away from an attack and then keep loosing arrows.

But he'd been late to the drill so he kept going even after he was the last one left, focused on perfecting his damage rotation, responding to threats, obeying Gorfram's orders about moving or changing targets, and accepting fresh quivers of arrows.

He was in the zone, the way he got on his best nights of raiding. And he felt like he had enough awareness of what was going on that he could've done this damage while leading a party of damage dealers.

Maybe even the entire raid, with practice; it would be a lot harder without headsets and voice chat.

Dare was vaguely aware that the others had stuck around to watch him. A few were murmuring, and some called out cheers. Apparently irked at their idleness, Gorfram yelled for them to pick up rocks and join the test. And he told Felicia and the other camp followers to throw harder and faster, not holding anything back.

A friendly "fuck you" to the new guy, huh? Dare grit his teeth and sped up, letting his damage lapse a bit as he focused more on survival, the way he would in those sorts of phases in a boss fight.

His Prey's Vigilance triggered as the attacks became impossible to completely avoid, and he had to begin using Roll and Shoot and even Pounce, leaping over to the nearest person and then running back into the target range. He heard people begin murmuring in admiration at his efforts, and even a few encouraging shouts.

Finally, though, rocks began landing painfully. Partly because he missed them in the fading light, and partly because there were just too many of them coming from too many directions.

At about the point one grazed his temple, dazing him, he heard

Gorfram shout a halt to the barrage. The rain of rocks quickly ceased, and with a grateful groan he slung his bow and rested his hands on his knees, sucking in huge lungfuls of cool, clean air.

Gorfram wandered over to stand beside him, inspecting his targets with a critical eye. "You'll do," he finally grunted. He stumped away towards the Irregulars' tents, raising his voice to bellow at the onlookers. "All right, you lot! Grub and then bed! And go easy on the ale . . . we'll be traveling hard tomorrow!"

Felicia trotted up to offer Dare a waterskin, expression awed. "Linia joked once that you could be a felid in disguise, but I didn't believe it until now." She patted the simple longbow slung over her shoulder. "I can't wait to catch up to you and show you I can be just as awesome!"

He chuckled as he gratefully gulped down half the skin. "Looking forward to you challenging me in the future," he said.

Gorfrom barked from the direction of camp, and the young catgirl jumped guiltily. "I need to go gather up the arrows," she said. "I'll bring them around so you can identify yours, or get replacements."

"Sure, thanks for the water." Dare retrieved his pack and started for camp.

He found Ireni waiting there with hot food and a skin of ale. She'd already set up her own tent, an elegant silk structure big enough for two, which seemed intentional.

"Your legend grows," she said with a grin as she held out a bucket of water. "Here. After you use one of Zuri's Cleanse Target scrolls you can change in the tent and hang your wet clothes on the line."

He felt his cheeks heat as he surreptitiously sniffed his pits. Yeah, he was smelling more than a little rank after that workout.

With a rueful chuckle he dumped the bucket over his head and used a scroll, thinking fondly of his goblin lover as he did and missing her and their daughter. He was excited for the raid, but he was eager to get back to his family, too.

The tent was as luxurious inside as outside, lit by a white glowstone and smelling of sweet scented herbs. He removed his shoes to step onto the clean soft groundcloth, looking around at the two beds made up on either side of the tent, piled with soft clean blankets atop comfy padded pallets.

He was relieved to see it wasn't one bed.

After changing into clean clothes he hung out his gear to dry and joined Ireni at the fire, accepting a plate of grilled meat and mashed buttered parsnips. "Thanks."

"You're more than welcome." She grinned and nodded towards a few curious onlookers at a nearby fire. "You've got some admirers after your show. Not that I can blame them . . . it was exciting to watch."

"Much as I enjoyed the challenge, I could've done without being pelted by a bunch of rocks," he said wryly, rubbing at his sore temple.

The petite redhead laughed. "Gorfram may be gruff but he's not the cruel sort. He made it hard for you once he saw you were capable of handling it."

"Well, hopefully I've proven I can pull my weight."

"That and then some," she agreed.

Her posture abruptly changed, becoming more assertive and familiar as the Outsider smirked and leaned close, breath tickling his ear. "Ireni's not the only one who was impressed. I was practically creaming myself watching you in motion. You have no idea how excited I am for you to get comfortable enough to make love to me the way I've dreamed of."

Dare felt his cheeks heat and glanced uncomfortably at the Priestess's tent. "You, um, aren't expecting that tonight, are you?"

She gave him a longing look, then sighed. "I'd be happy if you were willing, but I understand you need time." She bit her lip, looking almost shy. "Failing that, I'd love to cuddle with you as we sleep until you're ready to be lovers. We could always push the beds together."

He could admit he would love to cuddle the beautiful woman, and he thought he could be a bit more comfortable being that intimate with his benefactor, even if he still felt shy around Ireni. But the fact that the two shared the same body, and from what Ireni had told him also the same experiences, gave him pause.

"I'd be grateful if you'd be willing to share your tent, we're companions after all," he said. "But maybe we should wait on the rest."

The goddess nodded, although she was clearly disappointed. She gave him another longing look. "Can I at least hug you goodnight? You have no idea how much I've longed to feel your touch."

Dare couldn't refuse a request like that. He set down his plate and held out his arms, and with a delighted smile she rushed into them, hugging him affectionately. "It's good to finally be able to share your life with you, my beloved," she said, kissing his cheek. "I can't wait for all the adventures we'll have together."

The hug stretched on for almost a minute as she held him contentedly, then she stepped back and her posture markedly shifted as Ireni returned to the fore. The Priestess shifted bashfully and gave him a hopeful look. "Can I have a hug too?"

He couldn't help but laugh as he again held out his arms. Their hug was more awkward, and didn't last nearly as long. But her affection was genuine, and she looked content as she held him before finally kissing his cheek and stepping back. "I'm happy to be here too," she said. "I can't wait to share adventures with you like those I've heard about."

He shook his head wryly. "It's going to take a while to get used to you knowing so much about me while I know practically nothing about you."

"I know. But you will." Ireni returned to her seat and resumed eating. "Want to talk about video games? I know being part of a raid has you thinking of your past experiences with them. Maybe you could tell me what they were like."

Dare was more than happy with that topic, with finally having someone besides the Outsider that he could talk to about his past life and experiences. The slightly awkward atmosphere relaxed as they talked about his favorite multiplayer RPG games and some of the fights he'd taken part in or led, especially since Ireni was clearly very intelligent and had a great head for details, so she didn't get lost in his descriptions.

In fact, from how she talked he could believe she'd taken part in those same games herself. He wondered if the Outsider was talking to her as well and explaining anything she didn't understand.

The conversation continued seamlessly as they cleared up after the meal and retired to her fancy and very comfortable tent, where he was relieved to see Ireni had already made up two separate beds along either wall. Her blankets were high quality and incredibly soft, and the tent's interior was softly lit by a glowstone that provided enough white light to read by.

As if just as eager to hold the awkwardness at bay as he was, Ireni encouraged him to keep talking about his raiding experience as she undressed down to a modest linen shift and climbed into her bed, encouraging him to do the same. "Sleep however you're most comfortable. Since we're going to be companions, and hopefully more, we need to be able to relax around each other."

He appreciated that. But while he usually slept in his undershorts, or even naked if he was with his lovers, he was fine with wearing his clothes to bed.

The blankets were every bit as soft as they looked, and the pallet was surprisingly cushiony. He settled in anticipating a good night's sleep, listening to the soft rustling as Ireni turned off the glowstone and got comfortable in her bed.

"Good night, Dare," she whispered.

"Good night, my beloved," the Outsider said, voice subtly but noticeably different.

"Good night Ireni, Outsider," Dare replied, closing his eyes. He would've thought the silence would be awkward after that, but her soft breathing was surprisingly soothing.

Nirim

Besides, after the evening's training he was exhausted. He was more than ready to relax and let sleep claim him.

Chapter Five

Wyrm

They set out early the next morning, Gorfram's roaring voice rousing everyone at the break of dawn to take down the camp and prepare to move out.

As Dare sat up, fully roused by the dwarf's bellows, the glowstone lit up and he saw Ireni pull herself out of her blankets with a groan, soft auburn hair adorably disheveled. She rubbed her eyes with both fists as she peered across the tent at him with a smile. "Good morning."

He couldn't help but smile back; her beautiful face was a nice thing to see first thing after waking up. "Good morning, Ireni." He climbed out of his own blankets with a slight groan, muscles sore from yesterday's exertions, and reached for his boots. "Let me get a fire going and I'll cook breakfast for us."

"Let me," she said, smiling wryly as she reached for her robes and began pulling them on. "I'll let you take care of taking down the tent and packing our things onto the horses in the meantime."

He grinned. "Fair enough."

Outside Gorfram roared another order for everyone to get up, and Dare hurriedly finished pulling on his boots and ducked out of the tent.

In the camps for the other parties, as well as the finer camp in the center for Lord Zor and his entourage, others were similarly rousing the raid. Grooms were busily saddling mounts as camp followers took down tents.

As agreed, Ireni cooked breakfast while Dare took down the tent and packed up the horses. The smell of cooking meat drew Felicia, who seemed delighted to be invited to breakfast.

She reminded him more and more of his little sister Holly, and he had to admit that considering his relationship with the young catgirl's older sister and the fact that Linia was having his baby and Felicia would be the child's aunt, he was starting to think of her that way.

Irawn, the catgirl sisters' harried-looking guardian, joined them as well, seeming gruff but friendly enough. "I'll hunt us all something for dinner if you want," Felicia said as they finished off the meal with some honeyed scones. She seemed eager at the prospect of helping out.

The older felid grunted. "If you hurry up and kill an animal close to Terana, before they get too high level."

"Well duh." The pale orange catgirl ran off to finish preparing to leave, and with a sigh her guardian followed.

"Speaking of levels," Dare said as he and Ireni mounted. "I've been meaning to ask you-"

"How the hell I got from seven levels lower than you to equal level, as a Priestess with zero attack spells?" she asked with a grin.

"Yeah, that."

The bookish redhead laughed, adjusting her robes to gracefully sit sidesaddle. They were divided for riding and she wore thigh-length stockings, but even so she didn't seem eager to show off her legs.

Actually, unlike yesterday's form-fitting robes these ones were far more demure, hiding her figure without obviously doing so.

"I could say I cheated," she said, eyes dancing. "But only in the way a lot of people cheat to level up. Including you and your companions, helping each other get experience." She grinned and tapped her forehead conspiratorially. "Although it certainly helped to have someone along who could point us to which monster spawn points to farm. Justifying it by the fact that they were all spawn points you and your companions had used on your way north, so they weren't exactly a mystery."

"So you were part of a party?" Dare wondered where those people were now.

98

Ireni shook her head, lips twitching. "I was with two kind devotees of the Outsider who had classes ideal for leveling up. I would take turns inviting them to my party, and they'd each take twelve hour shifts so we could work around the clock to hunt monsters, while the other person slept or kept guard."

She'd been leveling literally nonstop? "That must've been exhausting for you."

"It was," she admitted frankly. "Although I did spend a lot of the time sleeping." She giggled. "I actually earned four levels while I was asleep. Which was certainly a pleasant way to wake up."

Dare couldn't help but laugh as well. "That happened to Zuri once, near the beginning when we were having her do her four hours at a time sleep schedule."

"I know," the petite redhead said as the Outsider came to the fore, smirking. "It was so cute watching her wake up to that pleasant surprise." Her smile widened. "And pretty hot what you two did together to celebrate."

He cleared his throat in embarrassment. "So you were watching that stuff, too? You're kind of a pervert."

She sniffed. "You can't call a limited omniscience deity perverted. We see all that stuff anyway." Her smile returned. "I just usually don't pay attention, except with you and your lovers." She paused, actually blushing a bit. "Although don't worry, I don't share *everything* with Ireni. That part of your life is private."

"You two all ready to go, huh?" Gorfram roared at them. "Get back down off your horses and help with taking down the rest of the camp. You're in my party now, you do your share."

Dare hastily dismounted and helped load the wagons with arrows, targets, and various camp supplies. Ireni got to work taking down tents with Felicia.

Everyone in the raid party and their entourages seemed to be competent and professional, doing their tasks quickly but well. Even so, large groups had their own inertia, and even with everyone moving quickly there were unavoidable delays with equipment breaking, mistakes, and miscommunications.

Finally, though, Lord Zor mounted and took the lead of their force of over a hundred people.

The tanks rode with him, then the healers, support, and spellcasters, and finally the melee and ranged damage dealers, just ahead of the camp followers and wagons. Although a few who could travel closer to the front chose their own place in the caravan, like Ireni riding beside Dare.

Or Felicia, who should be with the camp followers, walking between their horses. And Irawn trailing close behind, expression neutral.

The wyrm had appeared far from any town or village, which wasn't a surprise considering how spawn mechanics worked. That meant they were blazing a trail across the northeastern area of Terana Province, over plains and around hills and patches of woods, occasionally fording streams and rivers.

It also meant they ran into numerous monster spawn points.

This close to Terana, Lord Zor fearlessly led the way through the low level monsters, battering them down and leaving the camp followers coming behind to loot the bodies to go to the raid coffers; at the end of the raid everything would be appraised and funds equal to the total value distributed.

Which meant that if some good gear dropped Dare wouldn't be able to get it unless he was willing to pay its full price. Which sucked, but it meant if gear didn't drop for him, which was far more likely, he'd still get part of the profits from what did drop.

The monsters got steadily higher level the farther they went, until finally at the end of the day the raid leader announced that they'd be avoiding spawn points from now on, because the monsters were getting high enough level that if they encountered an unusually strong group of enemies it could threaten the raid.

To Dare's Eye the monsters were still only around Level 25, not a threat to anyone, but he supposed he appreciated the man's caution. He just wished he could break ranks and farm some of the monsters as they traveled, then catch up to the slow moving column that was bound to the speed of the wagons.

He doubted he'd get approval for that, though. And even if he could it would draw unwanted attention to him, as people wondered how he felt so comfortable fighting unfamiliar monsters.

On the plus side, it gave him a chance to get to know Ireni better.

Even better, she remained interested in talking about Earth. They had to be vague on the details, of course, since there were listening ears all around, but he could still frame things as if they used magic instead of technology.

The beautiful Priestess wanted to talk to him about games he'd played, places he'd been, his work and how he'd felt about it, and anything else he wanted to share with her. Even mundane, day to day things. And even though he found himself rambling more than once she always listened eagerly.

Dare supposed that if he had a chance to hear someone talk about another world with rules entirely different from his own, he'd be just as excited.

Felicia seemed mostly confused by a lot of what they talked about, although she gamely listened in, pale orange ears twitching back and forth between them. Irawn just stumped along impassively.

Feeling like he was dominating the conversation, Dare kept shifting the subject to Ireni where he could. And she was open enough about things like her class, the worship of the Outsider, and the brothel she'd run. She especially seemed eager to talk about Trissela and the other courtesans, obviously trying to entice him to accept them as lovers.

Although in roundabout ways, considering listening ears.

Her descriptions of beautiful women of other races was enjoyable enough, and a prospect to look forward to, but he felt like she was trying to distract him from talking about her past. Not because she was trying to hide anything, or at least that's not the feeling he got, but because the subject was one she preferred to avoid because it was painful.

Dare could sympathize with that, considering the things his other lovers had been through, and didn't press the issue.

That night they did more drills, this time Lord Zor insisting the entire raiding party of almost 40 people train together. They spent the next few hours coordinating moving around a field, with the shape of a worm hacked into the sod at the center of it as their target.

It wasn't particularly interesting but very important, with everyone learning to follow the directions of their party leaders, as they focused on the guidance of the Level 36 Paladin and his assistant raid leader Lady Ennara, a Level 37 Holy Warder.

Lord Zor cut a striking figure in his gold-enameled plate armor, wielding a massive tower shield and long hammer. He seemed competent enough, arranging everyone in smart configurations where each party could stay close enough together to coordinate and help the other parties, but far enough apart that random ranged monster attacks or area of effect damage wouldn't hit more than one or two people.

He would've done pretty well in most of the online games Dare had played.

That night the Outsider took the fore and asked him to go for a sunset walk. Even though they were out in the wilds and couldn't get too far from the raid party, it was still romantic. Especially when her small hand slipped into his, and she looked up at him with a contented smile.

They talked about Nirim Manor, and his other lovers, and their plans for the future. Dare did his best to include her in those plans, even though he still had his reservations about the arrangement with her and Ireni.

Which was why when she paused at the end of the walk and lifted her face to him, lips parted and expression quietly expectant, he hesitated.

This was his benefactor, his lover, and she was achingly

beautiful and he wanted nothing more than to kiss her. But the goddess was looking up at him with Ireni's sweet face. The woman he'd spent the day bonding with and had found himself becoming surprisingly fond of.

The Outsider sighed. "We'll get there, my beloved." She leaned in and gently kissed him on the cheek.

A moment later her posture changed as Ireni took the fore. She gave him a patient smile and held out her hand. "Will you go on a romantic walk with me, Dare?"

Dare nodded and took her small hand, finding a new route to walk with the petite redhead as the sky darkened and the first stars appeared in the sky. As well as what looked like a neutron star.

He couldn't help but laugh at that. "You realize your night sky's impossible, right?"

The Priestess smiled. "The Goddess mentioned that, and that it's a constant source of fascination and irritation for you, given what people on your world know of astronomy." She shook her head. "For us it's just the sky, beautiful and unexplainable. Honestly I'm content just appreciating its beauty."

He looked up at the checkerboard pattern of light streaming from the neutron star. "It's certainly beautiful." He realized as he finished speaking that his eyes had dropped to his companion's lovely upturned face, and felt his cheeks heat as he quickly turned his gaze back to the sky.

At the end of the walk Ireni hugged him, holding him for almost a minute with her face buried in his chest. "I know it might be off-putting to hear a relative stranger keep telling you she loves you," she murmured with her face still hidden in his coat. "But it doesn't change how I feel." She looked up and smiled at him. "I'm just waiting for you to catch up."

He smiled back, and on impulse leaned down and gently kissed her forehead. "Good night, Ireni."

"Good night." Grinning wryly, she turned and led the way into the tent they shared and made her way over to her bed.

Early afternoon the next day they reached the raid rated world monster.

* * * * *

"Magma Tunneler. Monster, Raid Rated. Level 35. Attacks: Bite, Devour, Crush, Tail Smash, Magma Spit, Molten Rain, Subterranean Fire Gout, Frenzied Roll, Burrow, Erupt, Granite Scales."

Fuck, that thing was beefy. Its stats made a party rated monster look like a regular monster 10 levels lower than it. A weak one at that.

The Magma Tunneler was slowly boring through the earth in a southwestern bearing along the plains up ahead, only occasional glints of a stony hide visible. But from what *was* visible it looked like a monstrous snake or worm, easily 60 feet long and as thick around as a man was tall, looking thin and sinuous. Which meant that it would not only be powerful but probably quick as well.

A bad combination.

Pretty much all the raid party and camp followers had gathered on a low rise overlooking the raid rated monster. They were waiting with great anticipation for a specific event: its path to intersect with a spawn point of Level 32-34 Cursed Gerons a short distance away.

There was some speculation about whether the monsters would actually fight each other, since they didn't always. But if so, they'd get to watch about 30 odd bird-like things only slightly lower level than the Magma Tunneler try to take it on.

It should prove informative. Or not.

The raid rated world monster burst into view when it encountered the first geron, earth and stones exploding in all directions as a head the size of a car rose into the air. Dare's impression of snake-like appearance immediately shifted more to worm, based on the triple-jawed mouth filled with spiraling rows of inward pointing teeth. It gaped wide to eat the first geron, swallowing it whole.

Then it rose high into the air, extending dozens of feet, before slamming back down in the center of the spawn point, crushing several monsters beneath it. It thrashed and rolled in a frenzy over the gerons flocking to it, swiftly smashing the life out of them.

The fight was over in less than a minute, at which point the Magma Tunneler dove back beneath the ground with shocking grace and speed and continued on its way, leaving a field of churned earth and broken corpses in its wake.

Ireni whistled. "I'm glad that aside from the healers and support assigned to the tanks, the rest of us get to stay back out of danger where possible," she said. Then she lowered her voice slightly. "I'm not getting any information from our friend from outside about that thing, probably since now I have you to tell me about monsters. What's it looking like?"

Dare glanced around, then leaned closer and murmured the information from his Eye. "We've got our work cut out for us," he concluded grimly.

"You sure do," Felicia said, joining them and staring down at the battlefield with wide eyes, tail swishing nervously. "I'm kind of glad I'm too low level to face that thing."

"Spoken like someone who means to surpass me one day," he teased.

Her big orange eyes blazed indignantly. "I will, just you see!"

"Enough chitchat, everyone!" Gorfram roared from nearby. "Lord Zor's sending a party to loot the slain monsters. The rest of us will set up camp a mile due south of here, prepared to make a quick strike on the beastie in the morning. Once we're settled in our leader is going to brief us on what his lore masters tell him about our enemy, then we'll do more drills."

Aside from the people sent to loot the gerons, those lined up on the low rise to watch the slow, steady progress of the wyrm reluctantly turned away, reforming their column at the chivvying of their leaders and heading south. There was an air of tense anticipation among raiders and camp followers alike, and Dare could admit he felt a bit of that himself.

Zuri had warned him raid rated monsters killed adventurers in almost every fight, and she wasn't the only one who'd told him that. This was going to be a serious fight, even more so than the wyvern boss of the dungeon they'd fought that had hurt Pella so terribly.

He was glad Ireni was going to be holding back outside of range of that thing. And also that they'd been practicing avoiding ranged attacks and AoE.

He wasn't going to die here, and if he could do anything to prevent it no one else would, either.

People worked hastily to set up camp, everyone eager to hear from the raid leader about what they were facing, and what the plan to beat the monster would be. They were still hours from dinner, but most ate a hasty meal of travel rations as they gathered just outside the camp.

The gleaming Paladin stood before them with the party leaders and two older men in robes with the Scholar class, almost posed as he waited for the group to quiet. He certainly looked every inch the leader.

Finally he stepped forward and raised his voice in a boom, clearly audible to all assembled. "Tomorrow, we face our foe!"

His words were greeted with a cheer, Dare and Ireni joining in as they embraced the spirit of the moment. Lord Zor let the sound carry for a brief time before raising his arms for quiet.

"But before the fight comes the preparation. My Scholars have identified the monster, and we are going to go over all their knowledge and plan an ideal attack. Then we will drill until we operate seamlessly as a team."

He looked around solemnly. "It will not be an easy fight, my brothers and sisters in arms. We're facing a Tundra Wyrm, which means it will primarily be using frost based attacks and-"

Fuck. Dare didn't want to interrupt the raid leader in the middle of an explanation, but the man had misidentified their enemy; that was a mistake that could get people killed.

"Your forgiveness, my Lord!" he shouted, darting into the open space in front of the Paladin and party leaders. He fell to one knee, fist on the ground. "The monster is a Magma Tunneler. I know its stats and attac-"

"Shut your idiot mouth, newbie!" a big, heavily armored man standing just behind Zor snarled, stepping forward to cuff him on the head with a gauntleted fist.

Dare didn't even need Prey's Vigilance to dodge the vicious but not terribly swift strike. Also he noticed that Ireni put up a Goddess's Grace barrier around him. His Eye identified his assailant as a Level 35 Warrior with mostly defensive and taunt abilities, which made him either the main tank or one of the more prominent off tanks.

Definitely not someone he wanted to antagonize.

"Hold!" Lord Zor shouted irritably. Although the look he shot Dare was scarcely less annoyed. "Explain yourself, Hunter. You make a claim countering the expertise of two eminent Scholars who've spent hundreds of hours pouring over monster compendiums and histories. What makes you think it's a Magma Tunneler?"

Shit. He couldn't exactly admit he had the Adventurer's Eye. Or he supposed he *could*, it would just be a reckless move. And nobody would believe him anyway because he was 20 levels too low to even have a chance of getting it.

"Reluctant as I am to contradict the wisdom of experts, I'm afraid I must. This monster matches what I've seen about Magma Tunnelers." Which was true enough, if vague, and should hopefully hint he'd read about them in a monster compendium.

"Why should we let this lowby who has zero experience in raids and almost none in dungeons waste any more of our time?" the same Warrior demanded.

Dare kept his respectful position on one knee. "I'll accept it if you choose not to believe me, my Lord. You have no reason to. But I give my word I'm telling the truth . . . at least allow me to tell you what we should look out for from Magma Tunnelers, so when I'm proven right we'll be prepared and no lives will be lost."

A rumble sounded from the crowd, although most seemed supportive; when it came to their lives, apparently people were willing to waste a little time.

Lord Zor briefly conferred with his party leaders and the two Scholars, then nodded. "All right, Hunter, let's hear it." He motioned impatiently. "And get up, by the gods' sake. Come stand here so everyone can hear you."

Dare made his way to the Paladin's side, uncomfortably aware of everyone's eyes on him. And more of them amused or impatient than friendly. "This Magma Tunneler will be around Level 35. It has roughly 200 times the hit points of a monster of that level, and does around 3 times the damage.

"Its close range attacks mostly involve biting and devouring with the head, crushing with the body, and if it surfaces fully lashing with the tail. For its ranged and area of effect abilities it spits balls of magma that must be avoided at all costs. It also erupts multiple jets of fire from the ground beneath our feet that also must be dodged. And finally it will also spit magma into the sky to rain down upon us, which again must be dodged."

One of the Scholars rubbed his jaw. "By your description it seems a variant of Tundra Wyrms."

The Paladin nodded grudgingly. "Although I mislike the thought of flame jets and lava rain. Those seem more dangerous to deal with than the ice spikes and driving hail of the Tundra Wyrm. Will we have to worry about more monsters appearing during the fight?"

Dare hesitated; none of the Magma Tunneler's attacks seemed to indicate that possibility, but that didn't mean it was impossible. "Not to my knowledge, no."

The raid leader grimaced. "I could've done with more confidence on that point. Anything else?"

"I'm afraid that's the extent of my knowledge, my Lord."

The man nodded curtly. "Very well, you are dismissed."

Dare bowed to him, and the party leaders and Scholars for good measure, then with some relief made his way back to where Ireni stood.

"Well done," she whispered. "Knowing what we're facing will make my job a little easier."

"All right," Lord Zor continued briskly. "We'll continue the planning, but account for the possibility of ranged attacks from either a Tundra Wyrm or Magma Tunneler." He motioned to a servant, who quickly unrolled and displayed a large diagram. "The heavily armored defenders will hold the monster's attention facing away from us, while the more lightly armored melee fighters attack the body from behind.

"The ranged attackers will array themselves at a safe distance in a cone behind the monster, so fewer will be caught by ranged attacks. The healers and support spell casters will position themselves to be able to reach as many people as possible with their spells, although there will be designated healers for the defenders, for the melee, and for the ranged, with targets switched at the discretion of the party leader."

The Paladin glanced at Dare briefly. "The compendiums indicate Tundra Wyrms do not draw or spawn adds, and from the sounds of it Magma Tunnelers are the same. However, in the event of the unexpected the ranged attackers should be prepared to switch to them, and Flankers and other more lightly armored, mobile defenders to draw their attacks away from the more vulnerable raid members."

A lovely older woman at his side who Dare assumed was Lady Ennara cleared her throat, and Lord Zor stepped aside for her. "The damage dealers are no doubt aware that their goal is to keep as much damage on the monster as possible. If you are too slow to bring it down we will surely fail. But that said, your number one priority is to avoid taking damage. Any damage you take will put more strain on already struggling healers and support, and you're less equipped to take that damage than the defenders."

Zor nodded. "Equally critical, *do not* do anything to catch the attention of the wyrm away from the defenders. If it suddenly turns around in the middle of the fight the entire raid will be in the path of its attacks, and I fear many of us will quickly fall."

He paused for a long moment to let his instructions sink in, then continued firmly. "Your party leaders know the plan in more detail. Everyone gather to them, and we'll prepare for our first mock battle."

As the group dispersed to the various leaders the Warrior from before roughly knocked Dare with his shoulder. Or at least tried to, since again Dare dodged with little trouble.

"Have fun in the fight, lowby," the big man said, sneering. "You'll die to the first hit you take."

"Then let's hope the Tunneler telegraphs his attacks like you," Dare shot back before he could think better of it.

Main tank, shit. The one person you didn't want to piss off aside from the raid leader, even more than the party leaders themselves. With their critical role tanks had a big dick to swing, and they could fuck you over with a word if you looked at them funny. As Dare had seen on more than one occasion in MMOs back on Earth.

The Warrior's eyes narrowed dangerously. "For your sake telegraph better mean "is swift, accurate, and massively powerful," he growled.

"Of course," Dare agreed quickly, lowering his head. "My apologies."

"Your apologies, *sir*," the tank growled. At first Dare was confused, thinking the man wanted to be addressed as an officer, until he continued. "I am Sir Ollivan of Trentwood, Knight of the Northern Wall. You will show proper respect."

"My apologies, Sir Ollivan," Dare corrected, bowing.

The man glared, obviously spoiling for a fight and irritated to not find a handy excuse. "Do not speak out of turn to your betters again, lowby," he growled. "My friend's nobility lends him a soft heart I do not share." He turned away and started towards where the tanks were gathered.

Relieved, Dare quickly caught up with Ireni, wanting to walk her to where the support party had gathered near the physical damage dealers party.

"You realize that guy's Level 35, an anointed knight, and a personal friend of Lord Zor, right?" she asked in a low voice as she slipped her arm through his.

"But he doesn't have toilets and sinks and hot baths in his house, or four beautiful women waiting for him," he said with a grin, some of his good humor returning now that the confrontation was over.

"Actually, it wouldn't surprise me if he had a harem of his own," Ireni said, smiling back. "Although I'm sure they're not as wonderful as us. Also it's six women, since you should be counting me and the Outsider. And seven if you want to count Lady Marona, although she's not really part of the harem, just a lover. And eight once you count Trissela. And nine with Lil-" she cut off abruptly, cheeks going pink.

"Who now?" Dare asked, a bit dazed by the list of names; now that she counted them all off, he realized his harem was growing faster than he'd realized.

"An absolute sweetheart, just like all your lovers are and will be," she said, squeezing his arm. "But you know we hate spoiling the future."

He gave her a cautious look out of the corner of his eye. "I have to admit, it's a bit unsettling that you know so much about me and my life, and apparently my future, when I know almost nothing about you."

Ireni laughed. "Believe me, it can't be half as interesting for you as it is for me. I got to talk to you about Earth today."

They parted to their parties, where Dare listened attentively as Gorfram laid out their role in the fight and gave some basic commonsense advice.

Or maybe not so commonsense, considering how the first fight went. Which was particularly ironic considering the speech Lord Zor gave before they began.

"All right!" he shouted, hefting his sword and shield. "It's safe to assume that at this level, all the morons have already gotten themselves killed. But since we all know that assumptions are something only morons make, we're going to repeat this mock battle until I'm satisfied no mistakes will be made.

"That includes very carefully going over this fight afterwards to make sure we all know what if anything went wrong, and what we're supposed to be doing next time from start to finish." He glared around. "And then your party leaders are going to quiz you to make *sure* you know it all before we go again."

The Paladin took the role of the wyrm for the fight, focusing everyone's attention and giving them something to converge on, although of course no one used real attacks against him. Meanwhile the camp followers supplied the simulated ranged attacks and AoE for the raid monster, throwing thin bags of sand that would burst on impact to bathe an area.

The first battle featured such gems as one of the off tanks accidentally using a taunt ability on Lord Zor because it would provide extra damage, causing him to turn around and begin shouting out names of people in the raid who were now dead until the main tank, Ollivan as it turned out, managed to taunt him back.

The healers also clumped too closely together, assuming they were safe, but unfortunately they clumped around the healers assigned to heal the tanks and were thus in range of the monster. A bag of sand bathed half of them and sent them all scattering, struggling in a frenzy to heal each other until Ollivan, who hadn't been receiving heals, died.

Although he cursed an awful lot for a dead man.

The secondary tank managed to pick up Lord Zor's aggro and the healers got their act together in time to keep the man alive, but by then the AoE from the boss was starting to take down the melee and ranged damage dealers. Many of whom had been focused on the chaos instead of their roles or avoiding damage.

The Paladin declared the raid dead a minute or so later, since the healers were having to overheal to keep the less well armored and leveled secondary tank alive, quickly running out of mana. Meanwhile enough of the damage dealers died that they could no longer kill the monster before the healers and support went OOM.

A somewhat dispirited raid gathered around Lord Zor as he looked around in stern disappointment. "Let's break down the fight, plan better, and try again," he said grimly. "And again, if necessary, as many times as it takes. I don't want to have a late night on the eve of battle, but we don't stop until we get it right. Remember, people, this is our lives at stake. And not just ours but the innocents of Bastion should we fail."

It was a late night.

Chapter Six
Battle

Lord Zor may have been stern, but he wasn't a fool. He let the raid sleep in until midmorning to make up for the late night of training.

That meant they had to travel a bit farther to catch up to the Magma Tunneler, and then wait until it left a patch of trees (leaving ruin in its wake) and was out on the open plains again.

By that point it was almost noon, so they ate a hasty meal of travel rations before making their final preparations and setting out to slay the monster.

Lord Zor and the party leaders again took a place before the raiding party, noble features focused and confident. "Today we slay a mighty foe!" he roared, raising his hammer. He waited for the cheers to die down before continuing. "Remember the plan, pay attention to your surroundings, and follow the commands of myself and your party leaders, and we'll all live to walk away from this as heroes."

"And hundreds of gold richer!" Ollivan, standing beside his friend, roared to guffaws and a fresh surge of cheers.

The Paladin waited for things to calm down with a tolerant smile. "Now is the time, my friends. We have lived this life from a young age, defeated countless enemies, and forged bonds that will last us til death. Now let us go test ourselves and prove triumphant once more! Take your positions!"

With a deafening roar the raid party split, moving into the formation they'd practiced the previous night. Ollivan and two other heavily armored men formed an arrowhead in front of the wyrm, ready to intercept it from its far side as it steadily burrowed closer underground. The rest of the raid arrayed themselves close enough

114

to begin doing damage the moment it surfaced, support spellcasters casting buff spells to boost their stats and defenses.

"Party leaders, final check!" Lord Zor shouted, waiting as each one shouted "Ready!" in turn. Then, clashing his hammer to his tower shield, he shouted, "Sir Ollivan, now!"

Dare had to hand it to the knight. He may have been a petty son of a bitch, but he ran fearlessly at the Magma Tunneler, bristling with protective barriers and defensive buffs. He didn't even flinch as the monster burst up out of the ground in a spray of earth and turned to snap at him, throwing himself to one side and clashing his shield into the scaled flesh around the monster's giant three-segmented jaws.

That turned the wyrm's back to the rest of them, and the Paladin roared, "Damage, now!" and led the melee damage dealers in a charge at the huge creature.

Dare had used Eagle Eye to inspect the Magma Tunneler's back when it had torn through that spawn point, searching for weaknesses in its Granite Scales. He almost would've preferred to be in front of the monster instead, so he could loose arrows directly down its vulnerable gullet, but then he'd end up getting a face full of molten spit.

There were two alternatives. One was to wait for the others to hack or blast an opening into the scales he could target, which he planned to do once they did. But until then his best bet for immediate damage was the gaps in the wyrm's segmented scales.

Since they overlapped, the only real place to find that gap was at the highest point of the monster's body before its head curved down towards the tanks, where the angle let him fire beneath the overlap and directly into the flesh beneath. He hoped.

It was a tricky shot, but Dare should be able to manage it consistently.

The dwarves around him loosed their huge crossbows at the Magma Tunneler's body, the heavy bolts punching into the scales and doing some damage in spite of the monster's massive damage mitigation. The other two bowmen's arrows plinked uselessly, one glancing off entirely and the other burying only as deep as the arrowhead.

Dare's first arrow buried up to the fletchings between two heavy scales, doing close to full damage. And with Rapid Shot already prepared his next four quickly followed. Then Rapid Shot again for four more, and into his rotation.

"Magma Spit!" one of the Scholars abruptly shouted as Ollivan caught the molten glob on his shield, which glowed with enchantments and held firm. "We face a Magma Tunneler!"

Lord Zor's voice roared over the commotion of battle. "It's a Magma Tunneler! Ware its Magma Spit, Molten Rain, and Fire Gout!"

No sooner had the raid leader spoken than the ground glowed sullen red beneath a dozen people's feet. Including Dare's.

Roll and Shoot got him out of the circle of growing heat almost before he realized the danger, Fleetfoot plus his hyper tense awareness saving him without even needing to rely on Prey's Vigilance. Which he wasn't sure would've saved him from an attack like this anyway.

By the time raw flames erupted out of the ground and ten feet into the air where he'd been, he'd already returned to loosing arrows.

Unfortunately, other people weren't as on the ball.

A dozen screams sounded all around the clearing as the pillars of fire shot upwards, and they were the truly haunting screams of people getting seriously burned. Most of them could be healed, but for the worst of the wounds there'd be scars.

"Get out of the fire!" Zor roared, backing away from the Magma Tunneler to use his weak healing magic to heal those in the most danger. "Damnit, you fools, get out of the fire!"

"My Lord, it grieves me to say that Lady Ennara just succumbed to the flames!" Ireni shouted.

The Paladin cursed, and for good reason; Ennara was not only his friend, but his second-in-command and the support party leader.

"She should've known better than that," he mourned. "Why didn't she escape?"

The petite Priestess was still desperately focused on casting, although her tone was sympathetic. "She was focused on protecting Sir Ollivan and didn't spot the danger in time."

Lord Zor cursed again as he dove back into the scrum at the base of the wyrm's body. "Jurrin, take over her role and leadership of the party!"

"Aye, my Lord!" another of the support party members shouted.

Dare's Rapid Shot came off cooldown, and as he activated it he switched his target to a spot lower down the body where the spellcasters' focused magical attacks had made a gap in the scales a few feet across. The Magma Tunneler's health was steadily dropping, but the fight was far from over.

"Melee scatter!" the Paladin screamed as the monster's body abruptly heaved out of the ground.

Melee fighters scrambled away in all directions as the monster's sinuous length began violently thrashing and rolling. A few people were caught beneath its crushing weight, but a combination of defensive barriers and healing kept them alive until the wyrm rolled off them and they were able to drag themselves to safety.

Dare noticed that along with the melee damage dealers currently out of the fight, many of the ranged had paused to gape at the sight. Or maybe they were just struggling to find a good target with all the thrashing. As for himself, he just switched back to the gaps in the heavy scales near the head, which remained fairly still as its focus remained on Ollivan.

The rolling finally ceased, Lord Zor leading the charge back at the wyrm's exposed flank, and for a precious half minute or so things stabilized.

"Arrows!" Felicia called from a safe distance away, tossing first one and then a second quiver at Dare. He caught them and slung them over a shoulder, tugging free the ties that bound the arrows together and to the quiver to keep them from falling out, then immediately got back to loosing arrows.

A few seconds later the Magma Tunneler threw its head back with a roar that made everyone on the battlefield stumble, and with a mighty convulsion began spewing magma directly upwards like an erupting volcano.

"Molten Rain!" the Paladin roared. "Eyes to the sky, even if it means slowing damage!"

For many it meant stopping entirely, even among the vital healers, as they stared anxiously up at the sky to track the falling gobbets of lava. Dare took one look up, determined the first wave wouldn't come anywhere near him, and smoothly kept doing damage.

The rain landed and more screams sounded, and at that point things went to shit.

Dare wasn't sure if Ollivan deliberately backed away to avoid falling lava, or if he'd panicked, or even if he assumed that with the Magma Tunneler's head in the sky he didn't need to tank for a minute. Either way he ran forward to join the melee damage dealers along the body, maybe assuming that since he was still on the far side that would be enough. The other two tanks followed.

At which point the wyrm abruptly abandoned its volcano impression. Its head swooped down with shocking swiftness, maw gaping wide, and slammed down over a swordswoman near Lord Zor, devouring her whole.

"Defenders!" Zor shouted, voice shaking with shock and grief. But rather than wait he used a taunt on the monster himself, taking its brutal attacks on his golden shield as the melee scattered to safety. He began sidestepping, trying to turn the Magma Tunneler away from the ranged and healers.

Before he could manage it the monster belched out a gob of Magma Spit that caught three of the fleeing melee together.

There was a reason Dare had warned them to avoid it at all costs; the more lightly armored men screamed as the molten rock pinned them to the ground, two dying instantly while one was barely saved with barriers and frantic healing. Although his gear was utterly destroyed and as he was dragged away to safety, still making a noise of torment to induce nightmares, his skin bore the sheen of horrific burns since healed, but that would never be restored.

Dare thought of the skin regeneration potion he kept on him for emergencies, one of the three remaining from the dungeon; if the man had no potion of his own and the healers couldn't help him, he intended to give it to the poor bastard.

But for now his focus remained on doing damage, using his cooldowns as they came up. Although he saved Roll and Shoot for the-

"Fire Gout!" he roared as the ground beneath him heated; just his luck it had hit him both times. Lord Zor was slow to raise the warning himself, distracted keeping the Lava Tunneler's attention, but he heard others taking up the cry.

Dare saw another glowing spot forming beneath a dwarf woman fifteen feet away, oblivious to the danger. With a curse he used Pounce to reach her, then grabbed her short, stocky body and held her tight as he used Roll and Shoot to get away.

It didn't quite work as intended with two people, but he managed to get them just far enough out of range that when the flames roared up into the sky it only singed their hair, not roasted them alive.

He hauled them both back to their feet and began sidestepping to put some distance between them in case of further attacks from the Magma Tunneler, back to drawing and loosing arrows as he went. Around him he heard more screams, but he kept his focus on his role.

They were getting close, and although things had gone badly they were starting to stabilize.

Lord Zor had met up with Ollivan and the main tank had regained aggro. That gave the Paladin enough time to spare to warn the melee damage dealers to back away *before* the wyrm once again lifted its body into the air and began rolling over them.

The ranged damage dealers were also getting their act together, grimly focused on doing everything they could to bring the monster down before it could claim any more lives. Dare watched as its health dropped below 10%, then to 9%, down, down to 5%.

The Magma Tunneler gave its deafening roar and started to rise into the air again for another Magma Rain, but just as it convulsed to produce the huge gobbet of magma its health ticked below 1%.

It thrashed a final time, knocking several people back but not overly harming then, and with a final trumpeting cry slumped lifeless.

Text appeared in front of Dare: "Congratulations, you have defeated raid rated world monster Magma Tunneler! 30,000 experience awarded."

"Completed 1/5 towards achievement Hero of Bastion: Slay 5 raid rated monsters."

"Objective completed for quest "Terror in Terana". Waiting for raid leader to turn in quest."

"Trophies gained: Granite Scales x12, Wyrm Head x1. Loot body to acquire."

Dare slumped to one knee, letting himself feel the exhaustion of the fight. Objectively it hadn't been anywhere near as strenuous as the practices they'd done over the last couple nights, but a real battle brought its own sort of weariness.

He didn't feel the same exultation as with the chimera he'd killed with Zuri and Pella, or even the grim satisfaction from the wyvern fight. With so many dead when it could've been avoided he mostly felt numb, glad it was over.

"Gather to the raid leader, lads!" Gorfram roared, stumping over to the woman Dare had saved. "You in one piece, Ulma?"

"Aye," she said, although she sounded shaken. She gave Dare a shaky smile, lovely broad features shining even more beautiful in that moment. "The Hunter used two fucking attack abilities to somehow get us clear, the madman."

Dare grinned back, relieved she seemed okay. "I couldn't let that pretty face get singed."

Both dwarves looked at him oddly, then Gorfram clapped the young woman on the shoulder and started her towards the fallen wyrm. "Come on, then!"

Ireni met Dare as they converged on the monster with the rest of the raid group and most of the camp followers, slipping her small hand in his. "Are you okay?" he asked her. "I wish I could've been close enough to keep an eye on you."

She gave him a shaky smile, looking drawn and weary; no surprise, considering what a chaotic time the support must've had in that fight. "Luckily I was far enough back to avoid any of the ranged attacks." Her expression fell as she looked over to where Lord Zor knelt beside the horrifically burned body of Lady Ennara. "I just wish I'd been alert enough to see the danger she was in."

The gathering group's mood was reserved but jubilant. Everyone grieved for the several lives lost, especially the Holy Warder's, but at the same time they'd fought against a terrible monster and emerged victorious.

Although some were simply jubilant. Like Ollivan and a few of his bodies, one of whom was the weaselly Armorer, Dorias. They were laughing and and pissing on the monster corpse while passing around a skin of mead someone had produced.

It seemed a bit insensitive, putting on that sort of display ten feet away from where two of their companions had been burned to a crisp.

Which reminded Dare, and he produced his skin regeneration potion and hurried over to where the horrifically burned man was lying on the ground, screaming around the leather-wrapped haft of a spear in his mouth while the healers struggled to aid him.

"Excuse me," he told their party leader, holding out the potion. "I earned this in a dungeon awhile back and wondered if it would help."

The woman's eyes widened. "It would restore and save him from an otherwise difficult and painful life, or ruinous expense seeking treatment," she said. "But that's a very valuable item . . . are you sure you wish to donate it?"

He pressed it into her hand. "Please."

"Malinet's blessing upon you then." She bowed slightly, then hastened to hold the burned man down, with the help of her companions taking the spear from his mouth and holding it open so she could pour the potion down his throat.

Its effects were shockingly swift, his skin becoming smooth and hale before their eyes. The thrashing man relaxed as if the agony scarred into his very flesh was easing, and with a final grateful whimper his wild eyes rolled back in his head and he slumped, unconscious.

Ireni wrapped her arms around him and kissed his neck. "And you wonder why we love you," she murmured.

The muted celebration around them stilled to respectful silence as Lord Zor strode through the group, flanked by party leaders and attendants. His face was haggard and drawn with grief, but his shoulders were straight and his bearing proud.

To Dare's surprise the man came straight for him. "It seems you were right about us facing a Magma Tunneler," the Paladin said grimly. "Tell me, is there hope for Helema, the Quickblade consumed by that creature?"

Dare checked with his Eye, but saw no signs of life. "I'm afraid not, my Lord," he said. "I'm sorry."

Lord Zor's shoulders sagged slightly. "I feared it was so. Those Devoured by Tundra Wyrms perish quickly within its gullet, and there was no reason to assume differently for this monster."

The man's features firmed into a controlled mask, shoulders straightening again, and with a nod he turned and strode to stand at the head of the group, the fallen Magma Tunneler at his back.

There he stood before the downed monster, head bowed, as the crowd fell still and solemn. "A good fight," he finally said in a loud voice, although he remained in his grieving position, "and a great victory! I only grieve it came at the cost of so many brave companions, particularly such a sparkling jewel as Lady Ennara."

After a few more seconds of solemn silence he straightened brusquely. "As previously stated, loot will go into the raiding party's coffers to be sold and divvied up in Terana." He motioned at the wyrm. "I need volunteers to cut open the monster and retrieve the body of Helema the Quickblade. She deserves a proper burial along with the other fallen, and we need her possessions to return to her family, or if she has none to give to the poor in her home city of Redoubt."

Gorfram and a couple of the dwarves stepped forward, producing woodsman's axes, and joined half a dozen of the bigger melee fighters and the two off tanks in struggling to retrieve the fallen woman's body. Although Dare noted that Ollivan made no move to help.

As the team worked Zor raised his voice for them to hear, along with everyone else. "We will have a funeral for the fallen, but let's take care of the last business of the raid first. Starting with post-raid statistics!" People perked up and began to crowd closer. "I'm accessing the raiding party data now. Those who top the boards on the various stats will receive a bonus of 200 gold."

The Paladin looked at nothing, obviously reading his command screens. "First off, highest healing . . . Berant of Esterwall." A healer stepped forward and inclined his head, and Zor gave him an approving nod as the group applauded and cheered; he was a popular man at the moment, considering the lives he'd surely saved.

"Highest damage mitigated through support spells goes to . . . High Priestess Ireni of Kor." There were a few surprised murmurs at that before the cheers and applause began, considering her low level. Dare patted her shoulder in congratulations as she stepped forward, blushing and looking pleased.

"Highest damage goes to . . ." The Paladin raised an eyebrow in clear surprise and glanced at Dare. "Our other newbie, Dare, Master of Nirim Manor."

Surprised, Dare stepped forward and nodded awkwardly to the group. Although to his chagrin there was little applause, the other damage dealers either surprised or furious; he supposed that made sense, considering healing and support were lifesaving, while damage was pure competition.

"Is this a fucking joke?" Ollivan growled with an incredulous laugh. "How did that lowby shithead get first?"

Lord Zor turned to his friend, expression sternly disapproving. "I beg your pardon?"

For once the knight displayed some tact, quickly bowing his head. "No, old friend, I beg yours. I meant to question the ##### #######, not you. Surely there must be some mistake."

"The ###### doesn't make mistakes," the Paladin said firmly. "Let us not poison the great accomplishment of our companion by such a display." He turned back to Dare. "Congratulations, Hunter. Well earned and well deserved."

There were a few grudging nods and some clapping, mostly among the Irregulars. Although Felicia put her fingers to her lips and whistled piercingly, grinning at him.

Ollivan, however, glared murder at Dare, as did Dorias and the knight's other cronies. It was obvious who they blamed for the Warrior getting called out for making an ass of himself.

Zor glanced into the air again. "Last of all, a bonus of 50 gold for those in the line of fire who took no damage." He grimaced. "A relative few, all things considered." He quickly listed off several names, including Dare's.

The raid leader's eyes focused back on the group as he dismissed the command screens. "As stated at the beginning, tanks will receive equal bonuses for the risk they take, regardless of damage taken. Their role sometimes requires them to act as backup or to tank adds. Again, everyone, well done."

"What about *most* damage taken by damage and support classes?" one of the dwarves yelled. "Who're we jeering at this time?"

An uncomfortable silence settled. Obviously that would be one of the dead, and just as obviously it would be in poor taste to point out their failure and death. Or even if he meant among the living, it was still tasteless given the losses they'd suffered.

Zor looked at the dwarf with narrowed eyes for a moment, then turned towards the wyrm's corpse to help with the work of cutting it open, not deigning to respond.

"Nice going, dipshit," the female dwarf, Ulma, muttered, elbowing her companion hard. "Nobody pays attention to that stat since someone almost always dies on these raids."

"That doesn't stop us from using it in our fights," the mercenary protested sullenly. "I meant among the *living*, of course."

"It's different outside the Irregulars," she snapped. "They live softer lives than we do." Shaking her head, she stalked away.

Ireni gave Dare's hand a last squeeze and moved away to help with the wounded, while he joined those trying to get at Helema's body, using his spear to pry at scales and try to create openings.

Finally they managed to drag the poor Quickblade free of the monster's gullet, wrapped in a cloak. She was solemnly brought to join the six other people who'd perished, and the same people who'd worked so hard to extract her immediately got to work digging graves near the Magma Tunneler's body.

Before Dare could join them Lord Zor intercepted him. "Well done again," he said, clapping him on the shoulder. He motioned curtly and one of his attendants hurried forward, producing a coin pouch. "Your portion of our earnings will have to wait until we sell loot and claim the reward for slaying the monster, of course. But it's tradition to give out bonuses immediately."

The attendant offered the pouch to the Paladin, who took it and in turn held it out to Dare. "250 gold. Congratulations."

"Thank you." Dare reached out to take the money.

The Paladin kept his grip on the purse, not relinquishing it as he met his gaze. "It strikes me as odd that you're one of the lowest levels in the raid, invited at the last minute because we're under strength, with fine but not great quality gear. And yet you topped damage . . . care to enlighten me?"

That was a good question, actually, and one that was worth some thought.

Dare knew why he'd personally done so well, of course. Fleetfoot had certainly helped, but even beyond that there were many other factors.

First off, even though this was technically his first raid in real life, he'd been part of, and led, *many* raids during his gaming career. He'd filled raiding parties, organized the various roles to best effect, led the fights, and taken care of the before and after raid business like buffs, materials, loot, and a fair loot system that spanned weekly or biweekly raids.

As a DPS he knew how to maximize his time doing damage on the boss and focus solely on his job, trusting in the other members of the raid to do theirs. He knew how to optimize a combat rotation that used all his highest damage abilities and cooldowns, and squeezed out every split second to make sure that no potential damage was left on the table.

He knew how to avoid boss AoE or special attacks, shed aggro, time things like tank rotation and boss phases, and countless other details that went into a successful raid. Individually he could pull his weight, and if the raid listened to him and did their jobs properly he could lead them to a victory.

Much of that seemed to be sadly lacking in Zor's raid. Granted, the man knew his business and was competent, but he'd put too much trust in inexperienced or untalented party leaders, as well as not taking time to properly prepare the individuals in the raid who were even more inexperienced and untalented.

Which was why Dare was able to out-damage people up to 5 levels above his, most of whom had better gear.

Honestly, he was looking forward to seeing what he could do when he finally decided he was high enough level to justify spending the gold to fully kit himself out, in the best items with the best enchantments available, and was in a raid he was the proper level for.

If he topped the charts now, he could probably crush them at that point, like in games on Earth where he'd doubled or even tripled the next highest person's damage.

Of course, that was when he grouped with scrubs, usually in pickup groups to beat easy dungeons where there were no stakes and people were phoning it in. And it was possible that at higher levels on this world people would be more experienced and professional and the talent gap wouldn't be so wide.

Although it was good to know that all his raid experience wasn't going to waste.

Hell, eventually he might even look into becoming a raid leader. In his previous life he'd occasionally sworn he'd never lead another raid, because it was like herding cats hopped up on catnip and was incredibly time consuming and stressful, not to mention usually being a thankless job . . .

But on Collisa it might be worth his while. He could get actual respect and renown, save lives by doing things properly, and as the cherry on top get extra shares for the extra responsibility he was taking on.

Zor cleared his throat, and Dare realized he'd been ruminating on his answer too long. He shrugged. "There's no big mystery. It mainly comes down to time spent doing damage to the enemy and the most efficient rotation of abilities to get the highest possible damage."

He motioned to the giant monster they'd just downed. "When the wyrm was shooting up fire and spitting lava, the others did a lot of running around dodging, slow to get back to doing damage. And even when it wasn't directly threatening them, they spent more time than they should've looking around at the rest of the battle. On the other hand, I was able to focus on shooting arrows and doing damage for nearly the entire fight. I may do less damage per second than anyone else, but I put the damage I could do to best effect."

Although with Fleetfoot, he wondered if he actually *did* do less DPS than the others.

"Hmm." Zor looked him over. "According to witnesses among the camp followers you were standing in the middle of one of those fire spouts on both occasions, and yet you managed to escape without harm. You even managed to save *another* member of the raid the second time. You would've had to respond almost instantly."

"I was blessed with excellent reflexes." Dare tugged on the purse they both still gripped. "Is there a problem with me doing well?"

"No," the Paladin said slowly. He released the money and Dare quickly tucked it away, although the man's hooded eyes continued to inspect him. "Well done again, Dare, Master of Nirim Manor. I hope we may hunt monsters again soon."

"As do I," Dare said as he bowed. "If I'm worthy of it, I'd like to serve as a party leader under you next time I have the honor of joining you."

Zor chuckled as if at a child's absurd dream. "If you prove worthy, certainly. Commoners have been given that honor before, such as Gorfram of the Irregulars. Work on the levels and the gear, get some more experience in raids, and befriend more raiders. And practice communication and leadership as well as caution and preparedness for the fight, but most of all boldness when the time calls for it, if you hope to hold the lives of others in your hands."

With a last wave the man strode off, his hangers-on hurrying after him.

Dare could admit that Zor wasn't wrong in his advice: leading in real life would be a lot different from leading in a game. Most of all in the stakes, and the way people would act in any given situation.

He knew as much as anyone about those sorts of factors when it came to games, and at least had a decent idea of how people worked and what they might do. But Zor was right, he needed more raid experience in real life. And more knowledge of raid rated monsters, so he'd know how best to lead the fight against them.

Assuming he really did feel up to being responsible for people's lives; even if he knew he was the best person for the job, that wouldn't help with the guilt if people died under his command. Especially if he made a mistake that got them killed.

Then again, the women he loved more than the world remained safe under his leadership when they leveled up. Aside from his fuckup with the wyvern, that was.

Then again again, they weren't fighting giant monsters that took upwards of 50 people to kill and could drop weaker raiders with one or two hits or a second's inattention while standing in the fire.

Yeah, better to save all that stress for when he was higher level or more experienced. For now he'd keep an eye out for any other raids starting up and consider joining them. After all, if they all gave bonuses for topping the charts and other good performance then he could make some good coin.

Especially with Ireni along, topping the charts right along with him.

Dare turned away to help with digging the graves and bumped into someone looming over him. A difficult thing to do, considering he stood a few inches over six feet on a world where malnutrition was still prevalent.

It was Ollivan, of course, along with his ratty little buddy Dorias and a couple melee damage dealers. "I don't know how you cheated to top the chart, Hunter," the Warrior snarled. "But you didn't win that."

Dare bit back a weary sigh. "What do you care, Sir Ollivan? You got your bonus as a defender."

"But my friend was cheated by your treachery," the knight snarled. He held out a gauntleted fist. "Hand it over."

Wow, seriously? Dare waved around them. "Are you going to rob me in the middle of the entire raid? In front of Lord Zor?"

Ollivan glared murder, but after a quick look around reluctantly lowered his hand. "You'd better watch your fucking back," he growled as he stomped away. Dorias gave him a rude gesture, and one of the knight's other companions actually tried to do a fakeout to make him flinch.

Dare watched them leave, equal parts pissed off and worried about further trouble; the guy really seemed determined to start something.

"He's going to be a problem," Ireni said behind him.

In his tense state he jumped slightly, then tried to play it casual as he turned. "I'm just glad the raid's over and we'll be heading home soon."

She nodded, expression tight. "Still, let's stay close to the Irregulars tonight." She shivered. "It's not just his one-sided fight with you, either. The way he's been looking at me from the start, him and his squire Dorias . . . let's just say I've seen that sort of look far too often, and it's not the sort you want to come from someone you're at the mercy of."

Dare grit his teeth. "If he touches you I'll kill him." It wasn't an idle threat.

"You'd be executed soon after." The beautiful Priestess looked genuinely worried. "We need to avoid a fight with nobility, Dare, it won't end well for us. Let's just stick close to our friends and avoid trouble until we get back to Terana."

He would've suggested leaving entirely, but they needed to be part of the raid for the quest completion and to get their share of the loot. So he nodded reluctantly, took her hand and kissed it, then made his way over to the graves being dug and grabbed a shovel.

Chapter Seven
Celebration

Say one thing about adventurers, or maybe Collisans in general: they might genuinely grieve their dead, but that didn't stop them from celebrating a victory afterwards.

Casks of ale and mead were broached from the supply wagons, courtesy of Lord Zor. Many produced musical instruments, the skill for which were all universal abilities, able to be learned by all. Although of course Bards and Minstrels and other entertainer classes got bonuses.

Which was clear, since there were some of those playing as well.

The camp was filled with music and laughter, the few women among the raid as well as most of the female camp followers drawn into dancing. Or into laps, laughing and returning the attention of the conquering heroes in kind.

More than a few couples went off hand in hand seeking tents, or even the dark spaces between tents, and whenever there was a lapse in music Dare could hear the grunts and moans of their lovemaking.

It was making him seriously horny, and he found himself wishing Leilanna had been able to come along so he could celebrate with her. It didn't help when the Outsider teasingly slipped into his lap, more than a little tipsy and giggling with full enjoyment of the celebration around them, and whispered breathy invitations in his ear between kissing his neck and running her hands over his chest.

He wasn't made of stone, and in spite of his reservations about the situation of two prospective lovers sharing the same body, he was very tempted to let the goddess lead him back to their tent like she suggested.

Dare was saved when Ulma, the dwarf woman he'd saved, dropped a chair next to his in front of the fire they shared with

Felicia and Irawn.

It was the same collapsible chair he was using, his own design which he'd introduced to the Irregulars; apparently its use was spreading among the mercenaries. "Well met, Hunter," she said in her gruff, husky voice as she held her hands out to the fire.

"Oooh, you're in luck," the Outsider whispered in his ear with a giggle. "This should be fun." Before he could ask what she meant she slipped off his lap and returned to her own collapsible chair, which of course he'd made for her as a new companion.

The dwarf woman was waiting for an answer, and he nodded politely as he gave her a closer look. "Well met, Miss Ulma."

The stereotype of dwarf females as stocky, often bearded, and deep of voice wasn't very accurate for Ulma. She was well muscled, sure, but those muscles were hard to see beneath an ample chest, hips, and ass, with womanly curves all over the place.

She wasn't stocky, but she was definitely thick. And her round face was pleasant enough, with a broad smiling mouth, big dark eyes, and a nose just slightly too bold for her features. Her long dark hair was pulled into a braid over her shoulder.

She was cute in her own right, and he hadn't had an opportunity to sleep with a dwarf before which made her even more attractive. And it was a plus that she didn't have a beard and a masculine build.

Also the fact that she was around four and a half feet tall made her proportions look even cuter.

Considering the couples groping and kissing around the fires, and the noise of sex drifting through the night, Dare checked the pouch containing Zuri's Prevent Conception scrolls. Just in case.

More suspicious, Felicia tugged on the Outsider's hand. "Come on, let's go dance!" Eyes sparkling with mischief, the young catgirl looked between him and Ulma as she dragged the petite goddess to her feet and led her away, Irawn silently following.

Leaving Dare and the pretty dwarf by themselves at the fire.

Ulma produced a flask and took a pull of it. "Got to say, Hunter, it was damn sexy watching you at work against that monster." She grinned, showing even white teeth. "Even before you literally pulled my oblivious ass out of a fire."

"Thanks." Dare said, grinning. "You're looking pretty sexy yourself."

She snorted and took another pull of her flask before offering it to him. "I'm a bit curious how you're that quick, though. I watched you and a higher level Archer standing in the formation beside each other loosing arrows, and I'll swear you got out at least four for every three of his."

"Oh yeah?" he asked casually, taking a sip; it was some sort of powerful spirits he didn't recognize, although they definitely packed a punch. He coughed a little before handing the flask back. "Guess he's just slow."

Ulma snorted as she took a deep pull, as if poking fun at his own reaction to the liquor, then offered the flask again. "Fine, be mysterious. It's not like we just bonded by slaying a giant wyrm or anything."

Dare shrugged, taking a deeper sip of the fiery drink. "It's not a secret that's going to help you shoot any faster, so there'd be no upside to sharing it for you, and a possible downside for me."

"Whatever." The dwarf hesitated, looking at him thoughtfully. "Not many humans would share a flask with a dwarf."

He smirked, taking another sip as if to refute her point before offering it back. "What, they're afraid of cooties?"

She scowled. "I don't know what those are but aye, maybe." She gestured at the camp. "Even among our raiding party, after defeating the foe and earning our reward, there's little friendship between our kinds. Humans see us as inferior, we see you as assholes."

"Well, from what I've seen about how humans treat other races, one of us is right," Dare joked.

Ulma shrugged. "To be honest, we're not much better." Her scowl returned with surprising fierceness as she took a deep gulp. "But it shouldn't be like that between humans and dwarves . . . we live in your cities, work alongside you, fight alongside you. Our peoples have lived in cooperation for centuries with almost no squabbling. So why the disdain?"

"I don't know," Dare admitted. "But people are all different. If most humans are jerks, find the ones who aren't."

"Like you?" she said in disbelief. Then, eying him defiantly, she spat in her flask and offered it to him.

He took it without a word and drank; alcohol sterilized, and more importantly if he could charm her like he wanted then they were going to be swapping a lot more than spit eventually.

"I make no boasts about myself," he said as she stared at him with open surprise, "I have my faults. But at home I have four women waiting for me, and they're all of other races."

Ulma eyed him thoughtfully. "That's more openminded than most, I'll allow."

"And I've bedded even more women of other races when the opportunity arose," Dare continued. "I'll befriend anyone who proves agreeable and trustworthy . . . I try to look at the behavior of people, not their race or class or anything else about them."

The dwarf retrieved her flask, although he was amused to note that she seemed reluctant to drink from it after spitting in it. She finally took a sip. "What races are your consorts?" she asked quietly.

"A goblin, canid, dusk elf, and hobgoblin. And I care for them all deeply."

Her round face twisted in surprise and derision. "A goblin as a consort?" she demanded.

Dare met her gaze firmly. "My oldest companion, the mother of my child, and someone I love with all my heart," he replied. "Just in case you were thinking of insulting her."

Ulma took another sip, longer this time, as she stared at him thoughtfully. "And me?" she asked as she handed her flask over. "Would you bed me?"

He grinned and made a show of looking her up and down as he took another gulp from the flask; it was getting close to empty and his head was starting to spin. "You think I've been flirting with you this whole time to get you to share this disgusting moonshine?"

She threw back her head and laughed, slapping her thigh. Which he couldn't help but notice jiggled nicely. "So you're not openminded, you're just a horny bastard."

"Hey, that's not exactly fair. I can be both."

The dwarf woman sobered and took her own turn looking him over closely. "You know, humans always strike me as frail pretty boys," she mused. "Tall skinny beanpoles, the lot of them. But there's something about you that's looking mighty good right about now."

"Could be my nine inch cock," he said with a grin. Which probably was a poor choice; the booze was talking at this point.

She roared laughter again. "All right, human, you're on!" she said, spitting on her hand and offering it to him. "You show me nine inches, and I'll let you put every single one of them in me."

"You sure?" Dare asked with a wide smile as he spit on his hand and held it out, just barely short of hers. "Because it means you're going to have the best sex of your life tonight, and you didn't even give me a demand if I lost."

Ulma thought about it for a moment, then grinned broadly. "Okay then. If you're shorter than 9 inches, you lick my hairy cunt and bush clean of all the sweat of today's battle."

It was his turn to laugh. "So I win either way?"

Her grin became predatory. "We'll see." She hopped to her feet. "Come on, Gorfram has a measuring tape."

Dare spotted the Outsider, Felicia, and Irawn returning and hesitated. Not so much at the worry about what the petite goddess would think, since she and Ireni had not only encouraged him to bed other women but all but insisted he do so.

But he'd almost forgotten that Ollivan had threatened him earlier.

The Outsider seemed to read his mind. "Don't worry," she said with a broad smile, looping an arm around the young catgirl's shoulder. "I'll stay close to Felicia, Irawn, and the rest of the Irregulars until you get back. Have fun."

Horny and with his head spinning, that was enough for him. "Okay, let's go," he said, taking Ulma's hand. She started with surprise, then smiled almost shyly and gripped him back with surprising strength.

When they made their request to Gorfram he scratched his bearded chin in puzzlement. "What do you need it for?" he asked a bit suspiciously.

"A bet," the dwarf maiden said, expression innocent.

With a shrug the old dwarf handed over a rolled tape marked with inches and feet. "Just bring it back before I need it."

Ulma eagerly led Dare to her tent, which was a bit cramped for two as they knelt facing each other on her unrolled blankets. She lit a candle, which flickered as she leaned forward expectantly. "All right then, let's see it."

He unlaced his pants and skinned them and his undershorts down to his knees, revealing his flaccid cock. She frowned at it. "I've seen bigger."

"Soft?" he said with a grin; limp he was still almost as long as he'd been back on Earth.

She hesitated. "So you're a shower not a grower."

Dare laughed. "We'll see." He gave her an innocent look. "You know, we can't exactly measure it if it's not hard."

"Oh, by Kurza's anvil," Ulma growled, although a smile played across her full lips. She grabbed him in her soft yet strong hand and began impatiently stroking him. She was a bit rougher than he would've liked, but the sensation was still enough to make his cock stir and stiffen in her grip.

"By Kurza's anvil," she said again when he was fully erect, staring at his manhood with wide eyes. She absently reached out with her other hand and double fisted him, expression one of amazed disbelief. "I'm going to lose this bet, aren't I?"

Nirim

"Only one way to find out." He motioned to the measuring tape.

The dwarf maiden unrolled it enough to measure his length, then sat staring at the result for several long seconds, grinning in delight. "Well?" Dare finally demanded.

She gave a long, deep belly laugh. "8 inches, 9/10s inch."

"Son if a bitch!" he said, snatching the tape from her. He quickly closed his eyes and imagined Zuri, Pella, and Leilanna lying naked side by side, legs spread wide and playing with each other's glistening petals as they waited for him to alternate between them.

His cock throbbed to maximum stiffness, and he placed the tape exactly at the base and held the end at the tip. He lifted it to his eyes, squinting in the candlelight: 8 inches, 9/10s.

His expression must've confirmed it, because the dwarf was already laughing her ass off. "All right, human," she finally gasped, motioning. "Guess we can put that away since you won't be needing it."

That took a while, since he had to wait for his erection to go down. Finally Ulma lost patience. "Forget it," she growled, skinning out of her own pants. "You lost the bet, so get that tongue to work already."

Dare stared at her crotch in something akin to awe; he'd been wrong about dwarf women not having a beard, they just kept it in their pants.

Ulma's brown pubic hair covered her entire lower abdomen, thick and curly, and continued on down her thighs for several inches below her pussy. Which couldn't be seen because of a thick curtain of more hair that hung down for a few inches below it.

He knew that no crotch smelled great after a day of hard work, especially in desperate battle, but hers had a particularly overpowering musk. Not entirely unpleasant; there was a hint of something enticing mingled in with the sweat and BO.

Then he noticed that the fur hanging down from her pussy was damp; not with sweat but with arousal.

"Well, human?" the dwarf teased, shimmying her hips in his

face. "What do you have to say now?"

Dare did his best to grin up at her, eyes on her damp pubic hair. "I say that I told you I'd win either way, and I was going to give you the best sex of your life." He dove into her bush, tongue extended.

"Gurran son of Kaszgoth!" she gasped; it was an odd curse, but her surprise was evident. "You really are horny."

He spat to one side and dove back in. All he had to say was that pubic hair might be lauded by some as holding a woman's heavenly fragrance, but when you were licking it and found yourself pulling a loose four-inch strand from your mouth, it might be excessive.

When you found yourself spitting out dozens of such strands as you basically tongue-washed a full beard transplanted to her crotch, you really found yourself longing to get to the good part.

He finally did, though, reaching the hairs around her pussy that were wet with her arousal. The damp patch had spread since he'd started, and now included the mats on her thighs; she was enjoying this.

The dwarf maiden tasted earthy and a bit smoky, like a barbecue in a smithy smothered with feminine pheromones. A surprisingly arousing taste, making his cock twitch as he kept lapping at her bush.

For a moment Dare thought his questing tongue wouldn't even be able to reach her lips through the jungle. But then he felt flesh beneath hair, parting beneath his probing, and his tongue slipped into a warm, soft, sweet-tasting heaven.

She was definitely a woman beneath all that hair, and his cock throbbed as he quested, searching for her clit.

When he found it she clamped her strong hands to his head and pulled him into her, hips bucking. "Kaszgoth born of the Mountain!" she roared, flooding his face with her juices.

Dare wondered how many dwarves or deities or whatever she was going to reference before he was done.

Laughing, he pulled her down onto her back on the blankets and dove in again. Her thick, powerful thighs clamped around his head, and she squirmed as he mercilessly tongued her bud until she squirted all over his face in another powerful climax.

Ulma finally released his head from the crushing embrace of her thighs, panting as she pushed him away. "Ganor's Forge," she said breathlessly.

Dare grinned at her. "That's that, then. I cleaned you navel to knee, and we both had a good time."

"That is is *not* that, human," she growled. Before he had time to be confused she bodily hauled him upwards on top of her, reaching for his cock and tugging it towards her pussy. "8 and 9/10s is close enough," she said into his baffled expression, spreading her legs wider. "And I said I'd let you put every inch of it in me."

Dare fumbled in his pouch for one of Zuri's scrolls and hastily read it, activating the spell. "Prevent Conception," he said to her curious look.

Ulma laughed. "Definitely not complaining, although I would've just had you pull out."

I only wish that worked for me.

Dare plunged eagerly into her soaked mat of hair, pushing between her flushed folds and into her warm, soft interior. She moaned eagerly as he stretched her, and he paused to give her a chance to adjust to his girth.

"No need to coddle me like your frailer lovers," she said, twitching her hips up to take him deeper inside her. "Dwarvish pussy is made to be pounded like pig iron on an anvil."

In that case . . .

Dare thrust forward until he bottomed out in one smooth motion, surprised at how deep he could go. He still had a few inches free, but for her size she could take him like a champion.

The dwarf maiden squealed as he fully penetrated her, then again when he pulled back and pushed in again. "Aye, just like that!" she panted, powerful hands gripping his back and pulling him harder into her with every thrust, short fingernails scraping his skin.

He pounded her soft wet pussy like she'd told him to, impressed as she urged him to go even harder. Until finally her walls gripped him with crushing force as she climaxed, the powerful grip of her pussy practically yanking his own orgasm from him.

With a groan Dare emptied inside her in pulsing throbs of pure pleasure, kissing her full lips as they climaxed together. She wrapped her short legs around him and held him tight, plunging her thick tongue into his mouth and wrestling his into submission.

When Ulma finally came down from her orgasm and her suddenly limp legs released him, Dare rolled off her and lay panting at her side, watching with satisfaction as their combined juices poured from her soft, hairy pussy to puddle on her blankets.

He'd thought she'd be out of commission for a short while after her orgasm, but almost immediately she purposefully reached over and grabbed his wilting shaft; he startled in surprise as her fingers trailed down it.

She grunted as she reached the base. "Dry. Thought so. You bottomed out with a few inches left outside."

Dare chuckled. "Surprised?"

Ulma growled. "Every. Inch. In. Me. That's what I said."

"How?" he asked. He looked at her hairy asshole, doubting he could fit all of it in there either.

"Every. Inch!" she repeated, and gripping him with one hand she bent her head over his tip, gently kissed it, then parted her lips to let him inside her mouth.

As it turned out, dwarves were good at deep throating. Or at least Ulma was.

She was the first woman he'd met on this world besides Zuri and Rosie (and slime girls and Ireni's mannequin he supposed) who didn't struggle to take his thick shaft into her throat. She didn't gag, either.

Although she *did* swallow repeatedly, tight esophagus rippling along his shaft. She began to hum, some surprisingly deep dwarvish chant by the sound of it, and the vibrations rumbled right down his length and into his body until his bones shivered.

Dare groaned at the pleasure and reached over to begin toying with the dwarf maiden's large breasts, freeing them from her shirt and teasing the nipples. She hummed deeper, nose buried in his pubic hair, then began bobbing up and down his length.

He grabbed her head, pulling her harder onto his cock, then finally surged up to his knees, bringing her along with him. She made an eager noise, guessing his intent, and her dark eyes looked up at him in approval as he held her head firmly and began to thrust his hips, fucking her tight throat.

She kept humming and reached up to fondle his balls, then squeezed gently but firmly.

That did it for him, and he yanked her nose into his pubic hair and poured everything he had down her throat while she swallowed eagerly.

Ulma pulled off his wilting shaft with a gasp, smirking in triumph. "Every. Inch," she repeated, crossing her arms in satisfaction.

He chuckled and pulled him into his arms, lying back on her blankets to cuddle. "Like a champ," he agreed.

Dare held her for a few minutes until she began to snore boisterously, then kissed her forehead, covered her with her blankets, and climbed out of her tent.

Only to find the Irregulars' camp empty and quiet around him, shattering the haze of drink and post-coital bliss he'd been enjoying.

* * * * *

Struck by sudden worry, Dare broke into a trot towards his and Ireni's tent.

Elsewhere in the raiding party's camp he heard voices and shouts, especially coming from the far side where the melee damage set up their tents. From the ruckus it seemed like there was some commotion over there.

But he didn't care, his full focus was on getting back to his

143

companion.

His fear exploded into full blown panic when he saw the fire where he'd left Ireni and the others and only Felicia was there, looking petulant.

"Where's Ireni?" he demanded as he entered the firelight. "Where's Irawn and everyone else?"

The young teenager folded her arms sullenly. "There's a fisticuff tournament going on in the melee section of camp and everyone went. I wanted to go, but Irawn said it would be too boisterous for me and told me I had to stay here."

From one of the nearby tents Dare heard a woman's muffled squeal; looked as if a couple looking for some fun had stayed behind instead of going to the fights. Although he dismissed the noise, focus on the young catgirl.

"Where's Ireni?" he repeated urgently.

"Relax, she's in the tent sleeping."

He started to breathe easier, then heard the woman's muffled voice again. Except it sounded more like a scream this time. And it was coming from his tent.

Dare crossed the distance to the entrance in what felt like an instant, barely aware he'd activated Cheetah's Dash, unslung his bow, and put an arrow to the string using Rapid Shot. All in a smooth series of movements, as if he wasn't breaking apart in panic.

He threw open the entry flaps and skidded to a halt, heart clenching in sick horror.

The silk back wall of the tent had been sliced from top to bottom and Ireni was draped half out of the opening, struggling frantically and screaming through a gag. In the light of the fire at his back he saw the entire side of her face darkening in a horrific bruise.

Through the opening he could see one man rolling on the ground, clawing at his eyes and screaming at the Priestess's Blinding Light spell, while an even larger man, heavily armored and roaring like a beast, battered at the protective barrier Ireni had hastily raised over herself.

Ollivan.

The petite redhead looked tiny and frail beneath her attacker, especially since she was dressed in her underwear for bed, and her eyes were terrified as she fumbled to cast another defensive spell.

Dare's vision went red, and it was all he could do to keep a sliver of control over his berserk rage at the sight of his companion under attack. He drew his first arrow and loosed, hitting a joint in the Warrior's armor and sinking the shaft deep into his shoulder.

Ollivan snarled in surprised pain and abandoned his attack on Ireni, straightening to face Dare.

"Hunter!" he snarled, fumbling for a knife at his belt with his remaining good arm as he rushed him in a Charge ability.

He brought the entire tent with him, threatening to bury Dare beneath the cloth, and in desperation Dare Pounced back to where Felicia stood in horrified shock by the fire.

The ability Tackled the young catgirl, but she barely had time to stiffen in surprise before he hauled her back to her feet and pushed her towards the center of camp. "Get Lord Zor!" he shouted as he spun, lifting his bow and drawing another arrow.

He managed to plant two more arrows in Ollivan's less armored lower legs as the man rushed him, then used Roll and Shoot to get out of the way just before the Warrior caught him in a tackle, putting another arrow in the man's back. Four arrows would've killed most even level monsters, but the heavily armored Level 35 main tank soaked them up like nothing.

Although he couldn't entirely shrug them off. Ollivan snarled and stumbled, wounded and slowed by the arrows just above his knees. Dare took the opportunity to point an arrow at Ollivan's eye, a wound that would likely permanently blind the man and put a critical bleed effect on him in spite of his high health.

"Don't kill him!" Ireni screamed, partially muffled by her gag. For a moment Dare thought she was talking to Ollivan, but then his loosed arrow bounced off one of her protective barriers.

Surrounding her attacker.

Dare gave her a look of shocked betrayal, but her bruised face was twisted in desperate urgency. "If you kill him we're both lost!" she shouted.

Ollivan didn't share the same qualms, and Dare's distraction nearly cost him his life as the Warrior threw his dagger in some sort of vicious ability. Only to be stopped by another of Ireni's barrier spells as it shimmered in front of Dare, the weapon bouncing aside.

Undeterred, the knight raised his fists and charged the remaining distance.

Don't kill him. Fine. But Dare was sure as hell going to beat him half to death for what he'd done to Ireni.

He slung his bow and retrieved his spear, diving aside as Ollivan roared past and jamming the weapon into the back of his enemy's leg in a Hamstring. As the big man stumbled Dare surged back to his feet and Hamstrung his other leg, further slowing him.

Then, dodging the slow, telegraphed punches the drunken Warrior threw his way, he began battering Ollivan's head with the butt of his spear, savagely ringing the big man's bell through his helmet over and over until Ollivan finally slumped to the ground, unconscious or dead.

Hopefully the former, although even with Ireni's warning it was hard to care if it was the latter.

Dare turned on the other assailant, who was groggily coming to his feet as he recovered from Ireni's Blinding Light spell. Dorias, of course, that piece of shit.

The man was Level 25 and an Armorer class with an Archer subclass, not much of a threat to him, and Dare went after him with the butt of his spear, chasing Dorias as he tried to run until the weasel was also limp on the ground.

Ireni had finished removing her gag and ducked back into the tent to retrieve her robes, and was pulling them on as Dare reached her and pulled her into a crushing hug. "Are you okay?" he asked anxiously.

"Alive," she mumbled thickly.

He started to reach for the ugly bruise on her cheek that had obviously come from Ollivan's gauntleted fist, then hesitated just short of touching it; the blow might've shattered her cheekbone or jaw, especially considering her trouble speaking. "It's okay, the fight's over. You have time to heal that now."

She shook her head firmly. "Evidence."

From her calm actions and tone, not to mention her posture, Dare had a feeling the Outsider had taken over. Although if she wasn't freaking out that made one of them.

"I should've been here," he mourned, frantically running his hands over her arms and legs checking for injuries. "I thought he might go after me, but I never imagined he'd be the sort of scum who'd lay hands on Ireni . . ."

In response the Outsider stumbled away and was noisily sick. Then she straightened with a frustrated noise. "Sorry, that was an uncontrollable response. This was severely traumatic for her."

No shit. Heart breaking for the gentle Priestess, he started to gather the Outsider into his arms again.

"Later, my lover," she said with a grimace. "The trouble's just starting, I'm afraid." She motioned to where a dozen men were rushing their way, Lord Zor at their head.

Fantastic, the man had finally showed up after the fight was already over. Just in time to assume the worst.

"Dare," the Outsider said with surprising gentleness, "Ireni's going to take over. She'll be more genuine in this confrontation than I could be." She rested a hand on his arm. "But you need to look after her. She's . . . not in a good place."

Nodding grimly, Dare gathered the petite woman in his arms, and after a few seconds she suddenly shuddered violently and huddled against him, shoulders shaking in wracking sobs. "Goddess," she whimpered. "I thought I'd put this behind me. I thought I was stronger than this."

"Shh," he said, stroking her hair and holding her tight. "It's all right. It's over now."

"Gods, Ollivan!" Lord Zor shouted as he arrived at the fire, staring down at the knight in horror, then over at where Dorias lay in a heap. He turned back to those following him. "Healer, now!"

A man ran off, and the Paladin whirled back to Dare and Ireni in a fury. "You assaulted my friend and his squire?"

Dare bit down his own rage, although his voice shook with anger as he answered, loud enough for the gathering crowd of onlookers to hear. "My Lord, I defended my companion when they cut into the back of our tent while she was sleeping and tried to drag her away."

Lord Zor glanced at Ireni, taking in her bruise and haunted expression. Although his eyes remained hard. "Your word against an anointed knight's and his squire's. And it's no secret there's bad blood between you."

Was this asshole serious? "Look at her!" Dare snarled. "I found her huddled on the ground, desperately hiding behind a barrier as that animal pounded at her with gauntleted fists! Five levels higher, a foot taller, and 150 pounds heavier! And she's a Priestess for the gods' sake! She doesn't even have attack spells, only spells to heal and succor others."

The Paladin looked away, although it was his friend his gaze strayed to. "Leave this camp, both of you," he said quietly. "I'll see your share of the loot reaches you."

Ireni let out a breath, seeming relieved, but Dare wasn't letting it go. "I need your assurance he's going to be punished for this, my Lord. That it won't happen again."

Lord Zor's head whipped around. "Are you insane?" he snapped. "He's an anointed knight and my friend. You should be glad I'm letting you walk away instead of clapping you in irons for assault or even attempted murder of a nobleman . . . whatever the feud between you, I have a hard time believing he was entirely at fault."

"Dare," Ireni said urgently, tugging on his arm.

He wrapped it around her protectively but refused to back down. "You're the leader of this group, my Lord. We're under your command and have done nothing but obey orders and help the raid, and you have a duty to protect us. He's under your command as well, and you have a duty to see he faces justice for his crimes."

He pointed a shaking finger at his tent. "He cut into our tent like a thief in the night! In the middle of *your* camp! Gagged and beat a defenseless woman before trying to drag her off to do only the gods know what to her!" Ireni whimpered and he held her tighter as he continued. "That's the man you call friend. That's the man you tarnish your honor defending! Is this the sort of leader you want to be?"

"Begone!" Zor roared, taking a step forward with his fists clenched.

Dare jumped as he heard a sharp tone from the world system, then text appeared in front of him. "You have been removed from Lord Zor's raiding party." From Ireni's expression she'd been kicked out as well.

Well, that was that.

He knew he was being a fool, but he had to get in one last parting shot as he ushered Ireni away towards their tent to pack up. "I'll gladly leave, as it seems your camp offers no protection to anyone but your lackeys. What a fine reputation to have."

The Paladin's hangers-on murmured in shocked outrage, but the man himself said nothing, turning his attention to Ollivan and casting his weak healing spells to help his friend. Dare did his best not to look back at him as he and Ireni returned to their ruined tent.

She finally healed the horrible bruise and other smaller injuries from the attack, her words coming more clearly afterwards, and it was a relief to know that physically at least, she was okay.

Her mental state was another concern entirely.

They gathered their things and saddled their horses, and he insisted his shaken companion mount up in front of him. He held her protectively as he rode out of the camp, leading her little mare behind him. In spite of the late hour he felt dozens of eyes on them, but aside from staying wary for potential attacks he paid them no mind.

"I fear more trouble will come of this," Ireni said quietly, face buried in his shoulder.

"If so we'll deal with it." He kissed her head. "How are you doing?"

She shuddered so violently he felt it through her whole body. "I'd rather not talk about it. Could you please just hold me?"

Dare held her, tenderly stroking her back as they rode south across the dark plains at a gallop. His heart ached at her obvious distress, and he wished there was more he could do for her.

After almost an hour she finally stirred and lifted her head, relaxed and alert. "She's sleeping," the Outsider said. "It should do her some good."

Dare nodded and kissed her forehead. "Thanks for looking out for her."

She glared fiercely. "Of course. I'd burn that camp to ash for her if I had to, and if it was allowed."

Allowed. "You didn't warn me she was in danger . . . because you can only talk through her, now?"

"Best to assume that going forward." The Outsider glared ahead. "You should petition for knighthood, my lover. It's our best defense against Ollivan manipulating the nobility or royalty, then using the full might of the region or even the kingdom as a weapon against you. People care more about who's in the right when it's a dispute between nobles, than with a noble and a commoner. Although wealth and influence still matter, and that fucker has them in spades."

"He who has the gold makes the rules," Dare growled.

"And might makes right." She looked up at him intently. "We should visit Lady Marona."

Right. She would at least have advice, if she couldn't help outright. "How much trouble are we in with this?"

The Outsider shook her head grimly. "As much as Ollivan can manage, I'm sure. But a lot will depend on the honor and fairness of the nobility of Bastion, and Haraldar in general."

Dare barked a bitter laugh. "In other words we're fucked?"

She just sighed.

Chapter Eight

Repercussions

Dare pushed hard for Terana, all through the night and into the next day.

He left the horses for the Outsider to ride while he ran with Cheetah's Dash, only mounting when he was on the verge of collapsing from exhaustion. Even with that the sturdy beasts began faltering by afternoon, forcing them to stop and rest.

At Ireni's insistence he gave in to exhaustion and dropped into fitful sleep for an hour or so, waking a few times with a cry of fear, desperately checking to make sure Ireni was still there and all right.

After the third time he gave up. His companion had cooked a stew with dried meat and root vegetables, as well as dipping into his stock of spices and cooking ingredients. It smelled delicious, and he ate ravenously with one hand while he gripped his spear tight with the other, looking around warily for threats and as he positioned himself protectively between Ireni and anyone who might be sneaking up on them.

"You need to relax, Dare," she said gently, small face worried. "If you keep going like this you'll push yourself to exhaustion. We're away, we're both safe, and you can finally breath easier."

"I can't relax," Dare admitted, looking into her eyes. "I failed you, Ireni. You put your trust in me and I let you down." His fist clenched tight around his spoon. "But I won't fail you again . . . I can't let my guard down. Not until we're among friends."

"It's all right," his companion murmured, resting a small hand his shoulder. "In the end you protected me, and I'm fine. It was just a bruise, easily healed."

"It's *not* all right," Dare said, staring into the bowl. "It was a terrible experience for you, and it happened because I wandered off to get my dick wet."

Ireni's posture shifted, and the Outsider shook her head grimly. "If you want to assign blame, Dare, I failed Ireni more than you did. I was just as eager for you to go with Ulma as you were, remember. And I'm the one who let my guard down, got drunk and then went to sleep when I knew you wouldn't be there to protect her."

Ireni took the fore again, giving him a strained smile. "And I didn't tell her to do any different. I think, even fearing what a piece of shit Ollivan was, I didn't quite believe he'd sink so low."

"I won't duck away from my own responsibility for all this." Dare looked deep into her big green eyes. "I'm so sorry, Ireni. That was the last time I'll fail to protect you."

The petite redhead's eyes softened. "I know," she said, resting a hand on his chest.

Dare savored the moment for a short while, then determinedly got back to eating; they needed to get going.

The rest of the day passed in a haze of exhaustion. The Outsider was too busy to stay with them the entire time, so as Ireni gave in to her weariness and fell asleep the goddess took over just enough to keep them in the saddle.

As dark fell he couldn't keep going another step in spite of his determination. The horses were in better shape after sparing them more, so he mounted up and pulled Ireni into his arms, and they continued on into the interminable night.

He wasn't sure what the hour was when Terana finally came into view. Late. It took time to wake the gate guards and get them to open up, mostly thanks to his and Ireni's levels and his claim that they had news from the raid to share with the Baroness.

Which was true enough.

Dare had the same problem at the wrought iron gate barring the driveway up to Montshadow Estate. He had to ring the bell, hoping he could get someone's attention. To his relief, after only a few rings the usual guard appeared from a nearby structure, looking tired and irritable.

"Sorry to intrude at this hour," Dare said as the man stopped on the other side of the gate. "It's a bit of an emergency."

The guard took in Ireni sleeping in his arms, not so much as stirring at his voice, and nodded, silently pulling the gate open. "Ride on up to the stables," he murmured. "A boy will rouse to help you with your horses."

"Thank you." Dare nudged his mount up the drive, Ireni's clattering along behind him.

True to the guard's word, as he reached the stable doors a sleepy stableboy opened them, rubbing at his eyes with one hand while holding a lit lantern with the other. He quickly came alert and hurried to take the horses as Dare dismounted, still cradling the high priestess.

"I need to speak to the mistress of the house," he murmured.

The boy looked at him with blank surprise, then nodded in the direction of the front doors. Dare turned with a start to see Miss Garena, immaculately dressed in her maid uniform in spite of the late hour, or hurrying towards him holding a glowing stone.

"Forgive the intrus-" he started to say.

She cut in briskly. "Nonsense, Master Dare. The Baroness instructed us to welcome you at any hour, and to send you straight to her chambers, day or night."

Wow. Was Lady Marona that eager to get him in the sack again, or was it something else? Either way he was grateful he wouldn't need to talk his way into her presence when it meant waking her up.

"Thank you." He looked down at Ireni's peacefully slumbering face; she was still out like a light. "My companion needs a room."

"Of course." The Head Maid briskly turned and started for the mansion, and Dare hurried to follow.

Inside she curtly barked instructions to a maid he only vaguely recognized, who ran off to wake up the baroness and inform her of his arrival. Then the stern older woman led him to the same guest bedroom he and his companions had shared before, turning back the covers and helping him tuck the sleeping Priestess in.

Then she briskly led the way up to the third floor and down the hall to Lady Marona's rooms.

The baroness was awake and waiting in her sitting room when Miss Garena ushered him through the door, wearing a thin slip of a nightgown that in most circumstances he would've found distractingly sexy. She immediately brightened at the sight of him, barely taking the time to dismiss her Head Maid before throwing herself into his arms.

"Great news, my paramour!" she said, beaming. "You've given me the child I longed for! I just got news of it yesterday, and was waiting eagerly for your return to . . ."

She trailed off, smile fading when she finally took in his expression. "What is it?" she asked, stepping back.

"I'm deeply happy for your good news, my Lady. Truly. I just . . ." Dare sighed and motioned to the loveseat, stepping over to sit down beside his lover. "I'm afraid I've gotten into some trouble."

Lady Marona assumed her usual focused and professional demeanor. "What happened?"

He told her everything from the start, about volunteering the information about the Magma Tunneler, the trouble with Ollivan, and finally the attack on Ireni. As he spoke her expression sharpened with concern, darkened with fury, then went pale.

"That motherfucker," she growled when he finished.

Dare blinked, surprised by the use of language from the elegant lady. Not that he argued the sentiment. "Just how much trouble am I in?"

The baroness sighed, leaning back against the armrest and staring up at the ceiling. "Officially? You defended yourself and your companion from an obvious and unprovoked attack. The law is firmly on your side."

"And unofficially, I came within an inch of killing an anointed knight," he finished, grimly shaking his head.

"Thank the gods you didn't," she said. "Lord Zor would've been obligated to arrest you, no matter the situation, and take you to face the judgment of Bastion's governor. Or in other words Ollivan's uncle, Duke Valiant."

"Fuck me," he blurted, then flushed in chagrin. "Sorry."

Lady Marona shook her head grimly. "The sentiment is well spoken. You couldn't have made a much more inconvenient enemy. Or a more brutal and dishonorable one." Her expression tightened with fury once more. "I had reason enough to despise Ollivan before learning of this . . . when he was my guest a few days ago he raped one of my maids."

Dare tensed in alarm. "Who?" he asked anxiously, immediately concerned for Belinda and Marigold. His heart went out to the poor girl who'd suffered that fate, of course, but he had a special bond with those two and was especially concerned for their welfare.

"Eala," she replied, a name he didn't recognize. "I issued a formal complaint to his family and the Governor and have barred him from my home in the future, but I fear he'll suffer no repercussions for his crimes."

He stood and began to pace, fists clenched at his sides. Whatever his lover said about the consequences, he felt some regret the man hadn't died to his arrows; Ireni could've suffered the same fate as poor Eala, if not worse, if he hadn't arrived in time to save her.

"So even though he's in the wrong, and has committed terrible crimes before, he'll likely come after me for this and be allowed to?" he grated.

"I fear so." Lady Marona sighed. "I'll take what measures I can to make sure he at least can't hurt you through official channels. Not anytime soon, at least." She took his hand. "In the meantime, I recommend you petition for knighthood. I'll sponsor you."

Dare nodded slowly. "Ireni suggested the same. That he'll have less weight to throw against me if we're peers. How soon can we make it happen?"

Her lips tightened. "I'm afraid the next trials for the Order of the Northern Wall, the official guardians of Bastion, aren't for almost three months, at the beginning of the new year." She squeezed his hand. "Until then I'll try to make sure that if he does come after you, it can only be personally, himself and any cronies he can scrounge up. Without any support from his uncle or any of the guards. You'll need to prepare yourself, though, either to fight or flee."

Fuck. Dare could accept danger to himself, but not to his loved ones. Not to his daughter.

He'd redouble his efforts to level up so he could meet Ollivan and any other scum he brought with him toe to toe. Him and Ireni and Ilin and Leilanna, and even Zuri and Pella if they could do it safely. And he'd evacuate the manor until this was sorted out.

He abruptly turned back to Lady Marona. "I need to get back to Nirim Manor. Can you keep Ireni safe until I get back?"

"Of course," she said, standing gracefully. "But I think you'd do well to rest for a few hours. No sense passing out from exhaustion halfway there and breaking your neck falling off your horse."

Dare shook his head, full of grim resolve. "Exhaustion won't touch me until I know my loved ones are safe."

His mature lover rested a hand on his arm. "The next week will likely be most dangerous for you, as the raiding party returns to Terana to turn in the quest, then disperses. If Ollivan intends to come after you instead of returning home, he'll likely go right away rather than sticking around twiddling his thumbs . . . he's not a patient man."

"We'll be on our guard," he assured her as he started for the door.

She accompanied him out into the hall and down the stairs. "I'll keep eyes on him the entire time he's in my town, and if he comes your way I'll send warning, or the good news if he departs back towards Redoubt."

Her lips curled upward in a hard smile. "I'll also have my maids dispersing rumors throughout the town, especially to travelers and merchants, about his attack on one of the raid's healers and the fact that he got his ass kicked by someone five levels lower than him. We'll see what damage he can do if his reputation is trashed as it deserves to be."

"Thank you." As they reached the manor's main doors Dare pulled the beautiful noblewoman into his arms and kissed her passionately. "I wish I could be here under better circumstances, and linger longer."

"As do I, my paramour," she murmured, melting against him. "I hope to see you soon, and with any luck by then all this will be sorted out. I'll be sure to keep you informed of any developments."

"You're a lifesaver, my Lady," he said, reluctantly stepping back. "I don't know how I can repay your kindness."

Lady Marona smiled gently and rested a hand on her belly. "I have to look out for the father of my child, do I not?" She motioned, and he jumped a bit as Miss Garena appeared as if from nowhere to open the doors. "Travel safely, my paramour, and bid all the lovely women of your harem my love as well. I hope to see them soon, and under better circumstances."

Dare hurried through the doors, then stopped in stunned surprise when he saw Ireni waiting with four fresh horses from the baroness's stables, mounts and remounts. "I thought I left you sleeping safe in the mansion," he blurted.

The beautiful Priestess smiled, but her eyes flashed with determination. "You think I'd let you leave me behind?" She clenched her fists. "That bastard's not just threatening us, he's threatening our family. I'm going to be there for Zuri and Pella and Leilanna and Se'weir and the baby."

Their family; whatever his reservations about the situation with Ireni and the Outsider sharing a body, the words felt right. He was touched to know the two women loved him and the others so deeply and would fight to defend them.

And honestly part of him was glad Ireni would be with him, where he could protect her.

They mounted up, and as Lady Marona waved from the door they urged their horses into a canter down the drive.

* * * * *

If the previous day had been brutal, the next day was punishing.

Dare ended up dozing in the saddle more often than he was awake, relying on his reflexes to keep him from sliding off the horse each time he jolted alert. He and Ireni took turns leading the mounts down the path beaten across the landscape, from all the laborers they'd hired coming to and from Terana, and spent their off time sleeping fitfully in the saddle.

A few times both of them ended up asleep, and the horses either stopped to graze or continued plodding placidly down the path. But all in all they made reasonable time.

Since they'd traveled all night they came in sight of Nirim Manor in the afternoon. Dare had spent the last few days imagining the worst for when they arrived, as if somehow Ollivan and his cronies could manage to reach his family before he and Ireni could. He'd pictured the manor burning, his loved ones fighting desperately.

But everything looked peaceful. In fact, the only excitement was at their return, as Leilanna abandoned her work in her gardens to announce their arrival, and everyone came pouring outside to greet them.

Dare had been awake for the last few hours and felt like a walking zombie, but as they rode through the gate Ireni perked up as if she hadn't spent the last few days pushing herself brutally.

Her surge of energy was probably thanks to her bubbling excitement at the sight of the others rushing forward to meet them, Ilin nodding in greeting but hanging back to give the family space for their reunion.

"Zuri!" Ireni shouted, leaping off her horse and rushing over to gently but warmly hug the surprised goblin. "I'm so happy to see you again! And Gelaa!" she tenderly brushed a finger over the sleeping baby's cheek. "She's so beautiful."

"Thank you," the little goblin said, looking surprised but pleased. She brushed a lock of auburn hair out of the Priestess's face, her nurturing side surfacing in obvious sympathy and concern. "You look like you're barely on your feet, you poor dear. Let's get you to bed, and a hot meal if you feel up to it."

"Soon enough," Ireni said, kissing Zuri on the cheek. "I've been waiting to meet you all properly for so long, I'm too excited to sleep yet!"

Dare was right behind the Priestess kissing Gelaa's soft cheek, and stood with his arm wrapped around his goblin lover as Ireni bounced around among the others, beaming with delight.

"Pella!" The petite redhead ran over to the dog girl, hugging her tight. "It's good to finally meet you! I can't wait to get to know you better." She backed away to look at her growing belly with tears shining in her eyes. "You're absolutely glowing, so breathtaking. Congratulations on your puppies!"

"And Se'weir!" She practically lifted the little hobgoblin off the ground and spun her around in her excitement. "I'm so happy you're going to be part of the family! I know we're going to be the best of friends."

"And Leilanna!" Ireni continued, although she wisely made no move to hug the glowering dusk elf who stood with her arms crossed. "I'm happy to see you again."

"Whatever." Leilanna turned to Dare. "I told everyone about Ireni and the Outsider. They're taking it surprisingly well."

"Why wouldn't we?" Zuri asked, puzzled. "She's Dare's benefactor and lover. Of course she's welcome."

Pella nodded firmly. "Although I'm a bit curious about Ireni. Is she part of the harem already? Is she going to be?"

Dare hesitated, but Ireni didn't as she moved over to wrap an arm around his waist and lean her head on his shoulder. "I dearly long to be, and I hope to be soon," she said as she smiled around at him and his family. "I love you all and dream of sharing my life with you as family. But you know Dare . . . he wants to make sure this situation is best for everyone and we can all be happy before he makes up his mind."

Leilanna snickered. "Yeah, that definitely sounds like him."

"At least you're being open about your feelings," Zuri said, pointedly nudging the dusk elf with her elbow.

"I'm sure it will all work out," Pella said, fluffy golden tail wagging. "After all you're not just beautiful, you're an absolute sweetheart. And anyone can see how much you love Dare. I'm sure he'll come to love you too in no time at all."

Ireni blushed, obviously pleased, and nodded. "I hope so. Until then thank you for welcoming me to Nirim Manor . . . I'll work hard to make it a wonderful home for all of us."

"Ooh, you're such a dear!" Pella said, throwing her arms around the petite woman and nuzzling her red hair. With her canid senses she'd obviously seen more of Ireni's deeper feelings than the rest of them, and liked what she saw. "I would love to have you as a fellow mate!"

"So would I," Zuri said, hugging her as well. "I'm sorry for our suspicion of you when we first met."

Ireni laughed, although there were tears of happiness in her eyes. "I can understand. Like I told Dare, we came on too strong."

Dare noticed Leilanna and Se'weir weren't joining the group hug. The hobgoblin's expression was carefully neutral, but the dusk elf looked pissed. "If she's going to join the harem, I'd better get a baby before her," she said, looking jealous. "It's only fair."

He stared at her in surprise. "Um, you always insist on using Prevent Conception. I didn't even know you wanted a baby."

She didn't seem to care for that point, putting her hands on her ample hips. "Of *course* I wanted one. Eventually." Her glower intensified. "Anyway I'm your *third* consort. *I* should get a baby before anyone else."

To his further surprise Se'weir nodded in agreement at that.

"It's not a race, Lanna," Ireni said gently. "We're all ready in our own time."

"Also technically the Outsider is Dare's second consort, and you're the fourth," Zuri pointed out. "Although I'm not sure why it matters."

"Whatever!" the dusk elf growled with a pout. "And don't call me Lanna, new girl! I don't know you." She grabbed Dare's arm and began roughly tugging him towards the manor. "Come on, you're going to give me a baby right now."

Dare barely managed a step before his strength gave out and he stumbled, nearly taking Leilanna down with him.

Pella and Ireni were there to catch him. "Easy!" the bookish Priestess snapped. "We've been riding almost nonstop for days to bring warning, and Dare pushed himself harder to spare me. He's dead on his feet."

"Why?" Zuri asked in alarm, clutching Gelaa fearfully. "What's happened? Are we in danger?"

"Maybe," Dare said, perking up enough at the reminder to push to his feet again. "I ran into some trouble on the raid, and I'm afraid it may follow us here."

Ilin finally came forward, looking concerned. "We'd best hear it then, my friend."

Dare nodded, and he and Ireni quickly explained what had happened with Ollivan. The other women all looked horrified and flocked protectively around the petite redhead when they heard what she'd been through, even Leilanna and Se'weir, while Ilin's normally cheerful expression became grim and full of purpose.

"I fear we may need to abandon the manor, at least for a while," Dare concluded when they were done. "And I believe we should take steps to all begin leveling up again." He glanced at Se'weir, who didn't have a combat class. "Those of us who can fight, that is."

She looked away, lips tightening.

Ireni swayed on her feet. "I think we'll be safe to stay here, as long as we're vigilant and ready to flee at short notice. Lady Marona promised to send word if Ollivan came our way, and at least for the next day or so our haste to get here has bought us a head start."

"In that case we need to get you two to bed," Pella said, firmly ushering Dare towards the door.

He balked. "I need to keep watch," he mumbled, although now

that the warning was given he felt himself beginning to collapse.

"Don't be stupid, you're going to be useless on watch in your state," Leilanna snapped, tone more worried than irritated. She lent him her shoulder as well, while Ilin gently lifted Ireni and carried her. The others hurried behind.

Dare reluctantly let himself be led to his bed, his lovers undressing him and pushing him beneath the covers. He was vaguely aware of warm bodies pressing around him, loving voices murmuring soothingly, and then he fell gratefully into blissful slumber.

* * * * *

Dare stirred awake to find himself alone, the bed disappointingly empty to either side of him.

With a groan he pulled himself into a seated position, looking around blearily. Through the window he could see sunlight, but considering it felt like he'd slept for a long time it couldn't still be the same day they'd arrived.

Had he slept through the day and night and it was morning? He must've been more wiped out than he'd realized.

His muscles were sore from the exertions of the previous days, but he climbed out of bed and dressed, including in his armor, then gathered his weapons.

He wasn't going to go unarmed while Ollivan might be a threat to his family. Although speaking of which, he needed to find them.

Dare smelled bread baking and heard the welcome sound of a baby cooing, and followed them to the kitchen, where Gelaa was wrapped snugly in a basket cradle on the table while Se'weir busied herself at the oven.

"Morning," he said, making his way over to pick up and cuddle his daughter. She looked up at him solemnly with her big yellow eyes as he tenderly leaned down to kiss her soft black hair.

There was no answer from Se'weir, and she kept her back to him.

Dare frowned; this sort of coolness wasn't like the gentle hobgoblin. "Um, so where is everyone?" he asked awkwardly.

After a pregnant pause she finally spoke, voice neutral. "They talked to my tribe about scouting around the borders of your land in case of threats, using a flag signal system Ilin showed them. Then they partied up and went to fight monsters and level. Ilin's going to take the damage while Zuri and Leilanna deal it, and Pella stays back in case she needs to protect the casters."

"What about Ireni?"

Se'weir stiffened. "She's there too."

Okay, this was obviously something he was going to have to address. With a sigh Dare gently set Gelaa back in her cradle, then made his way over to rest a hand on the shorter woman's shoulder. "Hey, are you okay, Se'weir?"

"Of course!" she said with forced brightness, back still firmly to him. "Why wouldn't I be?" She viciously slapped the bread she was kneading onto the counter, thumping it with her fists. "After all, I'm safe back here caring for Gelaa because I'm *useless*."

"What? Of course you're not useless, you're wonderful," Dare protested. The kindhearted hobgoblin just sniffed, and he frowned and leaned around to look at her face.

To his shock he saw tears streaming down her cheeks.

She looked away, shoulders hunching. "You should go level too. We need you to be strong." She pointed blindly. "There's a-a couple bacon sandwiches over there. Should be enough for breakfast and lunch."

"Hey, hey," he said, gently turning Se'weir around and gathering her into his arms. "What's wrong?"

His betrothed was stiff in his arms for several long seconds, and then she abruptly slumped against him and buried her face in his chest. "It's not fair!" she wailed, bursting into tears.

Dare blinked. "What isn't?" he asked, gently stroking her back. She didn't answer. "Se'weir, please, talk to me."

165

She finally looked up, pale yellow eyes shining and vulnerable. "Haven't I been a good mate, as much as you'd let me?" she asked miserably. "You've welcomed me into your house, treat me as part of the family, and I know you enjoy the time we spend together cooking. I even see the desire in your eyes when you look at me."

"Of course," he soothed, brushing his fingers through her soft brown hair. "You've been wonderful. You *are* wonderful. And so beautiful. And I'm happy you're part of the family."

"But I'm not!" Se'weir said, pulling away from him. "Why won't you mate me? Why won't you let me be with you like the others? Why do you make me wait a whole *year*, when life is so short and I'm surrounded by the others and forced to see how happy they are with you?"

Her face crumpled miserably. "And then you bring home a strange woman and *she* already feels more a part of this family than I do. It's not fair! I love you and want to have your babies, why won't you let me?"

Dare sighed. "It's complicated. With your father and brother pressuring for an arranged marriage-"

The beautiful hobgoblin shook her head morosely. "It's complicated, right. You've already told me over and over." She poked his chest with an accusing finger. "But you know what I think? I think you were bothered by the thought of having a stranger as your mate, someone who came to you instead of someone you met and developed feelings for. And you panicked and gave yourself a year to get used to the idea."

"I . . ." He paused. "Maybe you're right," he admitted.

"But that doesn't explain why you won't be with me," she continued in a small, sad voice. "After all, your agreement with my family was only that you'd *marry* me in a year. Nobody said anything about mating or having children. Which means there must be some other reason you don't want me."

Dare's heart broke for her, and he realized she was right. It wasn't that he didn't want her, he'd just been so focused on marrying her in a year that he hadn't considered any other possibility.

And he definitely hadn't been fair to her, or taken her feelings into account.

Gelaa began to cry, and Se'weir shook her head wearily. "We shouldn't be arguing like this in front of her," she muttered, hastily wiping her hands on a towel and moving over to pick up the baby. "Shh, shh, my courageous little one," she murmured, rocking Gelaa gently.

Dare stepped over and gently wrapped his arms around her again. "Se'weir," he said quietly. "You're right, I haven't been fair to you. You deserve all the love and happiness I can give you. Will you let me make it up?"

She said nothing, although she leaned against him slightly.

"Let me take you on a date this evening," he continued. "And if you'll have me, let me share your bed tonight. Just the two of us."

Hopefully Zuri and Pella and Leilanna would forgive him for not spending time with them, when he'd already been away for almost a week. Hopefully they'd understand.

The beautiful hobgoblin looked up, pale yellow eyes shining with sudden hope. "You mean it?" she whispered. "You'll breed me and give me a baby?"

Dare hesitated. He hadn't meant to take things quite that quickly. But to be fair he'd been willing to impregnate Rosie and Enellia right off the bat.

If Se'weir was part of his family and would soon be his wife, didn't she deserve the same? "I would be honored," he said, leaning down and kissing her softly.

Se'weir's lips tasted like honey and bacon, and she made a surprised, then happy sound as she kissed him back, mouth opening to welcome his tongue in.

Then she hastily pulled back, looking flustered. "I-I'll look forward to it," she said, blushing. "I mean I can't wait! I'm glad you gave me all day, though, so I have time to get ready."

She set Gelaa back in the cradle, then ushered him firmly over to pick up the bacon sandwiches. "Okay, go hunt monsters, my betrothed. I'll see you tonight."

Chapter Nine
Date

Dare always moved quickly and with focus when he leveled, of course.

He actually enjoyed the challenge, seeing how efficiently he could gain experience, optimizing his efforts to constantly improve the results. It was always satisfying to come home after a day of constant, deliberate effort knowing he couldn't have done much better than he had.

But now it wasn't just a challenge or a game. There was a Level 35 Warrior out there gunning for him, and the man would probably bring high level friends with him.

Dare needed to be ready for them.

He sprinted from spawn point to spawn point, using Cheetah's Dash when it was up, and demolished any monsters in his path that offered even the slightest experience. He even left junk loot behind once his pack and his horse's saddlebags were filled, burying what he couldn't take in a cache where he could come back for it later.

The experience required to gain a level jumped up significantly with each one. But it had also had a huge jump up at 20, and it jumped up again at 30. Even rushing as fast as he could he wasn't going to be able to manage the same speed he had before, but he was determined to do his best.

Unfortunately, the difficulty of monsters also jumped up at 30, same as it had at 20. Although thankfully this time it was a flat increase in health and damage, not more of the dangerous abilities monsters started getting at 20.

Dare could handle arrow sponges, especially now that he had Cheetah's Dash.

Thankfully he didn't have to worry about that just yet, since he could farm monsters in their high 20s for a while with only a small loss in experience. And maybe they could shuffle things around so Ireni leveled with him, since with her buffs and shields he'd be able to handle the tougher monsters much better.

He was so in the zone leveling that he almost failed to notice it was time to head back. He'd planned to make it an early day so he could clean himself up properly and prepare for his date with Se'weir.

To his surprise, on the way back he encountered the others also returning from their own leveling, and he got a chance to ask how the group of five had managed.

Slow, was the consensus. Having Ireni there let Ilin be a lot more confident in doing damage to monsters and not just kiting them, but aside from him Leilanna was the only real damage dealer, with Zuri's Healer damage sub-par and Pella unable to join the fight since she was melee and they couldn't risk it with her pregnancy.

Cautious pulling, low level monsters, and splitting experience five ways meant that even with pushing themselves hard the levels would be slow in coming. But still much faster than most adventurers on Collisa.

Of course his lovers seemed more interested in cuddling up to him as he walked, relieved to see him back on his feet after the condition he'd been in when he got home. They'd obviously missed him while he was gone as much as he'd missed them, and were wasting no opportunity to share their affection.

Honestly, if Ilin hadn't been there they probably would've tackled him to the grass and started an orgy right then and there.

It actually made Dare feel a bit guilty, because he had to interrupt their plans for a romantic and sexy night of lovemaking to tell them about his date plans with Se'weir.

"Good!" Zuri said, seeming excited rather than disappointed. "You finally got your head out of your ass. You just better make sure she has a good time."

Pella also seemed fine with it, happy for the gentle hobgoblin and eager to have her be part of the fun. If anything Ireni was most pleased of all, no doubt thanks to the Outsider's eagerness for him to grow the harem.

As for Leilanna . . . Dare should've predicted that she would have a problem with it. And to be fair, he probably should've approached her and the others to talk his plans through first, since any decisions he made with his love life affected them as much as him.

"What do you mean, you're going on a date with Se'weir?" she demanded, folding her arms beneath her large breasts. "Did you forget yesterday when I specifically told you that you needed to give me a baby next? It's my turn!"

He used the only card he could play under the circumstances. "Don't you want to go on a date with me, too? A romantic evening, and then a night together with just the two of us? I've already promised Se'weir, but we can go out next after her if you want, and I promise I'll do everything I can to make it special."

"Hey, what about me?" Pella asked, ears and fluffy tail drooping sadly. "Leilanna and Ireni both got to spend time with you recently, and Se'weir gets you all to herself tonight."

"Of course I want to take you out on a date too," Dare said hastily; damn, he was really handling this badly. "And Zuri too. I want to give all of you some quality time after how long we've been apart, not just together with all of us lovers but individually."

"I would like that," Zuri said quietly. "We haven't had a chance to make love since the baby."

He blinked. From what he knew of new mothers, you were supposed to give them time to recover from the birth before having sex. But he supposed healing took care of the physical recovery, and it had been a couple weeks.

"I don't like the idea of Dare having a date every night for most of the next week, though," Leilanna said, hands on her hips. "I'd love to have a night with him all to myself, but that would mean we won't all get to sleep together for a while."

171

The other girls considered that solemnly. "That's a good point," Pella said. "Maybe we should limit it to one date night a week in a rotation. And on the other days we all sleep with him."

Zuri giggled. "It would almost be like a rest night for him every week, since every other night we'll all be tiring him out."

Hoo boy. That sounded like paradise to Dare. Very, very strenuous paradise. Thankfully their bed was big enough for all of them, since it looked as if it would be everyone's moving forward. Not that it hadn't pretty much been shared by everyone already.

"Okay, but I get the next date night after this one," Leilanna said. She glanced at Ireni. "Unless Ireni or the Outsider wants to go first? I guess they still haven't had a chance to be with him."

That was uncommonly generous of her; was she warming up to the goddess and High Priestess?

Ireni gave him a somewhat strained smile. "That's all right. You go ahead."

Dare's heart went out to her. The Outsider had warned him that he should hold off on anything romantic, or at least anything sexual, with the shaken woman for a bit, until she recovered from the trauma of Ollivan's attack. From the sounds of it Ireni had things in her past she was still working through that the experience had brought back to the surface, and he needed to be patient and gentle with her.

Probably for a while.

Which he could do; he'd do anything for her, same as for the others. He hadn't known her long but he was already developing feelings for her, and his reservations about her arrangement with the Outsider were beginning to fade.

He just hoped he could give her the happiness she deserved.

"Good," Leilanna said. "I suppose I don't mind that Se'weir gets to go ahead of me, then." She put her hands on her hips and gave him a stern look. "But you *will* give me a baby the night of our date. And presents."

Dare chuckled and gathered her into his arms, kissing her softly.

"I can't wait."

The Outsider came to the fore and cleared her throat. "I'd like to share the bed with all of you too. I want to play with everyone."

"Of course you can, Outsider!" Pella said, hugging her; she seemed as adept at recognizing when the goddess was at the fore as Dare was, while most of the others looked a bit confused. "And Ireni will be welcome whenever she feels ready."

"Hey wait a second," he protested, shifting uncomfortably. "We still haven't, um, you know."

The goddess grinned at him. "That didn't stop you with Leilanna, when she wanted to be with Zuri and Pella until you two finally stopped being idiots and admitted your feelings for each other."

"Yeah!" Zuri agreed, gently but firmly. "Besides, do you really want to leave Ireni alone after what she's been through, the poor dear? She slept in our bed with us last night, you know."

Dare looked around at all his lovers, realizing he was outvoted. "Ireni?"

The petite redhead came to the fore, delicate cheeks flushing. "I'm not ready to get intimate just yet, even though I love you all and want to share that with you. But it would make me happy to know the Goddess is sharing that intimacy with you the way we both want. And Zuri's right that I don't want to be alone."

That seemed to decide things, and he wondered wryly if it was just a matter of time before he gave in and agreed to be lovers with the two women sharing a body. It seemed as if everyone else was already on board.

Besides, if this was what made Ireni happy he would have to be a total asshole to say he knew her feelings better than her. And as for his own feelings, he already considered Ireni and the Outsider as part of the family and could admit he wanted to be with them romantically.

So he sighed and offered a rueful smile. "I'd still like to give the Outsider my full attention our first time. Something more special than both of us ending up together in the passion of group sex."

"Actually, I wouldn't complain about that," the goddess said, taking the fore again. "I want powerful experiences and to try every new thing we can think of."

"Shh," Pella scolded her. "Of course your first time with Dare will be special. And Ireni's too." She bounced up and down eagerly, tail a blur. "And Se'weir's! I'm so excited for her . . . our family's growing so fast with such wonderful people!"

After that the girls were in a rush to get back to the manor. Pella and Leilanna wanted to help Dare prepare for his date while Zuri and Ireni went to help Se'weir. Ilin, looking equal parts amused and bemused by the whole thing, excused himself to his guest house to meditate for the night.

Dare was a bit bemused himself by how overboard the girls went. It was obvious they wanted this date to be special, not just for Se'weir's sake but to set the trend for date nights moving forward.

He was thoroughly washed, shaved, given a haircut, dressed in his nicest clothes, and the two women brainstormed ideas for activities and romantic spots where he and Se'weir could spend time together. They also very frankly talked about the sorts of positions he should try to give the beautiful hobgoblin a good time.

If he hadn't already been filled with nervous anticipation at the prospect of his first time with his betrothed, that would've done it.

Finally Dare was led to the front doors of the manor, where he waited for Se'weir to finish getting ready and emerge. Just like any date back on Earth, he thought with some amusement.

Although when she finally stepped through the doors it was worth the wait.

The beautiful hobgoblin looked like a princess, which he supposed technically she was as the daughter of a chieftain. She was wearing a beautiful evening gown the same light yellow color as her eyes, which tantalizingly hugged her voluptuous curves and was slit to either side all the way up to the hip, giving her ease of motion in case they planned to do anything more exciting than walk around.

Those slits also showed off her gorgeous legs in a way he found pleasantly distracting.

Her long, soft brown hair had been brushed until it shone and flowed loose down her back, a couple of pale yellow flowers cleverly braided into it. Her lovely face was lightly touched up with makeup that accented her pale green skin and made her eyes look big and bright.

The added blush to Se'weir's cheeks deepened when she saw how he was looking at her, and she gave him a shy smile.

"You look incredible," he said, offering her his arm. Her smile became radiant as she took it, leaning her soft body against his side.

The other girls looked as if they wanted to swarm the two of them with hugs and well wishes, but instead they disappeared into the manor with a few final bright waves and winks. Leaving Dare alone with his date.

"I set up a dinner in the gardens," he said. "Near the roses, in that spot you really like."

"Okay," she said, shyly looking at the ground.

Her usually bubbly personality was more subdued tonight, as nervous and excited as he was, and to prevent an awkward silence he kept going. "I used some spices I found in Terana this last trip. Imported from the south. I think they add some amazing flavors I'm excited for you to try."

"That sounds nice." His beautiful date bit her lip.

Dare chuckled and wrapped an arm around her. "Hey," he teased, kissing her head. "It's just me. No need to be shy or nervous."

Se'weir looked startled for a second, then giggled as her cheeks caught flame. "It's not that." At his questioning look she buried her face in her hands. "You're going to laugh at me."

"I seriously doubt that," he said, rubbing her back.

She made a quiet noise of enjoyment and pressed harder against his side. "I'm just really, really excited. Not just happy excited but *excited* excited, you know? Like, I know you have a lot of fun things planned for us but I kind of just want to get on my hands and knees and let you mount me right here."

Wow. Dare felt his own cheeks heat. "Well we have the garden to ourselves," he said with a grin.

The beautiful hobgoblin lowered her hands and offered him a radiant smile. "Let's at least enjoy your lovely dinner, first."

That seemed to break the tension, and they continued to where he'd set up a table with fancy plating, candles, flowers, and all the rest.

As they ate they talked about cooking, Gelaa, how the Avenging Wolves who'd moved to his lands were doing, what news she had of Gar and the others who'd stayed in the mountains, and a variety of other topics.

She'd never had much interest in his leveling aside from showing support in his efforts, knowing how much it meant to him, and her concern for his welfare. Although in a way it was nice not to talk about all that, since it tended to dominate his conversation a lot of the time with his other lovers.

Talking to Se'weir was down to earth and enjoyable, something he needed at the moment with all his worries about Ollivan.

Finally she pushed aside her plate, wiped her mouth with her napkin, and with a shy but eager smile stood. "The flower bed?"

"The flower bed," Dare said with a laugh.

Leilanna's garden was beautiful in a way he could only imagine elves and others close to nature were capable of. It somehow managed to seem natural and verdant but also symmetrical and tamed to ideal beauty. Not only that, but along with its beauty it was functional in many ways.

She had fruits and vegetables growing, for one thing, as if to invite people walking the paths to stop and pluck themselves a treat. And she also had benches placed along the paths to provide particularly lovely views across the gardens, inviting peaceful contemplation and appreciation of the beauty.

And deep in a secluded corner of the gardens, near a corner

where two walls of the estate met, was the flower bed. A thickly growing patch of ferns as soft as silk and resilient enough to handle people lying down on them, surrounded by verdant flowering bushes on all sides.

Leilanna had specifically created the place as a spot where they could make love, and it had become popular with the rest of the harem once the secret got out.

Se'weir skinned out of her elegant gown, revealing she was naked beneath, and practically dove into the ferns, turning onto her side to look up at him expectantly.

"Gods, you look like a goddess of fertility reclining in her garden in a deep forest glade," Dare said, taking in her lush curves.

He was surprised to find that her plump breasts were tipped with pale pink nipples, rather than dark green ones similar to Zuri's. They were already stiffening in the cool evening air. Her tummy looked just round enough to be enticing, hips wide and thighs thick and soft. Her pubic area had been shaved smooth and her plump labia were already soaked with her arousal, as were her thighs.

"I guess that makes you the fortunate traveler stumbling upon me by chance?" The beautiful hobgoblin giggled and rolled onto her back, spreading her legs wide to part the lips of her glistening sex, which gave him a tantalizing view of her soft pink interior.

Her pale yellow eyes were smoky as she looked up at him. "Come and breed me, my mate."

Dare eagerly skinned out of his clothes, shivering slightly as the cool breeze flowed over his rock hard cock, and wasted no time climbing on top of his sweet little lover.

She was soft and warm as she wrapped her arms and plump legs around him, pressing her silky skin to his. It didn't have the same lotion-slick feel as Zuri's, but it was smooth enough for his hands to glide over it as he cupped her full breasts and began kissing the soft, pillowy mounds until his lips found a nipple to suck and tease.

"Ooh!" Se'weir moaned. "I could enjoy this for hours." She squirmed beneath him, trying to position herself. "But I need you inside me now. And give it to me good."

Dare hesitated, looking between her plump little body and his big thick cock. "Are you sure?"

She giggled. "I'm goblinkin, my mate. I may have never had a mate or children, but I *have* been mated." She wiggled her hips, rubbing her warm, wet folds along his length. "And I like my mates to be enthusiastic."

Okay then. He moved until he felt himself at her entrance, then pushed in with a slow, smooth motion until he bottomed out with about two-thirds of his length inside her.

The horny hobgoblin buried her face in his shoulder and squealed in delight, plump hands grabbing his ass and eagerly guiding him back out, then in again. He kept it slow and deliberate at first, luxuriating in her warmth; she wasn't as crushingly tight as Zuri, but she was tighter than the others.

Se'weir bit his shoulder then pulled back, panting. "More, my mate! Show me the strength of your desire!"

Dare grinned and lifted up slightly, then began pumping into her with quick, firm thrusts.

She went nuts, squirming beneath him happily, and he had to admit she was a delight to watch. Her plump little body jiggled beneath him with every thrust, big boobs bouncing up and down hypnotically, and the slapping sounds their bodies made as they came together were sexy as hell.

After a few minutes the beautiful hobgoblin buried her fingernails in his back and began bucking beneath him like a bronco, wailing in orgasm as her walls rippled along his length and her overflowing nectar squelched out with every thrust. Her face scrunched up adorably in her pleasure, and he couldn't resist the urge to lean down and kiss her softly.

Then he trailed his lips down to nibble the base of her neck, driving her to higher heights as he continued to savor the pleasure of pushing in and out of her silky, tight tunnel.

His own orgasm caught him by surprise, so caught up in the moment that he hadn't realized he was on the verge. He plunged deep inside her again a final time and sucked on her neck as he began emptying in her depths.

When Se'weir felt him she erupting she hugged him close and wiggled joyously, warm walls eagerly milking him for every drop. "Yes, my mate," she cried. "Breed me! Give me your baby!"

That sexy encouragement squeezed out a couple more spurts, and then he rolled off her with a gasp and gathered her into his arms.

"I love you," he said, kissing her sweaty forehead.

She looked at him in open adoration. "I love you, my mate." With an excited wiggle she rolled onto her stomach and lifted her big round ass in the air. "Okay, now like this!"

Dare had been prepared for some cuddling and caressing before they went again, but either Se'weir wanted to make up for lost time or she was insatiable.

He was still hard as a rock, though, and with that invitation waving in his face he was ready to go again too. He positioned himself behind her and pushed in again, ignoring the sensitivity of his tip after just coming and immediately resuming his eager thrusts.

His plump little lover squealed into the ferns as his tip rubbed against different areas at this new angle, wide hips wiggling against him to try to press for every sensation possible.

He lasted maybe five minutes plowing the sexy hobgoblin from behind, while she squeaked and wailed and thrust her hips back in time with him. Her plump body jiggled delightfully with every thrust, his fingers sinking into her soft hips as he pulled her harder towards him.

"Spank me!" she gasped, turning her head to look back at him with eyes glazed with lust. The sight of her beautiful face peeking around her bouncing body was ridiculously sexy.

Dare grinned at his lover's naughty request and gave her round backside a firm smack, sending ripples across her pillowy cheek. She squealed in delight and pushed against him harder, encouraging

180

more, so he smacked her other cheek.

"Pull my hair too!" she begged, grinding back on his cock frantically.

Damn, this girl was kinky. He gathered her soft brown hair in one hand and used it to pull her back against him, while with the other he smacked her jiggling cheeks.

With a final cry of pleasure Se'weir's walls clamped down on him and she squirted all over his crotch and thighs. That was enough for him and he pulled her hips back against him hard, emptying himself directly against her cervix.

"Yeeessss!" she wailed, trembling her way through her climax.

He pulled out and rolled onto his side, pulling her back against him and kissing her neck. "You're so sexy," he whispered in her ear before kissing and nibbling her short pointy ear. She made a noise of pure enjoyment and began grinding her thick ass against his softening cock, and he stared at her profile in surprise. "And still not done?"

Se'weir giggled. "I want to make good and sure you put a baby inside me tonight."

They both knew he'd probably gotten her pregnant the moment his cock touched her pussy, but he was more than happy to oblige. He could already feel himself stiffening again against her plump ass, slipping in between her soft cheeks and sliding through that pleasurable groove as she continued to push back against him.

Finally he couldn't take it anymore and backed up enough to point himself at her opening, pushing inside her in the spoon position and biting his lip at the extreme sensitivity of his tip. It was almost too much, but he kept thrusting through it until it became pleasure and he got back eagerly rutting his insatiable lover.

He grabbed and toyed with the sexy hobgoblin's large breasts as she arched her back to give him a better angle, and she whimpered in sheer bliss as he rolled and pinched her nipples. Then he ran his fingers down her soft tummy and over her even softer, shaved mound until he found her clit.

"There, my mate!" she squealed, trying to push herself against his finger as she also pushed back against his thrusting cock. "Ancestors watching over us, how are you so *good* at this?"

Dare chuckled buried his face in his little lover's soft brown hair, thrusting harder until her back arched and her walls clamped down yet again, her nectar flooding their joined crotches.

He kept going, pistoning into her and playing with her pillowy breasts while teasing her clit. She went off again a few minutes later with another wail, and he let himself go with her, pouring his seed into her fertile depths.

That finally seemed to be enough for Se'weir, and with a contented moan she pulled herself off his wilting cock and turned to cuddle against him, grinning up at him impishly with her yellow eyes shining. "Glad you didn't wait a year for this, my mate?"

Dare laughed and kissed her softly, tasting her lips. "Very glad. Thank you for being so patient with me."

She sighed blissfully and rested her head on his shoulder. "It was worth the wait." She giggled. "Especially since we have the whole night ahead of us."

✳ ✳ ✳ ✳ ✳

Three days later, Dare returned from hunting monsters to find a commotion in the stable yard.

His first, panicked thought that the goblin sentries had sent warning of danger via flag signals was dispelled when he saw Morwal, the earth Mage who'd worked for them during the renovations, standing next to a horse and leading a loaded packhorse.

"Morwal!" he called, trotting up the drive and dumping his overloaded pack nearby so he could continue forward to clasp the man's hand. "We weren't expecting you, were we?"

"Not me, perhaps," the Mage said with a chuckle. He motioned back to the packhorse. "Lady Marona and Lord Zor hired me to deliver your earnings from the raid." His smile widened. "Although

I admit, there was the momentary temptation to take the money and ride for the border."

Dare laughed. "Were you given a tally for us, or is it up to us to count?"

"Even better." The man handed him a paper. "Signed by Lord Zor, Lady Marona, and Master Norril of the Terana Counting House as witnesses. Confirming that you should find 2,422 gold in that packsaddle. Yours and High Priestess Ireni's shares."

"On it," Zuri said, dragging the pack down and opening it up to begin counting the gold gleaming inside. "No offense of course, Master Morwal."

The Mage chuckled. "I'd think less of you if you didn't count it, just to be sure." He turned back to Dare, reaching into his pocket. "I have a paper for you to sign, confirming you received the delivery. I also have two letters, one from Lord Zor and one from Lady Marona."

Dare quickly signed the paper, Pella obligingly offering her back as a surface, then tore open the top letter which turned out to be from the Paladin. Inside was a short note:

"Hunter. Please find this delivered with your share of the earnings. Allow me also to extend my apologies for the unpleasantness after the battle. Sir Ollivan confessed he was drunk, as were you, and when he went to clear the air about the argument between you two the situation got out of control. He acted with excessive force when he was obliged to strike High Priestess Ireni during the ensuing fight-"

Dare ripped up the paper and wadded the pieces into a ball, tossing them onto the drive. "Leilanna?"

She obligingly burned them to ash.

Morwal arched an eyebrow. "Bad news?"

"Nothing surprising, unfortunately." Dare opened the letter from the baroness, feeling his shoulders loosen slightly as he read:

"Dare. I hope this delivery finds you well. Lord Zor and his noble retinue depart for Redoubt on the morrow, and none intend to remain. I'm sure you wish them a safe journey to their very distant destination."

He looked up at the Mage. "Thank you, my friend. You're welcome to stay the night in a guest house. Have you been paid?"

"I have."

Dare dug into his pouch and pressed five gold into his hand. "A tip for your efforts at least, and the welcome news and items you delivered."

"Much appreciated." Morwal snagged Ilin and walked away with him, apparently talking about the construction of the orphanage.

"So what was that about?" Leilanna asked, looking at the pile of ashes.

Dare grimaced. "Lord Zor very nobly informing me that the fight was pretty much my fault, but Ollivan feels ever so terrible about having to beat the shit out of Ireni even though it's her fault."

"Fuck that guy," the dusk elf said, spitting on the ashes. "Fuck both of them."

He shook his head grimly. "On the plus side, Lady Marona wrote that Ollivan is going with Zor back to Redoubt. If he's planning anything, he won't be personally involved in it."

"I'm not about to let my guard down even so," Pella growled, wrapping protective arms around Ireni. "I don't care how well equipped or high level that bastard is, if he comes after my family I'll tear him apart."

Dare hugged them both as the others gathered around to join the embrace. "We all will. This is a reprieve, at least, and while we don't let our guard down I say we make the most of this to level." He should be able to reach 31 tomorrow if he pushed.

"I like the sound of that," Zuri said, cradling Gelaa with her shoulder pressed to his side. "We need to be able to protect our children while Dare is away leveling."

"Not too far away," he assured her. "Not while there are

monsters I can farm close enough to home."

Ireni gave him an odd look, but didn't say anything.

"Come on," Se'weir said. "You've all had a long day hunting monsters. Let me get some hot food in you."

Pella giggled. "And then maybe Dare can get something hot in all of us."

They made their way inside the bright, warm, cheery manor. Although at the doorway Dare paused with a shiver.

Fall had begun almost a week ago, and winter would be close behind it. This far north, and with no protection from the winds blowing down from even farther north, it was probably going to get pretty cold.

In the morning he'd talk to Morwal about rigging up a central heating system for the manor, and arranging something for the outbuildings as well.

Zuri rejoined him, pressing herself to his side with Gelaa sleeping gently in her arms. "What're you thinking about as you stare off into the distance, my love?" she murmured.

Dare smiled and crouched to kiss their daughter's soft little cheek, then wrapped his arms around his lover's shoulders as he looked around their home. "Our future. The best one I can build for us."

"Mmm." She contentedly rested her head against his chest. "I like that thought."

Chapter Ten

Beloved

Level 31 wasn't a particularly exciting one.

Still, it was progress. Points to put in vital abilities, bridging the gap between Dare and a Level 35. And he wasn't the only one making progress.

Ilin and Leilanna had both reached Level 27. Zuri was 28. And while Pella and Ireni were still Level 30, they were making slow but steady progress towards 31 as well.

Still, he was leveling much faster than the others in spite of the difficulty bump at 30. And that would only increase with them making their slow, cautious progress as he blazed ahead.

While he still wished he could keep on adventuring with them, he now had plenty of motivation to get as high level as possible.

It was his duty to defend his family and provide for them. Against any threat, in any situation. And the best way to make sure he could do that was to get to a level only a few had achieved.

Then surpass them.

That evening everyone wanted to celebrate him gaining a level. Se'weir cooked a special meal, shooing him out of the kitchen when he tried to help, and they gathered around the table talking and laughing.

The group had also had a productive day, even if no one had gained a level. But they'd gotten a lot of loot and had some exciting encounters. Dare felt a bit wistful listening to their adventures, wishing he could be with them.

Maybe in the future, when their situation was more stable. When he was ridiculously high level and the loot he brought in from a week of farming could support the family for a year.

Unfortunately, it seemed his leveling was going to be slowed down.

At a natural break in the conversation Ireni cleared her throat, expression solemn. "My love, if you'll recall you promised to be there when Rosie produces her seed."

Dare blinked. "That's right." He glanced over at the simple calendar they'd hung on the wall at his suggestion, even more surprised at what he saw: it was already the 28th of Pir, the equivalent of September on Collisa. "Holy shit, it's already been almost that long?"

She smiled. "Time flies when you're having fun." The others looked confused by the Earth expression. "In any case you have enough time to get down there in a week if you leave tomorrow."

He looked around at his lovers and Ilin, frowning. "Now's not a good time to take a trip all the way down there, though. Not with Ollivan maybe planning to cause trouble, and the progress we've been making leveling."

Leilanna looked offended. "Are you saying you'd break your promise?" Given her people's insistence on honor that would be particularly appalling to her.

Pella nodded firmly. "You can't do that to Rosie. A promise is a promise."

"I wasn't planning to," Dare protested. "I'm just saying it's a bad time." He looked around. "Should we all go, then?"

Zuri and Se'weir both frowned. "I don't want to travel with an infant," his goblin lover said firmly, the gentle hobgoblin nodding in agreement. "And Pella's over halfway through her pregnancy and carrying multiple puppies. Now's about the time when she should be sticking closer to home anyway."

Dare glanced at the beautiful dog girl, whose tummy was already as round as many women approaching their due date. As a canid she handled her large belly a lot easier than other races would, but she still needed to take it easier.

"Besides, we need to keep leveling to try to catch up as best we can," Leilanna said.

Ireni seemed to guess his impending argument. "We should be safe enough with Ollivan headed back to Redoubt, and Se'weir's people keeping watch in all directions. And we'll be extra careful while you're gone."

He looked around helplessly. "So you're all fine with me ditching you and heading south."

"A promise is a promise," Ilin said. "We'll be fine while you're gone . . . I'll keep a sleepless watch over your family until you return."

"Besides, you'll be able to travel faster," Zuri insisted.

Dare took a deep breath, defeated. "All right, I'll get down there and back up here as quickly as possible."

"Take four horses," Ireni said, again surprising him; even as remounts, that seemed excessive.

But he just nodded again. "All right. Just be safe, all of you."

Pella abruptly leaned forward, tail wagging eagerly. "In the meantime, if you're leaving in the morning we need to make the most of tonight . . . you have a lot of women who're going to miss you for a couple weeks who you need to give a proper goodbye to." She glanced mischievously at Ireni. "Especially the Outsider."

Dare blinked and looked at the petite redheaded, confirming that the goddess had taken the fore. "Outsider?" he asked.

She glanced around, blushing. "The girls seem to feel like the situation when Leilanna was with the others but not you was hard on everyone, and they don't want to repeat it if we can avoid it. They want you and I to be together this evening and then rejoin them so they can finally be with me properly too."

It was hard to argue that. The Outsider had joined them in the master bedroom the last few days, but since she wanted him to see her for the first time when they were finally together she'd always worn her modest shift.

That hadn't stopped her from playing with the other girls, of course, although it was mostly her pleasuring them. And she'd quickly proved she was naughtier than Leilanna and liked it rougher than Se'weir.

And Dare got the sense she'd been holding back.

Even though he'd never seen any of the petite redhead's body bared above the knee or below the neck during her fun, it had still been hot as hell to watch. And also helped the goddess become closer to the others. Especially Zuri; the Outsider couldn't seem to get enough of the little goblin, and even when not kissing her or passionately entwined she still preferred to cuddle with her.

She really did have a special place in her heart for Zuri.

As for the tiny goblin, with her powerful libido she was more than happy to have fun with the beautiful redhead. And while she was a bit bemused by the sheer enthusiasm of the Outsider's affection and pampering, she seemed to enjoy it.

As for Dare, looking on from the other side of the bed by his own choice, he wouldn't mind being part of the fun. He wouldn't mind at all.

And it eased his worries to see how bubbly Ireni had been ever since the Outsider starting sharing their bed; even with the shadow of Ollivan's attack hanging over her, the fact that her goddess was able to enjoy intimacy with the people they both loved made the Priestess genuinely happy.

As if reading his mind, which she probably was, the Outsider gave him a keen look. "It's up to you whether you're ready to finally be with me, Dare, but all the girls agree it's time. Including Ireni."

"Including Ireni," the Priestess confirmed resolutely, returning to the fore. "If you're going to be leaving us for weeks, we want to be more cemented as part of the family. Besides, the Outsider's waited long enough." She hesitated, blushing even harder than the goddess had, and rested a hand on her flat tummy. "And we're ready to carry your child."

Dare stared in shock. Having his child really would cement them as part of the family, even more than becoming lovers. A lifetime commitment every bit as solemn as when he'd finally made love to Se'weir days ago.

Ireni and the Outsider weren't just asking for him to make love to the goddess, they were asking him to finally accept them as part of the family. And from the expectant looks of the rest of his family, they'd already fully given that acceptance to the two women.

Ireni gracefully rose from her chair and moved around the table to wrap her arms around his shoulders from behind, kissing his cheek before burying her face in his neck. "Thank you for being patient with me, my love. I'll be ready to be with you, with all of you, when the time is right. But I think the time is right for you and the Outsider, so please be with her with my blessing."

He looked around and received nods and smiles from all the women he loved, and felt his heart pounding with excitement as he realized this was happening.

He'd come to love the Outsider even more since she'd come to him with Ireni, and he unquestionably found her beautiful in her petite redheaded body. He wanted to be with her, and it looked as if it was time.

"Outsider," he started, then had to clear his throat with an embarrassed laugh. "My beloved, should we go for a walk?"

The arms around his neck tightened playfully as the goddess took the fore, and he felt her small breasts press pleasantly against his back. "A walk to the bedroom, lover," she whispered in a husky voice, warm breath tickling his ear. "No need to be romantic tonight."

Gulp.

To his embarrassment the others all cheered as the Outsider practically dragged him from his seat and began tugging him eagerly towards the staircase leading upstairs. He laughed, winked at his lovers, then swept the petite redhead into his arms.

She gave a giggle of surprised delight, then looked up at him with bedroom eyes. "Don't get lost along the way, my love," she teased, kissing along his collarbone while her small hands caressed his back and shoulders. "I've waited long enough."

Dare felt himself stiffening eagerly as he mounted the steps three at a time; she wasn't the only one who'd been anticipating this.

He burst into the bedroom and kicked the door shut behind him. The Outsider immediately squirmed out of his arms and lifted up on her tiptoes, pulling his head down at the same time to kiss him fiercely. There was no shyness there, and he reminded himself he was with the same woman he'd made love to in his dreams as a shadow and an alabaster mannequin.

Only now he was awake, and she was very real and warm in his arms. "Gods, I've missed you," he panted against her lips.

She gave a husky laugh and ran her hands over his shoulders and back, almost wonderingly, then pulled his shirt off with eager tugs and tossed it aside. "Oh Me," she murmured, staring at his muscles. "You're even more handsome when I have the senses to properly appreciate you. And the hormones, of course." She leaned in and delicately kissed his chest, then playfully ran a tongue across his nipple. "So sexy."

He couldn't help but grin, both at the compliment and at her unique version of profanity. "Well I have you to thank for that, since you're the one who gifted me these good looks and the body of an elite athlete."

"Yes, a gift." She drew back, green eyes dancing as she looked up at him. "One you've certainly benefited from, and without a doubt used to best effect." The goddess in the body of a petite redhead bit her lip almost sheepishly, resting a delicate hand on his chest. "I should probably admit something, though."

"Hmm?"

She gently stroked his skin. "Since I got to decide what you looked like anyway, I may have, um, decided to fashion you in the image of my ideal man." Her peaches and cream complexion flushed a rosy pink as she looked down at his crotch. "All of you."

Dare stared at her in shock. "What?"

"Just in case I ever got the chance to make love to you," the

Outsider said quickly, staring at his chest. "After all, it wouldn't make any difference to you and would be such a wonderful thing for me." Her brilliant green eyes darted quickly up to meet his, then just as quickly flitted away. "Does that bother you?"

That was a good question . . . did it? He'd come to view this body as his, every bit as much as his old one on Earth. His identity, him, Darren Portsmouth. Or Dare the Hunter now. "I'll . . . have to think about it."

The goddess looked a bit worried. "Because I mean," she continued uncertainly, "it's kind of the same thing, isn't it?" She ran her hands down her slender body. "Like I said, Ireni was perfect not just because I love her and we already shared such a deep bond, but because she almost perfectly matches your ideal woman."

She giggled, some of her confidence briefly returning. "And even if she'll probably be a little mad at me for telling you this, you match *her* ideal of the perfect man too. Although that's not as important to her as who you are inside. And honestly most women would agree you're everything they want, so it's not just us."

She bit her lip again. "But anyway it means our lovemaking will be perfect, won't it? Both of us getting exactly what we want in a partner? We'll have so much fun together."

Was it possible that the Outsider, who'd shown nothing but amused detachment and complete assurance before now, was actually worried about whether he'd accept her? Even after they'd already made love twice, albeit in very odd and somewhat disturbing ways.

Dare rested a gentle hand on her cheek. "I'm not sure how I feel about you making me your perfect lover," he admitted honestly. "But that doesn't change how I feel about you. You've been a friend and a helping hand ever since I arrived on Collisa, even if our conversations were limited through the information system. And the times we slept together before now were unreal." Literally.

A tentative smile spread across those adorable rosebud lips, which seemed far more pouty and sensual when the Outsider was in control. "Really?"

He trailed his hand down her cheek to cup the back of her neck, leaning forward to press his lips to hers, then stared into her eyes from inches away. "And it doesn't change how much I want you," he added. "You could come to me in the body of a toothless beggar and I'd still want you."

She giggled. "A nice sentiment, even if you're not sincere in that." Her green eyes danced. "And you certainly don't want me to take you up on it."

Dare grunted as the petite goddess abruptly shoved him backwards onto the bed. "Now that we've got that settled," she purred, shucking off her robes to reveal a lithe body with small, pert breasts and equally small pink nipples standing out proudly. "Time to experience all the sensations this new body is capable of. I'm going to take the lead the first time, if you don't mind."

"I don-" he started.

The Outsider threw herself on top of him, straddling him as she kissed him fiercely. Her tongue invaded his mouth with hungry eagerness, finding his and furiously wrestling with it. Meanwhile she began grinding herself roughly against his stomach, as if her panty-clad pussy was a garment she needed to scrub against his washboard abs.

She was certainly wet enough.

Dare ran his hands up her delicate body, her flawless pale skin soft and warm beneath his fingers. He cupped her small breasts, tweaking her hard little nipples, and she moaned and pressed her chest against his hands, moving faster.

"Oh Me, I've waited for this," the Outsider panted, perfect doll-like face scrunched up in pleasure and hungry need. She abruptly threw herself next to him on the bed, squirming to pull off her sodden panties.

The scent of arousal hit him in a heady wave, sweet and musky with a hint of the ambrosia he'd tasted from the goddess's alabaster mannequin form. He didn't know how it was possible, but his already straining cock twitched eagerly.

She grinned at him. "Don't I have the sweetest smelling pussy? I bet you'd love a taste."

Dare opened his mouth to answer, and the Outsider shoved her lacy green panties, drenched in her sweet nectar, inside before he could speak. His eyes widened, and he moaned against the soft, sodden cloth filling his mouth.

The taste of her was overwhelming, as was the eroticism of the situation.

"Suck them clean, Dare," his lover teased, green eyes sparkling as she got to work pulling off his pants and underwear. "It's only fair, since I made such a mess of them because of you."

Dare sucked at the drenched cloth and got a surprising amount of her love juices, sweet and slippery on his tongue. He savored her delicate flavor, wanting more.

"Good," the Outsider said, setting the undergarments aside. "But I hope you don't think you're done." She smirked and pointed at her thighs, which glistened with her nectar almost to the knees. "You need to clean this up as well."

He obligingly pushed her onto her back on the bed and gently parted her legs. As he began lapping at her thighs he kept his eyes locked on her beautiful pink pussy. It was flushed with arousal, her small labia pouting open to offer tantalizing glimpses of her glistening interior.

Dare was desperate to taste her at the source, to push his tongue into that soft, warm tunnel. To mash his nose into her clit and feel her buck against his face and squirt all over him as he drove her to new heights of pleasure.

Or just dispense with the formalities completely and slam his cock into her right now, so he could feel her vise-like, velvety walls rippling around his shaft as soon as possible.

Instead he kept licking, taking his time and savoring the feel of her soft skin beneath his tongue.

The key to real pleasure was buildup.

The Outsider moaned and squirmed, clutching his head and

pulling him eagerly towards her. Her nectar flowed freely, making a damp patch on the blanket beneath her, and he finally dove in to avoid further waste, lapping at her slit from base to clit and filling his mouth with her ambrosia.

"Yeeesssss!" she squealed, slender thighs closing tight around his head as she pushed herself eagerly against his questing tongue. "Oh, my lover, it's like fireworks going off!"

Dare got to work on her throbbing little button, making her squirm and buck even harder, until finally she went stiff as a board with a deep moan and he felt her delicate lips winking against his mouth in orgasm.

He had just a few seconds to savor the pleasure he'd brought his divine lover when she abruptly grabbed his shoulders and dragged him higher up the bed, pushing him onto his back again and climbing on top of him. He felt her folds wrap around his tip, soft and warm and impossibly tight, and with another whimper she pushed herself down on him.

"Oh, Me," she panted with a grin of pure bliss. "Your behemoth fits my tiny pussy perfectly. It's stretching me just like I want!"

Incredibly, that seemed true. Dare wouldn't have thought it was possible she could get his massive girth inside her small entrance without effort, but she was so drenched with arousal, and so relaxed and open as she accepted him inside her, that he penetrated her easily.

They both made sounds of pleasure as she slid down his length, stretching her tiny walls obscenely. He could see the outline of his tip moving up her flat tummy, an incredibly erotic sight, and then he bottomed out with a few inches of his cock left outside her.

"Now, my lover," the Outsider panted, quivering over him. "Hold off as long as you can before you pour your seed in me and give us a beautiful son."

As he was still processing that mind-blowing statement, she began bouncing up and down on him as if she wanted to break his cock, or maybe her own delicate little body, writhing in pleasure with warm nectar constantly flowing from her small pussy stretched obscenely over his girth.

"Oh Me!" she gasped. "I've wanted this, Dare, and it's everything I've hoped for!"

Dare groaned and couldn't help but involuntarily push his hips up against her, matching her rhythm. "Are you sure Ireni can-"

"*I* can take it," the goddess gasped. "She wouldn't want to, but I do." She increased her pace even more, rolling her hips slightly as if trying to get him to stretch and press against every inch of her impossibly soft, tight walls. "You can be as rough as you want with me, and I can take it. And don't worry, Ireni understands and agrees. She's even enjoying it all from the background . . . as you might say on Earth, this isn't her first rodeo. And our body will be fine . . . we're not made of glass."

She abruptly tensed with a sharp intake of breath, pausing her desperate riding to almost violently hump the tip of his cock against a certain part of her tight pink pussy. "So, so very good . . ." she whimpered through gritted teeth.

Moments later the Outsider squealed and fell forward on him, wrenching his cock almost painfully along with her. He felt her tight walls close around his girth in a crushing embrace, and arousal drenched him as she had a powerful climax.

The petite redhead clutched desperately at his chest as she rode it out, wide eyes glazed with pleasure. "I want it rough," she moaned. "I want to feel it all! All the sensations, as powerfully as I can. They're, oh Me, they're so overpowering." Her hand slipped between their joined bodies and found her little clit, mauling it mercilessly, and her muscles became taut as a bowstring as her small pussy somehow became even tighter, milking his cock desperately.

That was as much as he could take, and in spite of his best efforts he felt his balls surging. "Goddess!" he gasped, grabbing her small, perfect ass and pushing her down against his cock, while at the same time pushing his throbbing tip desperately against her core as he released inside her in one of the longest and most intense orgasms he'd ever had.

"Daaaare!" she screamed when she felt it, drenching his crotch, stomach, and thighs again with an even more powerful climax. Her limbs seemed to abruptly lose strength and she slumped down on top of him, velvety walls rippling powerfully around him as she sought to milk every single drop of his seed.

Dare held the trembling woman, rubbing her back as she whimpered against his chest.

In spite of the Outsider's insistent claims, her first time seemed to have worn her out. She looked content to just lay on him as her tight walls lovingly held his cock, which remained hard in spite of his recent orgasm. He kissed her soft auburn hair, her flushed forehead, her delicate nose, and finally her plump rosebud lips, gentle and loving.

"I love you," she murmured. "Thank you for giving me this. Not just in the bedroom but out there, able to explore the world with you and Ireni."

"I can't wait for the adventures we'll share together," Dare panted, wrapping an arm around her and dropping his head back to rest on the bed as he basked in post-orgasmic bliss.

The goddess giggled throatily and rocked her hips, moving him tantalizingly inside her warm softness. "So many adventures," she agreed. Her voice caught with sudden joy. "Including raising the son you just put in us. And more children to come in our long, blissful lives together."

"That sounds perfect," he murmured, holding her close and gently caressing her delicate little body.

To his disappointment she only wanted to cuddle for a minute or so before abruptly climbing off him, giving a soft sigh of regret as his hard cock plopped out of her gaping pussy, their combined juices flowing down her thighs.

"Done already?" Dare asked, heart sinking.

The Outsider smirked at him. "Done? We're just getting started . . . did you forget you have to leave tomorrow on a long trip, and all our lovers want to be with us tonight?"

He could only grin like an idiot in response; the sex had been so mind-blowing he almost *had* forgotten. "Still, I want to give you more attention than that. This is our first time, after all."

She grinned. "I don't mind. I was in so much of a hurry to be with you I just wanted to get you naked and let you screw me like a ballista bolt. But now it's time to include the others." She giggled. "So they can all watch while you screw me like a ballista bolt."

Oh hell yes.

The goddess started for the door to invite the rest of the harem in, but after a step paused and looked back. "One thing, Dare."

Dare sat up at her solemn expression. "Yes, my love?"

"Like I said, I love it rough. I love it dirty. I want all the experiences we can share together. But only me." She waved at her sexy body. "Ireni is my favored servant, not to mention very sweet and somehow unexpectedly innocent in spite of her past. And she's gone to very great lengths and made great sacrifices to help us obtain our desire."

She pointed an accusing finger his way. "You're going to court her as she deserves, and when she's ready you're going to give her a magical first time, complete with a gourmet dinner and candies and candles and flower petals and whatever. Or we'll both be displeased at you."

He was fine with that. "I only want her to be happy," he assured her. "If that's what she wants I'll spare no expense or effort, and if she wants me to spend the night buried between her thighs working tirelessly to give her endless orgasms, I'll savor the experience."

"That's what I like to hear," the Outsider said in satisfaction, then glowered at him. "And listen very carefully, because this is important . . . with her you *will* be gentle and loving. Understood?"

"Of course," Dare said, a bit confused. "That's how I want to be with her anyway. And I'd like to be gentle and loving with you, sometimes, too."

She made a face. "Boring." With a laugh she playfully slapped his leg. "Be right back with the others. You just lay back and rest . . .

we're going to be putting you through your paces tonight, my lover."

The goddess again made for the door, then again turned back after just a step. "And Dare?" she said, almost shyly. "Thank you for treating me as an equal, even though you know who and what I am. I'd hoped you would since people from your world, or at least your country, tend to act that way no matter what the rank or position of the person. But it's a relief to know."

"I suppose that is nice in a lover," he said.

"You have no idea." The Outsider grimaced. "The way my followers, and even anyone else, loses their minds when I contact them, was always too much. I knew that if I tried to take even the most arrogant or stupid of them as a lover, they'd just end up licking my feet and treating me like glass when I finally convinced them to take me. If they even would. Which is why I've never done this before."

Dare grinned at her. "Well, you can always count on me to ride you like an animal until you're a quivering mess on the bed, weak as a kitten and mewling like one too."

She offered him a wicked smile of her own. "I'll hold you to that." She teasingly wiggled her sexy little ass and disappeared out the door.

* * * * *

Since Dare and his lovers all shared the huge bed, pretty much every night and most mornings became fun time, with a least a few of his lovers wanting sex and the rest of the girls playing with each other.

Leilanna and Se'weir especially were popular, since they were so soft and cuddly. And although the dusk elf grew indignant whenever she was described that way, she never complained about the attention. Pella wanted to spend at least a little time with everyone, as did the Outsider, and everyone wanted to spend time with Zuri because she was so tiny, sweet, and adorable.

That night, however, was less a handful of relaxed couplings and lots of cuddling and more an outright orgy.

All of his girls wanted him inside them, often in quick succession as they piled on top of each other presenting their glistening entrances, or pressed together side by side in a line for him to work his way down. And the ones who weren't actively participating in the fun played with him and the others who were.

It was intense, it was incredible, and it was gloriously exhausting. He didn't think he'd ever been pushed to his limits like that as they teased one orgasm after another out of him, milking him again and again in their soft little mouths and pussies.

While Dare did his best to satisfy all his lovers, since he felt like he hadn't given Zuri and Pella as much attention in bed as the others recently, he did his best to more than make up for it that night. Especially since with the baby it had been so long since he'd really had these moments with his goblin lover and he wanted to make up for lost time.

And the fact that his dog girl lover's beautiful body, with her big round pregnant belly and enlarged, sensitive breasts, were so ridiculously sexy he had trouble keeping his hands off her. Especially since her pregnancy had made her even more horny than usual, and she squirmed delightedly at his touch, eagerly begging for more.

After a few hours Dare found himself begging too, for mercy as he was finally drained dry, too exhausted and sated to continue. His lovers laughingly relented, and he found himself in a pile of soft, warm bodies cuddling close, all wanting to hold him, with his head resting on Se'weir's pillowy breasts.

He'd spent the entire night telling them he loved them, and doing his best to show it, but he had to repeat it again as he rubbed Pella's belly and cupped the Outsider's sweet little ass. "I love you all more than words can say."

His girls murmured their own loving responses, kissing and caressing him and each other, and he fell asleep to the sound of them all breathing deeply in contented slumber around him.

Chapter Eleven

Promise

Dare kept to his word about hurrying south.

He didn't push himself quite as hard as he had on the trip back to Nirim Manor after his fight with Ollivan, making sure on this journey to get enough sleep and make better use of his horses. But he used Cheetah's Dash and ran a lot of the time, saving riding for when he wanted to rest and eat.

He managed to shave a day off the trip, arriving at Rosie's clearing in the late afternoon on the fifth day since setting out.

Dare's heart couldn't help but lighten at the sight of the adorable plant girl through the trees, as always naked as the day she stepped out of her budding flower; even though they'd only met a few times and been intimate for only a few days, he was surprisingly fond of her. Probably because she was so sweet and friendly.

Not to mention a ridiculously sexy lover.

True to her word, even though it had only been two months she was heavily pregnant, on the verge of giving birth. In spite of that her petite, gymnast's body looked just as slender as ever, aside from of course her swollen belly and maybe slightly enlarged breasts.

Although her soft skin, the color of new leaves in spring, had also darkened to a healthy fern green and she had the beautiful glow of impending motherhood.

Rosie turned at his greeting, and her adorable pixie-like features brightened with pure delight. "Dare!" she squealed, bolting towards him with an energy and spryness he wouldn't have expected from a woman about to go into labor. "You came!"

When she reached the limits of the stem extending from behind her like a tail, connecting her to her flower, she strained against it and held out her arms.

Dare hopped off his horse and ran forward to sweep her up in a gentle hug, kissing the top of her head. "I promised I would," he replied.

"Well yeah, but it's still great that you did." She buried her head in his chest with a contented sound. "It's good to see you."

"It's good to see you too," he said, running his fingers through her silky, fern-like hair, which grew in verdant curls and kinks down to the small of her back. It had tiny flowers growing as if woven in and remained as soft and fragrant as ever, with a fresh green smell reminiscent of summer and a flower garden. "You look even more beautiful than I remember. Motherhood suits you."

The plant girl giggled. "Thank you." She kissed him warmly, lips soft and moist and tasting of flowers and honey. But it was more in friendship than with any passion. "Although if you're hoping to have some fun I'm going to have to disappoint you."

He grinned and rested a hand on her taut belly. "Well yeah, most women aren't feeling too frisky just days before producing a seed."

She smirked. "True. But with florans we completely lose interest in sex about a month into the pregnancy, and don't get it back until about a month after sending our seed floating off to find a new place to put down roots." She nuzzled his chest again. "But I'd be happy to cuddle."

"That sounds great," Dare said. "Give me a few minutes." He tended the horses and set them out to graze, then she wrapped her arms around his waist and led him back towards her flower.

"It *is* great to see you," Rosie murmured, kissing his shoulder. "It's been lonely here since Enellia flew south to the Lepid Flower Fields."

"I can imagine," he said, feeling a surge of longing for his own family waiting back home. He hoped they were safe. "How was she when she left, and the baby? Healthy?"

She grinned. "Feeling great and looking forward to being a mommy. And I'm sure she's doing great now that she's returned home. The flower fields are a beautiful, paradisaical place." She patted his stomach. "Your child will be happy there with her, and hopefully they'll come visit us soon."

"I hope so." Dare patted her round tummy in turn, grinning back. "How about you? Do you know when the seed will come?"

"Soon. Maybe today or tomorrow, or the next day at the latest."

"I can't wait to see it." He kissed her cheek fondly. "I'm here for whatever you need, even if it's just moral support through the process."

Rosie gave him an odd look. "Wait, you aren't planning to stick around while I produce the seed, are you?"

Dare hesitated. "I, um, well if you want me to, of course it would be my honor. Where I'm from the father is often there for the birth. It's a beautiful event to be celebrated." He smiled wryly. "Although I'm aware that's seen as odd here."

"Uh huh no, I appreciate the offer but I don't want you there. That would definitely be weird." She laughed easily as she retracted her vine, making a rope they could climb to get up into her flower. "Honestly, most men just pollinate me and I either never see them again, or they wait until I've sent the seed off and am receptive again before returning to pollinate me some more. None have shown any interest in my childbirth or our daughter's life."

"So you wanted me to come for the childbirth, but you don't want me to be here for it?" Dare asked, puzzled, as he climbed up after her.

The plant girl sobered, not answering as they made their way down the silky soft, firm petals to where they met in a super soft floor. She settled down there crosslegged in a way he found highly distracting, and patted the ground beside her. He sat, and she leaned against him with a sigh and pulled his arm around her.

"Actually," she confessed, "the reason I asked you to come back is because I want you to take the seed back to your manor and plant her there."

Dare blinked. "Don't you usually send them to fly free?"

Rosie grimaced. "Well yes, but that's just because it's their best hope for finding a place where they can grow without competing with me for sunlight or mates to pollinate us." She looked up at him with big green eyes, far more lifelike and sparkling than you might expect for an animated plant. "But I figured you'd want our daughter to be close to you, and honestly I think it would be wonderful for her to be with her brothers and sisters. And her aunts or co-mothers, or however it is you handle terms like that in your harem."

He felt a surge of relief and happiness at the thought that he'd get to be part of his plant girl child's life after all. When Rosie and Enellia had asked him to impregnate them, and informed him that fathers weren't really part of child-rearing for their species (as seemed to be the case for a surprising number of races on Collisa), he'd felt a bit sad about it.

"It would be my honor to plant our daughter on my manor grounds," he said, affectionately rubbing her tummy. "Leilanna is especially skilled with plants, and I'm sure she'll take great care of her."

"That's good to hear," Rosie said with a grin. "Although I wouldn't worry too much . . . you have to mess up pretty badly to hinder a floran's growth."

"Well just in case, what can I expect with a plant girl child?"

She laughed. "Well first off, florans have a sort of passed on knowledge when it comes to language and interacting with people, and instinctive habits for survival. As well as fragments of our ancestors' memories. Which is nice since we often grow on our own, sometimes never even meeting other people until we're grown and ready to have seeds of our own."

The plant girl stared off into the distance, smiling fondly as she rubbed her belly, seemingly lost in memories. "It's an interesting life . . . we're better at dealing with solitude than most, although of course we get lonely and are always happy to meet new people. Our daughter will have a delightful time surrounded by family, and honestly I'm a bit jealous of her."

"Well I'll be sure to pass along messages from her," Dare promised.

The thought made her beam with gratitude. "Thank you," she said, cuddling closer. Her tone became businesslike. "Anyway, after the seed finds an ideal spot to grow and puts down roots, our daughter will put out her first shoot. For the first few years she'll basically just be a giant plant, aware of what's going on around her and able to hear what people say, but not able to speak."

A sudden thought occurred to him. "What if I needed to wait a bit to plant the seed, because there was some danger? How long could she wait?"

Rosie looked alarmed. "Is there some danger?" she asked anxiously.

Dare briefly explained his fight with Ollivan and his fears the man would seek revenge. "I'll fight to the death to protect our daughter, of course," he promised. "But I just want to make sure the danger's over before I plant her."

His plant girl lover relaxed a bit. "I wouldn't worry too much. Florans are more resilient than you'd expect, and people usually don't take notice of us as a target. Some of my ancestors grew in cities that have been burned to the ground, but they were left untouched."

She patted his stomach. "If you're really worried, though, as long as a seed is kept cool and dry and in the dark it can last for years. Decades." She pouted. "I hope you won't wait that long, though . . . most of my kind don't get to have much communication with each other, and I'd like to have lots of correspondence with our daughter."

"Don't worry, I'll plant her as soon as possible." Dare affectionately rubbed her pregnant belly. "What else do I need to know?"

"Well after you plant her, sometime within 2 to 4 years her flower will bloom, and she'll basically be a toddler, although one who can talk in full sentences. She'll continue to grow and develop about the same as a girl of any other race after that. Her mind will develop the same as any child's, but as she gets older, especially when she reaches adulthood, she'll start to unlock memories from her ancestors."

Rosie grinned up at him. "I trust you and your harem will see to her education same as your other children, reading and writing and all of that. And also ladylike comportment and proper manners."

"Absolutely," Dare promised solemnly. "Thank you for letting me be part of her life."

The plant girl climbed into his lap and cuddled him even closer, sounding almost plaintive. "No, thank *you* for giving her something more than just growing up alone in some random forest clearing, hoping people will stumble across her and they'll be friendly."

"Oh, Rosie," he said, hugging her sympathetically.

She giggled at him, her brief moment of melancholy disappearing. "Don't feel bad for me, I'm happy here." She poked his chest with a small green finger. "Just be sure to keep your promise to visit me often and let me be as much a part of my daughter's life as I can be."

"I will," he promised.

A peaceful silence settled for a while as they cuddled. Finally Rosie stirred eagerly. "Speaking of visits, how are Pella and Zuri and Leilanna doing? Is Pella showing? Has Zuri had her baby yet?" Her lips curled up impishly. "And have you guys met even more beautiful women to join your harem?"

Dare sheepishly rubbed the back of his neck. "I have, actually. And yes, Pella's showing so much she's probably going to have twins or even triplets. And Zuri's had her baby, a goblin girl we've named Gelaa."

"Ooh, tell me everything!" the plant girl said, cuddling closer and looking up at him expectantly.

He was only too pleased to give a report on his lovers and the baby and everything happening at Nirim Manor, going into detail. Rosie listened eagerly, seeming to enjoy every tidbit. Especially about Pella.

As night fell she closed the petals of her flower to make a snug room for them, and Dare slept blissfully with his arms wrapped around her warm little body; honestly, it was some of the most peaceful rest he'd ever enjoyed.

He had a bit of a rude awakening early the next morning, though, as the petals opened over his head to let in bright sunlight and his petite lover leaned over him, poking his shoulder. "Time to go," she said gently but firmly. Her face was flushed and she was breathing hard, almost panting. "I'm ready to produce the seed."

Dare scrambled to his feet, awkward and excited and terrified all at once. Same as he'd been with Gelaa's birth. "All right, I'll give you some privacy." He hesitated. "Is there anything you-"

"Go!" she said, dropping into a squat and breathing harder. "I'll be fine, this is an easy process. It's just really intense and requires my full concentration."

He obliged her and quickly climbed out of the flower, dropping to the ground below.

Almost as soon as he was gone the petals curled up to close tightly again. Just before they formed a tight seal he heard her voice. "No need to hang around waiting! How about you go fight monsters or something and come back tonight!"

The message was pretty clear; Rosie wanted to be left alone to have their seed.

Well, there was another visit Dare could make since he was in the area. He left the clearing behind, leaving the horses to continue grazing peacefully in the safety near the floran flower, and headed north a short ways.

Soon enough he stepped into another clearing, bowing his head out of respect for the dead.

He would've expected the garden Pella had so painstakingly cultivated over four years to be overgrown and shabby after being left untended since their last visit, but to his surprise it was as lovely as he remembered.

Even more so, if he was being honest.

Walking along the neat gravel paths, he admired the beautiful flowers and other ornamental plants. There were some new saplings growing beside the path, shade trees he thought, and near the grave an arbor had been created with a wide bench.

Dare settled on the bench, looking at the grave. There was now another gravestone alongside the one Pella had lovingly created for Lord Kinnran, a beautifully polished slab of marble carved with the details of the baron's life and a tender message from his loved ones.

"Perhaps some good came of Pella going back to your family after all," he quietly told the grave. "It's good to see them caring for your final resting place in her absence."

"Oh!" a feminine voice said with a gasp from the edge of the clearing.

Dare leapt to his feet, feeling a surge of chagrin at being caught here. As if he was an unwelcome interloper. He saw a familiar young woman standing there, one hand to her mouth in surprise, while behind her hulked a Level 22 Fighter who had the clear appearance of a bodyguard.

It was the old Lord Kinnran's daughter, Amalisa. The only one of Pella's family who'd been kind to her when she returned to them after her master's death. His Eye showed her as "Human, adult female. Class: Enchanter, Spellwarder subclass Level 15. Attacks: Arcane Bolt, Mana Bubble, Warp." So she'd apparently gained three levels since he saw her last; that was fast.

"Oh!" she said again, big hazel eyes wide with surprise. "It's you."

"I'm sorry for intruding, my Lady," he said quickly, dropping into a polite bow. "I was in the area and wished to pay my respects to your father. I'll go."

"No, please don't!" the young woman motioned to her bodyguard to stay back and quickly moved to join him, raising the skirt of her long, flowing light green dress. She gave him a tentative but heartfelt smile as she paused a few feet away, a bit nervously tucking a strand of her long dark brown hair behind her ear. "It's kind of you to come, even though you didn't know him."

That smile transformed her face, and Dare couldn't help but stare for a moment.

He remembered her as being a bit mousy, skinny and slightly awkward if kindhearted and passionate in defense of her loved ones. But she seemed to have matured since he'd last seen her; she was still willowy, but her curves were more noticeable and she had a lady's grace and poise. Although her elegant dress no doubt helped with that.

More than that, she looked more relaxed and confident, even happy. Her features were still pretty at best, but there was a warmth and kindness there that he was drawn to. She reminded him of a girl who'd lived down the street from him growing up that he'd had a crush on for years, although in spite of their solid friendship he'd never had the courage to tell her his true feelings.

She had that same sweet, innocent girl next door air about her.

Dare realized he was staring and quickly turned his eyes to the grave, feeling his cheeks flush. "Pella loves him, and I respect him for her sake. And also for the fact that he was kind to her when he could've been cruel . . . she's never had anything but good to say about him and her time with him."

"Yes, he was a good man," Amalisa murmured, expression sad and tears swimming in her big eyes. "I grieve that he was taken from us too soon."

She turned to her bodyguard. "I believe I'm very safe with Master Dare, Amin. You may return to camp."

The older man gave him a narrow look of clear warning, then bowed. "Yes, Lady Amalisa." He turned and clanked away into the woods.

The young woman made her way through the garden to join him paying respects at the grave, and a slightly awkward silence settled. Then the young noblewoman turned to him abruptly, brightening. "So did Pella come with you? Can I talk to her?"

Dare shook his head regretfully. "She's far enough along in her pregnancy to discourage such a trip."

"Oh, she told me last time we talked that she was having puppies!" She clapped her hands excitedly and her eyes shone.

"That's wonderful! I always thought it was a bit sad that Father wouldn't have puppies with her . . . she so obviously wanted them." She hesitated. "Or I guess I should ask, um, is it puppies?"

He chuckled. "Yes, going by her rate of development we're pretty sure."

The young woman smiled dreamily. "Oh, I would love to be there to see them when they're born. With such a beautiful mommy and handsome daddy they're going to be absolutely adorable." She blushed as she realized what she'd just said about him. "I'm sorry, that was very forward."

"It's all right." Dare smiled as he thought of his wonderful dog girl lover and the children they were having. "I can't wait to meet them, too. We already have a nursery prepared, and when we were renovating the manor Pella supervised painting and decorating it. The walls are covered in a beautiful mural of the nearby mountains, so they merge seamlessly with the view from the windows, except with a bright sun on the ceiling and fluffy clouds and rainbows and fanciful birds and butterflies."

Amalisa cooed as if picturing it, expression longing. "Oh, I wish I could be there to see it. I'd love to babysit the little dears. And I miss Pella so much." Her expression fell. "She's the only person who's been nice to me in a very long time, it seems like." She glanced after her departed bodyguard with a chuckle. "Aside from Amin, of course, but only because I pay him to be."

Dare felt a surge of guilt, thinking of the fright he'd given the poor girl that night he'd confronted Braley. He shifted uncomfortably. "Listen, I need to apologize for-"

"Threatening to kill my brother to protect Pella?" she said, expression twisting wryly. "Don't worry. I'd already guessed you were putting up a front for Braley and wouldn't have actually hurt him, even before Pella's last visit when she told me everything." She grimaced. "Although part of me wouldn't have blamed you for it if you had."

"I wouldn't have," he promised fervently. "I wouldn't dream of it, and not just because it would've broken Pella's heart. I don't like

211

hurting people if there's an alternative." He couldn't help but grit his teeth. "Although listening to your brother, hearing what he tried to do to the woman I love, it was harder not to want to beat him black and blue." For a start.

"I know." The young noblewoman scowled. "*He's* enough of a brute that he might believe you'd kill him even if it meant causing pain to the woman you love, since I could imagine him having no problems doing it himself."

She looked around forlornly. "After all, he banished me here."

"I'm sorry," Dare said. "What happened?"

Amalisa shook her head, expression bitter. "He never forgave me for taking Pella's side. After that he was really cold to me. I tried asking him a few times if I could come here and visit Father's grave, and finally he snapped that if I wanted to be here so much, I could stay here. He threw me from the house, and told the guards around Yurin I was forbidden from returning to his lands."

Dare couldn't say he was surprised; the man was a gaping asshole. "You deserve better," he said gently, resting a hand on her shoulder. "You're one of the kindest and gentlest people I've met, and Pella has told me a lot about the time you spent together . . . she misses you."

"I miss her too." Her big hazel eyes filled with tears. "I wish she'd come with you."

"So do I." He just hoped she and the others were safe back home, both from Ollivan and in their monster hunting.

A slightly awkward silence settled, then the young woman settled on the bench, patting the seat beside her. "You said you were in the area. What brings you here if your home is in Bastion?"

Dare coughed, cheeks heating slightly. "Pella's friend Rosie, a plant girl, lives not far away from here. We're, um, having a seed, and I came for the delivery. She wants me to plant our daughter at the manor so she can grow up with her family."

"Another child?" Amalisa's eyes twinkled, although her cheeks had taken on a fetching rosy hue as she blushed. "You've been busy."

Probably not a good idea to admit that by this point he had more than a dozen children on the way or already born across Haraldar. "It seems like you have as well," he said with a smile. "You're a few levels higher than when I last saw you."

The young nobleman blushed. "Thank you," she said. "Amin's been helping me." She grimaced. "I'm here around so many monster spawns anyway, and barred from going home. So I figured I might as well level up to where I can support myself with my profession, and not have to be dependent on Braley's dwindling generosity. Not to mention the materials I've been able to farm."

"So Amin knows the spawn points around here?"

"Up to Level 19," she said. "Even though he's 22 he won't touch the Level 20s or higher."

"Probably wise. They jump up sharply in difficulty."

"So I've heard." Amalisa gave him a keen look. "And at 30 as well?"

Dare chuckled wryly. "Yes, although in more manageable ways."

She bit her lip. "When last we met you were much lower level. Nine levels . . . and I thought Amin had been helping me level quickly."

"He has been, without a doubt." He gave her an encouraging smile. "I can't imagine leveling a combat subclass is easy."

The sweet noblewoman blushed a bit, looking pleased. "No, it isn't."

Another slightly awkward silence settled, and Dare cleared his throat. "Rosie told me to come back tonight after she's had the seed. I bet she'd be excited to meet a member of Pella's family if you want me to introduce you."

Amalisa brightened. "I'd love to! It's amazing to think she's made friends and is living her life now. I'm so happy for her."

He stood. "In that case, I'll leave you to pay your respects and find you this evening."

"Oh." She looked almost disappointed. "What did you plan to do?"

Dare gave her a crooked smile and shrugged. "Probably see if I can find some higher level monsters and farm them for a few hours. The grind never stops."

The young noblewoman returned his smile. "You're right. I should find Amin and get back to hunting monsters as well." She offered him her hand. "Until this evening then, Master Dare."

He took it and brushed his lips across the back of it, noting the blush that spread up her long, swanlike neck. "Until this evening, my Lady."

Chapter Twelve

Spark

Dare didn't want to stray too far, so when he found some monster spawns that were just high enough that he got some experience, even though it was drastically reduced, he got to farming.

It was only marginally better than sitting around twiddling his thumbs, but he picked up some loot at the same time. Still, he was happy to give up early and head back to Lord Kinnran's grave to pick up Amalisa.

She was wearing more practical leveling robes that sported a tear in the sleeve, which judging by the fresh blood and bandage underneath had happened during that day's leveling. "Don't worry," she said to his concerned look. "It's not bleeding and my hit points are already rising to near full."

Dare nodded, although he didn't think much of her bodyguard if he'd let a monster get at her in spite of his much higher level. "As a Spellwarder you're a hybrid offensive and support spellcaster, right? So no heals?"

"No heals," the young woman agreed. Then she jumped slightly. "How did you know my . . . oh, I guess Pella probably told you."

He didn't want her to think her friend had betrayed her secrets. "Actually, I have an ability that lets me tell people's class." It wasn't that he didn't trust her to know about Adventurer's Eye, he just didn't want to go through the rigamarole of trying to convince her of what should be impossible.

Maybe if they got to know each other better. "In any case, are you ready to go?" he asked.

Amalisa brightened. "Absolutely!" She turned to her glowering bodyguard. "Thank you, Amin, Dare will escort me for the remainder of the evening. I'll see you back in camp."

"My Lady," he said, bowing.

Dare led the way back to Rosie's clearing, where he found the flower still closed.

"Oh, it's beautiful," his companion said, staring at the giant plant in awe. "I've never met a plant girl before."

"Well hopefully producing the seed is going well and you'll see her soon." He headed over to the horses and checked on them, moving their pickets and preparing them to bed down for the night.

As he was doing that the pale pink flower in the center of the clearing gracefully opened, and Rosie appeared on one petal cradling a smooth dark brown object about the size of a coconut. Her stomach was as perfectly flat again as if she'd never been pregnant, which would probably inspire extreme jealousy in most women.

He couldn't help but notice that Amalisa was blushing at the sight of the naked plant girl, looking unsure whether to look away to be polite or whether that would be considered rude.

Rosie didn't seem to notice, her attention focused on the seed in her arms. "Look, Dare!" she said excitedly. "Our daughter!" Then she finally spotted Amalisa and stared at her curiously. "Oh hi, I haven't met you before. Are you one of Dare's lovers?"

The young noblewoman blushed even more furiously and glanced at him. "No!" she blurted, then looked chagrined at the strength of her response. "I mean, not that I think that would be a bad thing, it's just I'm, um, not."

Dare chuckled at her discomfiture. "Rosie, this is Amalisa Kinnran. She's the daughter of Pella's old master."

"Oh!" the plant girl said eagerly. "Pella talked about you all the time. She said you were an absolute sweetheart."

Amalisa blushed even harder, although she looked pleased. "Thanks. Were you good friends with Pella?"

"Yes, although it took time." Rosie smiled a bit sadly. "She was so heartbroken over your father's death, and spent so long grieving and staying by his grave. We're just glad she was finally able to move on with Dare."

"We?" the noblewoman asked, shooting Dare a curious look.

"Me and my girlfriend Enellia," the plant girl explained. "Although she traveled south to the Lepid Flower Fields to have Dare's baby and raise it there."

Amalisa was blushing again, although he wasn't sure if it was at Rosie's frank admission of having a female lover or at hearing that Dare had yet another child out there. "Lepids are butterfly girls, right?"

"Yep," the plant girl said happily. "The most beautiful butterfly girl in the world, which means the most beautiful girl, period. We always have so much fun pollinating." She paused, seeming to notice the other woman's discomfiture, and quickly changed the subject. "Would you like to hold the seed?"

"Can I?" the young woman said eagerly.

"Sure." Rosie gracefully hopped down to the ground, dancing over to place the smooth brown seed in Amalisa's arms.

"Oooh," Amalisa squealed, holding the seed gently. "She's so pretty. I bet she's going to be as beautiful as you."

Dare was torn between thinking it was a bit silly to make so much of a fuss over a big seed, and being well aware that that seed was his daughter and would grow into her once she was planted. It was messing with his head a little.

Especially since he was surprised to find himself already loving the little sprout, and kind of wanted to cuddle the seed like a baby as well. Rosie had said that the young plant would be aware of what was going on around her as she grew, and hear conversation, and he resolved to spend as much time with her as he could, talking to her.

"What are you going to name her?" the kindhearted noblewoman asked, finally handing the seed back to her mother.

Rosie shrugged and glanced at Dare. "My mother didn't name me, so I picked my own name. But I suppose we could give her one."

"How about Primrose?" he suggested.

Amalisa clapped her hands. "I like that, it's pretty."

"Or we could name her something not flower-related," the plant girl said, making a face. "How about Eloise?"

"I like that too!" the noblewoman said.

Rosie gave Dare an expectant look, and he smiled and rested a hand on the cool, smooth seed. "It's a beautiful name. Eloise it is."

"Yay!" Rosie tugged on her vine. "Come on, you guys, come up and join me in my flower." She took Amalisa's hand and tugged eagerly. "I want to hear all about Pella's time with you."

To be honest, he wanted to hear that too. His dog girl lover was always happy to talk about her past, even with the pain of losing her master, but it would be neat to hear another perspective.

The young noblewoman needed a bit of help climbing the vine, but once she was up she oohed and aahed at the beauty of the interior, as well as its softness and sweet floral scent. "You're so lucky to have this as your bedroom."

The plant girl giggled as she led the way down to the floor. "It's my body, you know. But thanks."

"Oh, right." Amalisa hesitated. "So what, um . . ."

"What's this specific part of me?" the petite green girl guessed with a grin, pointing at herself. Grinning, she stood up on tiptoes and whispered into the willowy noblewoman's ear. At which point Amalisa blushed even more furiously.

She was adorable.

Rosie seemed to have decided that being Pella's friend made her new guest her honorary friend as well, and as soon as Amalisa settled down on her mattress-like petal plopped right into her lap, still cradling the seed. For her part the prim noblewoman looked a bit discomfited by finding herself holding a naked woman, until she realized that the plant girl just wanted to cuddle.

It was an enjoyable evening. Dare got some food cooking for

him and Amalisa, then they all lounged on the pillowy flower floor chatting about Pella and a bit about themselves. It was pleasant and peaceful, and he was pleased to see the young woman coming out of her shell as she got more comfortable with them.

After dinner Amalisa looked up at the dark sky, yawning. "This was nice, but I should be getting back to my camp. If you could escort me, Master Dare?"

"Oh, you should just sleep here!" Rosie said. "It's nice and cozy once I shut the petals, and we can cuddle!"

Amalisa glanced uncertainly at Dare, and he realized the source of the well bred, proper woman's hesitation. He obligingly stood. "You know what, I should bed down near the horses to keep an eye on them. If you want to stay here then I'll bid you goodnight, ladies."

The plant girl giggled. "I'm a lady, huh? Princess Rosie of the pink flower?"

The young noblewoman looked relieved and inclined to accept Rosie's offer, but hesitated. "Amin will be wondering where I've gotten to."

"I'll let him know," Dare offered. "Go ahead and rest, my Lady." He nodded at her torn sleeve. "You've had a tiring day, I'd say."

"All right." Amalisa gave him a tentative smile. "Thank you, Master Dare."

With a bow he climbed out of the flower, leaving the two women to settle in to sleep.

Amin rose warily when Dare hailed him at his campfire. "Where's Lady Amalisa?" he demanded, hand going to his sword in spite of the fact that Dare was nine levels higher than him.

"Rosie offered to let her spend the night in her flower," Dare replied. "It's far more comfortable than a tent." He motioned to a log round across the fire from the older man. "May I?"

The Fighter glowered. "I suppose you'd best," he said. "I need to know your intentions for Lady Amalisa."

Dare blinked. He supposed he shouldn't be surprised that a bodyguard was protective of his charge, but the man's interest was clearly more personal; he genuinely cared for Amalisa. "My consort, Pella, was part of Lady Amalisa's family. *Is* part of her family, even though she's with me now. So I consider Lady Amalisa to be family as well. I wish only to be a friend and help her however I can."

"So you're not planning to bed her?" Amin demanded bluntly.

Wow. "I offer Lady Amalisa whatever she desires of me," he said carefully. "Although at the moment it doesn't seem likely."

The Fighter grunted. "If you hurt her in any way I'll find a way to slit your throat, no matter how much stronger you are."

"Then I have nothing to worry about from you, because the last thing I'd want is to cause her pain." Dare stood. "I'm going to bed now." He offered his hand.

After staring at it for a few seconds the older man grudgingly shook it, doing his best to crush the life out of his fingers in the process.

Dare returned his crushing grip and started away from the fire. But after a few steps he turned back. "It's not really my place to say, but thank you for taking care of her." If Braley had disinherited her and cast her out with nothing, the fact that the bodyguard had remained loyal spoke much about his character.

Amin grunted again and kept his gaze on the fire.

* * * * *

"Remember to find a big, open space with lots of sunlight to plant her," Rosie said as she gently wrapped Eloise's seed in the soft cloth Dare had given her, then tucked it into the top of his pack. "And be sure to visit her as often as you can and tell her that I love her and I'm thinking about her."

"I will," Dare promised solemnly, leaning in to kiss his petite lover's cheek. "And I'll visit you again when I can with news."

"And with some of Zuri's scrolls," the plant girl said, green eyes sparkling playfully. "I probably won't want another seed for a while, but I'm always up to have some fun. And if Enellia is here to visit we can all play together again."

Amalisa, standing nearby giving them space for their goodbyes, made an embarrassed sound, then blushed when he glanced at her.

Dare gave Rosie a final hug and kiss, then made his way over to the gentle young woman and offered his hand. "It was good to see you again, Amalisa. And under more friendly circumstances this time."

Rather than taking his hand she threw her arms around him and hugged him tightly, seeming reluctant to let go. "It was good to see you again too, Dare. Please send Pella my love, and that I hope she'll come visit as soon as she can. I'd love to meet her and the babies." Her eyes were shining, and she wore a look of intense longing.

At that he hesitated. "Listen," he blurted, "why don't you come back to the manor with me?"

Amalisa drew back, eyes wide. "What, um, are you asking?" she said hesitantly.

He blushed as he realized what she must be thinking; a logical assumption considering he had several lovers and had just invited her to his home. "Just that if you're exiled and have no home, Pella would never forgive me if I didn't invite you to come live with us. I'm sure she would be overjoyed to see you, and if it's what you want would love to be able to have you living where you could be together."

"Oh." The young noblewoman relaxed a bit, although she still looked a bit out of sorts.

Dare quickly continued, wanting to make her feel more comfortable. "And if you don't want to live at the manor we have guest houses nearby. You'd be more than welcome . . . you're part of Pella's family, which makes you our family."

To his surprise her eyes filled with tears and she threw her arms around him again. "Thank you," she murmured, burying her face in his chest. "I wanted to ask you if I could at least come for a visit, and maybe stay until the babies were born. But I didn't want to

221

intrude."

He awkwardly patted her back. "You could never intrude. I know Pella will want to share her home with you, and I'm sure the others will welcome you just as warmly." He hesitated. "Although I should warn you that there might be some danger."

Amalisa drew back, concerned. "What is it?"

He quickly explained his trouble with Ollivan. "So you see, the manor may not be completely safe for a while, although we'll do our best," he said when he finished.

Amalisa shook her head grimly. "He sounds like Braley, except more effective at being cruel with his power." She squared her shoulders. "It's all right. I'm facing trouble here too, and I trust you and Pella to keep me safe."

"What trouble?" Dare asked, feeling a sudden surge of protectiveness. "Is it Braley? Is he threatening you?"

"No." She laughed a bit bitterly. "I doubt he's given me a second thought since he banished me." She looked at the ground uncomfortably. "You'll probably think me spoiled, since you came from nothing and you know what it's like to struggle, while for me it's crushing me under."

"I only think the highest of you," he replied solemnly.

The sweet young woman gave him a tentative but brilliant smile, then took a shuddering breath. "I fled with little coin. I have no home, no employ, no prospects, and Amin's contract runs out in a month. I'm not sure what I'll do after that." She looked away. "Amin has been kind, and offered to take me in as his second wife. But while it's generous of him that-that's not what I want."

"All the more reason you should come stay with Pella and the rest of us." Dare patted her shoulder. "As an Enchanter I'm sure you'll be able to find business, especially in Bastion where so many adventurers have gear that needs improving. Including me and my companions . . . we'll always be happy to give you business."

He grinned. "And if nothing else, me and Pella could always take you on as a babysitter for the babies."

"Oh!" she said, brightening hopefully. "But I'd do that for free to spend time with the little dears." She squared her shoulders. "Thank you, Master Dare. I would be pleased to accept your offer."

Well, this might explain why Ireni had insisted he bring spare horses.

Dare gave Amalisa a hand up onto a horse, watching as she settled in sidesaddle with the same elegant grace Ireni showed. "Will you be okay like that?" he asked. "I'd like to push hard for Nirim Manor."

She gave him a warm smile as she stroked her mount's mane and murmured a friendly greeting to the patient animal. "Don't worry about me . . . I'd venture I'm a better rider than you. Father may never have taken me hunting monsters with him and Pella, but he loved riding his lands and hunting foxes and stags in the nearby wilds as well, and those he'd bring me along for. I practically grew up in a saddle."

Fair enough.

They swung by her camp, where his new companion quickly packed up her tent and other things. She had a surprisingly large bag of what he presumed were clothes and bedding, but it was comparatively light and the horses wouldn't have a problem with it.

Finally the sweet young woman gave her bodyguard a long hug. "Thank you for everything you've done for me," she said, tears in her eyes. "I'm releasing you from your contract . . . go back your family, and give them my love as well."

The older man gave Dare a suspicious look. "Are you sure, my Lady?"

"I'm sure," she patted his shoulder in reassurance. "Pella is his consort, which makes him family. And he's never been anything but a perfect gentleman."

"Aside from when he held your brother's own sword to his throat," the Fighter growled, although he didn't seem particularly offended by that action. "That could just as easily be you."

Dare looked at Amalisa's lovely, swanlike neck and couldn't help but think that the only thing he'd ever want to press against it were his lips. Then he felt his cheeks heat at the unbidden thought. "I give you my word as a landed gentleman and a prospective knight of Bastion," he said firmly. "I will protect Lady Amalisa with everything I have."

She gave her bodyguard another reassuring pat. "You see? Go back to your family with no fears, my friend. I'll be fine."

Amin looked a bit helpless. "I would've given my all to provide you with the life you deserve, my Lady," he murmured, gently taking her hand.

The young noblewoman's eyes softened and she patted his hand fondly. "I know. But that's not my path, nor is it yours."

She turned away hurriedly and mounted, nodding at Dare, and together they set off at a brisk pace.

True to Amalisa's word, she was a good rider. And she seemed just as eager to reach Nirim Manor and see her new home as he was, so she didn't complain about the pace.

When they were both riding he found her to be pleasant company as well, and enjoyed the time he spent with her. She seemed to enjoy it too, given how close she kept to him when possible.

Their evenings around the fire were relaxed and amiable, if brief before they both turned in to get an early start each morning. His new companion eagerly (if daintily) bolted down everything he made with obvious enjoyment and plentiful compliments; it was obvious she'd been starving for good, well made food since being banished from her home. Then they settled back in their seats (he'd made her a collapsible camp chair, of course) to talk for a while.

The gentle young woman had hinted at years of isolation and neglect following her father's death, and it was clear to see in her somewhat awkward social skills but eagerness for conversation. From how enthusiastically she spoke of Rosie, and how quickly she'd taken to the plant girl, he had to guess she'd been starved for human contact as well.

Luckily Pella was a great cuddler, and would no doubt be overjoyed to give her lonely friend all the affection she needed. As would the others, no doubt. Part of him even hoped that Amalisa might have some interest in him; she was sometimes reluctant to go to her tent in spite of her weariness, and he sometimes caught her staring at him, only to look away with a blush when their eyes met.

The thought of the sweet, innocent young women having feelings for him was a nice one, he had to admit. But he didn't complicate things with flirting while they were focused on traveling quickly.

In spite of Amalisa's best efforts she couldn't manage his best speeds, so it took another half day to reach Nirim Manor. It was just after dawn on the sixth day as he pushed his horse up a final rise to where he could catch his first view of home.

Only for his anticipation to turn to horror when he saw the billowing clouds of smoke rising from within the manor's walls.

No. Gods no! Every fear that had festered in Dare's heart since starting south smothered him in an instant, overpowered only by self-recrimination for leaving his loved ones behind, promise or no.

"Stay here!" he shouted at Amalisa, leaping off his horse and activating Cheetah's Dash. He shrugged out of his pack, carefully handling the precious seed inside, and gently handed it to her as he continued urgently. "If you see anyone but me or Pella headed your way ride like the wind for Jarn's Holdout!"

He would've suggested Terana, but Ollivan's cronies might've been lying in wait in that direction, or lurking within the town itself.

Without waiting for a response he unslung his bow and activated Rapid Shot, sprinting for the distant smoke cloud at speeds close to 40 miles an hour. He felt like he was flying, and crawling in slow motion at the same time.

He saw no signs of attackers around the walls, although that didn't much comfort him since it looked as if they were already inside. He had an arrow drawn and ready to loose when he burst through the gate, twisting and spinning to look for threats in all directions.

Instead, to his overpowering relief he saw Ilin poking around the charred, blackened eastern wall of the manor, while Zuri, Leilanna, Ireni, and Se'weir huddled nearby, his goblin lover holding their daughter tight to her breast.

They were coughing a bit from the smoke still drifting up from the recently extinguished fire, but there were no attackers to be seen, or any atmosphere of imminent threat.

Dare relaxed his arrow in the string but still held it ready in one hand as he went straight to Zuri and the baby, wrapping his free arm around them protectively. At his arrival his other lovers huddled around him, all doing their best to hold him close.

"Is Gelaa okay?" he asked anxiously, brushing the baby's soft cheek as she squirmed and wailed plaintively. "Did she breathe any smoke?"

"She's fine, my mate," his goblin lover soothed. "Leilanna acted quickly to save the house, breaking the storage tanks on the roof and directing the water with wind spells to put out the fires."

"What about you?" He looked around at his lovers. "All of you. Are you all right?"

"No one was harmed." Zuri opened her shirt and put Gelaa to her breast, who calmed and began to quietly nurse.

He breathed a bit more easily at the peaceful sight in the midst of the chaos. "What happened here?"

"Ollivan's weaselly squire, Dorias," Ireni said grimly, resting her head against his arm. "We think he was here to scout the manor for some future mischief, but when he saw an opportunity he set fire to it."

Dare cursed. "What about the goblin sentries? Did they give warning?"

Se'weir shifted, equal parts guilty and angry. "None. Goblins have excellent night vision and should've easily seen any humans blundering about in the darkness, but we saw no fire signals, heard no horns." She shivered, huddling against him. "Only the terror of

226

waking up to our home on fire."

He grit his teeth as he wrapped an arm around her and rubbed her shoulder. "We'll get to the bottom of what went wrong there when we have the time. Where is Dorias now?"

"He fled northwest towards Terana," Ilin said, joining them. "Pella's chasing him."

Dare didn't like the idea of his dog girl lover going into danger. Dorias himself probably wouldn't be a threat, five levels lower than her and with a crafting main class. And as a Tracker she'd be able to run him down easily.

But if Ollivan and more of his cronies were lurking around, and the squire had rejoined them, the group would be more than Pella could handle. Hopefully she'd be wary of the possibility.

Still, he immediately began disentangling himself from his lovers to go after her. "How long?"

"Ten minutes," Leilanna said. "She was able to activate Run Down, so he couldn't have gotten far before she caught up to him."

Dare nodded grimly. "You should all take what you need and head to safety. Amalisa Kinnran came north with me to stay as a guest . . . at the sight of the smoke I left her on the rise west of here. She'll be skittish, and I told her to run if anyone but me or Pella approached her, but see if you can pick her up and all head for the mountains for now."

"We'll probably be fine here," Ireni said. "The fire damage looks frightening, but it barely even touched the inside of the house. And Dorias is long gone."

She'd assured him they'd be safe if he left, too. And while technically they were all still fine, in his current mood he wasn't inclined to split hairs. "Just go, please!" Without waiting for a response he bolted back out the gate and went after Pella.

He found her after only fifteen minutes of travel, standing over two prone bodies near two skittish horses.

One must've been Dorias's companion, a Level 23 Skirmisher, and was merely bound hand and foot, with a few bruises from his capture.

As for the squire, Pella had beaten the shit out of him.

The man's face was almost unrecognizable beneath bruises and abrasions, eyes nearly swollen shut and missing teeth. The rest of him wasn't looking much better, showing cuts and burns from the lasso used to bring him down and likely used in the beating as well.

Dare could imagine the gentle dog girl's towering fury at seeing her loved ones threatened. He was just glad she hadn't killed the squire; he'd be a useful witness against Ollivan once they got him to talk.

"Dare!" Pella shouted when she saw him, lovely features sinking into deep relief. She gave Dorias a last kick before running to Dare and throwing her arms around him, holding him tight and trembling in his arms.

Her round belly, even bigger than before, strained her leather armor, and he felt an immediate surge of concern at her running around fighting in her condition. "Are you okay?" he demanded, anxiously running his hands over her. "Are the babies okay?"

"We're fine." His normally gentle lover's soft brown eyes flashed with dangerous fury. "Which is more than I can say for these two, once I'm done with them." She gave him a significant look. "They have questions to answer."

Ah. It looked as if she intended to be the bad cop. Or the worse cop, since Dare was in no mood to play good cop himself after what Dorias had done.

The Skirmisher thrashed as they approached, seeing their grim resolve. "Please, show mercy!" he begged desperately. "I'm not your enemy, I'm just a hireling!"

Dare spun his spear around and pressed the sharp tip to the man's chest to pin him to the ground, just short of breaking his skin. Or at least not much. "Hired by Ollivan to burn down my house with my family inside?" he snarled.

"No!" the Skirmisher squealed. "I had no part in the fire, and my master gave no such orders! It was all Dorias! I didn't even know the stupid fuck was going to do that! I was just sent with him to scout your manor."

"And that makes it better?" Dare said coldly. "Just left to scout a house full of pregnant women and a baby so you could prepare to attack it?" He leveled his spear at the man's throat. "Not another word until we're ready to get to you."

The man went ashen and swallowed, meekly keeping silent.

Pella was already working on Dorias, rolling him over and slapping him back to something resembling alertness in his current sorry state. "Where's Ollivan?" she growled, drawing her long knife and brandishing it near his eye.

Dorias coughed, all his focus on the weapon. "I-I don't know what you're talking about," he stammered.

She raised the knife and slashed it down between his legs, close enough to his crotch to cut the cloth of his pants. "I'll repeat the question after I cut off your balls, to see if you have the same answer," she snarled.

Dare was confident his gentle lover was bluffing, but in her current wrath even he had a sliver of uncertainty that she'd follow through on her threat.

The man who'd tried to burn down their home with women and a baby inside had a lot more than a sliver of uncertainty; a dark patch spread over his crotch as he pissed himself in terror. "Okay, okay!" he squealed. "My master is back in Redoubt. He wanted me to scout this place out, see how hard it would be to attack it and take you all out. I'm here alone with my companion."

Dare whipped his spear around to prod the Skirmisher in the throat again. "That true?" he demanded. "Anyone else with you?"

"Just us!" the man gasped, eyes wild. "We were supposed to return Redoubt with our findings."

Dare turned back to the squire, who was squirming away from the knife still buried centimeters from his balls. "What if he did attack? What could he bring against us?"

Dorias somehow found a sneer in spite of his terror. "He

wouldn't need anyone. At your levels he could take you all out on his own as long as you didn't ambush him like a coward again."

"That wasn't the question," Dare said coldly, nodding to Pella. She pulled her lips back to bare her teeth ferociously as she yanked her knife free and raised it.

"Half a dozen people!" the weaselly man blurted, kicking his bound legs desperately to get away from her. "All above Level 25. Two or three above 30. Maybe more, if he hires mercenaries."

That wasn't great news but it could be worse. Especially if they still had a few weeks to level and prepare ambushes and traps. "And what about if you fail to return?" Dare asked. "What would he do?"

The Skirmisher whimpered in terror.

Dorias went ashen, swallowing several times. "I-I . . ." He closed his eyes. "Mercy, please! I only acted on his orders!"

"Liar!" the Skirmisher shouted. "No one ordered you to set fire to the place, you're just a stupid vindictive fuck!"

Dare waved the man to silence, attention on the squire. "I can offer you justice in Terana if you answer our questions," he growled. "And you should be grateful for that, because I could just as easily leave you and your buddy in a shallow grave and nobody would know."

Dorias went limp in defeat. "If we don't return he'll probably send more scouts. He wouldn't waste his time coming all the way here unless he knew what he'd find."

"Good." That would buy them even more time before further trouble, hopefully. Dare looked over at Pella. "We should get these two up to Terana to face justice for their crimes. I sent everyone else west then south towards the mountains in case there were further threats . . . do you want to take the horses and go fetch them while I guard these two?"

His fiercely protective lover looked doubtful. "And leave the manor undefended?"

"Better than being there for another attack. Grab the legendary chest from the pump if you get the chance . . . it's the only thing we'd have trouble replacing." He wrapped an arm around her and rested his other hand on her round belly, smiling. "Also, I've got a surprise for you. She's waiting with the others." Hopefully.

She frowned at him, then furrowed her brow and sniffed. Then her face lit up in delight. "Ama!"

Dare blinked. Aside from the few times Amalisa had hugged him back before they headed north, and a few times he'd helped her up onto her horse, he'd had almost no contact with the young noblewoman. But Pella's senses were apparently keen enough she could still smell her friend on him.

He smiled ruefully. "Can't keep any secrets from you, huh?"

Pella squealed in delight and wrapped him in an enthusiastic hug. "That's not just a surprise, it's the happiest thing that's happened since I found out I was going to have your puppies!" She began eagerly kissing and licking his face with her soft, flat tongue. "Where did you find her? How did she end up coming up here with you? Is she safe? Happy? Oh, I can't wait to see her!"

Apparently she meant that literally, because instead of waiting for any answers she bolted to the horses and hopped on the nicer one, urging it into a gallop towards the south.

Dare grinned after her, although his smile vanished when he turned back to Ollivan's two thugs. "Up," he snapped. "We've got a long way to go to reach Terana, and I want to get there before dark."

"I'm in no fit state to travel," Dorias protested, hawking and spitting blood to one side.

"You'd better hope that's not true," Dare said darkly. "You tried kidnap and rape one of my consorts, then tried to burn down the house where my family was sleeping, including my infant daughter."

He loomed over the man. "So I dare you to give me an excuse to take my own turn beating your sorry ass."

The squire cursed, then with a groan of pain dragged himself to his feet and started in the direction of town.

Chapter Thirteen

Moments

Dare was a bit bemused when his weary group rode up to the gates of Terana to find them flung wide open, the streets full of celebrating people.

He knew whatever was happening in the town had nothing to do with the attack on Nirim Manor, and these happy townspeople had no way of knowing about it. But even so it irked him a bit to see them all laughing and cheering when his home had come dangerously close to being burned to the ground.

Everywhere he looked he saw people clashing mugs of ale together, or eating steaming sausages with grease dripping down their chins and fingers, or chomping down apples cores and all. Poles had been set up in squares and intersections and maidens with flowers in their hair danced around them. And it seemed on every street corner musicians played or other entertainers amused the crowds.

In spite of everyone's fear and exhaustion after the day's events, they brightened at the sight. "Harvest festival!" Pella said, clapping her hands. "With everything that's been happening I completely forgot!"

Ireni nodded, smiling tensely. "I wish we could've been here for it. Next year, maybe."

"No, this year," Dare said. He glanced back at the two men bound to their horses at the back of the group. "I'll take these pieces of shit to Marona and tell her what happened, you all try to enjoy the festival."

"Is that safe?" Amalisa asked nervously, kneading her horse's reins in her hands. She'd clearly been shaken by finding the house she'd hoped would be her new home on fire, as well as the full

232

explanation of the trouble with Ollivan.

Ilin gave her a reassuring smile. "Anyone wishing us harm would be a fool to try anything in these crowds. And I give my word I'll keep a constant vigil for any danger."

"Go," Dare urged his lovers and friends. "After all the misery of the last few weeks, everyone could use a chance to relax."

The others grudgingly relented and heeled their horses to a faster pace. Although he thought they seemed relieved to join the happy crowds and leave their worries behind for a bit.

All except Zuri, who cradled Gelaa gently as she nudged her horse up beside him. "I'd like to get Gelaa someplace safe and quiet," she murmured. "She's had a stressful day."

He nodded, feeling guilty that their daughter, barely a month old, had been forced to leave her home because of all this. Not to mention her weary mother. "We'll get you settled comfortably in Montshadow Estate and you can feed her and put her to bed," he said, leaning out to gently rub her back. "And you too."

His goblin lover simply nodded wearily, and Dare nudged his horse forward to where the guards waited, leading the two horses carrying Ollivan's thugs.

"Master Dare!" a familiar face, the guardswoman Helima who'd flirted with him and offered invitations to drink multiple times, only to have him always have good reasons to stand her up, called cheerfully. In spite of that she seemed genuinely happy to see him as she waved him forward. "Welcome to the harvest festival! By Baroness Marona Arral's beneficence ale, sausages, and apples are provided to all citizens of Terana Province tonight!"

She paused, then with a playful grin leaned forward. "I've been helping myself to the apples and sausages, but as soon as my shift ends I'll have a lot of catching up to do with the ale." She winked. "And if I happen to see you maybe we can finally share that drink, then *you* can share your sausage with me."

Wow, apparently the weathered but lovely guardswoman had decided to abandon subtlety.

Dare gave her a tense smile. "I wish I could, Helima. Truly. Unfortunately there'll be no celebrating for me tonight." He tugged on the leads to the two horses he led. "These two assholes tried to burn down my house with my family inside. I need to speak to Lady Marona."

Helima's smile vanished into a hard scowl as she took in the bound men, who were definitely looking the worse for wear after Pella's treatment and a long day of riding bound hand and foot with only the most grudging attention paid to their comfort.

"Is that right?" she growled. She nodded to her fellow guard. "I'll take them in." The man nodded and saluted her.

Since Zuri had the baby Dare pulled Helima up into the saddle in front of him. As they rode down the streets she roared for the celebrating crowds to clear the way, and at the sight of her and the two bound men the townspeople reluctantly complied. Although they were quick to pour back into the streets and resume their celebration after Dare's group passed.

They spotted the others from Nirim Manor before too long, clustered around an open grill where sausages were being cooked and apples and mugs of ale passed out. Ireni and Pella hurried forward to give Dare and Zuri a couple sausages and an apple each, which they gratefully tore into as they continued on to Montshadow Estate.

The mansion was lit up bright that evening, filled with carriages and milling guests that suggested the baroness was hosting a party. Dare hated to crash it, but Marona would want to know what had happened and frankly he needed her help.

So he nodded curtly to the familiar gate guard, who took one look at Helima and the two bound men and rang up to the main house to alert the staff of their approach.

Thanks to that Miss Garena was waiting at the door flanked by a handful of maids, two burly men, and a couple stable boys. The boys quickly took the horses, while the maids ushered Zuri and the baby into the house, fussing over them the whole time.

"Thank you, Helima," the Head Maid said curtly, inclining her head. "You may return to your duties."

The guardswoman saluted and strode off, armor clanking. Leaving Miss Garena and the two burly men to help Dare with Dorias and the Skirmisher.

"Into the basement," she said. "No sense drawing attention to this any more than we have to by disturbing the festivities." She gave the two thugs a severe look. "Ollivan's?"

Dare nodded. "I hate to disturb Lady Marona with this, but they set fire to Nirim Manor."

Miss Garena's expression turned genuinely concerned. "Are you all okay?"

"Yes, thank the gods. And the house was only burned along one wall thanks to Leilanna's quick thinking. Although we'll need to commission new water tanks for the roof."

"I'll send a boy in the morning to put in the order," she said as she led the way down a narrow, dank stairway into the basement. "Your and your poor household have enough on your minds right now."

"Thank you, but I feel like I'm going to be talking to the crafters anyway," Dare said grimly. "I'd like to get started on plans to improve the the manor's defenses while I'm here."

"Probably wise." The Head Maid motioned the two burly men with her to carry the prisoners into a dank room lit by a lantern. "Drop them in there. And soften them up a bit while we go find the Baroness, so they'll be inclined to talk when she arrives."

She spoke the words as dispassionately as if she was instructing scullery maids to get potatoes peeled for dinner, and Dare shivered a bit; her professionalism didn't extend to just running a pristine lady's household.

A brutal world, where even the good guys didn't pull their punches.

Miss Garena inclined her head to him. "If you'll come with me?"

235

As he followed the maid in search of Lady Marona, he heard meaty thuds and grunts emerge from the room behind him.

* * * * *

"That should be all we need," the baroness said with a grim smile. She motioned curtly, and her man stuffed the gag back into Dorias's mouth and bound it tight, then saluted and left the room, closing the door behind him.

"Thank you, my Lady," Dare said. He didn't just mean for his lover immediately welcoming his household and their prisoners into her home in spite of the party going on upstairs, but also her willingness to question Ollivan's thugs right on the spot.

She'd shown an unexpectedly savage side, too; both men were looking much worse than they had when they arrived hours ago, and that was saying something.

The baroness chuckled. "No, Master Dare, thank you for capturing two criminals on my lands and helping me bring them to justice."

Dare smiled wanly. "On the subject of justice, will we have to face reprisals for arresting these two?"

She immediately shook her head. "You have a right to defend your home and family, and it helps that these two aren't nobles, just the lackeys of one." She shot the arsonists a disgusted look. "In fact, I have excellent grounds to prosecute them. Dorias for assault and attempted kidnapping for his attack on Ireni, then arson and attempted murder, because the building he set fire to was occupied. His buddy will get time for aiding and abetting arson and attempted murder."

The stately woman smirked, giving Dorias a triumphant look. "In fact, it gets even better. This little shit fucked his master over good."

Unexpected as it was to hear the refined lady talking so salty, Dare liked the sound of that. "How?"

"Because while the idiot tried to burn down your manor on his own initiative, the fact that he's Ollivan's servant and was on an errand for him means the culpability ultimately falls on his master. That's going to turn a lot of people against Ollivan, and embarrass him among his peers."

"Wait, what?" Dare demanded. "Ollivan beat and tried to kidnap Ireni in front of a hundred witnesses, and *I* nearly got in trouble for stopping him. How is this any worse for him?"

Lady Marona shook her head grimly. "I forget you're not from Haraldar, and in spite of your clearly high level of education a commoner as well." She tapped her lip thoughtfully. "It would probably explain it best to repeat a common expression among the nobility, "Do what you want to the owners, but don't fuck with the property."

She grimaced. "A cruel, cynical, and fundamentally unjust saying, but it should tell you something of the mindset of Haraldar's peerage."

Dare wasn't a fan of the saying, certainly, but he didn't quite get it. "What's special about the property?"

"From a purely pragmatic standpoint, it's the only thing they care about," the baroness replied. "If the owners die, are enslaved, or are driven away, the land and house are still there, ready for the new owners to move in and pay taxes. And if livestock or other property is stolen, it still exists and can be taxed."

She shook her head. "But if you slaughter the cattle or burn down the house, you're taking tax revenue away from the province lord or lady, the viscount of the marches in question, the region governor, and half a dozen other nobles in the bureaucracy."

He shook his head in disbelief. "So if Dorias had murdered my entire family, nobody would've cared? But since he set a fire and burned the wall on one side a bit Ollivan will be in disfavor?"

"He will be after I relentlessly hound the issue from every angle," Lady Marona said, eyes flashing with quiet fury. "Which I will, because not only did he threaten people I care about but that was *my* land his lackey attacked. You're just the hereditary deed holder. And in turn the governor will feel the same way, and up the chain the King beyond him."

Dare felt the tension in his shoulders loosen. "Do I have anything more to worry about from Ollivan, then?"

She hesitated. "If so, it will only be another attack in person. He'll have even less power to turn the governor or other nobles against you, and with him in disgrace I doubt he'll find many friends interested in traveling to the corners of the region to harass random nobodies." She gave him a tight smile. "No offense, just how they think."

So it looked as if his priority should be to keep leveling, and encourage Ilin and his lovers to level as well, safely of course. That was a huge relief.

"On the subject of disfavor," his noble lover continued brightly, "you'll be pleased to know the rumors of Ollivan's awful behavior are spreading like wildfire, not just in Terana but other nearby towns as well. Perhaps even all the way to Redoubt."

"That's good." Dare snorted. "I don't suppose it'll increase the chances of him facing justice?"

She grimaced. "No, I'm afraid not. But while a lot of nobles are understood to be pieces of shit, they're not *openly* understood to be. Once their behavior goes from being common knowledge to being *public* knowledge, if you catch my drift, that's when the trouble starts for them as they begin to lose favor."

"Well, it's good to know that after all the terrible things Ollivan's done, at least his opportunities for advancement are drying up," he said, a touch bitterly.

Lady Marona sighed. "Sometimes it's the best we can hope for. And better than him being allowed to keep gaining power and influence, and one day perhaps becoming governor of Bastion." She arched an eyebrow. "Would you want *him* in charge?"

Dare shuddered. "Good point."

"Besides, with the way he is eventually he'll piss off the wrong person and end up dead, and good riddance. His uncle's power can only protect him so much." She motioned to Dorias and his companion. "In the meantime, I'll make sure these two get the justice they deserve. You need fear nothing more where they're concerned."

The baroness rapped on the door and her man stepped inside, saluting again. She gestured at the two prisoners, and he hurried forward to drag the two groaning men from the room.

Once they were gone Dare felt a weight lift off his shoulders, glad he would no longer have to worry about further danger from either them. With luck he'd never see them again.

"Thank you, my Lady. Truly."

"You're welcome. Always." The beautiful mature noblewoman tenderly rested a hand on his cheek. "It's a shame your visits always seem to bring excitement of late, and you're in too much of a rush to stay and enjoy my hospitality. My maids aren't the only ones disappointed you can't linger."

"I've missed you too," Dare admitted, pulling her into his arms and kissing her softly. She melted against him, and he rested a hand on her still flat belly. "How are you and the little one?"

She beamed. "Healthy and excited to be a mom." She nuzzled his chest. "And as I think of it, I realize I've never actually invited my paramour into my bed." She glanced up at the ceiling with a sigh. "I'm afraid the party will have died down by now anyway, and I find myself wearied by this grim business."

He smiled wanly. After the morning's scare and a hard day of travel he wasn't in the friskiest of moods. He mostly just wanted to pile into a bed with his lovers and hold them close, making sure they were all healthy and safe and there with him.

But Lady Marona was his lover as well, and he cared about her. Besides, he'd brought a lot of trouble to her doorstep; the least he could was spend some time with her. His girls would understand if he gave their host a few hours.

But she surprised him, taking his hand. "I've been given to understand that your consort Pella will be sharing a bed with Lady

Amalisa tonight," she said. "The two seemed eager to continue catching up."

Dare blinked. "This is the first I'm hearing of that, but I suppose it's not a surprise." His dog girl lover and her friend had been inseparable during the trip here, filling the air with happy chatter in spite of the grim circumstances of their trip to Terana.

Lady Marona hesitated, almost shyly. An unexpected look for the normally composed and in command woman. "In that case, would your other consorts mind if I took her place with all of you? It gets lonely in this big mansion, and while my maids make wonderful bedwarmers it would be nice to spend some time with my paramour and his harem while he's in town. Even if it's just sleeping, given your exhaustion."

That was even more surprising, but he liked the idea. "I think that would be wonderful, my Lady."

"Marona, please," she said, squeezing his hand. "After all, we're close enough now, aren't we?"

Dare lifted her hand and kissed it. "It would be my honor, Marona."

They walked hand in hand through the mansion to the guest room usually reserved for him and his lovers. He was vaguely aware of the few maids still awake popping their heads out from behind tapestries and around corners to stare, expressions ranging from excited to conspiratorial to jealous to outright horny.

His lovers were already in bed, cuddled together sleeping peacefully. Although Zuri woke up just enough to come hug them both before sleepily taking their hands and tugging them back towards the big four-poster.

"The maids are taking care of Gelaa tonight," she whispered. "They even offered the services of a wet nurse, although I insisted they wake me at least for feedings." She giggled. "Still, I'm looking forward to the best night's sleep I've had in a month. And I know Gelaa's in good hands with those sweethearts . . . they're gushing over her so much you'd think she was a princess."

Marona smiled. "No surprise, considering how fond they are of the dear girl's parents." She rested a hand on her belly. "Not to mention they're eagerly anticipating the birth of Gelaa's little brother or sister, and preparing to be the best possible caregivers for my child."

His goblin lover smiled back tentatively. "Thank you so much, Lady Marona, for being such a good friend to us."

"Oh, my dear, I hope you think of me as more than just a friend." The baroness gracefully dropped to her knees to wrap her arms around the smaller woman. "I'm sorry you had to leave your home so soon after giving birth. Rest easy in my home, Zuri."

Zuri hugged the taller woman fiercely. "Will you sleep between me and Dare tonight?"

Marona looked more pleased than he'd expected by the offer. "That sounds wonderful."

Before climbing into bed Dare paused long enough to strip down to his underwear, and the baroness stripped down to practical white panties, revealing her graceful mature curves.

He couldn't resist the urge to take her in his arms and kiss her softly, caressing her soft body for a few seconds. Then they let Zuri usher them into bed to join the pile of warm, cuddly bodies.

Marona backed into his chest until they were spooning, her shapely ass pressed against his crotch just enough to make his cock stir, but not enough to break through his drowsiness enough to do anything. He fell asleep with his nose buried in her silver-streaked dark hair, one hand cupping her small breast.

* * * * *

If Dare's lovers were surprised to find the lady of the house half naked in bed with them, they showed no sign of it.

Although they *did* look on with eager interest as Marona woke with a soft murmur, seemed to remember where she was, and with a moan of enjoyment began pushing her soft ass back against his morning wood.

241

In truth he'd been trying to slip out of the pile of cuddly women so he could relieve himself, but at that eager overture his piss hardon decided he needed a different sort of relief. He'd gone almost two weeks without sex on his trip down into Kovana, after all.

He pulled down his elegant lover's practical white panties, slipped his hand between her legs to fondle her plump labia until he felt them become damp, then freed himself from his own underwear so he could position himself at her entrance and begin sliding his tip up and down between her folds.

"Gods," she moaned, back arching. "I haven't woken up to a nice surprise like this in a long time."

"I know, right?" Leilanna said with a giggle, crawling over them to press her soft naked body against Marona, burying the mature woman's face in her pillowy ashen gray breasts. "You're so beautiful, my Lady. I'm glad you joined us."

The other women got in on the fun, and by the time Dare pushed his way inside his noble lover, still in the spoon position, she'd been well taken care of and was a quivering ball of pleasure.

He thrust into her slowly and gently, stretching her tight walls and making her moan into Leilanna's breasts and push her hips back into him. In his urgent need to relieve himself, in more than one way, he only lasted a couple minutes, holding out until he felt her sex ripple around him in a gentle climax and her arousal flowed down his length to soak their joined bodies.

With a last grunt Dare grabbed her hips and pulled her into him, then emptied himself inside her sweet pussy until it felt like she would overflow. He had a lot of pent up seed that had built up, after all.

Finally, kissing her graceful neck affectionately, he squirmed free of the press of bodies. "Hate to rush," he said in a sheepish voice, pulling on his pants.

Marona watched him languidly from amid the pile of affectionate women, expression amused. "I was married for decades, my paramour. I know why a man gets hard in the morning." She snickered. "I just wanted to make good use of it first."

Feeling his cheeks heat as his girls all giggled, he excused himself and found the nearest privy.

On the way back Belinda pulled him into a secluded nook and pressed her sexy body against him, lovely scales shimmering in a scintillating pattern in pure arousal. "I've missed you, Master Dare," she moaned, kissing him hungrily and pushing her slender forked tongue into his mouth.

"I've missed you too," he panted as her slender fingers worked the ties of his pants and freed his cock, still slick with Marona's juices. She began jacking him off with both hands, silky smooth scales sliding easily up and down his length.

Dare still had plenty in the tank, so he was happy to spin the beautiful dragon girl around, lift the skirt of her sexy black and white uniform and her tail as she eagerly thrust her ass out, and freeze reluctantly. "Scroll," he groaned.

She giggled. "Don't worry, I stopped by your room and got Zuri to cast the spell before seeking you out." Her eyes danced. "She really loves helping you get laid." She blushed even harder, scales shimmering faster. "Although I didn't expect the Baroness to be there, your seed dripping down her thighs as your lovers pleasured her."

His cock twitched at that mental image. "And what did she think of you waylaying me in the hall?"

The sexy maid giggled again. "She told me to hurry so you could clean up before breakfast." She bit her lip. "I'd be happy to help with that, too."

Dare chuckled and stroked her sexy thighs. "I have a feeling if you got me into a bath we'd be there all morning."

"Mmm, you're probably right." With an impatient noise the maid ground back against him, thick tail brushing teasingly along his length. "Come on, I need you inside me."

He wasted no more time plunging between her wet folds and deep into her warm, tight tunnel while she pressed her face to the wall and gasped. "Noble ancestors, your cock is a work of art. Give it to me."

Dare grinned and built up a steady rhythm of slow, powerful thrusts as she lifted up on her tiptoes and arched her back into him, whimpering and moaning her pleasure. It didn't take long for her soft walls to clench around him as she drenched his thighs with her nectar.

As Belinda came down she surprised him by pulling off his cock. "Now that I've got your manhood nice and slippery, I want to try the other hole," she said eagerly, bending even more and lifting her tail to display her cute little rosebud.

His eyes widened, and he couldn't help but grin at the prospect, cock throbbing in expectation. He stroked two fingers into her gaping pussy, gathering some of her copious arousal, then pressed them to her delicate asshole and gently pushed them inside.

"Ooh!" she murmured, sphincter briefly tightening around his invading digits. Her insides were warm and soft, and after pushing his fingers in and out a few times to loosen her up he inserted a third one, making her squirm.

"Don't worry, I've been getting ready for you," the sexy draconid said, giggling. "Miss Garena keeps asking where all the carrots and cucumbers are going."

Dare took her at her word and pulled out his fingers, eager to feel himself deep in her bowels. He positioned herself at her rosebud, gripping her tail and one hip for leverage, and then slowly pushed forward.

"Gods, you're huge," she moaned, quivering in delight with her face pressed against the wall. "I think you might be bigger than the cucumbers."

He wasn't sure about that, but what he did know was her asshole was so tight it took some gentle teasing and pressing to get his tip inside. He let go of her hip and moved his finger to her clit, rubbing gently to stimulate her as he slid deeper and deeper into her bowels.

It felt incredible, soft and hot and tight. Her squeaks of pleasure only spurred him on as he went deeper, deeper, until he finally bottomed out with barely an inch still outside.

"There," Belinda panted, clenching her sphincter around the base of his cock, then loosening it with obvious deliberation. "Now give it to me good."

Dare slowly pulled out, then pushed back inside, making her gasp and collapse against the wall, trembling and mewling with enjoyment as she urged him on. He pushed in her again, then again, gradually building up a rhythm. As he did he played with her thick tail and rubbed her clit.

Soon the sexy dragon girl was pushing back against him, on her tiptoes again and tail thrashing in his grip. He ran his hand down her smooth inner thigh, luxuriating in the silky feel of her delicate scales as he gathered up more of her arousal to slather on his cock as he continued thrusting.

Finally she pushed herself back against his chest and wrapped both his arms around her to support her weight, then lifted both her legs off the ground so she was fully impaled on him. At the sudden shock of the new position she squealed, and her asshole began winking around his shaft as she climaxed. He watched in amazement as she squirted powerfully against the wall.

That was enough for Dare to release inside her in a shared climax, pumping his seed into her bowels in a torrent that seemed like it would never end.

Afterwards she cleaned them both off with wet rags and soap, then hastily arranged her skirts. "Thank you, Master Dare," she murmured in a low, sultry voice. "I was a bit afraid I wouldn't like that, but you can fuck my ass anytime."

She kissed him passionately for a few moments, forked tongue exploring his mouth, then opened the door and led the way outside, every inch the demure maid once more. "This way to your room, Master Dare," she said with a polite curtsy.

Marona and the others were already dressed and ready when he entered, although Zuri was happy to cast Cleanse Target.

"Considering how long you've been without us, I'll just keep this spell handy for when you get drenched in the next woman's arousal," she teased as the others laughed.

Dare grinned gamely as he dressed in the expensive clothes the baroness had laid out for him. A gift from her, apparently.

Pella and Amalisa rejoined them in the dining hall, the two women looking bubbly and happy after their sleepover. Marona was very gracious to her noble guest, briskly ignoring Amalisa's protests that she'd been disinherited and treating her with all due respect.

Which certainly cemented the baroness's place as a fast friend in Pella's book.

Busy as Marona always was, it was a pleasant surprise when she joined them for breakfast, inviting him to sit at her right hand at the head of the table with the others gathered around them. The presence of the lady of the house might've explained why he didn't have a pink-haired gnome visitor beneath the table this time, although Marigold was one of the servers and he spotted her casting him inviting looks.

He hoped his return smile promised a rain check on future trysts, although sadly he didn't think he'd have an opportunity this time.

"Are you sure you won't stay for a few days at least?" Lady Marona asked as she bid him farewell at the door.

Dare grinned as he kissed her hand, then her cheek. "If you can convince the others to stay until I've taken a few measures at the manor, I wouldn't complain. But I need to get home and make sure our home is safe as soon as I can."

She gave him a wistful look. "I wish I had time to at least go with you on your business in town, but sadly I have to focus on running the place, a job that seems like it's never done."

"That commitment is why your town is as beautiful as its Baroness," He leaned in and kissed her softly, ignoring the giggles of onlooking maids.

The elegant noblewoman's cheeks went pink, and with a low laugh she ushered him towards the horses. "Go on with you, my paramour."

Dare's brief hope that his lovers would remain in the safety of Terana for a while was dashed when they all ignored his suggestion to stay and mounted up with him. Even Amalisa, who he would've thought would welcome a safe sanctuary in town while things settled down, seemed determined to stay by Pella's side.

So with a few final farewell waves they rode down the drive and into town, where Dare and his lovers parted to take care of business.

The girls were going to sell the massive collection of loot they'd built up over the last few weeks, which at Ireni's insistence they'd brought from the manor since they were coming here anyway. Then, since they'd leveled up a decent amount, they'd sell their old gear and purchase new weapons and armor so they'd have the best possible.

From the way they whispered eagerly and a bit conspiratorially amongst themselves, they also had other purchase plans.

Dare left them to it and made his way to the crafters' section of town, hiring laborers to come and repair the fire damage and commissioning new water tanks for the roof. He also stopped in at a jeweler's shop for a custom order, arranging for it to be delivered in secret with the next shipment of goods that went out to Nirim Manor.

He couldn't help but feel a surge of excitement as he made his selections, and the woman helping him smiled warmly and wished him the best as they settled the deal.

Then he went to a metalsmith he'd employed for previous fine work around the manor and pulled him aside for a less happy custom order. "Yes, I can do thin wire," the man said, stroking his beard. "I've got the molds and such. How much do you need?"

Dare had previously done the math for the dimensions for the wall, manor yard, the manor itself, and other pertinent details. So he ordered enough to completely surround the top of the wall with three lengths of wire, which would hang outward at an angle.

"And it's special wire?" the smith asked.

"Yes. Think caltrops or even smaller blades, honed razor sharp and attached to the wire every three or four inches."

The man's eyes widened. "That's a nasty idea. And you want this for a security measure?"

Dare smiled thinly. "Until I can be sure my home is safe." Razor wire was ugly and would give the place the look of a prison, but for medieval fortifications you couldn't do much better as a deterrent against climbing the walls.

The smith rubbed his jaw. "Affixing such blades to the wires will make the job take far longer and drastically increase the expense. Weeks and hundreds of gold, at a low estimate."

Dare nodded and dug into his coin pouch to pay an advance. "Get the first length of wire to Nirim Manor as quickly as you're able."

He ordered a few other specialty items from the smith, hired a few laborers for some more specialized jobs, including Morwal to use his earth magic to dig out a hole for a ventilated panic room, with a tunnel connecting to the manor and another tunnel leading out under the walls.

The gloves were off now, and if Ollivan came for his family or tried to send more cronies to make cowardly attacks, Dare was going to crush him.

Literally.

* * * * *

Dare had a lot of plans for how to improve the manor's defenses, such as reinforcing the walls and gate and digging out an underground panic room and attached escape tunnel. He also had a few nasty surprises planned for anyone who tried to come after his family again.

But since the laborers and craftsmen wouldn't arrive for a few days, once he'd spent an hour or so going over the walls and grounds taking measurements and considering options, he decided he should keep spending his time productively while he waited.

Which meant leveling.

His natural inclination was to stay at the manor to defend it, but his lovers insisted that the best way to do that would be to get strong enough that he could face any attackers. Which made sense. Also they were planning to level as well, bringing Se'weir and the baby along so nobody would be left at the manor while they were out.

The gentle hobgoblin would stay back a safe distance by the horses with Gelaa, of course, and Pella would be there to keep an eye on them.

As well, when they *were* at the manor they had worked out evacuation plans, and Ilin had promised to keep constant watch for threats. Between all those considerations, Dare had reluctantly agreed that he should get back to leveling.

They'd been safe enough while he was gone fetching Eloise, even with Dorias and the Skirmisher lurking around. Now that that threat was dealt with and Ollivan was far away in Redoubt, they were probably safe enough for a while.

Of course, he'd assumed the same before. At the very least he planned to level to the west, in the direction attackers from Redoubt would most likely come from if they didn't take the path directly from Terana.

To his surprise, as he saddled his horse Leilanna joined him leading her own mount, all geared for leveling. At his curious look she glowered at him. "I'm coming with you today. Consider it the date you owe me."

Dare winced. Their plans had been delayed by the events of the past couple weeks, but in spite of that his dusk elf lover had been unexpectedly reasonable and understanding about it. Although it looked as if her patience had finally reached its limits.

"That sounds great," he said. "Although will the others be okay without their main damage dealer?"

She sniffed. "We level so slowly together anyway it feels like a picnic, and I doubt dragging along Se'weir and the baby for their safety is going to speed things up. Zuri and Ilin can handle damage."

Her gorgeous dark pink eyes narrowed. "Besides, I've waited long enough for you to put a baby in me. I'm going to have you for a full day, and you're going to treat me like a princess."

Dare couldn't help but grin. "A naughty little princess who needs my big dick?"

If he'd hoped to tweak her nose a little with their usual playful banter, she just grinned. "Exactly."

He'd been planning to have a boring day of grinding experience, but it looked as if things were going to be a lot more interesting.

Before heading for the spawn points, Dare took a quick detour to the goblin village. He wanted to check on them, see how they were progressing, but most of all he wanted to find out why attackers had managed to sneak past their sentries.

The place looked peaceful and prosperous, far better designed and built than their hovels in the Gadris Mountains had been. Animal pens stood open while livestock grazed, small fenced gardens grew in most yards, and farther out fields of fall grains and other crops grew green and healthy.

Much of their success was thanks to Leilanna's help and guidance to the Avenging Wolf farmers, and as they rode past the fields she broke off to go speak to the goblins working there. That left Dare to ride on alone.

Chieftain Rek'u'gar met him just outside the village looking tense, even shamed. "Human," he called, dropping to his knees and lowering his head. "We beg your forgiveness for our lapse. Rest assured I have addressed the problem and delivered the required punishments. My people will not fail you again."

"I appreciate that," Dare said, dismounting and resting a hand on his soon to be brother-in-law's shoulder to urge him back to his feet. "What happened?"

Rek scowled. "Not a lack of vigilance, I promise you. More a lack of proper training, and focus directed in the wrong places." He waved vaguely towards the edge of Dare's lands. "We've been tirelessly patrolling your borders, but our gaze was directed outwards. If we had looked inwards just as keenly, no one who'd managed to sneak past our sentries would've been able to continue unhindered to your home."

He dropped his head again. "I blame only myself for this mistake. Because of it my sister and her unborn child were placed in danger. If you wish to beat me for my failure, I will understand."

"No need for beatings," Dare said, patting his shoulder. "But maybe we can go over a more detailed watch schedule and patrol routes, as well as what your sentries should look out for and better methods for signaling to each other and the manor."

He pulled out a sack of silver. "Here's payment for the sentries, and I'd like to hire more, at least for the next little while."

"Very well." The young hobgoblin solemnly accepted the money and motioned to a nearby tree. "Come, let us talk."

They spent the next half hour or so going over details and discussing protocols for sentries, as well as discipline and ways to spot impending danger. Then, when Dare spotted Leilanna heading his way after finishing her work instructing the goblin farmers, he quickly stood and offered Rek his hand. "I think that covers things for now. I'll swing by to check in on you as usual, but until then is there anything you need? Any issues I can help with?"

The chieftain returned his grip firmly. "Not at the moment, no. We prosper well on this land."

"Good." Dare hesitated, glanced at Leilanna to see she was still out of earshot, even with her elvish hearing, and lowered his voice anyway. "I wished to speak of the arranged marriage with Se'weir."

Rek gave him a cautious look. "Do you wish to cancel it? It seems unnecessary now that you've mated her and she carries your child. A pointless formality."

"A formality, certainly, but one with great meaning. A show of my love and commitment to your sister." Dare paused, again checking his dusk elf lover's progress. "I just wanted to ask your approval to move the date up to a sooner time, although I'll have to get back to you on exactly when."

The hobgoblin shrugged, looking disinterested. "It is your custom that you insisted on. As far as I'm concerned she's already your mate, and nothing more needs to be done. But yes, you have my approval."

"Thank you."

Rek hesitated, looking uncomfortable. "My sister is happy with you. I am pleased to call you a member of the family, and of the tribe."

It was probably the closest the proud, solemn young chieftain could come to expressing sentiment. Dare clapped him on the shoulder. "I'm pleased to be welcomed. May our friendship last until the end of days."

The hobgoblin grunted. "I will see to the sentries." With that he waved a curt farewell and started back to his village.

Dare mounted up and went out to meet Leilanna, who thankfully showed no curiosity about their topic of conversation; hopefully that meant he hadn't spoiled the surprise.

The ride to the spawn points Dare planned to level at was an enjoyable one. Leilanna was always fun to talk to with her quick wit, and he liked listening to her carefree laugh. Which he heard often since she was in unusually high spirits.

Their first spawn point was a sort of flying imp that circled lazily overhead, just in bowshot or spell range, and would swoop down in pairs when aggroed. Dare was pleased to see that Leilanna's damage, which had been impressive even when she was several levels below his, was now insane.

Although with the downside of not being as consistent as a bow, such as mana cost and a limited mana pool, as well as long casting times that were easily interrupted.

Still, they ripped through the imps with ease and moved on to the next spawn point. Then the next.

Between the mana regeneration from Leilanna's elvish heritage and what she got from her robes, along with her passive regeneration, her mana lasted for a surprising amount of time. Even so, given the cost of her spells eventually she ran out of mana.

To keep up their leveling pace as much as he could, he set up the tent near a fresh spawn point and had her bed down to sleep for her four hours to recharge. A schedule she still complained about, and reasonably so, but that was now able to easily stick to.

Dare half expected her to invite him in for some fun before she went to sleep, but she disappeared into the tent without a word; either she was too tired or she was planning something more special for later.

Either way, he left her to it and tried to be quiet as he hunted the giant scorpions in the spawn point, staying just close enough that she'd share the experience as she slept.

He was able to clear the spawn point in about an hour, not bothering to hurry since he was going to be twiddling his thumbs after he finished. He spent the rest of the four hours working on his crafting skills and hunting game for leather.

Part of him wanted to slip into the tent and cuddle Leilanna as she slept, but he didn't want to accidentally interrupt her sleep, and also he was in the mood to accomplish things; gaining proficiency in abilities didn't give much experience, but it gave *some*.

When his dusk elf lover finally emerged, silky white hair adorably tousled and cheeks flushed from just emerging from the warm blankets, she shivered slightly at the chill wind and practically climbed inside his cloak with him, pressing her soft body close for warmth.

"Gods, a storm must be blowing in directly from the north," she complained. Sure enough, he could see dark clouds looming ominously on the horizon.

Dare frowned. "Doesn't it usually get warm before a storm?"

Leilanna shrugged. "It was warm yesterday. Now the weather is just going to suck."

She wasn't wrong. As they moved on to the next spawn point and got back to leveling the wind picked up until it howled right through their fur cloaks and clothes and chilled them in spite of the sun. Although that quickly disappeared as the clouds rolled in.

His dusk elf lover still had mana left when the fall thunderstorm erupted in full fury, lashing chilly rain down on them that found its way through their cloaks and then their clothes. In spite of the discomfort she stubbornly insisted on continuing to level until her mana pool was empty.

Dare regretted agreeing to the idea within fifteen minutes, about the time it took before he was soaked and freezing his ass off. She must've been equally miserable, because she still had about 5% of her mana left when she finally threw in the towel and begged him to set up the tent.

They weren't making it home in this weather without a truly miserable time, assuming they didn't actually suffer hypothermia, so he wasted no time finding a more or less sheltered spot beneath a tree that kept out the worst of the wind and rain.

Since his pack was mostly waterproof the tent and bedroll were as well, and after he hastily set it up they wasted no time stripping out of their soaking clothes and crawling inside, shivering and huddling together for warmth beneath the blankets.

Chapter Fourteen
Putting Down Roots

Dare listened to the rain dripping onto the hide of the tent. "Unless this lets up soon, we're probably going to have to spend the night," he murmured, rubbing Leilanna to warm her up. In the light of their glow stone she looked unusually pale, and he worried she might catch a chill.

"F-forget whether we can make it home tonight," she said through chattering teeth. "I hope it lets up soon so I can go find a place to pee."

A gust of wind shook the tent around them, and he chuckled. "Unless you want to hold it, you'll either have to brave the storm or use the kettle."

His shivering lover gave him an incredulous look. "What?"

Dare wasn't sure what was so odd about that. "It's basically like a chamber pot, right?"

"You want me to pee in the kettle we use to make tea and coffee?" she said in disbelief.

"Why not? We can always use one of Zuri's Cleanse Target scrolls afterwards. Besides, urine is sterile."

Leilanna's lovely eyes narrowed. "I don't know what that means."

"It means it's clean." He reached for his pack. "Come on, I'll look the other way."

"I don't care about that," she said impatiently, "I'm just *not* pissing inside the kettle we eat out of."

Dare relented, although he filed away the tidbit that she wouldn't mind him watching her pee. "All right then, just a suggestion."

His dusk elf lover squirmed around to peer out the tent's entry flap, wincing at the splash of rain that blew inside. "Fuck it," she muttered. "I can hold it for an hour or so. Maybe it'll have died down by then." Shivering, she crawled back beneath the blankets and cuddled up to him again.

Now that they'd dried off and warmed up a bit the feel of her soft, sexy body was even more inviting. He leaned down and began kissing and nibbling one of her long, pointy ears, running his hands up and down her thick thighs and soft round ass.

"Mmm," she moaned, rubbing against his growing erection. "Perfect, I need a distraction."

"Distraction, huh?" he growled, squeezing one of her pillowy breasts and teasing her charcoal gray nipple as he moved down to kiss and gently bite her neck. He could feel dampness on her thighs, coating his tip and letting him smoothly slide between them. He shifted so the top of his cock was rubbing against her silky soft pussy as he fucked her thighs, making sure to grind his tip against her clit with every thrust.

Leilanna didn't need much of that before she began insistently tugging him with her as she rolled onto her back, spreading her sexy legs wide to invite him into her glistening pussy.

Dare tenderly kissed her plump lips, tasting her sweet blackberry wine flavor, and slipped his tongue into her mouth as he positioned himself at her entrance.

"Yes!" she gasped, grinding her hips up against him until his tip slid inside her. "Yes, my love! Give me your baby!"

He groaned at that sexy thought and pushed inside her with one long, smooth motion, her tight, hot walls stretching open to welcome him. "Are you going to be a sexy mommy?" he panted as he withdrew and plunged back into her.

"Yes!" the beautiful dusk elf squealed, squirming against him until their hips moved in sync. "I'll be your sexy girl with a round pregnant belly and big boobs!" Her hands lovingly caressed his back. "Oh, we'll have such beautiful babies."

Dare eagerly sped up and dipped his head to take one of her

eraser-sized nipples in his mouth, nibbling it teasingly. As she went nuts beneath him he propped himself up on one arm so he could rub her clit with his free hand.

It was surprisingly difficult to maintain his pace while doing that, but he was rewarded by his beautiful lover giving a low, throaty whimper and clamping her legs around him, holding him tight inside her as her walls milked his shaft and her nectar flooded where they were lovingly joined.

"More," Leilanna begged, relaxing her legs and pushing her hips against him again. "Take me higher. Give me an experience I'll never forget for the time we conceive our child."

Dare obliged her, playing her gorgeous body with all the skill he'd learned from his experiences on Collisa. He brought her to another crescendoing climax, then pushed her even higher as he hammered into her quivering sex and mauled her erect clit.

"Oh, fuck!" his lover wailed, back arching as her pussy clamped around his thrusting shaft with desperate force. "Oh fuck, oh fuck oh-" Her tone abruptly changed to one of surprise and mild panic. "Oh, fuck!"

Dare felt wetness flood their joined crotches, followed by the slightly pungent scent of urine, and realized that in her pleasure Leilanna had lost control of her bladder.

"Oh, fuck!" he gasped, and with a final thrust began pouring his seed deep inside her; gods, this was unbelievably sexy.

She seemed to think so too. "Damnit," she wailed, clawing at his back as her hips desperately lifted into him, legs clamping closed around his ass again. Her pee continued flooding out in a torrent, soaking them and the bed beneath them as they climaxed together.

Looked as if she'd really needed to go.

The beautiful dusk elf's skin was charcoal gray with mortification as she buried her face in his shoulder. "I-I'm an heiress of the noble line of Aleneladris," she moaned as her tight walls continued to milk his throbbing shaft. "I shouldn't be getting off to pissing all over you like a horny bunny girl."

That was something they did, huh? Looked as if his experience with Clover back near Lone Ox hadn't been a one time thing. Something to remember.

Dare kissed her silky white hair. "You're so fucking sexy," he said, holding her close as his cock gave a last spurt inside her.

Leilanna looked resigned as she sprawled spread eagle in the mess she'd made, panting for breath as she came down from her towering orgasm. Her dark pink eyes looked a bit uncertain as she stared up at him. "Y-you don't think I'm gross, do you?"

He chuckled and settled down beside her on the soaked blankets, gathering her into his arms and kissing her plump lips. "I think that was seriously hot."

"Oh." She bit her lip and rubbed her thighs together as their combined juices flowed out of her. "Is it something you'd want to try again?"

Dare's cock twitched at the thought. "I think we could have some fun with it," he said with a smile.

The beautiful dusk elf nestled against him contentedly. "Okay, just not with any of the others. It's too embarrassing."

He couldn't help but laugh. "I don't know, I bet some of them might think it's hot too. Pella would probably be into it. And the Outsider's ridiculously kinky as long as it provides powerful, enjoyable sensations."

Her big pink eyes narrowed. "Not another word to anyone," she growled. Then with a pause she added sheepishly. "Unless I say so."

"Okay, okay," Dare said, smirking. "No need to get pissy."

Leilanna glared for a moment, then abruptly giggled. "I love you, Dare."

"I love you too." He lovingly stroked her soft, urine-soaked skin. "I can't wait to have a child with you."

She groaned and buried her face in her hands. "I can't believe the time we conceived our child is the one where I ended up peeing all over us."

Dare laughed and kissed the backs of her hands. "Well, you wanted it to be an experience you'll never forget."

His beautiful lover squirmed away from him, still making plaintive sounds. "Nope, we're doing a do-over. We'll get this cleaned up and try again, and *that* will be the time I can tell the other girls about."

Suiting her words, she dug into his pack and produced one of the Cleanse Target scrolls. Then she threw open the tent flaps to let the cold rain pour in, using it to cast the spell and clean everything.

That resulted in clean but soaking wet and freezing cold blankets, not to mention them. Dare dug some spare leather out of his pack to lay out over everything, cuddling Leilanna for warmth as she ignited her hands and began heating and drying the tent with her magic.

"Didn't quite think that through?" he asked lightly.

"N-no, I d-did," she said through chattering teeth. She gave him a bright smile. "We'll j-just have to f-find a w-way to keep w-warm."

Which was exactly what they did. Multiple times, before the tent was finally dry enough for them to wrap the blankets back around them and fall asleep in each other's arms.

* * * * *

The practical side of Dare wanted to stick around in the area and do some more farming, save some time traveling by heading back to Nirim Manor that night. Which he probably would've done if there wasn't the looming threat of Ollivan and his thugs.

Instead he scrounged enough dry wood to light a small fire, cooked them the hot meal they'd missed the night before, and then broke camp so they could head for home.

Leilanna was in a surprisingly good mood given the uncomfortable night, and had been super affectionate from the moment they woke up together. To the point that when he mounted up, she insisted on riding with him.

"After all, we can always switch to my horse halfway home and it'll be about the same," she said as she snuggled into his chest.

Dare didn't point out that the weight of two people was probably more of a strain on the horse than the weight of one person for twice as long; both mounts were sturdy and could handle it for the relatively short trip back home.

As they rode his lover made contented noises and kissed his face and neck. "Our baby," she said dreamily, taking his hand and resting it on her soft tummy. She giggled, sounding a bit giddy. "Our baby."

He hadn't expected her to be so overjoyed about having a child, although it was adorable. He grinned and kissed her forehead. "May it be as smart and beautiful as its mother."

"And father," she said.

After an hour or so Leilanna's bubbly mood settled to her usual attitude, although she would still smile frequently and give him tender kisses and caresses.

Finally, though, she made a restless sound and pouted up at him. "I'm bored, do you know any jokes?"

"Of course I do," Dare said with a laugh. "I tell them all the time."

"Those are mostly plays on words or bad puns." His beautiful dusk elf lover poked his chest. "Come on, what about a dirty joke? Zuri and Pella say you tell funny naughty jokes, but I've never heard you tell one."

"I'm saving them for when I really want to yank your chain," he teased.

She blushed. "What sort of weird roleplay is that?"

Dare laughed. "Okay fine, here's one. What's the difference between a garbanzo bean and a chickpea?"

Leilanna frowned. "There is no difference, they're the same-"

"I've never had a garbanzo bean on me," Dare interrupted, grinning.

Her frown deepened. "I don't get it, you're saying you've had a chickpea-" She cut off as she got it, dark pink eyes narrowing dangerously. "Oh, you son of a bitch."

He threw back his head and laughed.

"You're never going to let me live that down, are you?" his lover demanded, slapping at his arm. "And it was *your* fault!"

Dare grinned and rubbed her back. "No need to be embarrassed, it was hot as hell and we both had fun."

She glowered. "You just better keep your word and not tell anyone else."

As it turned out, he didn't need to.

Not far from the manor Pella appeared riding their way, waving. Dare felt a stab of worry for a moment, until he saw that her tail was wagging and she had a smile on her face. "The laborers are here, Dare!" she called. "We've gotten them started fixing the manor's burned wall, installing the new water tanks, and reinforcing the wall and gate. But it would be better if you were there to direct the work since you know what they need to do."

She reined in beside them, giving Leilanna an expectant look. "Well?"

The dusk elf blushed but gave her an eager smile. "No Prevent Conception . . . I should be pregnant!"

"Yay!" the dog girl squealed, leaning over to hug them both. "You're going to have the cutest babies . . . I can't wait to meet them!"

"How long do dusk elf pregnancies last?" Dare asked, realizing he'd never thought to bring it up before.

"About a year," Leilanna said. "And of course if it's a human about 40 weeks."

He thought of what the Outsider had told him about making sure his first child with women of other races would always be of that race. "Let's plan on a dusk elf baby."

His dusk elf lover nodded. "Yeah, Ireni told us that-"

"You peed on him!" Pella abruptly blurted, leaning closer and sniffing as her tail wagged happily. "Wow, you peed on him *a lot*! That's so hot!"

The dusk elf glared, beautiful features darkening in a furious blush.

Undeterred, the dog girl turned to him, tail wagging so hard she shifted in her saddle. "I didn't know you liked being peed on, Dare!" she said with a grin. "My master used to love watching me pee and having me pee on him, and I'd love to do that with you." She brightened, tail becoming an excited blur. "Me and Lanna can pee on you together!"

It was Dare's turn to blush at the unbidden mental image of the two beautiful women both squatting over him. "That's okay," he said hastily, then paused. "I mean, it might be interesting to try . . ."

Pella giggled and turned her attention back to Leilanna, playfully swatting her knee. "And you! I knew you had a naughty streak, but I didn't realize you were that kinky."

"I most certainly am not!" his dusk elf lover said furiously. "It's only because I lost control while Dare was fucking me."

"Although once it happened you realized you liked it," the dog girl said with a knowing grin.

Leilanna muttered furiously and squirmed out of the saddle, dropping to the ground and stomping towards her horse. "I'm going to ride on ahead and give everyone the good news!" she shouted as she pulled herself into the saddle. "You just better not tell anyone, Pella!"

As she galloped away Pella turned to Dare, grinning. "Since we're alone now, if there's something you want to try . . ."

He laughed and leaned over to affectionately rub her tummy. "Sometime soon. Right now the laborers are waiting, and I need to make sure you and these little guys are safe."

* * * * *

Over the next five days Dare reinforced the manor's walls with the help of the laborers as well as Ilin and the girls, and also got started on the panic room and escape tunnel and other security measures.

The smith came through with the first delivery of razor wire, and Dare showed his family his idea for putting it around the top of the walls at an outward angle. "It won't completely stop a determined enemy," he said. "Especially not an armored one. But it'll slow them down enough to take other measures."

They also reinforced the gate, turning it into a short tunnel an enemy would have to go through to get into the manor yard. It was still the most vulnerable spot in the walls, as gates usually were, but Dare had a plan for that as well.

The ceiling of the tunnel was a section of bound together logs, supported sturdily enough to handle their weight but not *too* securely. When his lovers asked why, he deferred answering them until he could demonstrate his idea.

Which was why, before installing the newly reinforced gate, he gathered everyone at the manor to observe. "We don't need the legendary chest working the pump all the time," he said to the expectant group. "So when we close the manor down for the night when we don't expect anyone to be using the gate, we can do this."

He used a stick to slide the chest, currently the size of a peanut, into a groove above the bound log ceiling until it was in the center of it. Then he turned back to the others with a wry grin. "Obviously we'll take the chest out when we actually use the gate, to prevent accidents. Because we wouldn't want this to happen while someone was in the tunnel."

Dare tossed a rusty old breastplate they'd gotten as monster loot, stuffed with rags and straw to make a convenient target dummy, into the tunnel. Then he said, clearly, "Grow."

The entire ceiling broke through its supports and came down like a ton of bricks, slamming down to the tunnel floor hard enough to make the ground shake beneath their feet and completely pancaking the breastplate.

"Goddess preserve us!" Amalisa squeaked, hugging Pella's arm.

"No kidding we don't want anyone but an enemy in there!"

Leilanna stepped up beside him, stroking one of her long, pointy ears. "How did you do that? Even if the chest was full of rocks it wouldn't be heavy enough." She gave him a level look. "It's not full of gold, is it? What's the point of security if we're going to have our treasure sitting over our front gate?"

Dare chuckled and threw open the chest's lid. "Lead bars. About as heavy as gold, but much cheaper." He shrugged. "Since we're not using the chest for its actual purpose anyway, we can keep it loaded with this.

"And it's not just a security measure for the gate, either," he added. "Shrink."

The chest reduced to peanut size in an instant, and he picked it up and pointed at another dummy he'd set up outside the walls, like a menacing attacker. He chucked the surprisingly heavy little peanut (about four pounds, which was still vastly lighter than it would be thanks to the shrinking spell also proportionally reducing weight) towards the dummy. "Grow!"

The chest grew to full size just in time to flatten the dummy beneath it with terrifying force, in a way not even a boulder of the same size could manage.

Zuri shivered at the sight, clutching Gelaa protectively. "I'm almost scared to handle the chest after that," she confessed.

Ilin nodded grimly. "First the automated pump and now a devastating weapon, neither of which are its intended use." He whistled. "Your mind is awe inspiring, but at times also frightening."

"As long as I can use it to protect the people I love." Dare leaned down and kissed his goblin lover's head, tenderly brushing a finger over his daughter's soft cheek. "We'll all use the proper safety measures with it. And try not to move it around any more than necessary." He motioned to a small hole near the ground along the wall. "We can store it there or in the pump shed when we're not using it."

His lovers exchanged looks. "Does that satisfy you that the manor is secure?" Se'weir asked.

He hesitated. "Once the panic room and escape tunnel and the rest of the razor wires are done, I'll rest easier." He chuckled grimly. "I'll never be fully satisfied you're all safe, but that's my job."

"So we can get back to living our lives and leveling up?" Leilanna asked.

Dare flushed. He supposed that in his determination to secure the manor the atmosphere had been tense the last week. It had probably put undue stress on the women he loved. "Yes, of course," he said, gathering her into his arms. "As long as our sentries from the Avenging Wolves stick to the new patrol routes and protocols I gave them, I think we'll be fine against anything but an invading army."

"Which hopefully Marona will be able to warn us about," Pella said, tail wagging; the last visit had really cemented her friendship with the noblewoman.

Dare looked solemnly around at his family, Ilin included in that since he viewed the man as a brother after everything they'd been through together. "And the first thing I'd like to do now that I've made the place as safe as possible is welcome the newest member of our family."

The women all beamed, and together they made their way over to a bright, sunny spot between the yard and the garden. Just secluded enough for privacy, but still close enough to the center of activity to be part of things. It was surrounded by a circular footpath with plenty of benches for sitting, and outside of the path flowers and cheerful flowering bushes and vine trellises had been planted.

Then Leilanna solemnly produced Eloise's seed, which she'd been holding onto for safekeeping. She'd already prepared the soil and taken all the appropriate measures, but she left the actual planting for Dare.

He cradled the coconut sized object, kissing its smooth surface. "Sorry you had to wait a bit, Eloise," he said as he knelt in front of the hole they'd dug. "This place should be perfect for you, and we're eager to welcome you into our family. Grow healthy and strong in your new home."

Dare lowered the seed into the hole and tenderly covered it with the rich, loamy soil Leilanna had gathered in a pile, then dusted off his hands and stood. "Welcome to Nirim Manor, Eloise!"

The others cheered and gathered around him, looking down at the mound of dirt. "That was beautiful," Pella said, wiping her eyes. "Rosie will be happy to hear it."

"There's one other thing," he said, looking around at his family with a surge of warmth. "Something that's been too long in coming."

He ushered his confused (aside from Ireni who smiled knowingly) but expectant lovers to stand in front of him, smiling at them all.

Zuri, his first love, gentle and nurturing. Pella, playful and fiercely loyal. Leilanna, fiery and passionate but with a soft heart for those she let through her tough shell. Se'weir, warm and affectionate and quick to mother everyone, wanting her loved ones to be happy. The Outsider, mysterious and vigorous and freely affectionate with her family.

Ireni, sweet and gracefully strong and tenderly loving. She'd swept into their lives and organized a disorganized manor, brought the family together in shared purpose, and quietly invited them all to fall in love with her.

Which he had. He thought he knew how she'd answer, but he still felt his heart hammering at that barest possibility of uncertainty.

Dare knelt on one knee in front of Zuri, cupping her small face in his hands. "Zuri," he said tenderly, looking into her shining yellow eyes. "You always praise me for how I saved your life, but in truth you saved mine. You've brought me joy I never imagined I could have in my old life, made my life an adventure I wake up every day eagerly looking forward to."

He leaned forward and lovingly kissed Gelaa's head as she cooed and waved her little arms. "And you're the mother of my first child, our precious daughter. I love you more than I could ever express with words, and being able to spend the rest of my life with you fills me with happiness."

He took out one of the gold rings he'd had the jeweler craft, sized to her finger and set with a yellow sapphire. "I know we can't be properly wed thanks to the bureaucratic boondoggle in Haraldar, but I consider you my wife all the same."

Presenting the ring to her, heart pounding, he met her shining eyes. "Will you marry me?"

All the women there let out a collective sigh, expressions dreamy and tears shining in their eyes as well. Zuri sucked in a sharp breath, gave a laugh of quiet delight, and accepted the ring solemnly. "Of course, my mate," she murmured, slipping the ring onto her finger. "Yes, with all my heart."

Dare gathered her into his arms, tenderly holding her and their daughter, and kissed his betrothed tenderly. Then he held her for a brief time.

Finally he straightened, moved over to Pella, and dropped to a knee in front of her. "My turn?" she teased, eyes dancing.

The others giggled, and he laughed sheepishly. "Sorry if it's a bit clunky, I've never proposed to six women at the same time before."

"I doubt many have," Leilanna said dryly from down the line.

"Shh!" the other women said to her, waving her down, and she blushed and subsided.

Dare smiled up at his second love. "Pella," he said, taking her hand and kissing it softly as she beamed down at him, expression serene but fluffy tail's eager wagging showing her excitement. "You came into my life in a whirlwind, and every moment since has been an exciting adventure. I don't know how I got lucky enough for you to open your heart to me, but you did it fully and enthusiastically. The way you do everything."

There were a few quiet laughs, and the dog girl grinned.

He gently rested his hand on her round belly, leaning forward to kiss it. "I can't wait to be a father with you. To be a husband to you. To share my life with you. You bring our family together, embracing everyone who joins us and giving them your love without reservation." He smiled fondly. "And you protect us with the fierceness of a mother wolf."

Dare produced another ring, this one set with a diamond. "I love you, Pella. With every fiber of my being. Will you make me the happiest man alive and be my wife?"

There was another dreamy sigh from the women, just as heartfelt as the first. Pella's tail wagged so hard it thumped Leilanna beside her, tears of happiness glistening on her cheeks as she gave him a radiant smile. "Yes, Dare. Yes!" She slipped the ring on her finger and looked down at it in wonder. "I never thought I'd have this before I found you."

Dare stood and tenderly kissed her. There was a shared laugh as she enthusiastically licked his mouth as she kissed him back, then he held her close for a short while, heart full and savoring the moment.

Then he moved to Leilanna and dropped to his knee yet again. She folded her arms beneath her plump breasts and raised a snowy eyebrow at him. "I wouldn't have complained if you'd proposed to all of us more intimately, one on one," she said, although a smile touched her plump lips.

The other women groaned and playfully booed her. Dare grinned and took both her soft, elegant hands, kissing them. "Leilanna," he murmured. "We had a blast striking sparks off each other at the start, didn't we?"

"Why are you talking like we don't anymore?" she said, smiling.

He joined the light laughter. "But sparks lead to the hottest fires, and now that we've finally come together we make some beautiful fireworks, don't we?"

"You sure do," Pella teased, tail wagging. "I've seen you come together."

There was more laughter, and Leilanna scowled around. "Come on, you guys," she said plaintively.

They subsided, Pella and Se'weir to either side both patting her supportively. Dare sobered as well, kissing her hands again. "You bring brilliance and passion to everything you do, and you've brightened my life with every moment we're together. I'm honored that you let me into your heart, and I love you with everything I have. I want nothing more than to spend the rest of my life with you and have a family together."

He produced a ring set with a ruby and presented it to her. "Will you marry me?"

Again, the chorus of dreamy sighs. Leilanna tried to keep her expression stern, but her dark pink eyes were huge and sparkling with happiness.

"Since you asked so nicely," she said. She slipped the ring onto her finger, admiring it, then with a joyful laugh dropped to her knees with him and hugged him tight, peppering his face and mouth with kisses. "I love you too, Dare." She took his hand and pressed it to her tummy. "I can't wait to have a baby with you."

Dare held her tenderly, then moved on to Se'weir and dropped to one knee.

"Se'weir," he said, taking her hand and gently rubbing his thumb over the back of it as he looked into her pale yellow eyes, shining with anticipation. "You were willing to forgive me for being a big dumb idiot, and I'm the luckiest man alive that you gave me another chance."

Her eyes softened, and she took his hand with her other one, cradling it gently.

"I was afraid at first that being matched together meant we wouldn't find the strong feelings a husband and wife should have for each other, but I was wrong. Every moment I spend with you feels like home, and I cherish our time together. You wrap your arms around our family and hug us tight and we all bask in your love, and I can't imagine not having you in my life."

Dare kissed her hands, then produced a ring set with a yellow pearl. "I love you, Se'weir, and I'm eager to share a long life with you, full of warmth and laughter and tenderness." He offered her the ring. "Will you marry me?"

"Yes!" she squealed, drowning out the dreamy sighs from the others. She eagerly took the ring and hugged it to her chest, tears streaming down her cheeks. "Yes, my mate. My betrothed. My beloved. I can't wait to be your wife." She pouted. "Although I guess I'll have to."

He winced and grinned sheepishly. "Actually, I talked to your brother about moving up the date. We can have the wedding whenever you agree on."

"With everyone?" his hobgoblin betrothed asked hopefully. "All together as a family?"

Dare hesitated; he hadn't made any plans there, since that was something they'd all have to decide on. Although it looked as if a decision wasn't necessary.

"All together," the girls all agreed, in a tone that suggested that they were already making plans.

Dare leaned forward and kissed Se'weir, then wrapped her in his arms and held her close as she hugged him back warmly, soft and sweet.

Finally, he moved to kneel in front of Ireni and the Outsider.

"Me first," the Outsider said, not in a question but as if she'd already known. Which she had.

He grinned and took her delicate hands in his. "Same as you were first to greet me when I came to this new place, first to be my friend. And now you've become so much more to me. More than I ever could've expected when I first heard your soothing voice in my moment of panic in that gray void. And every moment since."

Dare looked into her sparkling emerald eyes, glistening with Ireni's tears but currently composed. "You freaked me out the first couple times we fucked," he admitted, ignoring a few surprised gasps from the others at the less than romantic choice of words. Although the goddess only grinned.

He kissed her hands. "But while you pretend to only care about the sensations, about the entertainment of my life and our time together, I can feel your love. Fierce, hungry, wholeheartedly giving. And I love you too. My benefactor, my friend, my lover. I love you with all my heart, and I want to spend the rest of this life you've given me with you."

He produced a ring set with a black pearl and proffered it. "Outsider, will you marry me?"

Rather than a dreamy sigh, the others all raised a collective cheer of delight. As for the Outsider, she offered him a secretive smile and leaned in close, pouty lips tickling his ear. "Merellesia," she whispered. "Sia, in front of the others."

Dare looked at her with wide eyes, feeling like he'd been given a great gift. "Sia," he said. "My beloved, will you be my wife?"

"Mmm. I'll permit you to be my husband." Big green eyes twinkling, she accepted the ring and slipped it onto her finger, smiling down at it.

She leaned forward and gave him a brief, heated kiss, running her hand through his hair. Then she briskly removed the ring and tucked it into her pouch, pulling him to his feet and ushering him away. "Ireni's turn."

The goddess withdrew, leaving a shy, nervous, eager Ireni standing there, nibbling her lip and idly toying with a strand of her long auburn hair.

She was so beautiful, so sweet, that his heart ached just looking at her.

Dare knelt in front of her, looking up into her shining green eyes. "Ireni," he murmured, holding out his hand.

Smiling, she took it and squeezed with surprising enthusiasm. "My love," she murmured, a happy tear slipping down her cheek.

He kissed the back of it, lips lingering on her soft skin, still holding her gaze. "The first time we met you offered me your full, unreserved love, and I ran away as fast as my legs could carry me."

"And me," Zuri added, to a few giggles.

Dare grinned but kept his focus on the beautiful Priestess. "I hope you'll forgive me, but any sane man would have trouble believing such a beautiful woman could love him that openly when they hadn't even met."

"I came on too strong," she admitted bashfully. "I'm just glad I didn't chase you away completely."

"Not as glad as I am." He took her other hand, holding them gently. "We haven't known each other as long, but every moment together has been a wonder. To feel your love, and feel my own grow as I've come to know your kind heart and gentle spirit."

He produced a ring set with an emerald that paled in comparison to her eyes. "I love you, Ireni. I want to spend my life with you. I want to share everything, to hold you close and make a home together and in our old age watch our grandchildren play at our feet."

He could already hear a few of the others cooing in delight as he held out the ring. "Will you marry me and share that life together?"

Ireni's smile hit Dare like a million watt floodlight, leaving him momentarily dazed.

A woman's smile was always a beautiful thing, but he didn't think he'd ever seen one as lovely as hers. It wasn't just her stunning beauty, either; the expression was so free and open that it could've come straight from the deepest recesses of her heart. Like a glimpse at a joyous, brilliantly shining soul.

"Yes," Ireni murmured, a few more tears slipping down her cheeks. She delicately took the ring from him and slipped it onto her finger. "Oh yes, Dare. With all my heart, for as long as I live, through whatever may come."

She wrapped her arms around his neck and settled down on his raised knee, cuddling close to his chest as she lifted her face expectantly.

Dare leaned down and kissed her tenderly. "I love you," he said again. "Thank you for coming into my life." After a few moments of holding her close he turned and looked at the others, who'd gathered around.

He held out his arms, inviting them all into a group embrace.

Phoenix

"All of you. I love you more than I could ever say, so much my heart is bursting. Thank you all for coming into my life and making a family with me."

His beloved, his betrothed, soon to be his wives, all gathered around him, wrapping him in their love.

Chapter Fifteen
Mountain Meadow

The rest of the day was spent in a whirlwind celebration, with the women eagerly making plans for a group wedding, debating on the date and what arrangements they'd make. The house and garden were filled with laughter and chatter as they played, ate, and basked in the glow of the moment.

Dare found himself showered with constant affection, his lap rarely empty when he was seated and his lovers cuddling him, showering him with kisses, and nuzzling his chest and neck throughout the evening. They were just as passionate with each other, showing that their love and desire weren't focused on him alone.

He was a bit embarrassed about the affection in front of Ilin and Amalisa, who at times blushed at the display. But their friends seemed pleased for them, and happy to be part of the celebration of this next step for the family.

He wasn't surprised that when the celebration moved to the bedroom, his lovers did their best to thoroughly tire him out again. Although the sex was more focused on tenderly expressing their love than fucking each other silly.

They saved that for the next morning, waking Dare up early and giving him a thorough workout for hours.

To their disappointment Ireni didn't take part, ceding control to the Outsider for the entire time. Not because she didn't want to be with them, but because she wanted her first time with him, then with the rest of them, to be special.

Understanding, they all showered the petite redhead with love and affection as they wished her goodnight, before she stepped back to let the goddess take over and they all headed to bed.

It was midmorning before Dare reluctantly dragged himself out of bed. With the security measures around the manor taken care of he wanted to get back to leveling, and his next goal was to check out the mountains to the south.

They were potentially a prime leveling location, since the abrupt elevation changes messed with the world system governing the spawn points, so they were far closer together than usual. The main downside was that those elevation changes also messed with monster levels, so you could find spawn points up to 20 levels apart within a hundred yards of each other.

There was at least some reason to the madness, where lower elevations usually meant lower levels and higher elevations were home to the stronger monsters.

Actually, that unpredictability was what excited Dare about finally checking out the mountains. The experience may be more consistent, or less, or random based on the day, but it should be fun.

Apparently he wasn't the only one who thought so, either, because when he announced his plans at breakfast Ireni insisted on coming with him, with the full approval of the others. And suspiciously, she also made it clear it was going to be an overnight trip and packed accordingly, while all the other women shared knowing grins.

He felt his heart begin to race at what that might mean; this was clearly Ireni, not the Outsider. And if this was like his hunting trip with Leilanna, did she intend for it to end the same way?

Dare gave the petite, bookish redhead a questioning look, and she blushed and gave him that million watt smile again. "Just the two of us," she murmured. As if to emphasize that point, she took Sia's black pearl ring from her pouch and set it on a nearby mantle.

It hadn't taken long for the woman and goddess sharing a body to settle that the best way for people to tell them apart was to switch the rings they wore. When there was time for that small gesture, that was. So even though they'd had the rings for less than a day, he'd gotten used to seeing Ireni wearing her emerald and Sia wearing her black pearl.

If the ring was staying behind then apparently the goddess would be as well. Or at least taking a backseat as an observer, to give him and Ireni a chance to truly be together.

He couldn't help but grin like an idiot as he made his own preparations to leave, pleased and honored that she felt ready to share her love with him.

During the ride to the mountains Ireni wanted to talk about Earth more. It was obvious the Outsider had told her a lot, a shocking amount actually, but she was clearly having trouble wrapping her head around things.

"So you hire these airplanes like you'd hire a carriage?" she asked. "People don't have their own personal planes, like higher level adventurers or the wealthy can buy flying objects?"

He shook his head. "Magical flying objects do most of the work for you, while a pilot requires lots of training to fly an airplane. It's not just a matter of wealth, most people don't have the time to learn to fly."

"Oh." She cocked her head. "So it's different from learning to drive a car?"

"Much different, and much more difficult. And even more so for helicopters."

The bookish redhead brightened. "Sia calls them whirlybirds!" She shook her head in amazement. "It's hard to imagine that thin blades spinning in the air can lift something heavy off the ground. I'm not sure I'd believe it if the Goddess hadn't been the one telling me."

Dare didn't often feel a pang for his old life on Earth, but he did now. "I wish I could take you there, show you everything."

She smiled wistfully. "There's no telling what may come in the future."

Just short of the mountains they encountered a Level 25-28 spawn point of giant rats. "What do you think?" Ireni asked. "Farm this? You're almost 32."

Dare grimaced. He'd been Level 31 for forever it felt like, and 30 before that. To be fair, though, compared to his other leveling it *had* been forever; he was leveling up like molasses.

It wasn't just the experience requirement bump at 30, either. He'd just been so occupied with other things the last few weeks that he hadn't gotten in a good day in a while. And technically, depending on how scouting in the mountains went, today would probably also be slow.

"Let's do it," he said. "I'd like to hit it today if possible." It meant they wouldn't be able to scout quite as far, but if they were going to camp out then they'd have tomorrow as well.

With his Level 30 Journeyman quality recurve bow he was able to kill most of the lower level monsters in two or three hits, with the occasional one-shot if he got a critical hit. Ireni barely even needed to shield him as they waded in among the giant rats, killing them quickly and working their way through to the other side.

The loot and experience gains were modest at best, but it didn't take long to clear the spawn point and mount up again, continuing on towards the mountains.

The spawn points doubled in frequency as they scaled the first foothill, the sharp elevation changes leading to a couple that felt practically on top of each other compared to the usual distancing. The first was around Level 15 and the next was around Level 20, both worthless for their purposes, but since they were in his and Ireni's path and they'd brought along a packhorse for loot, they went ahead and cleared them anyway. Or at least the middle of them where the monsters clumped.

Near the ridge was a Level 27-29 spawn point, which was worth pausing to clear. It took a bit longer, the humanoid bird monsters putting up enough of a fight with multiple adds that Ireni had to throw him a barrier on every pull. There were some decent tailoring materials among the loot, and a bit of treasure, which made searching each monster they killed a bit more exciting.

On the far slope of the foothill, after clearing another lower level spawn point, Dare perked up at the sight of a naked, transparent pink woman with her lower half dissolving into a viscous, amorphous pool, oozing her way down the stream below.

A slime girl.

"Did we stumble into a slime a spawn point?" Ireni asked, dismounting to approach the monster for a closer look.

Dare shook his head as he followed. "My Eye would've alerted me if we were in a spawn point." He checked his Eye and saw the slime was only Level 10, which made it a mystery how it was here, then chuckled. "Things tend to leave slime girls alone, aside from feeding them their come that is . . . do you think it's possible that a spawn point was ignored for so long that it overflowed and produced roaming slimes?"

She giggled. "It's been known to happen. Since they're harmless and provide a beneficial service communities have risen around them, and as the other nearby spawn points were hunted down until they disappeared the slimes remained."

He arched an eyebrow. "The women in those communities must be pretty chill with having a bunch of monster girls around for the men to play with."

The petite redhead slapped his arm. "I mean that they purify water and clean items placed inside them. They're basically living Cleanse Target spells." She gave him an impish look. "Although on the subject of playing . . . it's been awhile since you were with a slime, hasn't it?"

Dare laughed and put his arm around her, pulling her close. "Tempting, but I'm spending an enjoyable day with my gorgeous fiancee. I want to give her my full attention."

She blushed, looking pleased. "I want to give you my full attention, too," she said almost shyly, resting her head on his shoulder. They stood contentedly like that for a minute or so.

Then he had a sudden thought. "What about propriety? Physical danger isn't the only reason slime girls would be a problem in civilized society."

Ireni laughed. "Relax . . . you think people would have them around if they were oozing along the streets looking like naked women and randomly having sex in public? Think of them like pets in terms of intelligence and trainability. Except they clean up messes instead of making them."

She waved down at the topless pink slime. "Slimes can be trained to stay in a more socially acceptable blob form unless taken somewhere more private to "feed". Also, just like any living creature they can get full . . . if fed enough they revert to blob form and lose interest in feeding for a while, although that might take five or six loads."

"I think I could manage that," Dare said wryly.

His petite betrothed laughed. "Every day? I think your wives and consorts might have something to say about that . . . we need some loving too." She shook her head, sobering. "Anyway, as long as slimes are regularly fed at least a little, with proper training they're perfectly safe and acceptable in a community."

"That's a relief."

She smirked at him. "You're thinking of bringing her home to the manor, aren't you? Since you were talking about having Morwal dig us a swimming pool, and also an enclosed bath house. Having a resident slime to clean them would be useful."

She dug a small elbow into his side, grinning impishly. "If we were to swing back around on the way home and pick it up, would you be interested?"

"Oh fuck yes," he said, smirking down at the monster. "An adorable pink slime girl as a pool attendant? I'd be feeding her daily."

Ireni threw back her head and laughed. "You wouldn't be the only one, either." Her eyes sparkled as she looked up at him. "Guys aren't the only ones slimes draw secretions from. We could have a little bedroom for her near the pool where she stays when she's not cleaning, and we can visit her there to feed her whenever we want." She giggled again. "In fact, she'd probably be in blob form most of the time, she'll be eating so much."

Dare's cock twitched at the thought. "Ooh, maybe we should

visit her right now, then. We can have a threesome."

"Uh uh," his betrothed said sternly. "Like you said, I get your full attention today." She watched the slime girl meander along the stream. "Let's just hope she's still around when we get back."

He reluctantly mounted up again, and they made their way up the first slope of the Gadris Mountains.

They encountered a couple more spawn points, a Level 20 and a Level 39. The absurdly high level one they bypassed, of course, but after some debate they circled the lower level one as well, feeling in a hurry to scout and get some use out of their trip to the mountains.

As it turned out, their luck improved just on the far side of that first ridge.

In a hollow down below Dare caught sight of a giant bird, a hawk or an eagle. Like the slime girl it was on its own, but unlike that roaming monster this one had a reason for being alone; he checked it with his Adventurer's Eye, then felt his pulse race in anticipation.

He'd been right, it wasn't just an ordinary monster. "Lord of the Skies. Monster, Party Rated. Level 24. Attacks: Swoop, Talon Slash, Vicious Snap, Shriek, Tornado, Wing Sweep, Liftoff."

He quickly read off the stats to Ireni.

"What do you think?" she asked, grinning excitedly. "Can the two of us take it? It's a level lower than the wyvern from the dungeon, and with easier attacks, and you soloed like half of that."

Dare hesitated. Easy as the fight seemed, he couldn't help but think of how the chimera had pounced on Zuri, and only her Sheltering Embrace had saved her from serious harm. Then there had been the wyvern spitting acid on Pella; he still heard her agonized scream shivering in his nightmares, even months later.

There was probably no danger here against such a lower level enemy, especially with Ireni's barrier spell. The main strength of her class was *because* she could keep people from coming to harm rather than having to heal them when they took damage. Although she could do that too.

Still, his betrothed was carrying his child, and he'd sworn that he'd never make the mistake of putting his pregnant lovers in even the slightest danger again.

As usual, Ireni seemed to read his mind. "I know we've been needing to have this conversation, my love, so let's have it," she said, stroking his chest. "You want to talk about how adamantly opposed you are to the mothers of your children being put in the slightest danger. Which is an issue since you know for certain I'm now carrying your child."

Having a fiancee who read his mind was . . . an experience. "I do," he said firmly.

"Well don't worry, I feel the same way." She smiled gently. "Which is why neither I or the Goddess will ever put ourselves in danger. If there's any situation during our adventures where us or the baby might come to harm, we'll withdraw immediately. Or take appropriate action to ensure our wellbeing."

The petite redhead patted his cheek. "And it goes without saying that when we're far enough along in the pregnancy that we can't reasonably be running around fighting monsters, we'll return to Nirim Manor with the rest of the girls."

"That's all a relief to hear," Dare said, stroking her back.

She shook her head wryly. "I'll admit I feel better when I'm around to help manage things, anyway. The other girls are smart and well meaning, but inexperienced and hopelessly disorganized. I'm happy I can put my skills managing the brothel and chapel in Kov to good use."

He laughed ruefully. "We're all happy too. You've been an absolute lifesaver ever since you arrived."

Ireni's eyes softened and she leaned against him contentedly. "Thanks, that means a lot. But of course I'll do everything I can to make sure our family has the best life possible, just like you and the others."

She straightened determinedly. "Speaking of which, do you want to kill that party rated monster together?" She took his hand and squeezed it. "One kill closer to the Protector of Bastion achievement, which will help you with petitioning for knighthood. And more trophies to increase our reputation with visitors to Nirim Manor."

Dare couldn't help but grin. "In that case let's fuck the big bird up."

With most fights he would take some time to plan and prepare, but that was because it took some setup to get Zuri's Nature's Curse on the boss, and with multiple people they needed to figure out positioning and attack rotations and what to do about aggro.

With just him and Ireni, though, things were a lot more straightforward. She put up Bolstering Faith to buff their defense, cast her Goddess's Embrace barrier spell on them both as well, then got ready to respond to whatever happened as Dare made his own preparations.

Then he started damaging the Lord of the Skies down as fast as he could right off the bat, then activated Cheetah's Dash and sprinted to stay ahead of the monster as he used his spear to apply Hamstring and Wing Cripple. That gave him room to put some distance between them and continued loosing arrows.

Compared to the other party rated monsters the fight felt almost anticlimactic at first. Of course, the fact that they were several levels higher than the giant eagle made a difference.

It was quick, sure, and ferocious. Dare made full use of the barrier spell and used his defensive cooldowns, both Roll and Shoot and Prey's Vigilance, as he kept ahead of its blindingly fast beak. He also had to struggle to stay on his feet as it churned its wings and sent gale-force winds swirling through the hollow.

But ultimately it was a flying enemy and he was a ranged damage dealer. The abilities that would've caused trouble for a melee fighter were easier for him to handle, and with Ireni keeping him protected and healing the little damage he did take, he could focus fully on staying far enough back from the monster to deal damage.

The most frightening moment was when the Lord of the Skies turned on Ireni, who looked even tinier and more delicate beneath its fierce assault. But she stayed calm as she kept herself safe with one barrier then another.

That gave Dare time to Pounce in and Wing Cripple the monster with his spear again, drawing its attention back to him as his betrothed backed away to safety. He ended up getting a wicked gash along his side during the exchange, but it didn't slow him down.

Hell, he even finally got a proc from his Quill Shot ability, and got to enjoy the sensation of instantly pulling an arrow from the quiver, fitting it to the string, drawing, and shooting.

It made him feel like a badass as he dove away with Roll and Shoot, activated Rapid Shot again, and kept loosing arrows.

The biggest hurdle of the fight was that the monster had a lot of health. Even with his damage, having to stay ahead of its attacks made the fight drag on. Ireni healed the wound in his side, but he had to switch to his spear as the giant eagle again closed in on him.

Which earned him a vicious slash along his scalp that made blood sheet down across the side of his face. He got knocked tumbling, dazed by the attack, and lost his spear before he could roll to his feet and get away again. Although not before taking a talon across his back that burned like fire.

Fuck, maybe not so anticlimactic after all.

Thankfully the Lord of the Skies was only a few arrows away from death by that point. It also picked that moment to take to the air and use one of its wing attacks. *That* made the final moments a bit anticlimactic, as it wheeled away in death and plowed into the mountainside.

Text appeared in the corner of Dare's vision. "Party rated monster Lord of the Skies defeated. 14,000 bonus experience awarded."

"Completed 4/10 towards Achievement Protector of Bastion: Slay 10 party rated monsters in the region of Bastion."

"Trophies gained: Eagle Head, Eagle Foot x2. Loot body to

acquire."

Dare rubbed at his back, hands coming away bloody as he felt his skin stitch back together with Ireni's healing. It had hurt like a bitch for a moment there, but he was fine now. "You okay?" he called to his betrothed as he started for her.

"Untouched, as promised," she called back. She reached him and tenderly placed a hand on his cheek. "Sorry you got sliced up there . . . are *you* okay?"

He took her hand and kissed it. "Nothing these cute little hands couldn't wave away with a couple spells. Thanks for having my back."

"Mmm." The beautiful redhead buried her head in his chest. "This was fun, wasn't it?"

Dare grinned. "It was. Although now it's time for the best part . . . looking at the loot."

The Lord of the Skies itself didn't offer much more than the trophies and a whole bunch of golden feathers. Which no doubt Zuri would be happy to have for pillows and feather beds. But in their experience most of these sorts of monsters had more loot stashed nearby, so they went on a quick search.

Ireni finally called him over to a narrow crack in the hillside that had been stuffed with odds and ends the giant eagle had no doubt gathered. As they got to work dragging it all out into the sunshine they uncovered some treasure among the junk: there were some coins, a silver goblet, and an Exceptional quality belt that increased carry capacity by 20 pounds, just in the top layer.

As Dare rifled through the pile of loot his fingers brushed a small metal disk, and he jumped when text again appeared in front of him.

"Quest discovered: Mysterious Medallion. A silver medallion was discovered among the items collected by the Lord of the Skies. Investigation is warranted."

Frowning, he pulled out the medallion and looked it over. Ireni abandoned her own search and leaned closer. "Is that Goblin?" she asked.

There were words scratched faintly onto the front rim of the medallion. The translation stone was having trouble doing anything with them because they were nearly rubbed away, but after a bit of spit and buffing on his shirt they came out clearly.

"Wek'u'ko."

"Wek," the bookish redhead murmured, frowning. "As in Gar'u'wek?"

Dare nodded. "Se'weir's grandfather. Unless Wek is a common name."

Ireni played with a lock of her long auburn hair. "In that case it's pretty clear we should take it to her, or maybe Rek or even Gar."

They both gave a simultaneous start of surprise as text appeared in front of Dare's vision, and presumably hers as well. "Quest accepted: Mysterious Medallion. Return the silver medallion to its rightful owner and put the spirits of the past to rest."

"Well that's the easiest quest ever," he said as he tucked the item into his belt pouch.

"Not so much if we didn't already know the Avenging Wolves." Ireni shook her head sadly. "I feel bad for Se'weir, and Rek and Gar and the rest of their family. Wek probably just disappeared one day on a hunt and was never seen again."

"Well like the quest said, hopefully this will give them some closure." Dare motioned to the crack in the rock. "What do you say we get the rest of this loot sorted and loaded up, then see what else we can find?"

There were a few other items of note, and plenty of Trash loot they could sell. They loaded it all up, although Dare held back the carry weight belt. "Think this will work for the horses?" he joked.

His petite betrothed laughed. "Maybe, but I bet you'd rather use it yourself."

He blinked. "I'm not carrying anything right now, though."

"Aren't you?" She motioned to him. "Your armor, your

weapons, your clothes. It all adds up. And without it weighing you down you'll run faster and for longer." Her green eyes danced. "Also, if you were to carry me around like you have Zuri and Leilanna, I'd weigh less too. Which would be neat."

Dare raised an eyebrow as he removed his belt and put on the new one; sure enough, he immediately felt lighter and freer. "Are you saying you want me to carry you around while I run fast?"

"Yes, please! I've been looking forward to this for a long time!" Ireni shot him that million-watt smile that had left him dazzled yesterday and held out her arms.

Gods, she was beautiful.

When he recovered from the unexpected moment of heaven he found her looking at him quizzically. "What's that look?" She self-consciously brushed her hair as if afraid some bit of grass was there.

Dare felt his own cheeks heat. "What, you don't already know?" he teased.

"The Goddess doesn't tell me everything," his betrothed said, porcelain cheeks flushing rosy. She paused, then added something under her breath.

"What was that?" he asked; he could've sworn she'd said, "Like anything about your sex life."

"Nothing," Ireni said a bit too quickly. Then she recovered and her expression became stern, like a librarian who'd just caught him dog-earing pages. "So what was that look?"

Dare reached out and gently brushed her delicate rosebud lips. "I was just thinking that there's nothing more glorious than a beautiful woman smiling without reservation. And yours is the most incredible I've ever been lucky enough to see."

His betrothed's big green eyes went huge at his heartfelt words, and she became adorably flustered. "You're just saying that," she murmured, blushing furiously.

He grinned and nodded upwards. "Ask *her*."

Ireni shook her head, showing him a brief flash of that incredible smile again. "I don't need to," she whispered, stepping forward into his arms.

Dare held her tenderly for a minute or so, luxuriating in the feel of her soft warmth.

Then his betrothed wrapped her arms around his neck and shifted so he could hold her in a princess carry. "Zoom?" she said, eyes dancing. "We can go as fast as a car, after all."

He grinned back. "Zoom!" he agreed, picking her up.

But before he could take off she squirmed to face forward and pointed at the horses. "Take a stop off there first, though. I got a gift for you. For us, really."

Dare blinked, surprised, pleased, and more than a little touched. "You did?"

She nodded. "I've been meaning to give them to you, but I hadn't had a chance to be carried by you yet, and with the horses the other girls haven't really either."

Curious, he carried her over to her horse, where she dug around in the saddlebags and produced two pairs of goggles.

They were a bit crude, made of leather and glass and looking a lot like what the old aviators used to wear, back before airplanes even had closed cockpits. But they looked comfortable.

More to the point, they were probably one of the most useful gifts he'd gotten in a long time. Especially since he'd gained Cheetah's Dash and his passive speed increase with Power Up at 30 and could now run close to 40 miles an hour.

The wind at that speed was brutal on the eyes.

Dare grinned and hugged his betrothed tight as she put on his goggles for him. "These are perfect, thank you."

She flashed that brilliant smile again as she put on her own goggles; they made her look ridiculously cute. "Me and Sia brainstormed the best gift on the way to meet you. I'm glad you like them."

"Let's take them for a test run." Holding her close, he took off across the hollow.

Ireni shrieked in delight and leaned into the wind, grinning from ear to ear as they practically flew across the mountainside.

* * * * *

After another few hours of rolling the dice on spawn points, gradually finding higher and higher level ones as they got deeper into the mountains and higher in elevation, Dare finally killed the last monster he needed to reach Level 32.

At first he thought it was going to be another mundane level. Nothing exciting, putting points in Bows, Melee, various other passive class abilities. A few of the universal abilities he'd started working on, and-

He noticed in the universal tree that one of the new abilities he'd unlocked that level used mana.

Finally! 31 levels of having a mana pool sitting there uselessly, and now he finally had something. He eagerly put a point into the ability, then grinned like an idiot as he snapped his fingers.

A small, bright light appeared above them for a moment, using up about .5% of his mana pool.

Fucking awesome! With a laugh Dare raised both hands over his head and began snapping, the lights strobing like fireworks. His mana pool swiftly drained, but he didn't care. "Wooo!" he shouted, doing finger guns in front of him pointed at the monster he'd just killed.

He cut his celebration short at the sight of Ireni staring at him in bemusement; apparently she wasn't as excited by his new ability as he was. "Is that . . . Snap?" she asked, tone carefully neutral.

"Sure is!" He threw his hands out to the sides and spun as he snapped a few more times, making lines of light in a spinning blur.

"You used an ability point on that," she said flatly.

"Absolutely." Dare grinned. "I have access to a previously unused resource and can create light. How is that not badass?"

The bookish redhead remained unimpressed. "You can create a

moderately bright light for a moment. And considering your class, with no abilities to increase your mana pool and regeneration, you can use it what, a few hundred times until you're out of mana? That's worth a point?"

"You tell me." Grinning, he held out a hand to the side again and snapped his fingers. As the light briefly bloomed her eyes naturally followed it, and with her distracted he pounced with his other hand.

"Eeeee!" she squealed in surprised laughter, twisting away as he tickled her tummy.

"Gotcha!" Dare said, smiling even wider. "Light is never useless. You can use it for diversions, as signals over a distance or at night, as a quick counter to any sort of sudden darkness or to get a flash image of a dark room, the list goes on. Easily worth the price of a bit of mana and an ability point I otherwise probably would've put in Traps."

"Tickling, really?" Ireni asked with a great air of dignity, straightening her robes as her face went pink. "You realize I'm a High Priestess of the Outsider, right?"

"And you make the most adorable sounds when you're tickled," he said, wrapping his arms around her and pulling her close so he could kiss her rosy porcelain cheek. "And you can believe I'm going to remember it."

She pouted up at him with her adorable little rosebud lips, although her blush deepened. "Well, I suppose I don't mind if you tickle me."

"I'd rather kiss you." Dare leaned down and gently pressed his lips to hers.

"Mmm." Ireni's mouth opened invitingly as she kissed him back, her soft little body melting against his. Her small tongue slipped into his mouth and found his, lovingly caressing it as she continued to make quiet sounds of affectionate enjoyment.

The way she kissed was vastly different from Sia. The goddess was always passionate, even hungry, trying to rile him up with her lips and tongue as a prelude to vigorous lovemaking.

Ireni, though, held him softly and sweetly, her lips warm and tender. He thought she'd break it off after a few moments, but she seemed content to let the kiss linger as they held each other, bond deepening with every passing moment.

Dare gently stroked her silky straight hair with one hand and ran the other up and down her back, basking in the warmth of this beautiful, kind, brave woman's love. He would've happily held her like this forever, but then he felt her begin subtly moving her sweet little body against him in a way he was more than familiar with.

Feeling himself begin to harden, he pulled back. "I think we've done enough leveling for the day," he murmured as he looked into her big green eyes. "Ready to make camp?"

His beautiful betrothed nodded eagerly, looking breathless. "Let's find the closest flat spot close to a stream. I'll set up the tent and get ready, you cook dinner."

Chapter Sixteen
Precious Moments

Dare found an epind, one of the small cow-like animals with meat even more tender and delicious than beef, that must've strayed from its herd.

Up in the mountains surrounded by predators and roaming monsters, bringing down such a good meal was a lucky break. Or maybe a nod from Sia on the night she'd told him he needed to make special.

He certainly intended to, for Ireni's sake. It was no less than his beloved deserved.

As soon as they found a good campsite she used one of Zuri's Cleanse Target scrolls in the stream, set up the tent, then disappeared inside. He wasn't sure what his beautiful fiancee needed to do to get ready when she was already perfect, but no doubt she'd leave him awestruck.

In the meantime Dare got the steaks cooking and another skillet with frying potatoes, carrots, and onions, as well as a fireside pound cake. He left them to cook, grateful for the Collisa ability systems where cooking required far less supervision, and took a trip to the stream himself to use one of Zuri's scrolls and change into a new suit of fine clothes he found in his saddlebags, obviously her gift for the special occasion.

He could trust his sweet, beautiful goblin fiancee to think of those sorts of details. Probably a good thing, since he'd packed his usual evening clothes.

Fine enough for everyday wear, but this was a night he wanted him and Ireni both to remember.

Dare finally finished the last touches on dinner and called to his betrothed that the food was ready. Part of him expected to wait a few minutes, but to his surprise she emerged immediately, taking his breath away.

She had borrowed fashion from Earth and was wearing a gorgeous knee-length, strapless gown of the same emerald green as her eyes, the material thin enough to accentuate her delicate curves with every movement, as well as a fur stole for warmth in the cold air of a autumn evening in the mountains. As a nod to the temperature she wore white silk stockings and matching white calfskin slippers.

Her long auburn hair hung loose down her back, and her porcelain cheeks were flushed with the cold and excitement. She shivered slightly, from the chill or nerves he wasn't sure, and he quickly removed his heavy fur cloak and wrapped it around her, then hugged her close.

"I have no words," Dare said with a low laugh, leaning down to kiss her tenderly. "You're like a dream made flesh in this rocky mountain valley."

Ireni laughed ruefully. "And I'm well aware of it . . . this getup is seriously unsuitable for camping, especially in this season."

"It really is," he agreed with a smile, leading her to the fire.

He had a surprise of his own waiting for her there, one of the collapsible chairs he'd modified into a bench so a couple could sit side-by-side, as well as a blanket for them to wrap around them as they ate.

His fiancee looked grateful as he got her settled and snugly wrapped in the blanker, burying her face in the soft cloth. "This is great," she murmured. "I love how you're always trying your hardest to invent new things to give all of us a more comfortable life."

Dare felt his cheeks heat as he handed her a carefully arranged plate, then made up his own. "If I can provide you even a tenth of the happiness you've given me, I'll consider myself a great success."

She leaned against him as he settled down on the bench beside her and wrapped the blanket around them both, her body soft and warm. "It's a good attitude to have, my love," she said, kissing his shoulder. "One we all share. But I don't know if you realize just how happy you've made all of us."

Eating while cuddled together was a bit awkward, but he was content to accept the challenge and she seemed to be as well. He'd pulled out all the stops for this meal, at least as much as he could for something cooked over a fire, and he was gratified at her noises of appreciation.

Although he had to wonder if it was just enjoyment of the food that made Ireni eat as quickly as she could while still looking graceful and refined. She kept shooting him eager looks and shy, inviting smiles, and he wondered if she was as excited as he was for the night they'd both waited so long for.

Her even longer than him.

So he wasn't offended when she set aside her plate with several bites still left, then turned to him and dazzled him with that million-watt smile again. "I want to be with you, my love," she said, resting a hand on his leg. "I want to share everything with you."

Dare wasted no time setting aside his own plate, remaining food forgotten. When he turned back to his beautiful fiancee her big green eyes were looking up at him in eager anticipation, rosebud lips parted and glistening invitingly.

"I love you, Ireni," he murmured, then leaned forward and kissed her softly.

She made a quiet sound, somewhere between a sigh and a moan, and melted against him, arms wrapping around his neck and small hands grabbing his head to pull his lips harder against hers.

Her little tongue pressed into his mouth to teasingly play with his, while at the same time she lifted a leg up over him to straddle his lap, her soft little body pressed up against his. As he moved his hands down to her hips she moved against him with another moan, and he felt her warmth press against his crotch as the intimacy of the moment turned to pure heat.

"Ireni," he gasped when they finally broke the kiss for air.

His auburn-haired betrothed tugged insistently at his shirt as she hungrily explored his mouth with her soft little tongue. With some help from him she managed to peel it off and toss it aside, and she moaned as she ran her small hands over his chest, then reached down and began freeing his cock from his pants.

"I'm a romantic at heart, Dare," she panted as she continued to pepper his lips and face with sweet little kisses. "And I want nothing more than to make slow, gentle love to you and then fall asleep in your arms."

"Next time?" Dare guessed with a grin as she began unlacing his pants.

Ireni giggled. "Many times to come." She yanked his pants down hard enough to make him jump, small hands wrapping around his swiftly growing manhood. "But *this* time I've been waiting for you for a long time, and I've got a lot of anticipation to work out."

She leaned up to kiss him fiercely again as her soft fingers began working his shaft. Then he bit back a groan as she lifted up on her knees and pushed her hips forward, continuing to jerk him off as she rubbed her sex against the tip of his cock with only her soft dress between them.

She wasn't wearing panties, and he could feel her delicate lips parting deliciously as they pressed against his hardness.

The petite redhead moaned and teasingly moved against him in a way he wanted to feel more of, hands speeding up on his shaft. "I need you inside me," she breathed.

Dare groaned as his hands moved to her small ass, and his mouth worked entirely independent of his brain as he blurted, "I wish I could see you in glasses."

Her hands paused and her big green eyes stared up at him, smooth brow furrowing in confusion. "What?" Then she cocked her head as if listening to an unheard voice, Sia undoubtedly, and her rosebud lips parted in a delighted smile. "Oooh. Sexy librarian. And such a prim costume to hide my cute little body. I'd definitely like to make that happen with you sometime."

Ireni abruptly lifted herself away from him. "But I know of

something you want to see even more," she teased, reaching for the hem of her lovely green dress.

Dare watched eagerly as she lifted it up her slender body and over her head, tossing it aside to join his shirt. She was naked underneath aside from her thigh-high white stockings, and she was breathtaking.

He'd seen Sia naked and technically the two women shared the exact same body. But as he ran his eyes over his redheaded fiancee's delicate figure, small nipples hardening to points and flawless porcelain skin pimpling with gooseflesh in the cool evening air, he felt like he was seeing her for the first time.

He could've looked at her like that forever, but she shivered and pulled the blanket back up to cover them again, pressing her soft skin against him as her hard nipples pushed into his chest. He wrapped his arms around her, relishing the feel of holding her small body, and she moaned and resumed their heated kiss.

Ireni wasted no time running her hands over his chest and shoulders, and Dare was only too happy to reach up and take her small breasts in his hands, her nipples poking his palms like little diamonds as he played with her soft mounds and ran his thumbs over her nubs.

Then with a final needy whimper she raised herself over him again, taking his throbbing erection in her delicate hands and guiding him to her entrance. Her soft folds, warm and slick with her arousal, wrapped lovingly around his tip, and she gasped as she lowered herself onto him, guiding him inside her.

"Oh, Dare!" she whispered, burying her face in his shoulder. "This is everything I dreamed."

Dare held her tenderly, relishing the feel of her. All sex was intimate, and with his other fiancees he'd had this familiar feeling like they were joined by more than their bodies. But to experience this his first time with Ireni was indescribable, as they simply relished the feeling of being one.

Nirim

She must've felt the same; she may have claimed she wanted something wilder than slow, gentle lovemaking, but if that was the case then what she considered gentle lovemaking had to have been as romantic and loving as an old married couple cuddling on a loveseat watching the sunset.

Her green eyes stared deeply into his as she began to placidly rise up and down on him, her hands running lovingly over his chest. Just about every time she lowered herself back down his length she kissed him tenderly, and even her tight walls felt warm and inviting rather than hungry.

Even Ireni's arousal was different. She was certainly wet, but her juices didn't pour from her in a constant stream the way Sia's did.

Also, she kept making the sweetest little sounds, sighs and moans and contented "mmmm"s. Every now and then her sex would twitch around him and she'd gasp his name and wrap her arms around his neck, burying her head in his shoulder for a few moments.

It was sweet and adorable, and surprisingly enjoyable. Just the warm, loving feeling of shared intimacy with someone, with deeper feelings involved than just primal rutting. It was incredible to think he could already feel so in tune with her when this was the first time they'd been together.

And yet with those big green eyes looking at him with such adoration, such love and acceptance, he felt a powerful surge of emotion in return. "I love you, Ireni," he said, tenderly kissing her soft auburn hair.

Her walls rippled around his length in response, and her rosebud lips caressed the base of his neck as she gave another soft moan and sank into what had to be the gentlest climax he'd ever observed.

Their lovemaking was a slow burn for his sweet fiancee. Her pace increased so gradually that he almost didn't realize it was happening, and he was surprised when she took his hand and pressed his finger to her clit in a silent request to stimulate her as she continued to ride him.

So it came as an even bigger surprise when he finally realized that Ireni had sped up to an unexpectedly aggressive pace, and her hand holding his finger to her pearl was practically mashing it against her.

"Dare!" she gasped again, with far more feeling. Then, with a happy whimper, her sex closed tightly around him and began to milk him desperately. He felt her juices flow as if the floodgates had opened, and she collapsed on his chest and pressed her lips to his skin as she shook and trembled through a gentle but powerful orgasm.

Dare was almost surprised to find that the slow buildup to her intense climax had swept him along with it. He'd thought he could take her through multiple orgasms at this pace, but at the sight of her obvious pleasure and the feel of her tender walls massaging his shaft, his own orgasm rushed in out of nowhere and there was nothing he could do to stop it.

"Ireni!" he panted, wrapping his arms around his gentle lover and releasing inside her.

"I love you," she gasped when she felt it, trembling against his chest. "I love you I love you I love you!"

"I love you too," he replied as his pleasure engulfed him.

After they came down from their shared climax he gently stood, lifting her with him. He had to kick his pants off, but then he carried his beautiful fiancee to their tent as she practically purred against his chest, skin warm and steaming with perspiration in the cool evening air.

They both gasped as they crawled into the cold blankets, instinctively huddling together, and Ireni giggled. "And here I was careful to make sure the bed was perfect for our first time, and we didn't even use it."

With a low laugh Dare kissed her soft shoulder. "You really couldn't wait," he teased.

She blushed in the light of the glowstone. "I couldn't," she agreed with a happy smile. "I was so excited to finally be with you like I'd dreamed."

"I could tell," he said wryly, thinking of her gentle, loving movements. "You really had your way with me there . . . practically broke my dick in half."

To his surprise Ireni's face flushed. "Don't laugh," she said, sounding unexpectedly hurt. "That was wonderful and I don't want you to ruin it."

Dare hadn't expected such a strong response and stared at her in chagrin. "I'm sorry," he said hesitantly, hugging her closer. "It *was* wonderful. *You* are wonderful. I never meant-"

She sighed and dropped her head back to his chest, absently running her hand up and down his arm. "No, I'm sorry. It's just that I've never made love before and it's all I've ever wanted."

Dare frowned. "Never?" He could've sworn she'd told him . . . "I thought you and Sia said-"

"*Made love,*" his fiancee said fiercely. "I've *fucked* my fair share of times, and *been fucked* more often than I can count. But there was never any love there. Not even when there should've been."

She abruptly glanced up at him, looking almost scared. "I-I mean . . . I don't want you to think I'm a whore, even if I w-" She cut off in horror, expression crumpling miserably. "Oh Dare, you're not ruining this, I am," she whispered, big eyes filling with tears. "I'm ruining it and it was so perfect and now you'll hate me."

"Shh," Dare whispered, bewildered. But his heart broke for his gentle betrothed's obvious pain and he held her more tightly, stroking her back. "Shh, it's all right. I could never hate you, Ireni. Didn't I just tell you I loved you?"

"But that was before you knew!" she wailed, pressing her face into his neck. "When you thought I was a sweet, innocent librarian."

He couldn't help but smile. "Ireni, I found you running a brothel in a slums. I know you've lived your life, and I don't judge you for it."

Ireni just sobbed harder. "It can be such a brutal world, and Kov is such a cruel place if you have no one and nothing. I survived how

I had to, no matter what shameful things I had to do, until Sia's followers found me and took me in and saved me from that life."

Dare couldn't think of anything to say, desperate as he was to comfort her. He'd known she had things in her past that haunted her, had seen hints of her pain on more than one occasion. But since she clearly hadn't wanted to talk about it he hadn't pressed, just done his best to offer his support.

Only now he wasn't sure what to do.

She looked up at him, tears streaming down her cheeks. "After so long being used, after the life I've lived, I didn't believe anyone could ever love me. And I wasn't sure I'd be worthy to love them back if they did."

She hesitantly stroked his chest, looking lost and forlorn. "But I dreamed of it. Of having a man who would love me, who would be strong when he needed to be but always gentle and kind. And I dreamed of being able to love him back with all my heart, and share my love with him in the most wonderful ways."

"Ireni," Dare said gently, reaching to brush away her tears as delicately as he'd try to capture a bubble.

His sweet fiancee pressed her cheek into his hand. "The Goddess saved me, even more than her followers in all their kindly efforts could. She put me back together, showed me there was worth when all I'd been able to see was shame."

She kissed his palm. "And she told me about you. That of all her followers I was the one worthy to have you. Not just for my looks, but because of the person I am."

Ireni pressed closer to him, beautiful eyes looking up at him with fierce love. "And I got to be with you, to be part of your life and then be your friend and finally have the joy of feeling your love." She hiccuped, nuzzling his neck. "When you knelt in front of me and asked me to marry you that was the happiest moment of my life, no competition. And then we shared our first time and it was everything I'd ever dreamed it would be."

Her mood abruptly darkened again and her small fist clenched against his chest. "And I had to go and ruin it by showing you how soiled and worthless I really am. Now you'll only want to be with Sia and you'll cast me aside."

"Ireni!" Dare said firmly, so she looked up at him startled. "All you've shown me is that you were strong enough to survive a terrible situation you didn't deserve and shouldn't have had to suffer. Strong enough to get through it and still be the kind, wonderful person you are. Still able to leave me breathless with your radiant smile, and to open your heart and offer your love with such gentle sincerity."

He leaned down and kissed her forehead, then her lips, then drew back and looked solemnly into her eyes. "We haven't known each other long, and there are still probably a lot of things we don't know about each other. But there's one thing I'm absolutely sure of."

He hugged her closer, feeling one of the tears in his own eyes finally slip free in the depth of his emotion. "I'm sure that you're beautiful inside and out. That everything I've seen of you makes you a woman to love and admire. And I do." He kissed the top of her head. "If anything, I consider myself stupidly lucky to have you. If you'll have me, I'll always strive to be worthy of your precious love."

Tears flooded from Ireni's eyes again, and her shoulders began to shake as she buried her head in his neck. "I'll stay with you forever, Dare," she whispered. "I'll give you everything of me. Just please, please never let me go." She was unashamedly begging, voice more vulnerable than any he'd ever heard.

"I won't," he promised fiercely, pressing his forehead to hers. He abruptly chuckled, dispelling some of the heavy tension. "Besides, even if I could do such a heartless thing Sia would kill me, and if she didn't then Zuri, Pella, Leilanna, and Se'weir would . . . I'm not the only one who loves you and treasures you for who you are."

Ireni laughed as well, an uncertain hiccup, and finally smiled. Not her usual million watt smile, but like a slow sunrise growing brighter by the minute. "Thank you," she said, voice thick with emotion. "Sia told me you'd understand, that you'd accept me. I should've had more faith in her, and in you."

They held each other close for a long time in contented silence, peaceful and still aside from Dare gently rubbing her back. "I'll never tease you about making gentle love again," he finally said. "Now that you've told me what it means to you, having the honor of being the man worthy to share that with you makes it a precious thing."

"Precious," she murmured in agreement, settling softly against him. Soon he heard her breathing deepen in sleep, her beautiful face relaxed and peaceful.

Dare turned off the glowstone, but his own sleep was slow in coming as he held the woman he loved, grieving for her pain, humbled by her love, and full of resolve that he'd be the man she deserved. That he'd give her the sort of life that would make her troubled past a distant memory, overshadowed by happiness.

And with that resolve he finally settled into sleep himself, cradling his gentle fiancee in his arms.

* * * * *

Shortly after dawn the next morning Dare stirred awake to see Ireni lying on her side beside him, head resting on her elbow as she stared at him with a loving expression.

"Mmm, I can't think of a more perfect sight to wake up to," he murmured with a smile, rolling onto his side to face his fiancee and wrapping his arms around her. "Sleep well?"

She gave him her dazzling smile. "I got to lie in your arms all night for the first time. It was the best sleep I can remember having."

"Mmm, same here."

Ireni gave him a keen, knowing look. "Is that so? I get the feeling unloading my past weighed heavy on you."

Dare shook his head and gently stroked her soft back. "I'm glad you love and trust me enough to open up."

She smiled and leaned up to kiss him, lips warm and patient as she explored his mouth. Finally she pulled back, eyes shining. "We never got to make full use of this bed last night, and I'd like to feel you very gently loving me."

He returned her kiss, their passion building like a slow fire as they exchanged gentle kisses and caresses, exploring each other's bodies in a way they hadn't last night. Finally Ireni rolled onto her back, spreading her legs to reveal her glistening petals and holding out her arms to him.

Dare kissed his way up her slender legs, stroking her soft inner thighs with his lips as she sighed appreciatively and lovingly ran her fingers through his hair. Her intoxicating arousal, with the hint of the goddess's ambrosia, filled his head as he kissed around her dewy folds, across her smooth shaved mound, and then finally pressed his lips to her sex and kissed her tenderly there.

"Oh, Dare!" she murmured, delicate hands on the back of his head pulling him softly but insistently into her.

He continued to kiss Ireni's lower lips, tasting her nectar in a steady flow as he caressed her thighs, hips, and smooth soft tummy. All the while she moved contentedly against him, murmuring her enjoyment and seeming content to prolong this experience as long as they desired.

As it turned out, Dare desired to please her sweet sex for several minutes, only gradually slipping his tongue between her silky folds to explore her entrance, then sliding up to tease her delicate bud as she squirmed in quiet delight.

When she finally began pulling his head upwards instead of towards her, an unspoken plea, he kissed his way back over her soft mound and up her flat tummy. He paused for a moment to thoroughly cover her small breasts with more loving kisses, gently sucked on each erect nipple as she squirmed some more, then finally kissed his way up her delicate neck to claim her lips again.

Ireni wrapped her arms around him and stroked his back as he slipped his tip up and down between her petals, feeling her arousal coat him as her soft warmth invited him inwards. He took his time moving over her lips, nudging her pearl with every passage as she moaned into his mouth.

Finally Dare entered her, as slowly and tenderly as if he was moving in slow motion, feeling every millimeter of her tight, silky interior as she accepted him all the way in to her core. He stayed like that for a time, fully joined together and lovingly kissing and touching each other, murmuring tender words in each other's ears, before he began to pull out just as gradually to thrust in again.

Paradoxically, it seemed the more gentle he was the more pleasure she seemed to get out of it, and the happier she was. Until finally, without any demands for him to go faster or do anything special, he felt her once again reach her peak, soft pink walls lovingly caressing his slowly thrusting cock as her nectar flowed freely to puddle on the bed beneath her.

Ireni wrapped her legs around him and pulled herself up to his ear. "Come with me, my love," she breathed. "I know I've been carrying our child since your first time with Sia three weeks ago, and we've already made love once. But let me pretend this time is the one where you give me our baby."

The words were loving rather than erotic, but Dare still found himself tensing with a groan and, gently pushing until he was fully inside her, releasing in warm surges to fill her with his seed.

When Sia talked about him putting a baby in her, he imagined the gorgeous redhead's belly swelling with his child, her small breasts growing to make a nice handful. He imagined running his hands over that round tummy, and making her moan as he teased her tender nipples.

But as he finally finished inside Ireni and settled down beside her, gathering her in his arms, what he found himself picturing was holding her close in a nursery as they held a redheaded baby between them, watching in delight as it waved its little arms and legs and cooed contentedly.

"Oh!" his gentle lover gasped, and from the way she looked up at him Dare had a feeling Sia was sharing that image. Ireni smiled radiantly and hugged him tight, eyes glimmering with tears. "Oh, Dare, that's beautiful."

"It's our life," he told her, stroking her silky hair. "Our future. A joy and a wonder to look forward to."

"Our future." She shivered in quiet delight. "Our bright future. Together. Us and all our other beloved wives, and all the children we'll have."

The eastern wall of the tent brightened as the sun rose over the horizon, but they stayed contentedly holding each other for a long time before hunger drove them out to cook breakfast and break camp.

Chapter Seventeen

Home and Beyond

Ireni stayed close to Dare's side as they continued to explore the mountains, eager to give and receive affection. As if she'd been holding back before now, waiting until they became lovers, but now the floodgates had opened.

He was more than happy to return her attention in full, savoring his beautiful, sweet fiancee with every moment. Although neither of them let it distract them from their determination to explore and level.

Actually, she freely admitted that she'd been looking forward to adventuring with him like this.

There were more no big excitements like the Lord of the Skies, unfortunately. Plenty of spawn points worth clearing, interspersed with lower level ones they could either avoid or tear through quickly and higher level ones they needed to avoid for the moment.

They also found some absolutely breathtaking vistas, the mountains and the region of Bastion stretching out to the north stirring Dare's heart in a way he knew he'd never get tired of.

"We should build a summer cabin up here," he joked as they looked out over a ridge that offered a view of mountain peaks disappearing into the horizon to the south, east, and west, and the plains and woods around their home stretching out to the north.

Ireni laughed. "As long as you don't mind having freaky horse-lion monsters as your next door neighbors," she said, pointing to the spawn point a few dozen yards away that they'd just finished clearing.

"Meh, an excuse to exercise every morning." He wrapped an arm around her waist and pulled her closer as he continued to take in the scene.

She looked up at him soberly. "You really love it here," she said quietly, stroking his arm as her head found its way to his shoulder.

"It's a beautiful world," he admitted. "Even more so than Earth, which had landscapes that always left me in awe."

"Probably because the deities here don't always strictly follow the laws of nature," Ireni said with a snicker, pointing up at the blue sky overhead; a large orange moon hung pale on the horizon, one of several he'd seen so far.

"Or at least different ones." Dare made a final contented sound before turning away with an eager smile. "Speaking of which, ready to keep exploring this beautiful world?"

In a mountain valley that could've been a tourist destination back on Earth, stark terraced cliffs giving way to descending waterfalls that left the entire valley misty and lit with a soft light, they discovered a dungeon entrance. Not a crack in the mountainside or a cave this time, but what looked to be ancient ruins blanketing the terraces, breathtaking in their construction even in their obvious state of disrepair.

"Elvish, you think?" Dare asked.

Ireni shrugged. "Collisa is old beyond our knowing, with many who have come before who are gone or changed now, their stories lost to the mists of time."

Her words struck a sudden longing in him to explore the mysteries of his new home, finding the ancient forgotten secrets waiting in places such as this. "That's badass as hell," he said with a grin. "I bet archaeologists here have the sorts of adventures people back on Earth only dream of."

She was holding his hand, and squeezed it affectionately. "Speaking of adventures, should we see what this dungeon looks like so we can maybe come back to it later?"

"Oh hell yes."

To their disappointment, though, what he saw with his Eye of the first monsters waiting at the top terrace of the ruins was instantly a letdown. They were around Level 41, their strength for their level hinting that it would take a large party or small raid of a similar level to effectively fight them.

Exciting, once they got to that point, but it wouldn't be anytime soon. And they'd need to find a few real tanks first. That, and wait until their children were either older to go with all Dare's wives, or find other companions for him to lead.

"Well, in the meantime it's a fun secret to have," Ireni said, rubbing his shoulder.

He nodded glumly. Maybe he could recruit Rek and some of his warriors, help power level them the way he had with Leilanna. Having a ready raid party of Level 40+ adventurers would pretty much guarantee-

Text appeared in front of him, in a way it hadn't since Ireni and Sia had shown up and told him the goddess would be speaking through her priestess from now on. It was so unexpected and jarring he jumped in shock.

"You have been given great power. Do not abuse it or there will be consequences."

What the hell?

Dare whirled to look at Ireni, eyes wide. "Sia?"

Ireni looked back at him blankly; right, the goddess had promised she wouldn't be coming along.

"I just got a message through the world system," he told her, and repeated the cryptic warning before concluding, "That wasn't her, was it?"

His bookish fiancee relaxed. "You hadn't gotten that message yet?" She grinned. "You must've really been keeping your nose clean."

Had he? Dare thought back to how he'd killed over a dozen slavers, potentially breaking the laws of Haraldar to protect dozens of goblin victims. Apparently that didn't count, though. "What does it mean?"

She took a moment to consider her response. "Well think of it this way. The gods safeguard balance on Collisa." She gave him a wry smile. "You saw it yourself, when you turned Zuri's self defense spell into a fragmentation grenade and it was immediately nerfed."

"Yes, and I was Noticed for it," he said wryly.

Ireni smirked. "You sure were." She waved that away. "Anyway, the leveling system raises the potential for massive imbalance, and the subsequent abuses of power. For instance, the highest level hero on Collisa could visit Haraldar and slaughter the entire kingdom and we'd be powerless to stop her. She's closer to a god than a mortal at this point."

Her big green eyes inspected him soberly. "And it's not just at the highest levels. We're nowhere close to max level, but even at our level we could probably go into a few of the towns you've visited and slaughter everyone there."

As Dare sucked in his breath in horror at the unthinkable idea she hastily added, "Of course we never would, but people are people . . . there are some out there who have before, committing atrocities. And almost as dangerous is using the power of the Adventurer's Eye or your knowledge of monster spawn points to power level an entire army, which you then use to try conquering a kingdom or the like."

Dare winced. "I was thinking of doing that for Rek and some of his warriors so they could help raid this dungeon, and any others we find," he admitted.

His petite fiancee shook her head. "As a general rule, adventurers are expected to use their knowledge to benefit their own party, the occasional raid, and to help fledgling adventurers on their way or train a local garrison to protect towns. Anything other than that and you're toeing dangerous ground."

She grimaced. "That's why the Adventurer's Eye is so rare and precious, and why you have to tread carefully using it."

Good to know. And terrifying as hell, knowing he could get slapped down for using his abilities incorrectly. He rubbed his jaw. "What happens if you do abuse your power, as far as the gods are concerned."

"It depends." Ireni motioned vaguely at the world around them. "The gods don't like intervening in mortal affairs, obviously. They like people to have their freedom, and just as importantly they don't want their own kind abusing their power either. But in the case of serious abuses of power they'll resort to measures like calling holy crusades, inspiring clerics to give warnings to lords or kings, that sort of thing. Usually the wrongdoer has to be vile and persistent in their behavior for the gods to intervene, but it'll happen."

"So if somebody decided to become a dark lord and conquer the world, heroes would flock to defeat them?" Dare said.

"Exactly." She patted his arm. "There's no harm in training up Rek and a few of his people so they can defend their tribe and the rest of Nirim Manor's lands. The warning was just to let you know that you'd taken a step in a direction that could lead to a bad end, if you aren't careful."

He couldn't help but grin. "When did you get your warning?"

The beautiful redhead giggled. "When I leveled up twice in less than a day. Scared the blazes out of me until Sia explained things."

"And we're both used to being contacted by the gods," he said. He couldn't even imagine what it would be like for some random person to be going about their day and suddenly get a text warning like that.

Dare took one last longing look at the raid dungeon, then at the sun overhead, and reluctantly turned away. "It's about time to be heading home, isn't it?"

Ireni nodded. "Especially if we want to pick up our new slime girl pool attendant on the way."

They mounted up and found the quickest path north out of the mountains; cutting across the plains of Bastion back to where they'd entered the mountains would be much faster than retracing their steps. And also it allowed them to scout out some more spawn points, both of them jotting down notes on their maps and in travel journals.

As they rode along Ireni became uncharacteristically pensive, until finally he reined in to look at her. "What's wrong?"

She was slow to answer. "Nothing wrong, exactly," she said carefully. "I just don't think it's fair that I'm the only one who gets to share your past with you. All of it, your life on Earth and the truth of how you came here."

Dare tensed slightly; this was . . . unexpected. "Sia always wanted me to hold off on telling everyone."

"She did." His fiancee absently twisted her emerald ring on her finger. "But I think now's the time. After all, we have a home, we're all pregnant or have already borne your children, and we're all engaged to be married."

She was right. Their family was settling down to share a life together, and the women he loved deserved to know everything about him. "Sia's okay with this?"

Ireni hesitated. "She'll probably want to be there while we tell them, but I think so, yes."

"All right, then." His stomach fluttered with nervous anticipation; he wanted to tell everyone the full truth about him coming to Collisa, but he was also uncertain how they'd react.

Dare doubted they'd think he was insane, not with an actual goddess backing up his words. But would they view him differently if they knew he'd come from another world? A place so vastly different from Collisa and everything they knew?

He'd just have to have faith in their love and trust in him. Which wasn't hard, because his own love and trust in his fiancees had no limits.

They settled into a thoughtful silence as they rode on, both of them contemplating this momentous decision and how it would affect their family. It was almost a relief to be distracted by finding the pink slime girl oozing along the brook they'd left her at, far downstream of where they'd first encountered her.

Dare exchanged looks with Ireni, who grinned and shrugged, and they both dismounted and led their horses forward.

At their approach the slime girl formed long slender legs, ending in a plump, glistening pussy and small tight ass. Then she lifted one leg gracefully like a gymnast or dancer and hugged it to her body.

It was obvious she was inviting him to fuck her standing up like that, a position pretty much no woman could manage in real life.

Dare was eager to try it out, but he hesitated, glancing at Ireni. "So how do we do this?"

She smirked at him. "I assume you mean how do we bring her home with us, not how you fuck in that position." She shrugged. "We can do it the slow way or the fast way, I guess."

He was distracted by the slime girl toying with her pink pussy, spreading her labia to show her opening. Which of course he could see anyway since she was transparent. "Okay, what are those?"

"Well the slow way is to entice her along one step at a time until we get her back to the manor."

"Pass," he said immediately, looking up at the sun sinking quickly towards the horizon. He could just imagine having to spend the entire night kiting the slime girl at the best pace she could ooze along. "What's the fast way?"

Ireni grinned widely. "You start to fuck her so she gloms onto you, pick her up, and get up on your horse. Then you try to stay erect to keep her interested until we make it home." She giggled. "It wouldn't be the first time you've fucked on horseback."

Dare joined her laughter. "So the second option is better in every way?"

"As long as you've got the stamina for it, since you can bet she's going to be doing her best to suck you dry."

His cock, already stiffening in his pants, lurched at the thought. He quickly freed it and stepped forward, while Ireni led his mount close so he wouldn't have as far to go to climb up on its back.

Surprisingly, the horse showed no nervousness at all about being so close to a monster; further proof that slimes were harmless.

The pink slime girl kept up her pose, cheek resting on her slim calf as she swayed gracefully on one leg. Although she held out one hand in invitation as she continued to hold her lifted leg with the other.

Dare stepped into her soft embrace and wasted no time pushing into her warm, slick pussy at the unique sideways angle. Her transparent pink walls immediately began to grasp around him and tighten as she gathered slime around his cock to provide more pressure; it had been awhile since he'd fucked a slime girl, and he'd forgotten how loose they were to begin with.

Not quite as bad fucking jello (or so he imagined), but definitely nothing like a real woman's pussy. Although the more slime she packed around his thrusting shaft the better it felt.

Dare noticed her body starting to lose cohesion, and her remaining foot on the ground formed a puddle as she focused on where they were joined. Which was going to make picking her up awkward.

With a frown he wrapped his arms around her and tried to lift her under her ass, feeling like he was picking up a dense mass of pudding by the middle.

For a moment the pink slime girl quivered, obviously unsure whether to stay attached to the ground or attached to her food source. Then she flowed up around his grasping arms, around his chest and thighs, and as her slime continued to squeeze and stimulate his length the rest of her enveloped him and held on snugly.

Step one.

She was only a bit larger than Ireni, and he judged she weighed about the same. Nothing he couldn't handle as he carried her to his horse and with Ireni's help mounted up, then turned towards home and set the horse to a brisk pace.

The entire time the monster girl moved against him, pussy becoming tight enough for him to squirm and jerk his hips in pleasure as she continued to stimulate him. With no ground to latch onto she began reforming her full woman's body straddling his lap, arms and legs wrapped around him and transparent face buried in his shoulder as she rose up and down on his cock.

Dare was finding her ministrations harder and harder to resist, running one hand up and down her smooth, slippery back while he held his reins with the other. "Speed up a little?" he suggested in a strained voice as the slime tightened even more, walls rippling skillfully around his length as she continued to slide up and down on him.

Ireni giggled and sped up to a trot, and when his horse followed suit he found himself and his pink lover bouncing up and down more vigorously, increasing his pleasure.

"Fuck," he groaned in defeat after a few minutes of herculean effort, holding her warm slippery body tighter as he emptied himself inside her. Looking down through her transparent body he could see jets of his come shoot out into her abdomen and hang suspended.

There was a surprising amount of it as the pink slime girl milked him relentlessly.

Thanks to his literally goddess-given stamina he remained hard as they rode on, struggling to hold off another orgasm as the slime girl hungrily rode him, doing everything in her power to stimulate his shaft. She even began kissing and licking his neck with her soft wet lips and nimble tongue, and even worked her way up to kiss him on the mouth.

"Don't worry, non-toxic!" Ireni said with a laugh when she saw him tense.

Even so, it was a bit unsettling. Dare wasn't sure which unnerved him more, staring at the landscape through her see-through head or her blank, mannequin-like expression as her lips sucked and nibbled on his and her tongue slipped into his mouth.

She had an odd taste, more bland than anything, like sweet but mostly flavorless jello. Although with a hint of alluring pheromones. He enjoyed the sensations well enough, but it wasn't like kissing a real woman.

The pink slime girl seemed to sense it, with an almost sixth sense for how to best pleasure him, because she lowered her face to continue kissing and licking his neck as she focused on stimulating his cock with her slippery little body.

Dare made it another fifteen or so minutes before he grit his teeth around surges of pleasure and released inside her again, his previous load having been absorbed only to be replaced by a fresh one.

This was nowhere near as vigorous as some of his lovemaking with all his lovers at once, but it was definitely a marathon. By the time the walls of Nirim Manor came into view up ahead a few hours after nightfall, he'd come into his pink slime lover half a dozen times.

To his relief, at that point Ireni proved right that five or six loads would be enough to sate the monster girl's appetite, and she contentedly reverted to blob form and sat quivering in his lap, slime tentacles wrapped around his waist to keep her from falling off.

She seemed in no hurry to leave a willing and eager food source.

Dare couldn't help but shoot a glance at his redheaded fiancee at the sight of the tentacles, and she giggled as she guessed his thoughts. "Yes, they do that with girls," she confirmed. "Just like in those videos you've watched."

That was enough to make his weary cock twitch. "This I've gotta see."

"Oooh, looking forward to watching my cute little body get impaled in every orifice?" She grinned impishly at him. "I could take or leave it, but you can bet Sia will want to play with our new pool attendant. Don't worry, there'll be plenty of opportunities to watch her."

The manor, guest houses, and outbuildings were all dark and quiet by the time they rode up to the stable and dismounted. Dare closed the pink slime girl in an empty stall for the night, then carried the saddlebags and packsaddle and their gear to the manor while Ireni cared for the horses.

Not wanting to disturb their sleeping fiancees, they crashed in the guest room next door and climbed beneath the covers of the

315

slightly smaller bed. The adventures of the last few days had left them weary, and they were content to quickly settle down into peaceful sleep in each other's arms.

* * * * *

Dare woke to find Ireni again looking lovingly at his face. Or wait, no, it was actually Sia; he could tell by her bold smirk.

"I'm glad you had fun on your date, my beloved," she murmured, giving him a soft but passionate kiss. "And I am *very* pleased by how happy Ireni is." She kissed him again with unusual tenderness. "You took good care of her just like I expected you would, and it was wonderful to see and feel."

"Thank you for giving us that time together," he said, wrapping his arms around her and kissing her in return. "Although I'm happy to see you now that we're back."

"Mmm." The goddess's pouty lips curled upward. "I'd like to make you even happier, but there's no time this morning . . . you've got a busy day today." She turned unexpectedly solemn. "All the others will want a reunion and news about how your date went. And you and Ireni need to tell Se'weir about the medallion. But once the excitement settles down, probably after lunch, we have something to tell them, don't we?"

Dare nodded, feeling that nervous clenching in his gut again. "Yes, we do."

"Then I'd best let Ireni take over so she can go take a bath and prepare for the day." Sia gave him a last fond peck on the lips, then stood and stretched languidly in her underwear, the morning light streaming through the window highlighting her sexy body as she grinned back at him, well aware she was giving him a show.

Then with a last coy wave she disappeared through the guest room door.

Dare reluctantly rolled out of bed as well and pulled on yesterday's pants and shirt; at this hour his other fiancees might still be asleep in their room, and he didn't want to disturb them just to grab some clothes. So, following his dry throat and rumbling

316

stomach, he made his way down to the kitchen instead.

Pella and Zuri were standing by the changing table, chatting amiably as Zuri finished dressing Gelaa, who made sleepy sounds.

Pella's back was to the doorway, and she didn't seem to notice him as he entered and approached to hug her from behind. That seemed doubtful given her keen senses, so she was probably playing along. Especially given how her fluffy golden tail began wagging.

Dare stepped up behind his beloved dog girl fiancee and wrapped his arms around her. As she leaned back into him with a contented murmur he moved his hands beneath her big round belly and lifted it gently, taking some of the weight off her back.

"Oh, you wonderful, wonderful man," she murmured, nuzzling his chest with the back of her head, tail wagging harder between his legs. "Can you keep doing this for the next couple months?"

He chuckled. "As often as I can." He kissed her neck. "How were things here?"

"Good. Quiet." Her tail began thumping his legs in her eagerness. "How were things out *there*? I can smell Ireni on you, does that mean . . ."

Dare smiled. "Yes, we had a wonderful time together, including a wonderful night."

Pella squirmed delightedly in his arms. "Does that mean she's going to start sleeping with us, not always Sia?"

"I hope so, but you'll have to ask her." Dare reluctantly let her go and made his way around to gently pick up Gelaa, cradling her. She looked up at him with beautiful pale yellow eyes, and he leaned down and kissed her soft cheek. "How's my baby girl?"

She kept looking up at him, waving her little fists and cooing softly.

Zuri wrapped her arms around him and rested her head on his stomach. "Doing all the stuff babies do." She kissed his hand as he wrapped an arm around her shoulders. "I'm glad things went well with Ireni. We were all so excited for both of you."

"Thanks." He dropped to a knee to kiss her tenderly. "It was wonderful, but I missed you all."

"More like you missed the big, comfy bed," his goblin fiancee teased as she kissed him back lovingly.

Amalisa walked into the kitchen, saw the intimate scene, and started to back out again. At least until Pella bounded over and wrapped an arm around the slender woman's shoulders. "Ready to head out again today, leveling buddy?" the dog girl asked cheerfully.

Dare blinked, realizing that sure enough the young noblewoman was Level 16. "Leveling buddy, huh?"

"Yep!" Pella kissed her friend's cheek. "Back to doing what I love most, holding down monsters so my loved ones can beat them up." She pouted a bit. "I was getting bored sitting around while the others did all the work for me."

He frowned at that. "You're staying safe?"

"Against monsters 15 levels lower than me?" She rolled her eyes. "Yes, I'm being careful. And since Ama's as big a worrywart as you she's been casting her Mana Bubbles on me. For enemies that weak they can't even punch through before they're dead, even if they did get a hit off."

Making a happy sound, she wrapped both arms around Amalisa and cuddled her closer. "Won't it be great to have a high level Enchanter with us? We'll be so much stronger with good enchants on our gear . . . isn't she just the best?"

"Pella," the young woman protested, blushing. "You're praising me too much."

"For my beautiful, talented, sophisticated friend?" Pella said with a laugh. "Impossible." She turned to Dare and Zuri, tail wagging. "Now all we need is a high level Leatherworker and a Tailor and we'll be great."

"I've actually already asked Rek and he's volunteered a few people," Se'weir said, bustling into the kitchen with an armful of vegetables and immediately getting to work washing and cutting them. "As long as we help them level, they'll keep us supplied. And it'll be a great source of income for the tribe, too."

Dare kissed Gelaa one last time and passed her back to her mommy, then went over and wrapped his arms around his hobgoblin fiancee from behind, kissing his way up her neck and then her plump lips as she turned her head to smile at him.

"Good morning," he murmured. "You look beautiful as always."

"Mmm," she said, slipping her soft tongue into his mouth. "Keep talking like that and I'm going to need to take a break from cooking breakfast so you can bend me over the nearest surface." Amalisa made a choking sound and Se'weir blushed pink. "In private," she added hastily.

"Speaking of privates," Leilanna grumbled as she strode into the room, flushed and with tousled hair and her nightgown hanging askew, "is there a reason a pink slime girl ambushed me in the stables? I was in there investigating an unusual thumping, opened what I thought was an empty stall, and the next thing I know she was hugging and kissing me and trying to get under my clothes."

Amalisa made another squeaking noise, blushing furiously, and Pella giggled and hugged her friend closer.

"Sorry," Dare said, feeling his own cheeks heat. "We brought back the slime to be a pool attendant for when we hire Morwal to make the pool and bath house."

"Hey, I'm not complaining," the beautiful dusk elf said, smirking. "Far as I'm concerned, riding slime tentacles in both holes until I squirt like one of your sinks is a great way to start my morning. Just wouldn't have minded a heads up . . . I nearly had a heart attack until I realized it was a harmless slime."

They all laughed, and he made his way over to gather her into his arms and kiss her plump lips. "Harmless unless you're an ascetic who's taken a vow of celibacy," he said with a grin. "We're going to need to warn Ilin not to go into the stables unless he wants a surprise."

They all laughed again at the image of the reserved, in control

Monk's reaction to an amorous slime girl appearing out of nowhere.

"Or better yet fence in a spot for the pool and baths where the slime can be contained while she cleans, at least until she's trained to stay in blob form and only feed at appropriate times," Ireni said, joining them in the kitchen with her cheeks flushed from her bath and her auburn hair wrapped in a towel. "And a bedroom where we can keep her the rest of the time, and where we can have fun with her if we're in the mood. We need to observe propriety, after all . . . the manor's host to guests and will soon have children running around."

The rest of the harem immediately flocked to the petite redhead, eagerly asking questions about her overnight trip with Dare and offering congratulations amid a flurry of hugs and kisses. Dare was left exchanging a somewhat sheepish shrug and smile with Amalisa.

After a few minutes of the happy reunion, however, Ireni broke away from the huddle and produced the silver medallion they'd found from her belt pouch, joining Dare and nodding towards Se'weir.

The sweet hobgoblin, who'd gone back to chopping up vegetables as she participated in the conversation, gave them an uncertain look as they approached. "What?"

"Is your grandfather named Wek'u'ko, Se'weir?" Ireni asked gently, handing over the medallion. "We found this in the stash of a party rated monster."

"Yes. What's this?" Se'weir wiped her hands on her apron, then took the medallion and inspected it, brows furrowed. "Oh. Oh my. We'd thought this lost forever."

"What is it?" Zuri asked, crowding closer. To Dare's amusement she also shifted Gelaa around so the baby could see, although Gelaa seemed more sleepy than curious.

The beautiful hobgoblin displayed the medallion for the others as they also crowded around. "It's the mark of the Chieftain of the Blightfang Tribe. It was last seen with my grandfather, Wek'u'ko, a very long time ago."

"I'm sorry for your loss," Dare said, resting a hand on her shoulder.

Se'weir shrugged, looking more regretful than grieved. "I suppose it is a loss, but it's hard to feel too strongly since I never got to meet him. Father and the rest of the tribe always spoke highly of him, but he died before I was born."

She traced a thumb over the name engraved in the medallion. "He was a great chief, however, one of the highest level goblins in the Teeth of Gadris for generations, and a brave hunter who ventured far into our ancestral hunting grounds."

The beautiful hobgoblin shook her head with a sigh. "Too far, it seems." She looked up at him and Ireni, pale yellow eyes sad. "Where did you find this?"

They quickly described their fight with the Lord of the Skies and their discovery of the medallion. When they were done Se'weir quietly tucked the medallion away in the pocket of her apron, then turned back to her cooking. "After breakfast, could I trouble both of you to come with me to visit my brother? As the future chieftain of the Avenging Wolves, and the heir of Father and Grandfather before him, he'll want to hear of this as well."

"Of course," Ireni said, giving her a brief hug.

Pella cut in, tail wagging. "I want to hear more about your fight! That's amazing just the two of you killed a party rated monster."

"And about the other stuff you found in the mountains," Leilanna added. "Maybe the story of how you found the slime girl that double penetrated me earlier."

Dare grinned. "Actually, we found something even better . . . a high level raid dungeon. Ruins that looked as if they could've been elvish."

The conversation turned to their trip as they gathered around the dining room table, Se'weir joining them after she got breakfast cooking with her abilities. Soon after Ilin made an appearance as well and found a seat beside Amalisa, at the far end of the table from where Dare and his fiancees had inadvertently made a huddle.

Although every effort was made to include them in the conversation. Especially as Dare described the raid dungeon to him and asked his opinion on it.

It was a relaxing morning full of warmth and laughter as they ate and prepared for the day. But all too soon it was time to get to work, and Dare felt himself tensing as Ireni cleared her throat and shot him a significant look.

"We need to visit the Avenging Wolf village with Se'weir about the medallion," she said solemnly. "But when we get back Dare and I need to speak to you all about something important."

Half a dozen heads turned to him, expressions curious, and he nodded his agreement. "When we get back."

He was finally going to tell his loved ones where he'd come from, and how. Hopefully they'd understand.

Chapter Eighteen
The Truth

"Landgiver," Rek called solemnly as Dare, Se'weir, and Ireni rode up. "Welcome. The sentries continue their watch on your borders and throughout your lands, and have discovered no threats. Although we remain tireless in our vigilance."

"Good," Dare replied as he and his fiancees dismounted. "Thank you, Chieftain Rek, for your hard work . . . we all sleep more easily knowing you're out there." Although just in case Ilin meditated atop the manor roof, alert to any intruders.

The young hobgoblin nodded solemnly. "What brings you to Wolf Den village? Have you come to inspect the new livestock?"

Dare looked over at the pastures and pens where cows, sheep, pigs, goats, and chickens milled around. As well as several mares to both help the goblins with plowing fields, hauling logs, and other labor around the village, and for breeding to grow the manor's herd.

Ireni had arranged for the purchase of the livestock from Terana, and she and Se'weir had worked out a deal with the Avenging Wolves for them to tend the livestock in return for a share of the eggs, milk, butter, cheese, wool, meat, hides, and other products, as well as every second animal born.

The goblins had eagerly accepted the chance to grow their own herds. Several of the lowest level had even taken the 10% experience loss, which wasn't much of a loss for them, so they could shift over to Ranchers, Herders, and other classes dealing with animal husbandry.

He certainly wanted to check on their progress, both at the prospect of bringing in quality products for his family and in his interest as a cook wanting new ingredients, and ones he was more familiar with. He also wanted to discuss helping the livestock handlers get a few levels, both to make up for the experience loss they'd taken and to help improve the quality of the goods their livestock produced.

Which would also be a good time to discuss leveling up the crafters Se'weir had organized, as well as Rek and a few of his people as a defense force for their lands.

But that was a matter for a less grave occasion. "At some point, yes," he told the hobgoblin chieftain, reaching out to take Se'weir's hand. Ireni came up on her other side and rested a hand on her shoulder.

Se'weir solemnly dug into her pouch to produce Wek's medallion. "Rek'u'gar, my brother, Dare and Ireni have recently ventured into the Teeth of Gadris to the south, to the ancestral hunting grounds. There they defeated the Lord of the Skies, and from the monster recovered the medallion of Wek'u'ko, chieftain of the Blightfang tribe."

Rek reached out to take the silver disk, reading the name carved onto the front. "Our revered grandfather," he said quietly. "Father often spoke of him, and it was to my regret that I was never able to meet him." He looked up at them. "You brought it to us, first?"

Dare nodded. "Chieftain Gar and his warriors can be hard to find these days, and we wanted to confirm it belonged to your grandfather."

The young chieftain grunted. "Father will want this, not just in memory of his lost sire but as a symbol of authority. He had to fight even harder to solidify his place as Blightfang's new chieftain without it."

He bowed low to them. "Thank you, Landgiver. I regret we're not in a position to properly reward you for such a great service, particularly since you refuse to accept the gift of laborers or females as mates. But on my honor as leader of the Avenging Wolves on your lands, and speaking on behalf of my father who will be equally grateful, we will show our gratitude as soon as we are able."

Text appeared in front of Dare, and he assumed Ireni as well.

"Quest Completed: Mysterious Medallion. 5,000 experience awarded. The regard of the Avenging Wolf tribe for you has increased as a result of your service."

He nodded to the chieftain and squeezed Se'weir's hand. "I'm just happy I can return such a treasure of your people to you, and provide you news of the fate of your grandfather. Even if it's grim news."

Rek tucked the medallion away. "It is appreciated, and your kindness will be repaid in time." He turned towards the livestock. "I will personally go and find Father to deliver this, but before I leave shall we inspect your animals?"

Dare looked at his fiancees. Ireni nodded, likely just as eager to check up on their investment, but Se'weir shook her head and gave him a brief hug. "I'll leave you to it. I want to go check up on my friends and the people of the village."

"Pella's given us some great advice on animal husbandry," Rek said as they walked towards the pens. "Her experience is mostly with horses, but it's been helpful even so."

"Good." Dare inspected a sheep that wandered over to look at them. "I'm not much of a judge of livestock . . . what would you say the quality and condition of these are?"

"Not exceptional, but good enough," Ireni said. "Good breeding stock, and they should provide quality animal products."

Rek nodded. "The village is already prospering from the eggs, milk, butter, and cheese they provide. I hope your house is as well."

"It's been a welcome change from dry goods carted in from Terana, and the game and wild forage Dare provides," Ireni said, smiling and resting a hand on Dare's arm. "Delicious as those are."

"It is," he agreed. "There's a reason we keep these animals as livestock . . . the stuff they produce is tasty." He motioned towards a nearby barn, newly erected and reasonably sturdy. "Show me how you've set things up."

* * * * *

Lunch was a bit quieter than usual.

The joy of Dare's and Ireni's successful date was offset by pensiveness at what their news could be. Ireni didn't seem to think it was her place to answer any questions, and he followed her lead until they could sit down and really talk about it without the distraction of food.

Although he offered them multiple reassurances that it wasn't going to be bad news. Just something important.

Soon after they finished eating Sia came to the fore, making a show of removing Ireni's emerald ring and putting on her black pearl one so everyone would know it was her. That seemed to signal an end to the meal, and even those still with food on their plates sat back.

"Let's all head to the parlor," Dare said. Then he hesitated, glancing at Sia.

"Ilin and Amalisa too," she confirmed.

Everyone looked uncertain as they followed him and the goddess into the parlor and settled down on the plush furniture. He would've happily pulled Zuri into his lap or held Gelaa, probably while a couple of his other fiancees cuddled around him, but he wanted to face them all in a more formal setting, fitting what he had to tell them.

As a silence of tense anticipation settled he looked around at the assembled group, the women he loved and their friends, all looking back expectantly. Then he took a deep breath. "There's something I need to tell you."

"If it's that Ireni's going to finally be joining us tonight instead of Sia, we kind of guessed," Zuri said wryly to some light laughter, partially easing the tension.

Dare smiled at her, but stayed serious. "It's about where I came from. I've been vague on the details, partly because the full truth would be a bit hard to believe."

"And mostly because I told him to," Sia said, taking his hand and squeezing gently. "For good reason, as you'll see. But now it's time for you to know it all."

She fell silent, leaving it to him, and he took another breath. "Collisa is a large world, with many secrets and places that have never been discovered or explored. But there is more beyond it, including at least one other inhabited world. Earth, a place with no magic. No world systems or abilities or levels or monster spawns. A place of animals and humans with inventions so advanced many here would likely view them as magic, but they all follow natural laws."

Dare looked around at each and every one of his loved ones, meeting and holding their eyes. "I'm from Earth. I died there, and Sia brought me here and gave me a chance to be reincarnated in this body . . ." he frowned, doing the math, "over half a year ago now."

His words were met with dead silence.

Finally Zuri, cradling Gelaa close, cleared her throat. Her eyes were huge as she stared at him. "You were brought back to life? With your former memories?"

He was surprised that was the point she wanted to focus on, but he supposed it made sense. "Yes. I lived 27 years on Earth before dying in an explosion at my job."

"I've never heard of anyone being reincarnated with their memories," Ilin said, tone unusually flat. As if he'd fallen into his stoicism in the face of this news. "As far as I know reincarnation has never even been proven real. And I certainly haven't heard of people coming from other worlds."

"I didn't even know other worlds existed," Pella agreed, looking unusually pensive. "Although I guess it makes sense."

"Not to me," Se'weir said, huddling up to Zuri as if seeking comfort from the smaller woman, her eyes wide. "Sometimes I feel like I barely understand *this* world."

Dare gave her an apologetic look. "I know it's a lot to hear all at once, but I want to tell you everything and answer any questions you have. To share my past with you, what Earth was like and what I did in my life there." He laughed self-deprecatingly. "Although it wasn't much in the grand scheme of things, mostly just playing games and doing manual labor with little hope for advancement."

Sia affectionately rubbed his leg. "Games that allow you to excel on Collisa. And which made me fall in love with you in the first place."

He blinked. "The games?" That seemed hard to believe.

She beamed. "What can I say, I'm from a world that's very similar to them. Also I'm a huge nerd."

"Sorry, what the fuck are you two talking about?" Leilanna said, skin flushed to a deep charcoal and beautiful features drawn in a tumult of conflicting emotions. "You died somewhere else and a *goddess* gave you a new body? You've been wandering around Collisa for half a year in a second life? And you're *already* Level 32?"

"I-I'm sorry," Amalisa cut in, looking bewildered. "I was still getting used to the idea that Dare's engaged to Sia, to the Outsider, an actual goddess, and she's having his baby. I have no idea what to make of all this."

"Join the club," Leilanna snapped, folding her arms and glaring at him and Sia. "Don't you think you should've been truthful from the start?"

"Come on, Lanna, they already explained why he couldn't," Zuri said, carrying Gelaa over and climbing into Dare's lap so he could hold them both. She looked up at him solemnly, although a smile teased her lips. "If you're from an entirely different world that explains why you sometimes say and do such bafflingly odd things."

Dare laughed. "Mystery solved." He tenderly brushed Gelaa's soft cheek. "But no matter where I'm from, the important things are the same. Like the love I have for my family."

Pella also made her way over to cuddle him, pressing against his side, and smiled as she looked up at him with her big brown eyes. "If you're from a place where it's only humans, and there *can't* be anything else, that would explain why you're always so excited about meeting people of other races." She giggled. "Especially women."

Dare grinned and hugged her close. "We have stories there about many of the races on Collisa, but we all believed they were just made up." He gently stroked her soft floppy ears. "Which just makes meeting them all the more wondrous."

Se'weir also made her way to cuddle with him, Sia scooting aside to make room for her on his other side. "I still don't completely understand how it's possible," she admitted, head on his shoulder. "But it doesn't really change much, does it? You're still from another place, which we knew. You're still you and we're still your mates and soon your wives."

She tenderly kissed his cheek. "And we still love you, and know you love us."

He felt a lump in his throat as he hugged the tenderhearted hobgoblin. "Thank you," he said.

Leilanna glowered at all of them for a bit longer, then sighed and made her way around the couch to wrap her arms around his chest from behind, pulling his head back into her pillowy breasts. "I guess even though it changes everything, it really doesn't change anything important." She paused a moment, then added sternly, "Although you still should've told us."

Ilin, left sitting near Amalisa, chuckled wryly as he took in the scene. "Reincarnated otherworldly traveler or not, you're still my friend."

The young noblewoman nodded. "And Pella's betrothed, which makes you family."

Dare looked around at everyone, heart full. "Thank you all. Having you in my new life makes it the wonder it is."

After a warm moment of quiet Leilanna bopped the top of his head with her chin. "Well, aren't you going to tell us more about Earth? I want to hear all about these fantastical inventions there."

Sia cleared her throat sternly. "Probably best if he doesn't go into too much detail, to preserve world balance. But he can certainly tell you some of it."

Almost speaking over her, Ireni came to the fore, looking at him with shining eyes. "But he can share the wonder of his world, at least. It's a place like we can hardly imagine."

Dare shifted his hand from Se'weir's hip to rest on his redheaded fiancee's back, giving it an affectionate rub. "I could say the same about Collisa." He grinned at her. "Although here you don't have a way for everyone to communicate with each other, anywhere on the planet, on little flat boxes they carry around with them. And you can't travel to pretty much anywhere in Collisa in less than a day."

The others expressed clear disbelief at his claims, peppering him with questions, and he settled in with his family gathered around him to tell them everything he'd longed to about the world he'd come from and his past life.

There was so much to share, like the floodgates had opened.

* * * * *

Any intentions of getting anything else done that day were brushed aside as Dare gave a brief introduction to Earth, its lands and peoples and history, and a brief but necessarily vague explanation of the technology.

He also used the opportunity to finally ask some questions about Collisa, its people, and their everyday lives that would've made him seem beyond strange if the people he was talking to didn't know he was from another world.

Things like what life was like for children before they got their class and started at Level 1 at the age of 12. Which as he'd expected was pretty much the same as on Earth, although they still used most of the informational features of the world system. And they had to be extra careful about not venturing into the wilds and wandering straight into a spawn point.

Dare was also interested to find out how children were prepared to select their class, although as it turned out most just looked at the available non-combat classes and picked the one they wanted or had the most aptitude for. That, or the one the community most needed or their family demanded of them, especially for family farms and businesses.

Also pretty much what he'd expected. And surprisingly not much different from Earth, aside from that picking a profession class and working at it required less education and honing of skills than it would without the leveling and ability systems.

A common saying on Earth was that to master a skill required 10,000 hours of effort. That was very much not the case on Collisa. Instead the mastery came from the difficulty of leveling up and obtaining materials to gain ability proficiency.

As Dare had expected, the literacy rate here was pretty close to 100%, because people needed to be able to read to use the information systems. Even the blind could see the information systems in their heads, and there were methods for teaching them to read.

The very few exceptions had access to a spoken prompt similar to how Sia had contacted Dare before she began sharing Ireni's body, but it usually required a circumstance beyond simply an inability or unwillingness to learn to read.

Which was rare, since even if the parents or community were lax in teaching kids to read, there was a surprisingly efficient reading tutorial in the systems, found with the tutorials for using the systems and how classes and leveling worked.

Tutorials that, to Dare's chagrin, he'd never found and hadn't read. Which led to some laughter at his goodnatured cursing as he finally did, with directions on how to find them from Zuri and Leilanna. Thankfully the tutorials were basic, and mostly included stuff he'd figured out himself through context.

The conversation continued through dinner and into the evening, and Dare felt like a barrier had been torn down between him and his loved ones as he was finally able to share the secret that had been weighing on him.

They'd accepted him and still loved him in spite of the impossibility of his story, even if a few were still having trouble wrapping their heads around it all.

About the time when they'd usually head to bed, though, the mood shifted as the focus returned to Ireni finally spending the night with them. Ilin said his good nights and returned to his guest house, and Amalisa excused herself to her room on the other side of the manor. Zuri put a sleeping Gelaa to bed in the nursery, and then they all eagerly gathered in the master bedroom.

Ireni, who loved the other women in the harem with all her heart and had won their love in turn over the last month, found herself in the middle of an affectionate crowd of lovers who took turns warmly hugging and kissing her as they helped her and each other undress.

Leaving Dare to lie on the bed in his underwear, appreciating the sight.

Although he didn't remain an observer for long; to his bemusement his other fiancees all wanted to watch him make love to Ireni, and as the press of soft feminine bodies moved to the bed he found himself in their midst, stripped and cuddling his blushing redheaded fiancee.

She seemed happy to share this moment with the other women, though, and after some loving kisses and caresses rolled onto her back and guided him on top of her.

Dare had resolved that unless Ireni gave him a cue indicating she wanted something else, he would give her the tenderest lovemaking he was capable of. Which was exactly what he did, taking his time and showing his beautiful bookish fiancee all the love he felt for her with every touch and movement.

He would've thought the other girls would get impatient at the slow pace. But they all seemed entranced as he moved gently inside the petite redhead, her hips rolling sweetly to welcome him, exchanging soft kisses the entire time.

Until finally she pulled his head down to the nape of her slender neck, and as he kissed and nibbled her soft skin she held him close and showed her appreciation with quiet sighs and gentle exclamations, murmuring his name in moments of heightened pleasure or stronger feelings of closeness.

He shared loving words of his own as his lips moved down to her breasts, feathering the soft little mounds with light kisses and briefly teasing her small hard nipples.

Finally Ireni's back arched and her slender arms and legs wrapped around him as she held him tight. He felt her tight walls ripple along his shaft in a quiet but intense orgasm as she buried her face in his neck.

"I love you, Dare," she murmured, voice muffled. "Oh! I love you so much."

"I love you, Ireni," Dare said, and as her hips guided him into her core he released his seed inside her in unexpectedly intense surges of pleasure.

As they both came down from their shared climax the room was oddly silent as the other women all stared at them.

"I want that," Leilanna finally said.

"I want that with Ireni," Se'weir agreed, shyly resting a hand on the gentle redhead's shoulder.

Zuri didn't say anything, just wrapped her arms around them both and held them lovingly, yellow eyes shining with tears of wonder.

"I want that with both of them!" Pella said, tears in her eyes as well and tail wagging softly. "That was the most beautiful thing I've ever seen."

They all seemed to agree with that sentiment, and Dare felt like he was drawn into a wonderful dream as he shared intimate love with all his fiancees, connecting with each of them in that same deep, soul-bonding way.

Zuri, vise-tight little pussy opening sweetly to his tender motions as she caressed his back. Looking up at him with shining eyes as he ran his hands over her large breasts, lotion-slick skin soft and warm. Murmuring loving words between soft sounds of pleasure until finally her small tunnel rippled around him, and her heady nectar flowed over where they were joined. They cried out each others names at the same time as he released inside her in a shared climax.

Pella, giggling as he kissed and stroked her large pregnant belly, then sighing in contentment when he trailed his lips down through her golden bush to her beautiful glistening petals, tasting her arousal. With her tummy making it awkward for him to be on top like with Ireni and Zuri, she rolled onto her side and he hugged her close to him from behind, pushing inside her slowly and gently moving inside her while caressing her belly and large breasts.

She turned her head so he could kiss her, murmuring loving words between lapping at his face with long, affectionate licks of her soft flat tongue. Her orgasm seemed to catch her by surprise, and with a happy whimper she moved his hand down to her clit to rub her there as she trembled in his arms, until finally he emptied in her warm core.

Leilanna, soft and welcoming as she pulled him into an embrace and ran her elegant hands over his body, pressing herself against his own caresses with quiet sounds of enjoyment. Her arousal flowed freely over his fingers and then his lips, filling his mind with the heady scent and taste of rich blackberry brandy.

When she was ready she rolled Dare onto his back and lowered herself tenderly onto his shaft with a throaty whimper, doing her best to press her whole body against him as her hips rocked languidly, making small gentle movements around his shaft. She kissed and sucked on his neck as he softly stroked her silky ashen skin from shoulders to thighs, tenderly moving with her.

Until finally her tunnel lovingly caressed his length, and with another contented whimper her nectar flowed over his crotch and thighs and she held him tightly, her large dark pink eyes looking deeply into his, shining with happiness. It was the love there as much as the sensation of her soft walls milking his shaft in orgasm that caused him to release his seed inside her in a surge of his own contented pleasure.

Se'weir, rubbing affectionately against him as he ran his hands over her small plump body, making her best effort to glide her full lips over every inch of him. When she finally welcomed him inside her she held him tight with her arms and thick thighs, looking lovingly into his eyes as her walls tenderly milked him from the start.

Her orgasms were quiet and gentle and seemed to come one after another, until finally she buried her face in his neck, lips lovingly nibbling him, and with a final whimper she squirted on his cock as her rising peaks culminated in a soft but powerful climax. That was enough for Dare to fill her with his seed, panting loving words in her ear as his pleasure rippled through him.

All that time Ireni had been beside him making love to each of their fiancees in turn with equal tenderness, petite body moving gently as she and her lover explored each other with fingers, lips, and tongues. Through it all they exchanged loving words, contented moans, and the occasional exclamation of pleasure.

While the sight of Ireni with each woman was ridiculously sexy to Dare, mostly it was beautiful as they each became her lover in the truest sense of the word, binding their family together as she was tenderly welcomed into it by every one of them in turn.

When they'd all been together and had dissolved into a warm pile of kisses and caresses Sia came to the fore.

Ireni had been cuddling Zuri, and the goddess leaned over and groped for her black pearl ring sitting on the nightstand with the others. Then, once she was sure the little goblin realized it was her, she almost shyly asked Zuri to share those moments of loving intimacy with her as well.

He wasn't surprised Sia wanted that with Zuri; there'd always been a special place in the goddess's heart for her. And the sweet goblin was happy to lovingly hold and caress Sia, a far different experience than the usual eager, intense fucking the goddess preferred.

The other women were drifting off to sleep in each other's arms when Sia gently guided a peaceful and happy Zuri to cuddle with Leilanna. Then she slid over to Dare and rested a hand on his cheek. "Will you make love to me, my love?" she whispered.

He answered with a soft kiss as he pulled her close, lovingly caressing her familiar curves. He could feel the goddess's restrained heat, holding back from her usual intensity as she sought something deeper, and he brushed his lips down her soft little body to her delicate sex and began tenderly kissing her petals the way he had with Ireni.

Intimate lovemaking or not, Sia's arousal flowed far more freely than Ireni's. The goddess's nectar always had a stronger taste of that heady ambrosia, as well. Although this time instead of a haze of lust he felt as if he was wrapped in warmth, a deep and abiding love that was personally for him.

Sia reached her peak twice with his gentle ministrations, then softly pulled him upwards to lovingly kiss her breasts as he positioned himself at her entrance and she welcomed him inside her.

Dare kissed his way up to her ear as he pushed gently and patiently towards her core. "I love you, Sia," he murmured.

"I love you, Dare," she turned her head to kiss him softly but deeply, joining in his tender movements as her soft walls rippled around him in a quiet climax. "Every moment is a wonder. Thank you, and thank Ireni, for showing me that the sensations don't have to be intense and powerful to be wonderful."

They made love, possibly for the first time rather than intense fucking, for what felt like a very long time, in their own world together as the other girls slept peacefully or sleepily watched them. Until finally Sia reached a long, deep climax and he released his seed inside her in shared pleasure, whispering his love into her ear.

At last they lay in each other's arms, Se'weir and Zuri to either side of them cuddling close now that they'd stopped moving. Ireni returned to the fore long enough to kiss him and wish him goodnight before resting her head on his arm and drifting off to sleep.

Dare lay for a moment listening to the soft breathing of the women he loved. His brides to be, the mothers of his children. The most incredible women he could ever hope to meet.

Smiling in contentment, he closed his eyes and slept as well.

Epilogue
Call to Arms

Two days later Dare was back at the firbolg camp; they really were the most convenient things to farm at his level.

Aside from the Alpha and two lieutenants, that was, who were still Level 36 and 37. He could only suppose they were so absurdly higher than the rest of the monsters in the spawn point because they had that treasure they were guarding.

Which was still empty until the camp could be cleared again, courtesy of his previous cheesing. As he'd already checked for the fun of it using the trick of kiting everything away and then running back to loot the camp.

He supposed it didn't matter too much since his current focus was on farming experience, not treasure. Although of course he'd take any treasure he could find to support his growing harem.

But whether it was loot or experience, Dare just wished all spawn points offered up monsters like these slow, high hit point ursine creatures; they were basically moving targets and offered next to no threat to him.

Heck, once he finished with them he planned to recommend them to the girls and Ilin as a great leveling location. And maybe at some point they'd even be able to kill the Alpha and lieutenants and fully clear the camp.

Leveling had gone well the last couple days. He'd been able to ride out, focus hard on clearing spawn points and getting experience, and return home in time for dinner and a relaxing evening with his family. Followed by a more vigorous hour or two before bedtime.

The experience gains still felt painfully slow, but he was confident he'd reach Level 33 within the next several days at this rate. And it was surprisingly pleasant to go out and fight monsters in the beautiful wilds of Bastion, then have a warm home, a delicious meal, a soft bed, and most important of all a loving family and good friends to return to every evening.

Ireni and Se'weir had even talked to members of Rek's tribe about starting up a brewery and distillery, although that was something to look forward to in the future. It was low priority at the moment since aside from the goblins and Volen, the elderly and mostly retired caretaker of Nirim Manor, he was the only person there who drank. Aside from Amalisa who'd have a glass of wine every now and then.

Although to be honest, Dare wasn't much more of a drinker himself. Still, it would make a good export to Terana.

There'd been no further trouble from Ollivan since Dorias and his buddy had been arrested, and Marona hadn't sent any warnings of potential threats. As far as her agents knew the knight was still in Redoubt, and any mischief he might have planned was likely not going to happen anytime soon with the days growing colder.

Although the goblin sentries remained on high alert, just in case Ollivan decided to act now rather than next spring or sometime during the winter.

Actually, with the looming cold Dare's biggest worry was winterizing the manor and guest houses, as well as stocking up on food to last them until spring. There were plenty of trees on the land for firewood, although he'd have to plan for sustainable logging by planting new trees to replace the ones they felled. And Leilanna's fire spells would definitely make a huge difference, even with something as simple as dumping heat into a heat sink like a water tank or even a big rock and then letting it warm the house all day.

Thankfully even though winters this far north could be harsh, the autumns remained relatively mild thanks to a wind that blowed in from the southwest around this time of year. They'd probably have until late Lin or early Pol, the Collisan names for November and December, before the first snows fell. And probably a few weeks more before the weather really turned cold.

Of course, after that the winter turned brutal, staying below freezing and dipping down to below zero regularly for a few months before the cold started to recede.

Still, they had over a month to prepare as long as the snows didn't come early. He intended to make full use of it.

"See, I told you," a girl said cheerfully from behind him.

Dare jumped half out of his skin and whirled, abandoning the firbolg he'd been about to pull and lifting his bow to face this potential new threat.

Then he relaxed as he spotted large, soft fox ears covered with fine, midnight dark fur poking up from behind a nearby bush. Beneath them came a flow of shimmering hair of the same color, then a beautiful round face with big, curious golden eyes, a flawless peaches and cream complexion, and vulpine features that gave her a mischievous air.

Or maybe that was her grin.

After a moment he recognized the fox girl he'd saved from the furbolgs on the day of Gelaa's birth, about a month and a half ago; it looked as if she'd come back. Or maybe she'd been around the whole time, since he'd only recently returned to this area to level after being gone for a while.

Another fox girl's head popped up, as snowy white as the first was midnight dark, like an arctic fox. She had similar golden eyes, pale skin, and mischievous vulpine features, although by the height differences she was taller than the first. "I never said I didn't believe you," she replied, tugging on the first girl's ear.

The midnight-haired fox girl twisted away with a pout. "I know, but didn't I tell you? I totally did."

The arctic fox girl smirked. "Okay yes, you did. He's ridiculously handsome."

"He sure is!" The bushes rustled as the first girl leapt out from cover, revealing her slender, petite body. She was wearing a short dress of soft rabbit fur, the skirt hiked up in the back by the fluffiest tail Dare had ever seen; he had the sudden urge to stroke the sleek black fur and feel how soft it was. She was barefoot, delicate feet covered in the same fine midnight fur.

The second fox girl quickly followed, revealing a taller body with lean strength that reminded him of Pella. When she wasn't heavily pregnant, that is.

His Eye identified the arctic fox girl as a Distracter, Level 19 like the first girl. She was wearing tight leather clothes that showed off her slender curves, showing that in spite of her athletic grace she had medium sized breasts and wide hips with an inviting round ass. She wore leather shoes, so either she had no fur on her feet or preferred to keep them covered anyway.

Unlike the first girl, the arctic fox girl had *two* tails. And if the midnight-haired girl's was the fluffiest he'd ever seen, these two snowy tails were in their own way even more inviting, looking as if they'd be impossibly soft. Dare wanted to hug them to him.

Both girls looked to be around his age, maybe a bit older, and were as sexy as they were adorable.

"Ladies," he said with a bow, making them giggle. "I'm Dare. To what do I owe the pleasure of this visit?"

"Hi," the midnight-haired girl said, biting her lip shyly. "I'm Seris."

"And I'm Selis!" the arctic fox girl said more boldly, her two tails swishing back and forth. "It's good to meet you." She waited a moment, then pointedly nudged the smaller girl with her elbow.

"Oh!" Seris said, blushing slightly. "I wanted to thank you for saving me. Your plan was very clever, like a fox, and I'd be in a firbolg's stomach right now if not for you."

"I'm just glad I happened to be around at the right time, and you're okay," Dare said. He glanced back at the firbolg he'd been about to target. "Although I'm a bit surprised to find you so close to the camp again after your ordeal."

"Well we wouldn't be if you weren't here," Seris said, resting a hand on her lush hip. "We came to talk to you, obviously."

"Although we live nearby, so we kind of have to be in the area unless we want to leave our den," Selis added with a frown, snowy tails swishing in displeasure. "We're just glad you've been clearing this spawn point regularly so they don't send any more roamers around to our den to catch us by surprise."

The midnight-haired fox girl shuddered. "Not a great way to wake up from a nap in the sunshine," she agreed.

The arctic fox girl sternly tweaked the smaller girl's big soft ear. "Serves you right for letting your guard down. It could've just as easily been a tundra wolf or dire bear, or even a white tiger."

"Stop that, dummy!" Seris complained, twisting away again. "I was using Stealth, obviously."

"Well Stealth's not going to do a whole lot of good if the monster or animal's like ten levels above you." Selis turned her displeasure on the other girl's dark fluffy tail, tugging it firmly. "You scared me half to death."

Dare couldn't help but smile, charmed by the two beautiful women; if he'd known they were around here he would've come back sooner. "Well I'll probably be in the area for a while, clearing these spawn points and any animal predators. And even after I level past here I'd be happy to come back regularly, just to make sure the spawn points aren't left neglected long enough to produce roamers that might threaten you."

Both girls brightened, tails swaying in unison. "Really?" Seris asked eagerly. "You'll come back and visit?"

"You should definitely come back and visit," Selis agreed. "We can show you our den! It's so comfy!"

The smaller girl nodded happily, giving him a shy smile. "Yeah! And then I can tha-"

Again in unison, the midnight and arctic fox girls both whipped their heads around to one side, fluffy tails bristling in alarm. Without a word they dove into the undergrowth, vanishing with barely a rustle.

Literally, in Seris's case, as her body rippled and faded into the background with Stealth.

"Come back and visit like you promised!" Selis hissed from somewhere in the bushes. Then with another soft rustle Dare got the sense he was alone.

Almost half a minute later he heard the thump of hoofbeats, and looked through the trees to see Pella and Amalisa riding his way. The two were wearing their gear and equipped for leveling, but they wouldn't have come here where the monsters were so powerful when the young noblewoman had just barely turned Level 17.

They had to be here for him.

"Dare!" Pella called as they pulled their lathered horses to a halt in front of him. "Morwal's at the manor!"

Dare frowned. "To do the digging for the pool and bath house?" They hadn't even sent to town for the man yet, unless Ireni had once again thought ahead.

His dog girl fiancee shook her head. "No, there's trouble and he-" She abruptly paused, sniffing. "Why do I smell fox girls?" She brightened, fluffy golden tail beginning to wag. "Aroused fox girls! Did you find new lovers to play with? Can I meet them?"

He hadn't been aware Seris and Selis were horny, although that made the prospect of returning for a visit even more appealing.

But now wasn't the time for distractions. "What trouble?" he asked. Hopefully the fact that Pella was willing to change the subject meant there wasn't any immediate danger to their family at the manor.

"Oh, right." His dog girl fiancee frowned. "There's trouble in the north of Terana Province, a monster horde he said. Which can be a serious threat."

Amalisa nodded. "Lady Marona has called for reinforcements. Morwal came to the manor to deliver her summons."

A monster horde. Dare had heard of them before, but mostly vague references to them laying waste to the countryside, and requiring a strong response to stop them before they grew out of control. They sounded more like an invading army than the usual behavior of monsters, even roaming ones.

Which was more than worrying, it was terrifying.

He wasted no time moving Pella over to his mount and Amalisa's saddle to the packhorse. Then he led the way on foot as they hurried back to the manor.

Morwal was in the dining room, eating an early dinner courtesy of Se'weir, who'd happily joined in with a snack of her own; Ireni, Zuri, Leilanna, and Ilin were apparently still out leveling.

"Hi!" Se'weir said as Dare, Pella, and Amalisa entered the room, waving them to the table. "Come have some cakes and mint water."

But Morwal was already rising, wiping his mouth on his sleeve. "I'm afraid there's no time, Miss Se'weir," he said politely as he turned to Dare, expression grim. "There's a threat to the north . . . a monster horde has begun to rampage. Baroness Arral calls for all combat classes and subclasses over Level 10 to gather to meet the threat." He glanced at Pella and shifted uncomfortably. "Pregnant women, mothers of young children, those under the age of 18, and the infirm elderly and crippled are exempted."

That pretty much ruled out most of the people at Nirim Manor. Dare himself could answer the call, of course, and Ilin and Amalisa. As well as maybe a score of the goblins from the Avenging Wolf tribe; Rek couldn't go based on his age, since he was only 17, and most of the others were similarly exempted for one of the listed reasons.

"We'll answer the call, of course," he said. "How long do we have?"

"I leave immediately, even if it means camping halfway back to town," the earth Mage said grimly. "Given the urgency of the situation I suggest you waste no time . . . a rampaging monster horde could lay waste to every settlement in Terana Province, then beyond, if not stopped before it grows too powerful. Including Nirim Manor and the Avenging Wolf village."

Se'weir sprang to her feet, as solemn as Dare had ever seen her. "I'll find Rek and help him gather as many warriors as we have," she said, rushing out of the room. "Gelaa's in the nursery napping, watch her until I get back!"

Pella also headed for the door. "I'll find the others and bring them back."

Amalisa wrung her hands. "I'll pack up my things and watch the baby until Se'weir or Zuri get back."

Dare nodded. "And I'll get the horses ready and pack up whatever we might need for what could be a campaign lasting weeks." He wasn't sure what fighting a monster horde would entail, but better to be ready. "You're welcome to travel with us, Morwal."

The man shook his head and gathered his staff and pack, then offered a firm handshake. "If you catch up to me on the road north to Terana, certainly. Otherwise I'll see you there."

Dare followed the Mage outside and headed for the stables.

* * * * *

"I still think we should go," Zuri said, crossing her arms unhappily. "He said pregnant women and young mothers are exempted, not forbidden."

"Absolutely not," Dare said. "This sounds like a situation spiraling out of control. You and the others need to stay back where it's safe and protect the manor and goblin village if needed, or if it comes to it be ready to evacuate to the goblin ravine and escape into Kovana. And we can't forget that Ollivan might still be a threat . . . when we're all distracted by a monster horde would be the perfect time for him to cause trouble."

"He's right," Ireni said firmly. "We may be high level and could help in this situation, but the danger's too great. Me and Sia swore that we wouldn't risk ourselves and the baby, and that applies here."

"But it's okay for Ama to go?" Pella said, clutching the slender young noblewoman protectively. "She's ten levels lower than us!"

"Commanders of battles against monster hordes take level into consideration," Ilin said, patting the distraught dog girl on the shoulder. "And I think we can trust Lady Marona to be a canny leader. Besides, Lady Amalisa's a support class so she'll be protected

345

in the back." He smiled at Amalisa. "And I give you my word I'll do my best to protect her."

The young woman's cheeks turned pink and she smiled back tentatively.

"Well if we can't go, Dare should at least take the legendary chest," Leilanna insisted. "He's got those tricks for using it in combat that could save his life."

His family all seemed to agree with that, and the dusk elf hurried to retrieve the item for him, returning minutes later to personally tuck it into its secured carrying pocket on his belt. "Be safe, my love," she said, kissing him fiercely. "Your family needs you to return to us."

"I'll be careful," he solemnly promised. "Nothing on this world could keep me from coming home."

Se'weir, Rek, and the goblin reinforcements poured into the manor grounds, nineteen in total and geared for war. Including their chieftain.

Dare frowned as he met the war party. "You're exempted, Rek."

"Fuck that," the hobgoblin snapped, glowering as he clutched the hilt of the long sword strapped to his back. "I'm their chieftain and war leader . . . they're *my* responsibility. If the humans of Terana forbid me from fighting in the battle itself I'll obey, although under protest, but I'll lead from behind like a coward if I have no other option."

Dare glanced at Ilin, who shrugged. "He's right that even if he's not allowed to fight, his people would benefit from having him there as a leader," the Monk said.

"All right, then, let's go." Dare turned back to exchange a few hasty goodbyes with his fiancees, and hold Gelaa for a few precious moments.

"Be careful!" Zuri cried as she held him tight, eyes wide with fear he hadn't seen from her other times he'd left to hunt monsters, even the raid rated monster. "A monster horde is unlike anything you've faced before. They can be the bane of entire kingdoms if allowed to grow too strong."

Ireni nodded grimly as she hugged him with equal fervor. "Entire continents, even. On the other side of the world Nil, the Lost Continent, has been completely overrun by monsters, many of them max level. Only the ocean prevents them from spreading to destroy all intelligent creatures on Collisa."

Dare stared at her in shock. The deities of Collisa had actually allowed such a thing, when Sia had told him before he'd even come to this world that max level had never been achieved, and few had even come close?

Sure, it was possible for lower levels to take on higher levels, if the gap wasn't too great. He'd done it himself, especially in a party with the others. But still, were there even enough people on Collisa high enough level to form a party to hunt max level monsters? Would there ever be?

If so that continent would never be reclaimed. Or at least not without some worldwide effort or major change in circumstances.

A part of him couldn't help but fantasize about what wonders were to be found on the Lost Continent that had possibly not been seen in ages, if ever. A sudden longing struck him to do the impossible, reach a high enough level to hunt max level monsters, and visit the place.

Although at the moment his focus needed to be on the monster horde threatening his family and home, as well as his friends and lovers in Terana.

Dare hugged and kissed the rest of his fiancees, cuddled Gelaa close while she cooed and clumsily reached for his nose, then reluctantly pulled himself away from his family to mount up, nodding to Ilin and Amalisa.

Rek and his goblins fell into loose formation behind them, and together they departed out the gate and started up the path to Terana.

It was safe to say that with the goblins marching on foot they didn't catch up to Morwal. In fact the journey that usually took less than a day, and which honestly Dare could manage in half that time if he pushed on foot using Cheetah's Dash whenever it was off cooldown, took over a day and a half.

They'd left in the late afternoon and marched all the next day, so it was morning on the day after that before they reached the town.

As they got closer to Terana Dare spotted parties of adventurers farming the well known spawn points, faces set in the grim determination of people desperate to get stronger in the short time available. Just outside the town itself he saw a growing camp, the nearby fields full of men and women drilling relentlessly to gain proficiency in combat abilities. Both to be more effective with the abilities themselves as well as to gain the modest experience they could gain from it and level up.

A harried Miss Garena met them outside the camp, surrounded by young teenagers she was obviously using as runners. "Thank you for answering the call, Master Dare," she said, looking over his group with a critical eye. "I'd hoped for more."

"This is everyone at Nirim Manor who wasn't exempted," he said.

"I suppose that's true, given your acumen for putting buns in ovens." She sighed, then turned briskly to Rek. "You are now under the banner of Baroness Marona Arral, with her guarantee of protection and provision as well as compensation for your service. I require your oath your people will cause no trouble and follow orders."

The hobgoblin glanced uncertainly at Dare, who nodded. Straightening his shoulders, Rek turned back to the Head Maid. "I give my oath my people will cause no trouble and follow orders, until the threat to our homes is dealt with."

"Good." She gestured curtly. "Report to Guardswoman Helima for assignment. The tall woman in plate armor leading the drills." As the goblins moved away in a wary clump she turned to Amalisa. "You're a healer?"

The young noblewoman also glanced at Dare before answering a bit timidly. "Spellwarder subclass. Modest damage and barrier spells. I'm also an Enchanter main class, if my services can be of use."

Miss Garena nodded and motioned to a large tent. "Report to Master Jurrin with the healers and support. If there's a spot available you'll be invited to an adventuring party to try to get you some levels. But since you're a combat subclass, unless you're already close to leveling up you'll be at the back of the list, likely doing drills and skill proficiency exercises as a substitute."

"That's fine. I just want to help." Amalisa gave Dare and Ilin quick hugs, then hurried off in the direction of the indicated tent.

That left him and the Monk. The Head Maid waved them on towards the nearby gate. "The Baroness has requested you see her personally at Montshadow Estate. With your higher levels and skillsets she has a particular task for you."

That was true, given what Dare had seen of the levels of those in the camp; not many were over 20, and he'd only seen a handful over 30.

He just hoped there wouldn't be any much higher level monsters in the horde, or better yet that Marona had more powerful adventurers with her at her mansion. Otherwise Terana was fucked, and so was Nirim Manor; they'd have to evacuate and hope to escape the rampaging monsters.

Montshadow Estate was a beehive of activity, with runners and soldiers milling about on important tasks while the baroness's most senior maids directed the activity. A stableboy rushed out to take Dare's and Ilin's mounts, although rather than taking them to the stables he cared for them right there on the drive.

Apparently Marona didn't intend them to stay.

A harried Belinda brightened when she spotted them, but was so busy she could only point them to the baroness's study on the first floor, with not even the time to exchange pleasantries. As it turned out the study was empty when they arrived, and they had to wait almost ten minutes before Marona hurried in.

Dare couldn't help but think that his mature lover looked closer to her age than usual, weary and drawn and clearly worried at the threat to her town. Maybe it was that, plus Ilin's presence, that kept her behavior stiffly formal.

"Thank you for coming," she said, not offering them a seat. She turned to the Monk. "Master Ilin, would you be so good as to find Miss Belinda? Please inform her I need her to pick out two runners and a maid suited for a journey into the wilds, and ensure they have provisions and mounts. I've already spoken to her about their purpose."

"Of course, my Lady," Ilin said, bowing and departing the room with his usual economy of motion.

The moment the door shut behind him Marona sagged as if strings holding her up had been cut, and without a word stepped forward and wrapped her arms around Dare, burying her face in his chest. "I'm glad you're here," she murmured.

"I came as quickly as I could," he said, stroking her back. He could feel her trembling, from fatigue or fear or overwhelming emotions he wasn't sure. "How can I help?"

The baroness grimly pulled him to the table, seating him in a chair and settling into the one next to it facing him, so their knees touched. Her dark eyes met his worriedly. "As you've no doubt heard, a monster horde has appeared in northeastern Terana Province, close to where you fought that Magma Tunneler." She snorted grimly. "It's possible the two are even related, although I'd be at a loss to explain how."

"What do we know about it?" he asked, resting a comforting hand on her knee.

She shook her head with a sigh. "A shaky eyewitness report from a couple wood elf travelers crossing into Bastion from Elaivar. Here." She leaned over to a map laying on the table and dragged it between them, pointing at a spot near the Tangle that formed the border. There was a circle drawn there, large enough that he presumed it was indicating the horde's possible current location.

"They reported upwards of a hundred monsters traveling in a

group in our direction. Although as you can guess, at the sight the two were so terrified they didn't linger for a specific count or to try to identify any of the creatures, but rushed straight here to give warning. After which they immediately kept going in the direction of Jarn's Holdout."

She snorted grimly. "If I had to guess, once they reach it they'll keep running south or west to get far away." Her shoulders sagged. "I can hardly blame them."

Dare rubbed her knee soothingly as he took in that news. A hundred monsters. That could be a pathetic force or enough to wipe out Terana depending on their levels. "How far out?"

Marona hesitated. "From what we know of the pace monster hordes usually travel, since they follow the speed of the slowest among them, maybe a week if they aren't slowed or diverted."

A week. To gather an army, call for help from nearby towns, and to get her recruits a level if they were already close.

Dare swore softly. "What are we looking at in the fight itself? Will they behave like usual monsters?"

"I wish," she said grimly. "A monster horde breaks the rules, or I suppose more accurately they follow different ones. Which means they can be a huge danger."

His lover tapped the map near the circle that indicated the possible location of the horde. "First off, they can "recruit" monsters. Roamers naturally tend to flock to them, and when they encounter a spawn point there's an even chance the monsters in it will join as well and be able to leave their usual boundaries. Depending on the type of monster, it seems, and whether the horde has intelligent leaders. Which they usually do."

Dare whistled. In that case a horde could grow dangerously fast; no wonder his noble lover was so eager to stamp it out before it got out of control. "Do they still follow the usual rules for aggroing and bringing adds?"

"I wish." She sighed. "In many ways they're the same as your usual stupid monster, yes, but in others they behave more like an intelligent army. Or at least a less constrained one. One of the biggest threats they present, to answer your question, is that their aggro becomes line of sight . . . if they see you, they'll go for you."

"All of them?" he asked incredulously.

"Depending on how close they are to the rest of the horde, yes." Marona idly traced the circle on the map. "They behave like an army, and it takes more than just a party of adventurers whittling them down by pulling them a few at a time with adds. You have to bring an army yourself, and the battles are usually brutal."

Dare was more and more glad his fiancees had stayed behind. "I can see how hordes can overrun towns."

She nodded. "Which is another way they differ from roaming monsters . . . they usually head straight for the nearest village, town, or city. Although thankfully they seem to need to send out scouts to find the places, while otherwise they generally head in a predictable direction." She grimaced. "Which by design or luck usually seems to be towards the largest population center in a province."

His lover abruptly straightened, pushing away weariness with what looked like pure determination. "Which brings us to what I need you and Ilin for. A task that's important, but dangerous. You're some of the most mobile people I have, and I need you to act as advance scouts and skirmishers, taking out targets of opportunity and bringing back information."

She briskly tapped the map. "Especially the horde's scouting parties, if you can, to keep them blind and moving predictably. And also if possible clear spawn points in their path, so they can't recruit those monsters and swell their numbers further."

"Me and Ilin can handle that," he assured her, stroking her knee. "Assuming they're not all stupidly high level."

She sighed again. "There's no way to know until a monster lore expert can clap eyes on them. A horde will pull in whatever monsters they come across that join their ranks instead of fighting, so depending on how far away from a population center they started they could have some very high level enemies."

Marona absently took his hand in hers and held it in her lap. "Usually the most powerful monsters will stay with the main body of the horde as leaders, though. If their strongest monsters turn out to be more than we can handle, our only options will be to either evacuate, or slow them enough by slaying their scouts and using careful diversions that we can call in for more powerful adventurers. Which may take awhile, since they'd have to come from farther north along the border, or from Redoubt."

"Then I'd better get going," Dare said grimly. The quicker he got out there and got to work, the more they'd know and the faster they could respond.

"Thank you." Marona leaned forward and kissed him softly. Then she abruptly stood, tone becoming brisk. "I'll send along a few of our low level conscripts to act as messengers for you, so you don't have to abandon your efforts to deliver information back to me. They'll have mounts and the supplies they need, so they shouldn't slow you down."

That was probably the message she'd had Ilin deliver to Belinda. Fair enough, as long as the messengers could keep up, and probably a good idea. "Anything else I should know?"

"Mostly just about renumeration." She smiled tersely. "Since you're acting as a defender of Terana you'll be given a small daily stipend until the threat is dealt with, to be paid as the province is able. It's based on your level, so it should be some compensation for your time away from your own pursuits. You're also eligible to receive all the loot from the monsters you kill yourself."

His lover's smile became grim again. "Although if you're fighting as part of the army you receive a portion, similar to loot rules for a raiding party. Although the province of Terana will take a larger cut." She brightened. "Oh, and also if you didn't know, since the horde is far more dangerous than your average roaming monster or those in spawn points, traveling in numbers and far more aggressive, experienced earned for them is doubled. The loot is usually better as well. It's a good way to level and earn coin, if you survive."

She winced. "Sorry, I shouldn't have said that."

"It's fine, I appreciate you being honest about the risks." Dare frowned. "Speaking of which, do monsters in the horde all mix together, or is there some order according to level?"

"There's some," Marona said. "Usually. In most hordes the monsters form in packs of numerous weaker monsters, with fewer stronger monsters as leaders and their lieutenants and bodyguards. So usually the weakest enemies will be on the outside of the pack, clumping around stronger lieutenants, who'll be clumped around the toughest leaders and their bodyguards. Although sometimes the most dangerous monsters rampage through the battle, depending on their nature."

She motioned to some of the markers she was using for various units. "The usual tactic is for our strongest melee fighters to go in the front, cutting through the weak monsters until they encounter resistance. Then while our weaker soldiers take care of the weak straggler monsters we send more of our tougher adventurers to assist the melee fighters and clear out leaders, then mop up the weaker enemies."

"And hope you don't run into stronger monsters that plow through whatever you've got."

"Yes, true." His lover's shoulders sagged, and her voice became small and frail. "I wish Orin was still here. He would know just what to do in a situation like this." She hiccuped a sad laugh, dabbing at her eyes. "Hell, him and his party could've probably handled a small, low level monster horde by themselves."

Her lips twisted bitterly. "But instead my people have a coddled, Level 4 Strategizer to look to in this time of peril."

"No, Marona, your people have one of the best leaders I've ever seen. Who they love and have wisely put their trust in. And I know you won't fail them."

The baroness looked at the map and hugged herself miserably. "What if I do?"

"You won't." Dare stepped forward and wrapped his arms

around her slender shoulders, pulling her close and guiding her head down to his shoulder. For a moment Marona stood stiffly, then she sank into his embrace and began to weep softly but intensely. Like a slow leak in a dam steadily growing as she set down the mantle of leadership she wore and allowed herself to be vulnerable, scared, and grieve her lost love.

He wished he could do more for her than simply hold her and rub her back. Although he was determined to do everything in his power to eradicate this monster horde before it got anywhere near Terana, for Marona's sake as well as that of his fiancees and their home.

His lover clung to him for a few minutes, then finally pulled back and gave him a tremulous smile. "Thank you, Dare. It's nice to have a shoulder to cry on again."

He tenderly brushed her cheek. "I'm here for you, Marona. Whatever you need, however I can help."

"Actually, I'm counting on it." She gave him a keen look. "I've heard enough to indicate that you have some knowledge of the monsters you face. A veritable expert on monsters in your own right." Her expression turned hopeful. "Maybe enough to go after them with more confidence than most adventurers? Can I count on you to assist me in determining the danger we face, so I won't be throwing the lives of good citizens of Terana away?"

Dare wasn't sure if that was the extent of her knowledge, or if she knew about his Adventurer's Eye and was being circumspect. But he nodded. "Of course, Marona. I'll do my best to identify the monsters in the horde, their levels and anything else I know about them."

"Good. Then I suppose I have no more excuse to keep you." She gave him another kiss, sweet and vulnerable. "Go safely, my paramour. For my sake, and the sake of our child, take no foolhardy risks."

"I promise," he assured her, holding her tighter for a moment. He rested a gentle hand on her belly. "You be careful out there too, for your sake and that of our child."

His lover laughed. "No fear on that count. Some great warriors lead from the front, but I prefer to stay alive to direct the battle." She made a wry motion above her head, as if indicating her almost impossibly low level considering her age, courtesy of the sheltered life she'd led. "Not that I'd be much use anyway."

Abruptly sobering, she stepped away with a reluctant expression. "I can't linger, my paramour. My maids have been a tremendous aid, but even so the burden of what needs doing is wearing me down." She patted his shoulder as she guided him towards the door. "Although it'll be a comfort to know you're out there keeping tabs on the horde, so they don't catch us by surprise." She gave him a strained smile. "A boon of having a competent lover."

Dare only hoped he was powerful enough to make a difference. After giving her a final quick peck on the lips he hurried out the door and through the manor.

Ilin was waiting on the drive with the horses, along with a fresh-faced young man and woman who must've been Marona's messengers, leading their own mounts and an extra packhorse laden with supplies.

And Marigold, mounted on a sleek mountain goat.

"You're one of the messengers?" Dare asked her, arching an eyebrow.

The gnome maid blushed and fiddled with her ankle-length pink hair, which she'd bound up in an elegant braided circlet to keep it from being a nuisance as she rode. "And to assist you however I may," she said, blue eyes twinkling mischievously. "I figured that with the nights getting colder you may want a bedwarmer to keep you company until my duties take me elsewhere."

The other two young messengers made choking sounds and shifted uncomfortably, and Dare couldn't blame them; that had certainly been . . . straightforward.

Although he could admit that he wouldn't complain about having someone soft and warm to share his bed, especially since his fiancees had all stayed home.

That said, he hoped the plump little gnome was made of sterner stuff than she appeared, given the task they were about. He assumed she had to be, if Marona had approved her coming along; his noble lover had assured him the messengers would be able to keep up.

"So we're facing a horde?" Ilin confirmed, all determined business. "Our companions tell me the Baroness wishes us to scout its strength and hunt down any scouts it's sending out."

"That's the plan," Dare said, mounting up. "As well as thinning its numbers if we can, and clearing spawn points ahead of it so it doesn't grow any larger."

The Monk snorted. "Well, I'm glad we'll have enough to do to keep us busy."

"Let's just hope we're up to the challenge." Dare glanced at Marigold and the two messengers, got their nods of readiness, and nudged his horse forward down the drive.

To find and defeat a monster horde.

End of Nirim.
The adventures of Dare and his family
continue in Horde, fifth book of the Outsider series.

Thank you for reading Nirim!

I hope you enjoyed reading it as much as I enjoyed writing it. If you feel the book is worthy of support, I'd greatly appreciate it if you'd rate it, or better yet review it, on Amazon, as well as recommend it to anyone you think would also enjoy it.

As a self-published author I flourish with the help of readers who review and recommend my work. Your support helps me continue doing what I love and bringing you more books to enjoy.

About the Author

Aiden Phoenix became an established author
writing stories about the end of the world.
Then Collisa called, a new and exciting world to explore,
and like the characters in his series he was reborn anew there.

Made in the USA
Monee, IL
12 January 2024

51672107R00208